IN THE SEEING HANDS OF OTHERS

NAT OGLE

First published in Great Britain in 2022 by
Serpent's Tail,
an imprint of Profile Books Ltd
29 Cloth Fair
London
EC1A 7JQ
www.serpentstail.com

1 3 5 7 9 10 8 6 4 2

Printed and bound in Great Britain by
Clays Ltd, Elcograf S.p.A.

A CIP catalogue record for this book is available from the British Library.

ISBN 978 1 78816 835 9
eISBN 978 1 78283 867 8

IN THE SEEING HANDS
OF OTHERS

COPIED POSTS FROM CORINA SLATE'S BLOG, 'WITNESS'

AUGUST 2016 (1)

Blood flowed beyond their bodies. There's about 250ml of blood in the machines at any time. Losing that much isn't lethal, but it's definitely sub-healthy. Weakness, dizziness, nausea, along a short scale of severity. It's not something we usually think about, let alone expect. But the lights cut out. The machines sounded an outage alarm. I had to rely on moonlight to find the nurses' station, the headlamps in a drawer. I handed one to Tasha and we both went down the beds, checking the machines. The backup batteries kept blood flowing, but it wouldn't be long before the batteries died. A temporary lifeline.

Then we checked on the patients. I tried to stop my trainers squeaking across the floor. I tried to hold the calmness in my voice. I told them what I was doing as I did it. It's amazing how much this reassures people. It points to a route away from failure, illness, pain. I smiled into their faces. I promised a standby generator, forced myself to pat their knees. Confidence can be an effective medicine, whichever way it's administered. Sometimes I think treating them is medicine for me. Or I mean I hope it is.

They had their own ways of telling me they were scared. 'How long will it be?' 'This better be a drill.' 'Corina? Are you there? Corina?'

A frowning man with black tooth cavities, shrunken gums, possible gingivitis, maybe a dependency on fizzy drinks, new to dialysis, asked me why this would even happen. I told him I didn't know. Then there was the fire alarm. He said, 'I assume you know what that is?'

Before, I would have let it go, but I said, 'I assume you don't want me to leave you here?'

He just shook his head, held on to a twitchy smirk, like that would save him.

When the batteries died, their blood began to clot in the machines. The only thing to do was cut and clamp the lines, move them to another unit. The younger patients were timid, obedient. The older ones were woozy now, or agitated, like when people wake up after a coma. That little moment of wild potential before they become themselves again. I struggle not to cry when I see someone wake up. Maybe because you didn't.

We went back and forth with wheelchairs. There was a woman I'll call Audrey. 76 years old, 6'1", only two deep wrinkles cut from the corners of her eyes. A bubbling giggle that lets you hear what she was like as a girl. During her treatments, we'd play trumps. We were fascinated by each other's hands. Mine are ashy, over-washed. Hers soft. She'd laugh when I envied her hands. I let her touch mine. She told me she was scared by saying my name. When I wheeled her out, she asked me faintly if this was anything to worry about. I told her, 'No, you'll be all right soon enough.'

But it was extreme hypotension, shock, heart failure. She died.

In the toilet after, I let Tasha hug me. We had a cry, checked our watches. She said, 'We're only two hours in.'

I said, 'At least it went by quickly.'

———

In the past week there have been three kidney failures, four heart failures, all fatal. The power cut made it eight. That's a lot of dead people, in case you thought it might be common. Eight dead in a week in a hospital isn't as unusual as eight dead in a nursery, but it comes close when it's a renal unit we're talking about. The second anniversary of what your brother did was on the third day of the week. On that night I needed help so I watched an American YouTuber talk about her own experience. 'Because the worst thing,' she said, 'is if you lose your sense of humour.' I wasn't thinking about my sense of humour after the power cut, a sixteen-hour shift. I was standing in the toilet slapping my cheeks to rouse the blood in them.

The problem with surviving is what to do next. Leaving the hospital means facing a life that doesn't feel like my own, to ailments I don't know how to heal, to myself, not yet back to who I was or on to someone else. I can remember laughing off a sixteen-hour shift. It was ridiculous, hugging other nurses, an honoured kind of feeling. I remember laughing a lot, being silly. I don't think you could've called me a pushover. I didn't have to sleep facing the bedroom door. I didn't feel like there's someone with a big mouth who knows an awful secret about me that could ruin my life if it got out. It was easy to care for others.

A relief to find the break room empty. I stared through gluey eyes at leaflets on the coffee table. I put another teabag in my half-drunk mug, watched it turn in the microwave. There weren't any spoons so I plucked the bag out with my fingers, but it wasn't much warmer or stronger than before. I chucked it, washed the mug. Then I washed up Tasha's mug that looks the same as mine. I did this quickly, wanted to get out before someone else came in, but behind me the General Manager of the Kidney Service Team chirped hello. I went over to my locker. Talk to the General Manager of the Kidney Service Team for long enough and she'll extract something painful.

'It was a pipe that burst in the basement,' she said, getting one of her yoghurts from the fridge. 'It flooded the electrics. Actually, one of the firemen was electrocuted.'

3

I glanced over at her, saw she had new acrylics, red swirls, glitter. She was wearing her Dior coat. She's a woman with a Dior coat, fur hood, real fur.

'You look good, Corina, considering.'

She pierced the foil lid on the yoghurt pot with a biro, dragged it around the rim. I've put on a stone this past year, but every other day she asks if I've lost weight. Not long ago she said, 'You probably can't gain weight, no matter what you eat.' Once, when I brought in some rice for lunch, she talked to me about rice for twenty minutes, how cultures who eat rice live longer, stay thin, so I don't bring in rice for lunch anymore. When a cry is coming I'll go to the toilet and she'll see me after and say, 'God, you look fucking great today.' She's white and nicer to me than she is to white women. She'd probably like to say that she has me as a friend.

I closed my locker, looked at her. She was right in front of me now, making the I'm-so-sorry face that's taught in palliative care seminars. I could see the pores on her nose. She put her hand on my shoulder. I looked at it. She pulled it away. She sipped from the pot, said, 'I can look at the rota, you know, and maybe give you a day off soon. Maybe get you some more day shifts, too.'

'It's fine,' I said.

'Well, if you need any help,' she said.

'I don't need any help.'

I pulled my cigarette tin from my coat pocket, but she wanted something more from me. I suppose she'd finally diagnosed a cause of my pain. She said, 'But, you know, last night. Hadn't you gotten close to—' but she waved her hand in place of her name.

'Audrey,' I said.

She nodded. 'It must have been—' she said, widening her eyes, her mouth, yoghurt slime '—really bad.'

4

We stared at each other for a moment.

I said, 'Yeah.'

Then the General Manager of the Kidney Service Team filled her thermos from the tap and left, as quick as if I wasn't there.

———

No deaths today. But I still smelled death in the corridor. Past the prayer room, by the staff toilet, where a young man stood plastic-eyed cradling a cane and a purse, there was a sweet, vinegary, turned-fruit smell. That's the smell of death approaching. I've only met a couple of other nurses who say they can smell it. It's not a mystical nurse power. It's probably just an olfactory sensitivity to some chemical building up in the dying body, maybe excess acetone in the bloodstream brought on by ketosis. I don't know if Tasha can smell it. She likes to mythologise nursing even less than I do. When we met, in our first year at King's, twelve years ago, Tasha said her mum wanted her to be a doctor, like she is, but she went for nursing because she didn't want to be like her mum. One time, when we were in oncology, she got angry with a woman with stage one lung cancer who said she couldn't stop smoking. This woman requested another nurse. The consultant lectured Tasha about 'best practice'. Tasha was determined to quit, saying she's too hard, unfeeling. But I think she just lacks pity. I think many nurses quit because they've confused pity with care. I don't think you can properly care for someone if you pity them. Same with empathy. I think the nurses who talk about empathy only care for patients who are easy for them to empathise with. Tasha cares using an instinctive understanding that you have to keep your hand on someone's back for a few moments after you've heaved them onto a bed. Some nurses use common sense to care. A Sister once told me, 'Common sense is hit-or-miss, and we're not here to fucking miss.'

When I went into the staff toilet before going home, I heard Tasha shout my name from inside a stall.

'How did you know it was me?' I said.

'Heavy steps.'

She asked me why I was still so mopey. I leant my bum against the sink. I looked at the lino that had come loose, curled up, beneath the stall door. If I told Tasha why, she wouldn't be able to help telling everyone. We've toured the units together since graduating, both gravitating towards nephrology. She worked for years at Chelsea and Westminster before coming back to Guy's and St Thomas' a few months ago. We've drifted apart, especially since your brother did what he did, but we can't admit it. Maybe if I could tell her what he did, we'd be close again. But maybe the secret to having friends is avoiding important situations where someone can let you down.

I made up something about getting a cold. I could hear her pissing.

'I had a guy in my GP year who kept getting colds,' she said.

'What was the matter?' I said.

'All he ate was ham.'

'Was he trying to lose weight?'

'Nah,' she said, 'his childminder beat him for not eating or something. Fucked him up.'

'Shit,' I said. 'I hate ham.'

'It's all a bit grim,' Tasha said. I heard her tear off some toilet paper.

We were supposed to go out with the graduating students tonight. Tasha said they were going to Shoreditch. I would've had to find something Shoreditch to wear. I knew that another nurse, let's call her Grace, would be going. She's the kind of person who never forgets a compliment. She'd judge my Primark heels. She'd say something like, 'I love how you don't feel the need to wear any make-up, like, at all.' She'd get men to talk to us.

'I wouldn't know what to wear,' I said. 'I've got nothing I like the look of.'

The toilet flushed. Tasha came out wide-legged with her zip undone, her hands held up as if in surgery prep. She said, 'I haven't pooed in thirty hours.'

'I'm bunged-up, too,' I said.

'I need a night out. I need to not remember going home.' She washed her hands.

'Can't you sleep?'

'Like the dead.'

'I can't,' I said. 'I close my eyes and I just keep seeing the bad stuff. I think I've forgotten how to distance myself.'

'We got paid yesterday, didn't we?'

'I haven't looked.'

'I think we got paid.'

She dried her hands. She pinched and pulled her tunic at the back to see how flattering our uniforms could be. 'Are you coming out, or what?' she said.

I planned the route to Shoreditch. Two buses there, night buses back. I'd be alone.

I said I needed to take my mother to her oncologist in the morning. A half-lie. It was in the afternoon.

Tasha took off her glasses, put her lenses in. 'So, no?' she said.

'Yeah. No.'

'Well, I've got to go church tomorrow morning. Got to show my face.'

Her voice suddenly seemed to get so loud. It seemed to ring around the toilet walls, in my head, after she'd left. I got rid of the smile she'd put on my face. I washed my hands. I stood at the toilet door. I wondered if the automatic lights would go off if I just stood there very still. I knew I wouldn't go to Shoreditch. I wish I could go to Shoreditch. That I felt comfortable in Shoreditch, in the night-time in Shoreditch, in the night-time outside. That I didn't have to take the longer way out of the hospital to avoid the security guard who calls me darling. That I could stop seeing innocent things, like cars, crowds, handshakes, smiles, laughter, jokes, flirting, food, the Internet, the world, as infected, violent. That I didn't hate and feel afraid. I don't know if writing this will come to mean anything, if it'll be any good. I know it won't be seamless. Showing the scars, my own sloppy stitches, that's the point, if there is a point. This won't be a well-made, thought-through thing.

No deaths today, except yours always.

COMMENTS

Unknown
This comment has been removed by the blog administrator.
Reply

Unknown
So is this guy (if there even is a guy . . .) did this guy go down for what he did (if he even DID anything . . .) or what???
Reply

TRANSCRIPT OF TEXT MESSAGES FROM CAMERON STRUTH TO SAMUEL STRUTH

28 MAY 2014
12 WEEKS BEFORE ASSAULT

20:03

Contrary to your advice I've drunk excessively after a shite rehearsal and wandered over to Guy's to wait outside for Cor and ended up following someone I thought was her along the river until the Tate only to discover it was actually an amazingly svelte South American bloke. Probs for the best. She had the grace to Skype the other week, saying how she was in love with someone else and I thought she was only saying it so that I would hate her and move on, but in fact her expression said 'I'm in love for the first time.' That hurt. So I've gone up the London Eye. Mate I'm on the London Eye

20:10

Why don't you answer your phone man? Mam text earlier about you, I didn't know what to make of it as per

20:12

Full moon! When you notice it it's like peering up from your book on the underground and bam! There's someone looking at you. Look up at the moon Sam! Can you feel it? We're interfacing

20:19

8 miss you man. Christ I thinkninjust heard your eyes roll. It doesn't really bother me that much that you don't like that sort of talk (I don't really either evidentially), but what does brotherhood mean in

9

all your philosophy? Is saying 'I miss you' the same sort of thing as saying 'I'm there for you' when you're not actually at hand?

20:29

On me way down now. It's not long up here like! Those red lights cranes have turned on. When they finish London it's going to be tremendous

20:30

Only just noticed a magnificent church by the opera house that's got a rose window all lit up, and for some reason I just imaged how wonderful it would feel to grow a brick through that

20:32

In rehearsals I had my first scene with the guy playing a policeman and duck me and call me halitosis. It's unacceptable man. It's impossible to concentrate when there's an open sewer in your face. Savage. It makes you want to sew their mouth shut and sew their ducking nose while you're at it

20:34

We were running through the scene, just reading it out really, and instead of saying 'clumsy male hands have dressed her' I said 'lovely male hands have dressed her' and this donkey makes some joke that everyone feels obliged to laugh at, I could've crushed his face against the wall. This cunt wears a t shirt with FEMINIST on it makes me sick. He's fucked his way around the crew of course. If he wasn't so repulsive I think I'd admire him

20:37

Oh yeah what Mam text me was 'you've killed your brother'. You know what she's getting at? Rev Michael must've turned her water into whiskey again

20:38

Ere – when I saw Cor last she seemed sort of weird with me. I wouldn't say scared, but. Maybe I'm just ducked and para but you know I was only joking when I said all that stuff last month yeah?

Not saying you will have told her owt, obviously, but I was only joking. You know right? You know I wouldn't do anything like that

COPIED POSTS FROM CORINA SLATE'S BLOG, 'WITNESS'

AUGUST 2016 (2)

A girl has taken Audrey's bed. Anorexia has led to diabetes, electrolyte imbalances, anaemia, hypotension, causing repeated pyelonephritis, chronic kidney disease. Vomiting. Too tired to hold the bowl herself. If tolerated, an anti-emetic before a small meal of favourite food. Fish-finger sandwich with tomato ketchup. 25 years old. She has been here a few times before. Last year her mother had agreed to donate a kidney. The girl was wheeled to surgery, but when they went to move the mother, her gown lay on the bed, hasn't been heard from since. The girl went on the transplant waiting list. She'll get a new kidney in two years, if she's lucky.

EPO injection. Phosphate binders and Alfacalcidol with meals. Aggressive treatment of hyperlipidaemia. Possible dialysis.

She fell asleep. I took a student nurse aside, the one who'd started crying when this girl went into hypoglycaemic shock, who I'd told to get the fuck off the ward to pull himself together. I apologised for that. I told him tears are fine. It's good that he feels.

You might wonder where these outbursts have come from. Last night I dreamt of the room where your brother did what he did. I woke up, pinned by the bedsheets, sweating, didn't trust my sleeping mind to let me stay out of that room, so I kept myself awake, out of the room of sleep. Is there any beating it? Not long after it happened I moved into a flat across the city because I couldn't sleep in that room. Now I sleep to get rid of my body, my memory of it, but sleep uses my memory to take my body back to that room, that oven.

Glomerular filtration rate >40ml/min. Tipping point before progression to end stage, renal failure. IV iron. Aiming for ferritin >150ng/ml. Obtain daily weight. Clip nails, avoid acute paronychia. Don't make it all about quantitative development.

The girl's stool was slightly more solid than the day before, floating in the water. Her hydration was better, blood pressure up. She wears a crucifix with a long gold chain that gets sharp bends in it from her clavicle. She reads a filthy Gideon's Bible, close up to her eyes, as she mouths the words, replacing pages that fall now and then. She's 50 years younger than Audrey, but their silhouettes are indistinguishable. Her hair is thinning, falling out. Elsewhere, on her body, she's furry. Except for extremely underweight people, only new-born babies have this kind of down. It's insulation the body grows to protect itself.

In the morning, the girl wept openly over an untouched sandwich, kind of forcing it out, like clearing your throat, exhausted, saying, 'I just want to fucking disappear.'

She managed a bite a few hours after that. I asked her if she wanted more. She 'went monster'. That's what she called it later. Suspicious, frustrated, prickly, nasty. She apologised. Her voice sort of frothed. It smelled of mouthwash. Her name is Ali. She doesn't mind me writing about her, though she said she couldn't see why I'd want to write about her, or myself, in the first place. She asked me where I could find this blog. I didn't tell her. I asked her what Ali is short for.

'Alistair.'

'Really?'

'No.'

I tried to hide how cross it makes me when I'm the butt of a joke. I asked her again what Ali is short for.

'Alien.'

———

It took 55 days for the word to begin to lose its dread. 66 days to manage the cinema, in the afternoon, alone. 94 days to imagine a day that I wouldn't feel dissolved. 98 to go to a pub. 135 to go to a busy bar. 159 to go to a busy bar, have a few drinks. 162 days to go to a busy bar, have a few drinks, let a friend, a girl, stay over with me in my bed. 188 days to walk the ten minutes from Turnpike Lane Station to my flat instead of waiting for a bus. 201 days to say, once, without doubt, that it wasn't my fault. The 268th day was the first day I realised that a memory of what happened hadn't made me sweat. The 371st day was the first day I could remember remembering your brother's face and not feeling scared, vulnerable, and then wanting to smash my fist into his nose, crack the ethmoid in half, flatten the septum, the cartilage mushed, skin burst, until it couldn't be called a nose. No, I just felt a vague nausea, a kind of regret, almost like disappointment, which turned eventually into the black emptiness I feel seeing a stocky macho white bloke with kanji tattooed on his arm. The 548th day was the first day I slept without a knife hidden between my mattress and headboard. On the 578th day I put the knife back. On the 581st day I heard that a girl I knew from uni had gone through something similar. I thought about messaging her to ask if she wanted to meet to talk, but I couldn't find the words.

COMMENTS

Unknown
Something happened to me and I just never want to think about it.

I don't want to talk about it, I'd rather pretend it never happened. I've been depressed ever since and I want to be okay again but I don't know how. This is a really good blog, thankyou for writing it. *Reply*

Unknown
This comment has been removed by the blog administrator. *Reply*

———

Many times when my mother appears in my head, e.g. a picture of her calling the council with a speech written in bullet points over takeaway menus that come through her *NO JUNK MAIL NO EXCEPTIONS* letterbox, or pouring herself a Guinness on a Saturday evening, or arranging flowers on the kitchen counter, I yawn. When I think of her, it's like watching someone yawn. When she calls, I answer, 'Hi, Kaasan,' and she says, 'What's the matter now?' and my voice is thick with yawn, saying, 'Nothing. I just said hi.'

'*Hi*. That is how you said it. *Hi*. What's the matter?'

I called her every other day for a couple of weeks after she was first diagnosed. One day she called me. Two days later she called me again. It's become a kind of custom, whether I like it or not, whether this dosage of interaction is useful or not for either of us.

'Have you eaten yet?' she says.

'Not yet.'

'I suppose you must have slept in.'

I tell her I got home late from work before I realise I should lie. I'm never more earnest or humourless than with her.

'I've had my meal,' she says. 'It should last me all day.'

'You don't get hungry?'

'I never get hungry. I don't think I've been hungry in my life.'

'That's ridiculous.'

'"Ridiculous" is a bit dramatic. I wasn't hungry this morning and I had an orange. But I suppose that is personal information you don't need to know.'

This could take us, if I let it, to one of three long-contested diagnoses.

    1) I am just like my father.

    2) I resent having my mother in my life.

    3) I don't value anyone's opinion other than my own.

She tells me that Polina, another housekeeper at the Stratford Premier Inn, has given her some Russian face cream. 'I cannot read the bottle at all,' she says, 'but Polina says it will get rid of any wrinkles.'

'You don't have wrinkles,' I say.

'Thank you for saying.'

'What's wrong with having wrinkles?'

She makes the sound you shoo a cat with.

'There's nothing wrong with wrinkles,' I say.

'Of course not.'

'But then—'

'But what?'

'Why don't you just try it on your hand if you're that worried?'

'I am not worried,' she says.

'Concerned.'

'I'm not concerned.'

'Whatever you are, then.'

'Well, Polina was the one who sneaked her boyfriend in one of the rooms.'

'And what?' I say.

'Well,' she says. 'A woman like that.'

'A woman like what?'

Now there's a certain silence that even my mother knows not to cross.

'I'm about to make some food,' I say.

'What did you have last night?'

'I went to a kebab place. It was late.'

'Kebab?'

'You know what a kebab is.'

'I do not.'

'It's a Turkish thing, and you do.'

'Turkish food is unhealthy,' she says. 'It makes you sluggish. It's addictive.'

'I don't have it often.'

'Expensive. Extravagant.'

'I don't have it often.'

'Your grandmother ate like that. She was an elephant. When my father died, she didn't know how to look after herself, and—'

'And she didn't even notice the gas leak.'

'Yes. I have told you many times. But it's worth repeating. A woman must know how to live completely by herself. That is why I am here and not in Aomori picking apples.'

And because of the family fruit shop that was swallowed by the earth. Because of the pain of seeing her mother's face – a 'strange thing,' she once said, 'like it was made of gauze' – since Obaachan had been 'mistreated' by an American soldier in Tokyo, lost everyone in the air raids and moved north with Ojiichan, a man constantly ashamed of whatever 'unspeakable' things he'd got away with in China. Because the foreign white investment banker she met at a Michael Jackson concert, my father, had a Western offer.

In this silence, I see her checking the list of things she wanted to talk about, making another bullet point at the bottom, but scribbling over it.

'Well, I don't want to take up your time,' she says.

'I've got to make some food,' I say.

'That's what you said.'

'What are you going to do today?'

'I'm not sure. Some things.'

'How do you feel?' I say.

'Good enough for some things.'

'Do you need a hand with anything?'

'With what?'

'Anything.'

'I'm going to call Sally about the living-room wall again. She says it's damp. It's my responsibility, she says. But the wall is wet again. *Wet*. That is a leak. That is not damp.'

'I can come over, have a look.'

'You could get a haircut,' she says.

I don't say anything. I hold out my silence, full of pain, hoping she'll diffuse it with asking how I am. 'Kaasan?' I say, readying the question, the subject, that I can never bring up.

'Because that would be a good thing to do,' she says.

'Kaasan?'

'What is it?'

But I can't say anything. I can't ask her.

'Because I saw a picture of you and wondered if people might think you are sloppy. I think if someone looks sloppy, they look lazy.'

'Okay,' I say.

'Okay?'

'Okay. I'll get a haircut.'

'That might be for the best,' she says.

'Okay. Well. Talk soon.'

'Okay.'

'Okay. Bye, then.'

'Yes. Bye.'

'Bye.'

'Bye.'

'Yeah, bye,' I say, but I don't hang up.

'Are you still there?' she says. 'Hello? You're still *here*, but, hello? You must have gone. Now how do you—?'

I should hang up first. I suppose that's the daughterly thing to do.

While she tries to end the call, I swab the condensation on my bedroom windowsills. Black, flaking with mould. Dust has clogged with rain, crusts the glass outside. The light that tries to come through comes through a little dirtied.

I guess it's an obviously motherly thing, but it still amazes me to think that after every time we speak on the phone, she plans and awaits our next call. More and more these days I think about what she gets up to. I know she wakes up at 5:30 on workdays, 7:00 on her days off. I know she has big breakfasts, usually rice, smoked fish, omelette, fruit. This became her routine when she started working for Premier Inn. With no payment for overtime, they practically pay housekeepers by the room, not the hour, so she works through the shift without a break to finish her schedule in time. I know she has a bath when she gets home. I know she often calls her property manager, the council, about problems with the flat. Leaks. Mould. I know she arranges flowers. I know she meets other women with cancer in a café once a week. I know, once a month, she drinks with women she doesn't like but can speak Japanese with. I know she often has dinner, watches TV, has sex, I think, with Leonard Down the Corridor, whose wife died some time ago. But this is strictly private information. I can tell by the way she says hello to Leonard Down the Corridor when we pass him on her floor. 'Hello, Leonard,' she says, flatly, without looking at him. 'Hello,' he says with a smile.

I know she thinks about the money she wants to leave my brother and me. I know she thinks about the cancer the size of a five-pence piece in the only breast she has left. I know she must worry about it. She must worry about when blood will drip from her nose after chemotherapy. She must worry about when or where she will need to throw up. She must worry about looking like a person with cancer. She must worry about having a daughter who has a mother who has cancer, how that daughter will be if the mother dies. She might not worry about leaving her own life, but maybe about leaving her daughter's life.

What she must not worry about is how the daughter was raped. She believes the lawyers who argued that the drunken stories don't add up, that not putting up a fight, what I felt I needed to do to save my life, is evidence of me not telling the truth. She believes the witnesses who vouched for your brother's sensitivity, his affability, his history of respecting women. She doesn't understand why I would throw my bedsheets, my pyjamas, evidence, in the skip, how I could be too disgusted by them to think they could be useful dirty. But she does worry about the daughter lying about such a serious thing. About the daughter getting so drunk she could've got raped. And the daughter worries, between all this worry, about her mother having cancer. She worries about wishing her mother didn't have cancer. She worries because she wishes her mother didn't have cancer, partly so she could say how much the mother has hurt her.

COMMENTS

Unknown
I was sexually abused by my stepfather from 8 years old to 13. I never told anyone. Now I'm 50 and I still haven't properly. I wish I had told someone. If this is happening to you or if it has, please, please tell someone. Like Corina, don't hold it inside.
Reply

Unknown
This comment has been removed by the blog administrator.
Reply

Anonymous
You invited your ex to a party; you got drunk and flirted with him; he was still in love with you, God knows why; he passed out in your bed; you could've told him to fuck off but you let him stay there; you got in bed with him . The whole thing stinks of bullshit. You only posted this for publicity as a means to grow your online brand or whatever you think you'redong. Gtfo with your BS and put your face on . . . tramp
Replies

> **Corina**
> Is that you, Your Honour?

denial

I would like to let all know that the size of your Penis really matters in your relationship or marriage. I got married to my wife about 1 month after we met on a photo studio, we lived happily for the first 3 months of our marriage until I and my wife started having quarrels at home because I couldn't satisfy her on bed with my little penis. Actually my penis was very small, it measured about 4.5 inch long on erection and I am 39 years old. My wife said it was forbidden by the women of this world. My wife started sleeping with other men outside. Sometimes I will return from work without finding my wife at home and whenever I call or ask her where she was, she will always snub at me and sometimes just tell me to go get a larger dick. All this continued for a long time and it hurt me so much that I was at the edge of breaking up on the marriage till when I read about a doctor calledDR. OMOHAN. online. I never thought I could smile and be in a happy marriage again if not for the help of DR.OMOHAN. I got the doctors Emails: (dromohanherbalmedicine@gmail. com) on the internet and I emailed him, and he got back to me with some encouraging words, he got me some herbs cream which I use for just 8 days and I began to feel the enlargement of my penis, and without surgery! This went on for a little period of about 10 days and to my surprise my wife keeping screaming that she love my big dick now. Now my wife no longer cheat on me, and my penis is now about 10.5 inches long on erection and off course very large round. And now my wife uses breasts, hips and bumsenlargement. I and my wife are very happy for the help rendered to me byDR.OMOHAN , and I want to say a bif thanks to Doctor for the help. You can contact the Doctor now on his Email ☹ dromohanherbalmedicine@gmail.com) Am thankful to the doctor for helping me.

his whataspp number +2348164816038

DOCTOR OMOHAN CAN AS WELL HELP THE FOLLOWING
PROBLEMS:

HIV/AIDS SPELL

HERPES SPELL

CANCER SPELL

IF YOU WANT YOUR EX LOVER BACK SPELL

IF YOU NEED A BABY SPELL

LOW SPERM COUNT SPELL

get all your problem solve. No problem is too big for him to solve.
Reply

———

When someone is raped they're never raped once, never just by one
person, never just by a person.

COMMENTS

Unknown

This comment has been removed by the blog administrator.
Reply

SCAN OF RECORD OF INTERVIEW WITH CORINA SLATE

18 SEPTEMBER 2014
26 DAYS AFTER ASSAULT

RECORD OF INTERVIEW

ROTI

	URN	01	YR	00673	14

Person interviewed: Corina Slate	Police Exhibit No: CS/01
Place of interview: Fulham Police Station, 6 Heckfield Place, Fulham, London, SW6 5NL	.... 🖉 ....
Date of interview: 18 September 2014 (180914)	Signature of interviewer/transcriber producing exhibit

Time commenced: 1902   Time concluded: 1911   Duration of interview: 09.10

Audio tape reference nos.:   Visual image reference nos.:

Interviewer(s): Det Insp 2514 Nneke Anyaegbuna, PC 6732 Eleanor Davidson

Other persons present: Megan Greene, Special Prosecutor, CPS

Tape counter times	Person speaking	Text
00.01	DI 2514	Okay, my name is Nneke Anyaegbuna, Detective Inspector for the Metropolitan Police and we're back in the interview room with Corina Slate after two short breaks to talk through an alleged rape committed against her. The time is 19.02. If you can say your names again, in the interview with us is.
00.21	PC 6732	Eleanor Davidson, Police Constable for the Metropolitan Police.
00.25	DI 2514	Thank you and.
00.27	MG	Megan Greene, Special Prosecutor, CPS.
00.31	DI 2514	Thank you. Now before we start again I just want to make sure you're okay to continue Corina. You can come back another day if you don't feel up to it.
00.42	CS	I'm fine now. Thank you.
00.45	DI 2514	Okay. So if you could, could you talk about what happened afterwards? Did you tell anyone what happened to you?
00.56	CS	Yes I told my mother.

Signature(s): ....

2014/09

Person interviewed: Corina Slate

Tape counter times	Person speaking	Text
00.59	DI 2514	When did you tell her?
01.01	CS	The week after.
01.03	DI 2514	Do you know the date?
01.05	CS	It would've been the 31st.
01.10	DI 2514	The 31st of August.
01.11	CS	Yes.
01.13	DI 2514	And that was the first time you spoke to her since it happened? That was the first time you spoke to your mother after?
01.20	CS	No. I spoke to her the day after it happened as well.
01.24	DI 2514	Do you remember what you said?
01.27	CS	Not exactly no.
01.29	DI 2514	Or just what you told her.
01.33	CS	Well I tried to tell her. I tried to tell her then what happened. On that Sunday. She doesn't work Sundays. But she was waiting for her property manager to come around because the walls in her building were leaking or something but she couldn't talk because she was doing a crossword while she waited.
01.56	DI 2514	She was doing a crossword?
02.00	CS	Crosswords are important to her.
02.07	PC 6732	Why did you wait a week to tell her?
02.11	CS	I don't know.
02.14	PC 6732	Did you want to tell her?
02.16	CS	Not really. I thought maybe I just wouldn't tell her.

Signature(s): ....

Person interviewed: Corina Slate

Tape counter times	Person speaking	Text
02.20	PC 6732	Why not?
02.23	CS	I didn't want to. I didn't want her to know. I didn't want to bother her with it.
02.30	PC 6732	But you did tell her.
02.32	CS	Well I thought not telling her is about as easy as telling myself it didn't happen. You know.
02.39	PC 6732	And how did you tell her?
02.43	CS	We were on the phone. A different time.
02.48	PC 6732	What were you talking about?
02.51	CS	I don't know.
02.53	PC 6732	So you called her and told her?
02.59	CS	I think we were talking about my brother at that time.
03.03	PC 6732	Okay and what's your brother's name?
03.06	CS	Hiro. With an I.
03.08	PC 6732	Older?
03.09	CS	No.
03.10	PC 6732	Younger?
03.11	CS	Well yeah.
03.13	PC 6732	And you were talking about your brother before you told her?
03.17	CS	Yeah.
03.19	PC 6732	And you'd planned to tell her this time?

Signature(s):..

Person interviewed: Corina Slate

Page No. 4   of 7

Tape counter times	Person speaking	Text
03.23	CS	I don't know if I'd planned it. I wasn't going to tell her then. I was going to hang up actually.
03.31	PC 6732	You were going to hang up?
03.33	CS	It's not important really.
03.34	PC 6732	It might be.
03.39	CS	Well he owes me some money. She was trying to convince me to let her sub for him. She was trying to convince me that it's all the same to me where the money comes from even though she definitely doesn't believe that herself.
03.51	PC 6732	And you didn't hang up?
04.23	CS	Well I suppose she likes that we talk often so. Anyway.
04.27	PC 6732	What else did you talk about?
04.29	CS	Well what was she going on about? She was going on about drowning squirrels in her building's water butt or. And I'm saying it's barbaric or. Well I didn't say those words, but something like that. Then she tells me this. This story about how I would stand on a chair and drown the squirrels myself when I was little or. I know I wouldn't have done that but. But something about the thought of it made me need to tell her what happened. To me.
04.57	DI 2514	And how did she react?
05.01	CS	She thought it was a joke at first.
05.03	DI 2514	A joke?
05.06	CS	She laughed.

Signature(s):...................

Person interviewed: Corina Slate

Tape counter times	Person speaking	Text
05.08	DI 2514	Then did you.
05.11	CS	I told her it wasn't a joke. And then she went quiet. Shocked I guess. Horrified maybe.
05.15	DI 2514	Did you name Mr Struth?
05.17	CS	Yeah. I told her it was him.
05.22	DI 2514	How did she react?
05.24	CS	Well she didn't understand how it could be true. You know. She asked me if I'd gone to the police.
05.30	DI 2514	And you told her.
05.35	CS	I said no. And she said good. She said we've all done things we regret. No, we've all had bad ones, that's what she said. Then I didn't say anything. She doesn't like it when I don't say anything. She said I was being silly. She said I'd probably just built it up in my head. Then I started to cry. I couldn't help it. She never liked it when I cried. She said I was being childish. She asked me if I cry. As in generally as a human. She said. What was it? She said. Yeah she said I'm happy to listen to you talk but I won't waste my time being cried at. Then she told me to call her back once I'd pulled myself together.
06.16	DI 2514	And is that why you took so long to come forward? Is that why it took so long for you to tell anyone else?
06.25	CS	Partly.
06.26	DI 2514	Have you told your brother?

Signature(s): ....

Person interviewed: Corina Slate

Tape counter times	Person speaking	Text
06.29	CS	No.
06.30	DI 2514	Why is that?
06.32	CS	Well if I told him I couldn't be sure he wouldn't do something stupid.
06.36	DI 2514	Like what?
06.39	CS	Like hurt him.
06.42	DI 2514	Mr Struth?
06.43	CS	Yeah.
06.45	PC 6732	But he'd believe that Mr Struth is capable of something like that?
06.48	CS	More than my mother would. My mother liked him.
06.49	PC 6732	Mr Struth.
06.50	CS	Yeah.
06.53	DI 2514	Can you say why? Did she ever say what she particularly liked about him?
07.00	CS	He was polite. He smiled a lot. He made her smile.
07.05	DI 2514	And what about your brother?
07.08	CS	They. Actually they got on as well. You know. With him. Cam. Hiro can get kind of cocky, macho. Hiro gravitates to that kind of guy.
07.20	DI 2514	He's like that himself?

Signature(s):...

Person interviewed: Corina Slate   Page No. 7   of 7

Tape counter times	Person speaking	Text
07.22	CS	Not really. But he was with him. I think Cam can see in you what you need him to be and he can be that for you. Do you know what I mean? I used to think it was an act of generosity like an effort to make the other person comfortable which everyone was around him.
07.39	PC 6732	And what do you think of it now?
07.45	CS	I don't know.
07.51	DI 2514	Do you have enough support at home Corina?
07.56	CS	Support? I don't know. It is what it is. You know. I'll manage.
08.04	DI 2514	What I mean is we can set you up with someone to talk to.
08.09	CS	I don't think that'll be necessary. No. I'll be fine. I will be fine. As long as I don't see him I think. I think I'm fine. Well not fine but. You know. I don't know. Seeing someone like that I. I don't know. But no. I don't think that will be necessary.
08.34	DI 2514	Are you sure? Okay. Well I think it would be best for you just to go over some things we don't have time to go over here. Okay? Okay. Now if there's not anything more you'd like to add I think we can stop there. Is there anything you'd like to add Corina?
09.04	CS	No.
09.07	DI 2514	Okay. The time now is 19.11. You did great. Thank you. What we'll do now is have you write a statement. Then what will happen is we'll get Mr Struth in for a chat. Then we'll talk again to you at another time. Okay? Okay. Stop the recording there please.
		End of tape.

Signature(s): ....

32

COPIED TRANSCRIPT OF CONSECUTIVE VOICE MESSAGES FROM CORINA SLATE (C.SL.) TO CAMERON STRUTH (C.ST.)

15 AUGUST 2014
8 DAYS BEFORE ASSAULT

22:53

C.Sl. [whispering]: Hello, stranger. I'm hiding in the toilet where we met. The unisex toilet in the, er, that Hackney pub. If you've forgotten that. I'm feeling very, like, [unintelligible]. I think I'm older than everyone in here. Like I'm wearing someone else's dress. It's a bit too small for me. Bitch. No. But, er, I can't even remember the last time I went out out, you know. It was probably with you. Maybe it was. Er. The students are on the wards these days and like, I didn't want them to think I'm all serious, you know, and past it. I didn't want them to talk badly about me. Like I don't know why I care so much really. Like they just keep screaming shots, shots, shots. I'm like again? Already? They look at me like they don't know if I'm joking. And now I think about it [unintelligible]. Like. What's happened to me, man? Well I can tell you so far tonight I've managed to crack a filling on a lemon pip, I've spent like ninety pounds, and a table of drinks tipped over onto a little man in a wheelchair with a nasogastric tube and I can't say for sure it wasn't my fault. So some, er, glasses broke over his head I think. I tried to help clean him up but he kept pushing me away. I said I'm a nurse but he didn't like seem to think that was relevant. He just said good for you and he wheeled himself out. I'm, er. A couple

33

of people took a picture of me stood there not knowing what to do. They weren't laughing though I felt like they were, they were just taking pictures. The, um. I saw the guy in the wheelchair in the smoking section. I tried to say sorry but he flicked his cigarette at me so yeah I've also got a burn on my neck. Oh. And two guys have hit on me. Yeah. Forgotten what that's like. First one just sort of asked for my number out of the blue. I said no thanks but he just kept on asking why so I told him I had a boyfriend and he seemed to respect that. The second one. He called me cute. Fucking cute. White guy obviously. I asked him why he would use that word. I asked him if he'd ever used that word in his life. He didn't know what to do. I just fucked off back inside. It's, well. When we met here we were like twenty-seven or something. This would all make for a good story I guess but, like, [unintelligible] gracefully. I remember [unintelligible] you were, um, you were putting on eyeliner in front of the sink. Do you remember? You grinned at me through the mirror when I came out a cubicle. I remember thinking something like what a beautiful boy and laughing at that in my head. I don't think I really wanted anything to do with you. You said. You said it smells like Tinkerbell's kidney stone in here which is a wild thing to say. I said you've smelt a kidney stone? You said only Tinkerbell's. You said, Have you? And I said yes. You said what's a human kidney stone smell like then? Like I imagine caviar smells. I.

22:56

C.Sl. [whispering]: Shit. Sorry. This was supposed to be one whole thing. It was supposed to be a quick thing. I'm only doing these because I can't be arsed to type. Must be. It will be quick I promise. The people I, er, came with will come looking for me. I hope. I'm, er, so I let the students take me out because the. The guy I was, er, seeing, we were in love actually, ha, love actually, [unintelligible], no, but, er, so he, er, like, he left me, I guess, [unintelligible]. You don't know him. I'm here in, like, the toilet because I, er, I just got my period actually. So I feel a bit stuck. My. My feet hurt. I'm. I'm sad. I'm a bit sad. I, um, I thought of you. I was already thinking

34

about you actually. I was already thinking about you because, well, I'm here, you know. I, like, I've imagined you turning up all night but I. I'm messaging you, a bit drunk maybe, yeah, I, like, because I see you're coming to ours next week. Yeah. So. I wonder if you thought this message was to tell you not to. It's not. Really. Like maybe I should've said that first. But, no, like I'm glad you're coming. I think. I've, er. I've been thinking about you, us, more often these days. Like I don't know how I feel about seeing you again. Excited. In a kind of, um, scared shitless way. I looked at a picture of you the other day. It was weird. Like. Not weird weird just I don't know. I realised that you were actually alive, a, you know, walking, talking, thinking kind of person, which is obvious but I guess you were only kind of, sort of theoretically alive before that, you know. It was like seeing a picture, like, a new picture of a childhood friend or. I can't think of the word, like, well, it's probably affection isn't it? Because even though there was so much horrible shit between us, there's a lot of me that's still you, you know. If that makes sense. Because I. I don't know what I want, or if it means anything but, like, except I do think we could, you know, use each other these days, because, I mean, do you? I mean I wonder, like, why are you coming? Like. What does coming mean to you? You know. Like. I mean, fuck, maybe this is a mistake. I don't know what this is. Maybe it's nothing, maybe you'll make it into something or what it actually is [unintelligible] don't know but I don't know. There was something else I wanted to say. It was. It was. Sam. Fuck. This is. Fuck. I'm sorry about Sam. I'm sorry about your brother. I heard, er. So is he. Can you tell me.

22:58
C.Sl. [whispering]: Sorry. So. The girl in the next cubicle has been crying for ages and just stopped. Shall I. Like. Hold on.

C.Sl. [to Doe]: Are you all right?

Doe: [unintelligible].

C.Sl. [to Doe]: Do you want to talk about anything?

Doe: [unintelligible].

C.Sl. [to C.St.]: Hold on, I'm.

23:01

C.Sl. [to C.St.]: Weird. So I went out to talk to her but she was already gone. I just looked in the toilet. Don't know why. It's clear. So. I better go, man. There's so many people I have to say bye to. Or maybe I'll just leave now. Fuck is this a big. I. Hold on. I've just realised the other messages haven't sent. I. There's no signal in here. So, like. Um. So I wonder if I'll send them later when, not so or maybe I'll remember what I've said and just delete everything or. I, er, which would mean I've been talking to myself this whole time. So. Well. Okay.

[End of transcript.]

COPIED WORD DOCUMENT FROM CAMERON STRUTH'S PERSONAL COMPUTER

LAST SAVED 24 SEPTEMBER 2014
32 DAYS AFTER ASSAULT

On the 5th August 2014, Ms Corina Slate invited me via social media to attend her housewarming party, and late on the 15th of August, she sent me various voice messages intended to encourage my attendance. By virtue of my having to rise early the next morning for rehearsals—I am the lead in a production of *Crime and Punishment* at the Young Vic—along with the fact that I was feeling poorly and black mould had grown in patches of my room's ceilings and walls (probable cause), so that when I breathed my chest sounded like a kettle boiling, which, after checking the symptoms online, led me to believe I had a chest infection—and also because my brother had tried to kill himself three months before the night in question and remains in a coma to this day—I did not believe I would be an especially charming guest and I decided not to go.

To be honest, these factors coincided with the crucial fact that Ms Slate and I had separated following a two-year-long relationship in February. The invitation was our first point of contact since then and I was led to believe that she had not taken the split too well. On various occasions, mutual friends and friends of hers had contacted me to communicate as much. On the 30th of May, for instance, a couple of days after my brother's failed attempt at suicide, I remember Ms Sophia Doldross messaged me something to the effect of: 'Corina won't stop crying. She won't leave her room. Do you know anything about this?' Likewise, a message from Ms Sade Cully the next day saying: 'She's crushed about something. You need to do something.' The invitation, I believe, was either sent out of mere courtesy or a fear of appearing bitter, and her subsequent effort to encourage my attendance seemed only the result of excessive drinking, and thus I believed that it would only exacerbate any residual hostility between us.

Nevertheless, my eventual decision to go followed a discussion with Ms Tasha Johnson, a colleague and friend of Ms Slate, in which the former assured me that the latter had recovered from the break-up. Just after 19:00 on the night in question, she messaged something to the effect of: 'Fuck, dude, she's over you, okay? Good lord.' Confident, then, that there would be no bad blood, as well as eager to piece together a friendship, I intended to alleviate the symptoms of my illness—whenever I felt unwell as a child, which happened often after my brother had locked me out of the house one winter night and I experienced hypothermia and subsequent pneumonia, my mother would have me drink a glass of brandy, and so, on my way home from rehearsals that night, I bought a 35cl bottle of brandy from an off licence on Barking Road, at approximately 20:30—and I intended to arrive early so as to talk with Ms Slate somewhat clear-headed.

When I got to Ms Slate's house, around two and a half hours later, on account of travel time and losing my way through Clem Attlee Court estate because a group of young men had given me false directions, I had drunk about half the bottle of brandy, but I did not feel inebriated. In the hallway there were scores of people I didn't recognise. As I made my way to the kitchen at the back of the house, I felt distinctly overdressed in brogues and an Oxford shirt, having earlier fancied myself a kind of authoritative cultural professional, like an editor or curator perhaps, but now I imagined that I looked merely bland, out of touch, in light of the worker's jackets, the five-panel caps, the over-the-shoulder bumbags, and perfectly grubby white Reeboks abundant in the vicinity.

In the kitchen I met Ms Johnson, who pulled me by the sleeve into some furtive and slanderous seminar, immediately complaining that Ms Slate had invited her neighbours and word must have spread around the estate. These interlopers had set up enormous speakers in the living room and a stall in the corner of the kitchen for selling pink dollar-signed pills and balloons bloated not, I assume, with helium.

Again, with rehearsals the next day, I did not partake in these chemical extravagances, but I did accept a beer that a girl, about whom I can't remember much except that she had the appearance and mannerisms of a sparrow, had offered me from an old camp cooler. She said we'd met many times before. If that was true she must have been totally forgettable on each occasion. Her name eludes me still because I didn't want her to think that I'd forgotten her and so I didn't ask her to remind me. To be honest, I don't believe she'd been invited or that she even knew the hosts. The beer tasted like there were coins in it so I asked her if it was out of date. In retrospect, I believe that one of these uninvited guests had spiked it. She said she didn't know, and gave me a thumbs-up. She asked me if I wanted a piece of gum. She herself was chewing manically.

'Sure,' I said. It was stale and soft and bubble-gum, which I loathe, but I didn't spit it out, so as not to offend her—maybe the gum was what was drugged—and she asked me if I felt okay. 'Sure,' I said, looking for someone I knew in the unnervingly contented crowd, and I asked her why she'd asked. She couldn't say; it was neither necessarily the way I looked, nor the way I was acting, she said. As far as I was concerned I felt as if I seemed perfectly normal—self-possessed, even—but she went on to suggest, seriously, that I spend time sorting myself out and acquiring some composure.

Affronted slightly, since emotional control is precisely that upon which I pride myself and even base my career, I spontaneously recited all twenty-two lines of my favourite soliloquy—that's Edmund's from Lear (1:2)—while holding this girl's gaze for every word, except, strategically, on the words 'curiosity', the second use of 'base' and also when I addressed the 'gods', specifically to emphasise the command I have of my expression in any given moment and in general, and after this, I asked her if that sounded like someone who needed to sort himself out and acquire some composure.

She said, 'Yes.'

We stood there looking at each other. Her eyelids dipped sleepily so I asked her how she felt. 'I feel fine,' she said, giving me another thumbs-up. Upon this gesture, she said something to the effect of: 'I feel bright. I feel like I'm a Christmas tree. Or I feel like a bonfire. I really feel like Guy Fawkes or someone in a Christmas tree. When I close my eyes, I do.'

This is when I began to suspect that she was on drugs—probably methylenedioxymethamphetamine, since every now and then she would break her frightened reposing expression with a smile so abrupt and vast it was as if others were watching us and the smile held a secret only I could know, and as such, her opinion of me clearly couldn't and can't be trusted.

'Cool,' I said.

She told me to close my eyes.

'No, I'm cool,' I said.

'You,' she said, a finger jabbing at my chin. 'You might as well be dead, man.'

'What's that?'

She said (and I remember it exactly), 'I'm sorry but your life is going to be meaningless for forever. I can tell.'

Then she stepped back from me and turned away, and though I called after her, she lifted her middle finger above the heads. The crowd resisted me coming through them, and by the time I got past, the girl had disappeared. From here I could see Ms Slate in the living room with Ms Johnson and a man I didn't recognise. Ms Slate had been growing out her fringe, as I'd seen from photos, but that night she had a box fringe. This means, I know, that she'd just turned the corner after a stretch of what she would deem unhealthy and careless living. She looked cute and happy.

Now this is where my memory frays. What I do remember is talking to Ms Johnson outside by the recycling bins. We were discussing the Israel–Palestine conflict, particularly the fact that President Nassar had threatened Israeli annihilation, but Ms Johnson was adamant that this was not the case. We did not talk about Ms Slate, I don't think, though I wanted to know why she had been so insistent that I attended that night. The next thing I remember is vomiting multiple times in the toilet. Whether my pulmonary affliction had climaxed or I'd decided to eject the drug with which I'd been spiked, I don't know, but it certainly had a positive effect. My head felt flushed and rinsed, but with that came the painful clarity of knowing the party had all but ended and that now, sometime around 3:00, finding somewhere to sleep ahead of rehearsals was imperative, so I looked to see if the room next to Ms Slate's room was empty. Cracking open the door, Corina's other housemate, Ms Louise Prieditis, and another man I didn't recognise, both sat up in the bed and asked me what I wanted. Apologising, I said I needed a place to crash. 'Have you got a spare sheet or pillow?' I said.

'No,' said Ms Prieditis.

'Honestly,' I said, 'I won't be a bother. I'll sleep on the floor over here. Please.'

She said she had nothing for me.

'I don't want to be a pain,' I said. 'I don't, but I've seen you do yoga, Louise. Don't you have a yoga mat I could use?'

'No,' she said. 'I don't. Try Corina.'

'She doesn't do yoga,' I said.

'Just try her for a blanket or something.'

But I didn't know if that was appropriate.

'She won't mind,' Ms Prieditis said. 'Believe me.'

'Really?' I said. (The way she said 'Believe me' communicated the affirmation that Ms Slate would actually embrace it.)

'Yes,' she said. 'Yes. I'm sure she won't. Yes. I'm sure. Okay? See you later. See you.'

'Okay,' I said. 'Sorry for bothering you both.'

Despite the assurance of Ms Slate's willingness to welcome me into her room—in fact, I didn't, at that moment, expect to share her bed—I did not want to disturb her. From memory I knew she

41

had a box of spare sheets under her bed, and there was a cushion on the vanity table chair. The room, when I opened the door, seemed empty, for Ms Slate made no shape in the bed, totally starfish flat as she is when she sleeps, but I knew she was there because I heard her snoring lightly. With the door closed behind me, I stood there for probably up to a minute trying to acclimate my eyes to the dark. Somehow Ms Slate sensed my presence and woke. She asked if it was me. It was, I told her, me.

'What were you looking at?' she said.

'Nothing. Just the dark,' I said, which, in retrospect, might have sounded a little creepy.

She asked me if I was okay.

'Sure,' I said. 'I'm just trying to find a place to crash. I can sleep in the tub if you don't want me here.'

'No,' she said. 'Don't do that.'

She pulled back the duvet, opening a space for me. Once I was beside her, she said, quietly, with what seemed to be affection, 'I thought you'd left.'

'You missed me, have you?' I said, but joking, obviously. She didn't say anything, though I heard her lips part into a smile.

After that we talked idly about the events of the night and what we'd been up to since the separation. Our voices reached each other via the dark, and, in my memory, this produced a kind of tender detachment from the world, an unburdening of our proximity to the anxious demands of being seen and seeing, which thus engendered the dreamy release that people feel in the confessional, I imagine, or in those lovely dwindling moments of a childhood sleepover, before the sky outside shifts tones to pink, eventually reversing this disembodiment with clarity, the clarity of reciprocated intimacy and, crucially, for the matter at hand, consent.

We had sex. But briefly, unsuccessfully, on account of my unexpected and residual intoxication, and not to mention my infant cryptorchidism—that is, an undescended testicle—which means I'm often unwilling in this regard, especially in conjunction with alcohol. To reiterate, though, there was no point at which it appeared to me that Ms Slate had not consented. Even without verbalising it directly, the case seemed, quite palpably, the contrary.

After that, we went to sleep, and the next thing I remember is waking up in Ms Slate's bed. She was asleep beside me. My phone, I remember, told me it was 10:52. There was a text from my mother, which said that my father and she were giving my brother until November to wake up or they would have to let him go. For months I'd dreaded the text saying he'd died as well as the text saying he'd woken up, but I didn't know how to feel about this, the text that seemed to promise both.

Without waking Ms Slate, I dressed and left. Music still played in the living room but there was no one else awake. After having taken the tube, then the DLR to Canning Town, I walked home. I texted Sam asking him if he was okay. I don't know how I could've forgotten. I was sober. It must have been habit, or maybe wishful thinking. Four days later, I texted Ms Slate a smiley face. Or at least I tried to, but accidentally I sent: 🙁

There was and is no doubt in my mind that what little had occurred between Ms Slate and I was consensual. From my confident perspective, it was only somewhat messy. *It was only somewhat messy*. **It was only somewhat messy.**

COPIED POSTS FROM CORINA SLATE'S BLOG, 'WITNESS'

AUGUST 2016 (3)

The week after our mother's cancer came back, Hiro told me he'd tracked down our father. We were in The Drum, a pub on Lea Bridge Road. He pinched the skin on his knuckles, looked around with a kind of restless pleading expression, hoping to find something else to talk about, hoping that it was enough simply to tell me, that I wouldn't pry or test him.

A woman passed our table. He looked up at her, then quickly away, deciding not to check her out, which I guess he thought was chivalrous. An earring bounced off the floor. The woman didn't notice. Hiro picked it up, called after her. She took it back with a look of suspicion, as if he'd nicked it in the first place. As a kid he was often presumed to be up to no good, which maybe made him get up to no good more often. At first kids called him names to hurt him, make him feel his outsiderness, but then they called him names to watch him throw a chair, grab someone by the throat, instigate a fight just so the white kids could say he started it after they'd battered him. Our parents would tell him to ignore them. I would also disapprove, mainly of his getting into trouble, but now it's more because he's what they want and expect him to be.

He wrapped his hand around his pint, swilled up a fizz. He glanced back to where the earring fell, muttered, 'Should've fucking kept it.'

'Have you talked to him?' I asked.

44

'Just found his name on a bus tours thing in Greece.'

'You going to call them?'

'Thought about it. Then I thought about him hanging up.'

'How do you know it's him, then?'

'There's a picture on the website as well.'

'Well, fine,' I said, feeling hollow. 'So what?'

'I want to go see him.'

'But why?'

'I don't know. I miss him.'

'You barely knew him.'

'That's what I miss, man.'

'But why now?'

'I just told you.'

'Don't do that. Don't play stupid.'

He angled his head to the floor and sneezed.

'Cover your mouth, man,' I said. 'You know how far germs spread?'

He took out his phone, looked at it.

I said, 'I just don't know why you want to see him now.'

'Oh my days—'

'I'm only asking—'

'What?'

'I'm only—'

'Oh, nah, not you. There's this video of a bulldog puppy leaping off a sofa and into its owner's arms. You seen it?'

'Yeah, it's adorable. Put your phone down.'

'All right. Calm.'

'I'm only saying I don't know what good seeing him would do. For you. For Mum. You know she—'

'You just don't want to be left alone with her.'

'No.'

'See how quickly you said that. See that.'

'No. Because it's not true.'

'You just want to feel like the good daughter, holding us all together, and you need me around for that.'

'Don't say that. I'm just saying there's no use reopening scar tissue.'

'Speak English, man.'

'How's what I'm saying unclear?'

'Listen, yeah, I want—'

'Sounds like you want Mum to freak out.'

'Freak out?' he said.

'That you'll leave for good like him and that she'll pay your rent if you don't go or something.'

'You're chatting shit, man.'

'Because she would, you know. She would for Little Hiro.'

'Well, it looks like nothing's fucking happening with Mother Corina around.'

'All right. So are we finished talking now?'

'I'm going to get money off him,' he said.

'What money?'

'His money. Our money.'

'We don't need his money.'

'But we're owed it.'

'We don't want it.'

'Why?'

'Because it's his.'

'Doesn't matter where it's from,' he said. 'If it's legit.'

'It won't be.'

'So what?'

'Just think about what you're saying, Hiro. The words you're saying.'

He shook his head. I knew if I told him he couldn't go and see our father, he'd rent a car, drive to wherever-the-fuck by himself. He was looking hench that day. He'd had more time to fill at the gym.

'And this is the only reason?' I said. 'The money?'

'That's all, man.'

'And it's for us, yeah? Mum?'

'Us. Mum. Who else?'

'Yourself.'

'I'm part of us, aren't I?'

'You finding work, Hiro?'

'Course I am.'

'What work?'

'I got some software repairs. Some hardware. Hardware pays better, styll. But yeah. Loads of things.'

'Legal things?'

'Listen. Right. The money I get from him will be for Mum. And you. There'll be some for you, Cor.'

'Have you talked to Mum about it?'

He looked in his lap.

'Hiro?'

'I don't want to lie to her about it.'

'Well, I don't see any other way without it hurting her somehow, especially now.'

'But I'm going,' he said. 'I'm going.'

I looked in his eyes until I couldn't look in his eyes. I wondered how many people had seen him grapple back tears at Comic Relief, or when he's wrongfully accused. I felt the ulcerous burn I feel when I think of him not talking to me, avoiding me, leaving me alone with our mother.

He said, 'Don't you ever want to see him?'

'No,' I said. 'I don't.'

'But you can get why I want to, though.'

'Not really.'

'He never actually hit her.'

'Well, in that case.'

He breathed heavily. 'I can't not tell her that I'm going,' he said. 'And I am going.'

'So just go, man. Go get wrapped up in whatever dodgy scheme he's got going on. Go score his coke for him. Go place his bets.'

'It's not something I can just do, though, is it?'

I didn't know what to say. He waited to see if I was going to say anything. Then he looked at his phone. His face relaxed into his basic expression. Confused by the complexity of the world, annoyed that he is confused, that it is confusing. I've often wished we had not grown up so close, that he was remote enough for me to be awed by him sometimes. Actually, that isn't quite true. My jealousy of how his coolness can become arrogant but fun, attractive, in spite of the softness he hides, has often come close to awe.

He licked his thumb, checked that no one was looking, and scrubbed a smudge on his trainers. He said, 'Thinking about getting a dog, you know.'

'It's expensive, having a dog,' I said.

'I'd get up bare early to walk it.'

'Demanding, too.'

'It could come on runs with me.'

'It seems sort of cruel to have one in a city.'

He grinned at his phone screen. 'Oh my days.'

———

The chain on my door doesn't work. The bolt at the end of the chain has rusted, ground down so much that it just slips out the bar. I answer the door one morning, someone explodes into my flat. That could happen. I'm not paranoid. Well, I am, but it does happen. I've heard about it happening. I call the estate agents, ask to speak to the property manager. 'I'm afraid we're just closing up for the day. We open at ten on a Saturday so you can speak to someone—'

'I'm not going to wait till then. I want to speak to the property manager.'

'As I said, madam, we're—'

'What time do you close?'

'On Fridays we close at seven but—'

'So you're still open.'

'It's seven now.'

'It's one minute to.'

'Yeah—'

'So you're still open?'

'We're closing now, and by the time—'

'My flat's just around the corner. And I have an urgent problem.'

'Urgent?'

'Yes.'

'What seems to be the problem?'

'The problem is that the chain on my door doesn't work.'

'The chain lock?'

'I guess. Yeah.'

'And is the door lock faulty also?'

'The door lock is fine.'

'Well, as I said, madam, we open at ten tomorrow so you can—'

'Is the property manager still there?'

'Well, yes, she's—'

'I'm coming over there now.'

'But we're—'

It's dark out so I slot a screwdriver under the waistband of my joggers, run out, down Green Lanes, slapping puddles up my legs.

I meet them outside their office. Someone is locking the door. Others are smoking, fastening their jackets. A young woman says, 'That's—'

'I'd like to talk to the property manager,' I say.

The eyes turn towards one woman tying the belt around her trench coat. Her hair is up, pulled back tight.

'Is that you?' I say to her. I cough the warble out my throat. 'You're the property manager? I have a problem.'

'Sorry?' she says, leaning towards me and frowning.

Did I speak too quietly?

'I have a problem,' I say.

'With the chain on your door?'

'Yes.'

'Yes and we're closed now, I'm afraid. If you tell me where you live I'll be happy in the morning—'

'I want it fixed now, though.'

She makes a face like I don't understand her language.

'I want it fixed right now,' I say. 'Okay?'

She looks at the ground.

'What if someone breaks into my flat?' I say. 'What if I call you at ten tomorrow and I've been broken into? What's your policy on that? I assume you'll accept responsibility.'

'There's nothing right now that—'

'There's a DIY shop still open just by me.'

'Then I'd suggest that you—'

I pull out my hand, still holding the screwdriver. They shift away. Eyes move quicker. 'This is your responsibility,' I say. 'It is your responsibility to ensure that my flat is properly equipped. Okay? I'll fit it myself,' I say, looking at the screwdriver pointed at them, something I wish I'd thought of not doing before doing it. 'I'm not mental,' I say. 'I was fixing something.' I lower it by my thigh. They nod slowly. I say, 'I'm sure as fuck not paying for it myself. Okay?'

The property manager checks her watch. I check mine. 19:03.

We walk together, me a little ahead, to the DIY shop. The property manager has to get cash out along the way. She knows exactly where the door chains are. We don't say anything till I say thank you quietly on the street. She lifts her eyebrows bluntly, turns, walks away. I walk home so fast my shins hurt.

COMMENTS

Unknown
This comment has been removed by the blog administrator.
Reply

—

RE: Tenancy Renewal

Dear Ms. Slate,

I hope all is well.

Your Assured Shorthold Tenancy Agreement is due to expire on 9th November 2016. Please let us know if you would like to renew the tenancy for a further term of 12 months, by phone or email.

If you wish to renew the tenancy agreement we will then approach your Landlord accordingly to obtain instructions and review the current rental. Should you proceed with the renewal an administration fee of £120.00 inclusive of VAT will be applicable.

I look forward to hearing from you.

If you require anything else, please do not hesitate to contact us.

Kind regards,

Ana Thompson

Residential Lettings Administrator

———

We were testing the dialysate tanks, the water quality, ahead of the day shift. I can tell we're close to clocking off when Tasha's uniform comes undone. I was watching a lace flop on top of her trainers, waiting for it to unfurl.

'You been on any dates recently?' she said.

I shook my head.

'But wasn't there—'

'No.'

'No one on the cards then?'

'Nope.'

'What's up?'

'Nothing,' I said. 'There's no one on the cards.'

'All right, all right. Nothing wrong with a dry spell.'

I told her I was tired. She told me about her friend's recent dates. 'So I'm getting these voice notes from her,' she said, 'and she's getting progressively more pissed, and I can hear other people in the background, it sounded busy, and she's basically shouting into her phone, "I'm going to fuck tonight! It's happening!"'

I binned my gloves, checked my watch.

'Cor?' she said.

'Yeah?'

'You hear what I said?'

'Yeah,' I said.

Tasha sighed as if to tell me I'm hard work.

'So you're just tired,' she said, taking off her gloves. 'Nothing else going on?'

I said, 'My rent's going up and I'm starting to hate the place. There's mould on the windows that won't fuck off.'

Tasha told me her brother was moving out of the flat her parents gave them. 'Why don't you come live with me and Seb?' she said. Seb is her boyfriend. He's easy-going, flirty, white, speaks with his hands like an MC, 6' 7". Once after a druggy night, we ended up in a threesome situation but I left because his dick is hilariously big. I've been on the outside, in the middle, of some savage arguments, mostly about one of them flirting with someone else. 'It's perfect!' she said. 'When do you have the tenancy till?'

'I don't know,' I said. 'November sometime, I think.'

'That'd be great, wouldn't it?' she said.

I made an affirmative sound.

'No?' she said, but the General Manager of the Kidney Service Team saved me.

'Morning, all,' she said, toasting us with her thermos. 'Any fires?' When we shook our heads, shifted ourselves into a calmer and more careful manner, she said, 'How about the new girl?'

'Ali,' I said.

'She's no walk in the park,' said Tasha.

'GFR is around 60,' I said. 'It'll have to be checked more often. I would screen for microalbuminuria. She's been given ACE inhibitors.'

'What about treating her personality?' Tasha said.

'What about it?' I said.

'You mustn't have borne the brunt of it.' Tasha whistled.

'I quite like her,' said the General Manager of the Kidney Service Team. 'Reminds me of my cousin.'

'She's fine to me,' I lied.

Tasha peered into my face. I knelt to retie my laces.

'If GFR goes down anymore,' Tasha said, 'it's because she's not eating.'

I suggested counselling.

'I was thinking appetite stimulants,' she said.

I couldn't be bothered to respond with more than a nod.

'Well, we'll cross that bridge,' said the General Manager of the Kidney Service Team, already walking away.

In the break room Tasha changed her socks, saying, 'That phrase has always bothered me. "We'll cross that bridge when we come to it." It's like, yeah, what else are we going to do at a bridge? Should be *if*, right? Cross that bridge *if* we come to it.'

I was mopping a spill of tea on the floor, can't remember what I said. Tasha frowned at me, asked me what I wanted to eat. I told her I'd eat at home.

'I guess I'll eat on my own then,' she said.

'I guess,' I said.

'You've been in there a long time,' my mother said. 'The doctor is ready to see me.'

The toilet in the oncology unit was pristine. Not just clean; it looked new, refurbished. I wondered if people only came in here to cry, for a break, like now. I was sure that there'd been vomit. Anxiety vomit. Chemotherapy vomit. Toxic urine. If there were a window I'd have thought about climbing out of it.

'I don't want to keep the doctor waiting,' I heard my mother say.

I broke my own gaze, sanitised my hands, opened the door. She looked quickly away. I'd forgotten she was wearing a woolly hat, a fluffy bobble on the top. We walked together down the corridor, feeble in our own ways. I wanted to hold her hand. Her hands, rough, nicked, ridged, like nettle leaves. She would have swatted away my hand with a tut. She held back on affection, didn't spare us any suffering, to strengthen us up. It's not like she never comforted us when we needed comforting. It's more that comforting us was no different than changing our nappies. Once, when I won a prize at Sports Day, my father treated me and my friends to McDonald's. That night I overheard my mother say to him, 'Only kiss the baby when it's sleeping.'

I overheard her giving him this advice a few more times. I've heard women talk about getting to the age when they can share their intimacies with their mothers. It's always been embarrassing, irritating even, for us to see the other falter. More maybe for me. For the times she stumbles over a word, or speaks too quietly. But I can't tell her, e.g. how her difference used to embarrass me, how I blamed her for the names I got called, for the pictures I found taped to my locker. It's not that I can't tell her how I hurt, but that I hurt at all. Now it's too late because I'm afraid that it, the sharing, the intimacy, the response, might in some way destroy me.

In the corridor, my mother stopped. I stopped, too. She looked at me, around us. 'What's up?' I said. She scratched her collarbone, fingers glancing over the plastic chemotherapy port above her breast, a vascular opening for cytotoxic agents.

'I was just,' she said, blinking, lips twitching. 'I thought maybe there was . . .'

'What?'

But she turned, rigid, looked down towards the exit. Her head shook. I'd like to be able to say that I knew what she was thinking. It reminds me of the time we watched news coverage of the Fukushima Daiichi Nuclear Plant after the earthquake. The Japanese government had advised some towns near the plant to stay indoors, but the Western specialists said these towns should have been evacuating. I kept asking my mother why they weren't leaving. I'd become sort of breathless since the tsunami, checking the news constantly. 'Why aren't they leaving?' I'd said to her. 'I don't get it.'

'You can't understand,' my mother had said, 'because you're not Japanese.'

'I can't understand anything to do with Japan?' I'd said. 'Is that what you're saying?'

'Not really.'

'But you're Japanese. Can't I understand you?'

'No,' she'd said. 'You can't.'

What other pains, hers, mine, ours, have we not been able to share? What other silences, hers, mine, ours, have always laid between us?

In the oncology corridor, it seemed to be raining behind her eyes.

'Kaasan?' I said.

'No. It's silly,' she said. 'I was thinking I could just, or maybe there was, but no.'

We carried on to the consultant Dr Datta's office. He'd not even sat down behind his desk when he said, 'We are not happy with your progress.'

'I see,' my mother said.

A sinking silence. My mother looked like Dr Datta had told her a cooking tip.

'Yes,' he said. 'I'm afraid to say.'

He sat forward, hands together on his desk. I could smell his aftershave. I sat back in my chair.

He put his mug on the desk. Tea slopped over the sides. I waited for him to mop it up, but he didn't.

'Do you have any suggestions for progression?' I said.

'Don't interrupt,' my mother said quietly.

Dr Datta's eyebrows went up.

'I didn't,' I said.

'Dr Datta was about to speak. Weren't you?'

'Yes, but—'

'See?'

She pulled down the sleeves of her shirt. I looked at the sunflower painting leaning against the wall on the floor.

'Please go on, Dr Datta,' she said.

'Well,' he said, 'you're not responding to this course of chemotherapy as well as we'd hoped. The carcinoma, the cancer, keeps returning.'

'What are my options?' she said.

'Well, first, there's to do nothing.' He smiled, tried to clear his throat. 'But that's not something I'd advise.'

'No,' my mother said. 'I imagine not.'

'The course we've put you on, as you will know, has been a very heavy dose-dense cocktail, if you understand me.'

'It's not been too bad.'

'Yes. You yourself have been remarkably formidable. You've put up a good fight.'

She tilted her head, a little shrug.

'But your body is a different matter, I'm afraid to say. If we carry on this dosage, it will do you more harm than good, in many ways, and there's no evidence the cancer will not recur.'

'So radiation surgery?' I said.

'Do not interrupt,' my mother said. 'For the last time now.'

'It's okay.' Dr Datta stroked his upper lip, tried to clear his throat, then pointed at me. 'And yes, Corina. We would like to perform a radical mastectomy of the right breast, removing the tumour and more lymph nodes. It is radical, as I say. Quite drastic. But necessary, I think. It will be a painful recovery.'

'I see,' my mother said.

'And of course we would like to prepare you for the psychological impact.'

'Psychological impact?'

'It's my understanding,' he said, swallowing dryly, 'that the loss of a breast—'

'I've already lost one,' she said.

We were silent. Dr Datta and I were in the same silence. My mother's silence confronted ours.

Finally, Dr Datta said, 'Well, then radiation is the next step.'

'Radiation,' my mother said.

'Yes, the—'

'I don't want that.'

'I understand your trepidation. My first piece of advice is to avoid Google Images.'

'I don't want that.'

'But of course we will treat your skin for denaturing and radiation burning, so—'

'No, Dr Datta, I do not want it. Thank you.'

'Radiation therapy?'

'Yes. I do not want it.'

'But, Kaasan—'

'Please. I have made up my mind, Dr Datta. I do not want it.'

'Well, I have to be honest,' Dr Datta said, looking down at his desk, 'I cannot recommend this decision.'

'I'm sure.'

'Because, if you don't accept the radiation therapy—'

'Radiation doesn't hurt,' I said. 'It's—'

'Corina-chan,' she said. Her eyes were frozen leaves. Her hand moved over onto the arm of my chair. I watched it there.

I put my hand around hers, turned to Dr Datta. 'Are there any other options?' I said, knowing there weren't.

'Well, more chemotherapy, I suppose, but in a lower dosage. Less toxicity, and thus, in all likelihood, less impact.'

My mother was looking out the window behind him. At the trees, maybe. The summer trees, full of light.

Dr Datta studied my mother. 'Is that how you would like to proceed?'

She lifted her chin, said, 'Yes.'

Dr Datta tapped his lip, scribbled in his notepad. On his desk I saw a child's drawing of a volcano. Bright blue cloud shot out the top. Orange lava flowed down the sides in thick loops.

Dr Datta looked up, gripped his pen. 'I would not be doing my job if I did not prepare you properly,' he said.

My mother moved her hands to her lap. We both straightened in our chairs.

'It is more than likely that the chemotherapy will slow the growth of the main tumour,' he said, 'but it will not stop it from spreading. It will spread, most likely. Your body will of course fight the cancer, but the cancer will likely win.'

We didn't say anything. The fact of what he had said was making no impact on me. If she'd said that she was immortal I would have defended it.

Dr Datta shook his head, let out a little cough. 'I've spent my life fighting this,' he said. 'It's not like your fight, but in my own way. I hate to see it win.'

My mother pulled her hat over her head. 'I have always disliked a sore loser,' she said.

SCAN OF LOUISE PRIEDITIS'S WITNESS STATEMENT

22 SEPTEMBER 2014

WITNESS STATEMENT

Criminal Procedure Rules, r 27. 2; Criminal Justice Act 1967, s. 9; Magistrates' Courts Act 1980, s.5B

| URN | 01 | YR | 00673 | 14 |

Statement of: Louise PRIEDITIS

Age if under 18: Over 18   *(if over 18 insert 'over 18')*   Occupation: Data Protection Officer

This statement (consisting of 4 page(s) each signed by me) is true to the best of my knowledge and belief and I make it knowing that, if it is tendered in evidence, I shall be liable to prosecution if I have wilfully stated in it anything which I know to be false, or do not believe to be true.

Witness Signature: *L. Prieditis*   Date: 22.09.14.

I am the above named person and this is my statement in relation to an incident which occurred on the 23rd of August 2014 when Corina Slate was allegedly raped.

I wasn't around Corina that night because we had drifted apart over the past year and we are still amicable but not particularly close anymore. We'd had a fight about her living at Cam's most of the time when they were together. Having an empty room in the house seemed wasteful to me. It was the first significant fight of our friendship and it changed it. I don't want to say we were avoiding each other, but that's probably what we were doing.

So I don't think I'm the best person to ask about her specifically, we don't figure much in each other's lives anymore.

But I did spend time with Cam that night.

I saw him in the kitchen talking to Sophie, it will have been before midnight.

Sophie had taken MDMA. She was leaning on the wall, she wasn't standing up on her own.

Cam didn't seem to have noticed.

This is not uncommon for Sophie, I often end up looking after her.

I straightened her up and Cam and me talked until Sophie had come around.

Cam was talking in a strange 19th Century voice, it sounded like he was reading from an old book.

Witness Signature: *L. Prieditis*

Signature Witnessed by Signature: ....

Page 1 of 4

64

Continuation of statement of: Louise PRIEDITIS

I asked him why he was talking like that, he said he was playing a character who talked like that and it helped him to prepare for a job.

Sophie came around eventually but then she started saying strange things to Cam, she sounded like a palm reader.

Cam got her some water and I asked her if she could stand on her own. Her mind was all over the place but she wasn't falling about.

Cam handed her the water but she just walked off. Cam asked if she was okay on her own like that and I said if she's walking she's okay but we better keep an eye on her so we followed her out to the front of the house.

She stood on the pavement looking across the road, Cam and me smoked on the doorstep.

For a long time Cam and I talked about Israel and Palestine, he got annoyed because I said it had nothing to do with us, as in the UK. We would've fallen out over it but the bizarre accent he put on was making me laugh.

He asked me if Corina was seeing anyone. I told him she wasn't but I knew she was, she'd been seeing his brother. I didn't condone it, seeing his brother without telling him, but that's none of my business so I didn't say anything.

My boyfriend Jordan turned up around two-thirty in the morning, he works security at the O2. When he turned up we went to bed.

At three in the morning Cam crept in my room asking if he could crash there. I asked him to go but he stood there laughing and talking in that voice, he pretended not to hear what I was saying. I got annoyed, I raised my voice. He said 'Okay, that's all you had to say.' Jordan was going to have a word with him but I told him not to.

I didn't see Cam again.

I didn't hear anything from Corina's room either, mine is right next to hers.

Cam was odd that night but he is odd. I never really know if he's joking or not. Earlier when

Witness Signature: L. Prieditis

Signature Witnessed by Signature:

65

Continuation of statement of: Louise PRIEDITIS

we were talking outside the house, he said, 'I don't think dwarves should be allowed to have children' and when I said 'What?' but he just said 'Hah?' like an old man with bad hearing. It's easier to laugh it off with him.

I went to bed and didn't get up until 1pm the next day.

I've asked Sophie what she thinks about it all but she can't remember anything obviously. Tasha said Sophie will have walked out right into the river if people weren't looking after her all night.

There's nothing else I can add about that night except the next day I couldn't find the hand mirror that I keep on the dresser next to my bedroom door. I used it that night before bed and put it back there, I'm convinced that Cam stole it.

Witness Signature: ... L. Prieditis ....

Signature Witnessed by Signature: ....

Witness contact details

Name of witness: LOUISE PRIEDITIS   URN | 01 | YR | 00673 | 14

Home address: ▮▮▮▮▮   Postcode: ▮▮▮

E-mail address: ▮▮▮▮▮   Mobile: ▮▮▮

Home telephone number: ▮▮▮   Work telephone number: ▮▮▮

Preferred means of contact *(specified details for vulnerable/intimidated victims and witnesses only)*:

Gender: ▮

Date and place of birth: ▮▮▮▮▮▮▮

Former name: ▮▮   Ethnicity Code (16 + 1): ▮▮▮

DATES OF WITNESS NON-AVAILABILITY:

Witness care

a)   Is the witness willing to attend court? YES   If 'No', include reason(s) on for **MG6**.

b)   What can be done to ensure attendance?

c)   Does the witness require a Special Measures Assessment as a vulnerable or intimidated witness? *(youth under 18; witness with mental disorder, learning or physical disability; or witness in fear of giving evidence or witness is the complainant in a sexual offence case)* If 'Yes' submit **MG2** with file in anticipated not guilty, contested or indictable only case. NO

d)   Does the witness have any particular needs? If 'Yes' what are they? *(Disability, healthcare, childcare, transport, disability, language difficulties, visually impaired, restricted mobility or other concerns?)*. NO

Witness Consent (for witness completion)

a)   The Victim Personal Statement scheme (victims only) has been explained to me   Yes ☐   No ☒

b)   I have been given the Victim Personal Statement leaflet   Yes ☐   No ☒

c)   I have been given the leaflet "Giving a witness statement to the police…"   Yes ☒   No ☐

d)   I consent to police having access to my medical record(s) in relation to this matter *(obtained in accordance with local practice)*   Yes ☐ No ☐ N/A ☒

e)   I consent to my medical record in relation to this matter being disclosed to the defence   Yes ☐ No ☐ N/A ☒

f)   I consent to the statement being disclosed for the purposes of civil, or other proceedings If applicable, e.g. child care proceedings, CICA   Yes ☐ No ☐ N/A ☒

'I understand that the information recorded above will be passed on to the Witness Service, which offers help and support to witnesses pre-trial and at court'.

Signature of Witness: *L. Prieditis*   PRINT NAME: LOUISE PRIEDITIS

Signature of parent/guardian/appropriate adult.   PRINT NAME:

Address and telephone number (of parent etc.), if different from above:

Statement taken by: ELEANOR DAVIDSON   Station: FULHAM

Time and place statement taken: 22/09/14 @ FULHAM POLICE STATION SW6 5NL

SCAN OF RECORD OF INTERVIEW WITH CAMERON STRUTH

19 SEPTEMBER 2014
27 DAYS AFTER ASSAULT

RECORD OF INTERVIEW

ROTI

Person interviewed: Cameron Struth

Place of interview: Plaistow Police Station, 444 Barking Road, London, E13 8HJ

Date of interview: 19 September 2014 (190914)

Police Exhibit No: C DS/02

..........Joln Finch.........................

Signature of interviewer/transcriber producing exhibit

Time commenced: 0648   Time concluded: 0658   Duration of interview: 10.19

Audio tape reference nos.:   Visual image reference nos.:

Interviewer(s): Det Insp 7871 John Finch, PC 3009 David Chaplin

Other persons present:

Tape counter times	Person speaking	Text
00.02	DI 7871	This interview is being recorded and conducted in an interview room at Plaistow Police Station, London. The time is 06.48 in the a.m. I am John Finch, Detective Inspector for the Metropolitan Police. PC Chaplin would you introduce yourself with your name and collar number please?
00.19	PC 3009	David Chaplin, Police Constable, 3009, for the Metropolitan Police.
00.28	DI 7871	Thanks. At the conclusion of the interview PC Chaplin and I will give you a notice explaining exactly what will happen after the interview. Do you understand?
00.37	CS	Yes.
00.38	DI 7871	Right, that voice was and the next voice will be the interviewee's voice. Can you state your full name and address please?
00.48	CS	Cameron Struth, residing currently at 89 Comyns Close, Canning Town.
00.53	DI 7871	Postcode.

Signature(s): ......John Finch...

2014/09

Person interviewed: Cameron Struth   Page No. 2   of 9

Tape counter times	Person speaking	Text
00.55	CS	E16 4JJ.
01.00	DI 7871	Right. Now Cameron I will explain the specific allegations to you shortly but do you yourself understand the nature of this interview and the reasons why we've brought you in here? But before you answer I need to formally caution you. You do not have to say anything unless you wish to do so but it may harm your defence if you do not mention something asked of you which you later rely on in court and what you do say may be given as evidence. So do you understand the reason you were arrested this morning, this morning being September the 19th 2014.
01.33	CS	No. No clue.
01.37	DI 7871	Right so. Is the chair too hard for you Cameron?
01.43	CS	No. It's all right. It's more a lack of cushioning on my part.
01.49	DI 7871	Right. So an allegation was made by Ms Corina Slate last night in reference to an incident that took place on the evening of August 23rd this year. Do you know Corina Slate, Cameron?
02.00	CS	Yes. What happened?
02.03	DI 7871	Well Corina came in last night quite upset.
02.06	PC 3009	She stated that she's been raped and named you as the person responsible.
02.10	CS	Raped?
02.11	DI 7871	That's right.
02.12	CS	That I raped her?
02.14	DI 7871	Yes. Corina came in last night.

Signature(s): ....

Person interviewed: Cameron Struth

Page No. 3   of 9

Tape counter times	Person speaking	Text
02.15	CS	You must have the wrong person here. There's someone else you should be talking to.
02.19	PC 3009	Is there another Cameron Struth that Ms Slate knows?
02.24	CS	There must be if one of us has raped her. I haven't seen her since.
02.29	PC 3009	Since August 23rd, her housewarming in Fulham?
02.32	CS	Well aye that's right aye but I haven't raped her. This is absurd. Honestly you're truly mistaken here.
02.40	PC 3009	Well that's what we're here to find out.
02.43	CS	I can't believe this.
02.44	DI 7871	Now Cameron do you still understand the circumstance of this interview and what I mentioned in the caution?
02.50	CS	Yes. Aye. I'll answer anything you ask. I've not done anything wrong. If you've not done anything wrong then you're okay.
03.00	PC 3009	That's one way of looking at it.
03.01	DI 7871	Now what do you understand by what we're talking about here Cameron, that word, rape?
03.09	CS	It's. This is mad. It's. Rape involves sexual intercourse wherein one person. Rape is, obviously, having sex, penetrative sex, with someone without their consent.
03.28	DI 7871	Right. That's a good enough generalisation as to what we're talking about. Now can you tell me how you know Corina?
03.40	CS	This is mad. Yeah. We were in a relationship for a few years.
03.47	DI 7871	How many years?

Signature(s): ......John Job......

72

Person interviewed: Cameron Struth

Page No. 4   of 9

Tape counter times	Person speaking	Text
03.48	CS	Over two. A month or so over two years.
03.52	DI 7871	How did you meet?
03.54	CS	Tinder. The Tinder app.
03.56	DI 7871	And how would you characterise the relationship in general?
04.02	CS	Good. Excellent. The most meaningful relationship I've had. Honestly this is mad. This is absurd.
04.10	DI 7871	Why did you break up?
04.12	CS	Why did we break up?
04.15	DI 7871	Why did your relationship with Corina end?
04.19	CS	I wanted to focus on my work.
04.22	DI 7871	So you broke up with her?
04.25	CS	More or less. I had mentioned to her on several occasions before then that maybe a break from each other would be best for both of us.
04.34	DI 7871	And why's that?
04.36	CS	Because I wanted to focus on my work.
04.38	DI 7871	But how was being with Corina detrimental to your career at the time?
04.43	CS	Well I wouldn't say detrimental.
04.45	DI 7871	How would you describe it?

Signature(s) ....

Person interviewed: Cameron Struth

Tape counter times	Person speaking	Text
04.47	CS	Well I wouldn't say detrimental because that implies she was deliberately damaging but well. I wasn't the first choice for the role I'm in now at the Young Vic and as a matter of fact I wasn't even the second choice but anyway my point is I was lucky to have the role and I wanted to dedicate myself to it 24-7. This meant that we didn't see much of each other. Most evenings I was out with the cast bonding or whatever and so Corina was alone. When we were together my mind was on the play. I know I wasn't a good partner to her then. I can admit that.
05.24	DI 7871	Did you live together?
05.26	CS	Yes. Well not officially. Technically she lived in Fulham but she stayed at mine most nights.
05.32	DI 7871	Why was that?
05.25	CS	She wasn't on good terms with her housemates.
05.38	DI 7871	How come?
05.41	CS	Well I'm not exactly sure but Louise, Louise Prieditis, she has always been flirty with me.
05.49	PC 3009	What do you mean by that?
05.51	CS	Well Louise flirts a considerable amount with me and it was obvious to me that Corina took issue with that. Corina doesn't hide her suspicions very well.
06.01	PC 3009	So what was your relationship with Louise?
06.05	CS	If you're asking if I flirted back you'd have to ask Louise. Certainly I wasn't aware of flirting with her.

Signature(s): ....

Person interviewed: Cameron Struth

Tape counter times	Person speaking	Text
06.11	DI 7871	So this factored into the reasons why you broke up?
06.15	CS	Sure.
06.15	DI 7871	Right.
06.17	CS	No. Sorry. It only factored insofar as Corina felt isolated and kind of glum and maybe a little jealous.
06.24	DI 7871	Right. And was the break-up on good terms would you say in general?
06.30	CS	Sure. We were on the same page about our problems. Quite quickly I came to terms with it.
06.37	DI 7871	What about Corina?
06.39	CS	Well she hadn't taken it very well as I understand it.
06.42	DI 7871	Why do you say that?
06.44	CS	Her housemates told me as much.
06.46	PC 3009	But why do you think she took it so hard given the fact that you were on the same page about your problems as you just said?
06.53	CS	Well that's something I've wondered myself. I mean what worked between us was that we didn't really need each other. We weren't In each other's pockets as my mother would say but when I wanted to focus on my work I think it made her realise that she relied on me or that she needed someone as such. From my understanding she's been the needed one her whole life professionally and in her family and she hated feeling needy and as a consequence she resented me and our relationship for making her feel needy which is partly why I didn't want to attend the party.

Signature(s):......[signature]..

Tape counter times	Person speaking	Text
07.25	DI 7871	The night of the incident?
07.27	CS	No not. Well that night you said before. August 23rd was it?
07.31	DI 7871	Right. So let's go over that night now. Give us your account of the incident and then we'll go over Corina's statement okay?
07.43	CS	Okay. Where do you want me to start?
07.47	DI 7871	Whenever you feel is relevant to start.
07.50	CS	When I was invited?
07.52	DI 7871	If you like.
07.55	CS	Okay. So aye. Roughly three weeks before the party Corina invited me to the party via social media and approximately a week later, a week before the party, she sent various voice messages to me in order to persuade me to attend. By virtue of.
08.13	DI 7871	How did she try to persuade you?
08.16	CS	Sorry?
08.17	DI 7871	How did she try to persuade you to attend?
08.20	CS	Oh. Well. She said she wanted me to come. She sent me those messages specifically.
08.34	DI 7871	Right.
08.35	CS	So. So from my perspective that's indicative of an attempt to persuade me. Right?
08.41	DI 7871	Right.
08.42	CS	Aye.
08.46	DI 7871	Go on. Please.

Signature(s): ...

Tape counter times	Person speaking	Text
08.47	CS	Aye. Aye. What was I saying?
08.51	DI 7871	You were saying.
08.52	CS	No. Aye. I was saying the invitation was the first contact we'd had since the break-up and that I didn't initially want to go.
09.01	DI 7871	And why's that?
09.02	CS	Well because I felt unwell and because I thought the invitation was sent out of not wanting to seem bitter and because I thought going there would make things worse between us.
09.13	DI 7871	But you said things ended on good terms.
09.17	CS	It did. It did. But just in case there was any residual hostility is what I mean to say.
09.24	DI 7871	So why did you go in the end?
09.26	CS	Louise.
09.27	DI 7871	Louise. Louise Prieditis?
09.28	CS	Aye. But because I talked to Louise about the situation. Of my attending I mean. And she assured me that Corina has recovered.
09.37	DI 7871	Recovered from what?
09.38	CS	From the break-up. Louise said she was over it and naturally because I didn't personally feel any bad blood or any acrimony or any. Well I looked forward to piecing together our friendship.
09.52	DI 7871	Right. So what time did you arrive?
09.59	CS	Is there any chance I can go to the toilet?

Signature(s): ⟨signature⟩

2014/09　　　**RESTRICTED (when complete)**

Person interviewed: Cameron Struth

Page No. 9   of 9

Tape counter times	Person speaking	Text
10.06	DI 7871	Now?
10.07	CS	Yes. I really need to use the toilet. I didn't get the chance to go before you came this morning.
10.16	DI 7871	Right. Sorry about that. Yes. Sure. Let's pause the recording there please. The time is 06.58.
		End of tape.

Signature(s): ....*John Juul*..

COPIED POSTS FROM CORINA SLATE'S BLOG, 'WITNESS'

SEPTEMBER 2016 (1)

Ali's piss is brown, stinky. Medically speaking. That's better than no piss at all. The fire is still outside the house, as my dialysis tutor said. There's enough potassium leaving her body. One thing death row inmates receive in lethal injections is IV potassium because it works in massive doses to contract the heart into a fist. Cardiac arrest. Medically speaking. I tell Ali that this might be the thing most likely to kill her if she enters the oliguric phase. She nods. Her mouth hangs open, not from shock or disbelief, it just hangs open, dry, grey, brown, a clay cave. If that happens we'll give her dopamine to open up her renal arteries, then a bolus of IV fluid, then a diuretic.

'I know that sounds a little contradictory,' I say.

'Not really, mate. Like tossing a bucket of water down a blocked loo.'

'But hopefully it won't come to that.'

'Hopefully.'

'How are you feeling?' I say.

She groans, smiles one-sided.

'Is there anything you'd like?' I say.

'Cup of tea?'

'Herbal?'

'Can't I have a proper one?'

'Afraid not.'

'The caffeine?'

'That. You can't have milk, either.'

'But that's good protein, isn't it? Good for my bones.'

'The problem is you can't absorb calcium very well.'

'Shit.'

'You can have soy milk.'

'Fuck that.'

'Well, that's your answer.'

She folds her arms, chews the inside of her mouth. 'Mate, now it's in my head,' she says, 'I'd fucking kill for a cup of tea.'

'Then you better hire a hitman.'

'Are they expensive, like?'

'Cups of tea?'

'Hitmen.'

'It depends on the quality of the hitman.'

'Sounds like you could sort me out.'

'What kind of guy are you looking for?'

'Trustworthy. Tall. Funny.'

'I used to know a guy like that.'

'You still got his number?'

'I do.'

'Mates' rates?'

'Mates' rates.'

———

We met in the damp beery bar of Network Theatre, down in one of the arches under Waterloo. I'd come to see your brother in a play. You and your parents had come too. Your brother never wanted me to meet your parents. He'd told me stories of abuse, neglect that he seemed to exaggerate but it's not something you question someone about, is it? I'd seen him bend the truth with people he'd just met. He was exciting, smart, fun. He could be whatever you wanted him to be, convince you it was only a blip whenever the mask slipped.

Your parents were sitting next to each other on a sofa, looking sort of aggrieved. You were standing next to the sofa sipping a pint of orange juice. Was the wall behind you orange or is that just how I remember it? When I think of you I think of orange. It's like the air in the memory is orange.

You were wearing a tuxedo. I found it funny though I didn't yet know it was a joke. I'd not met you before but I recognised you from photos. I was at the bar. When I turned back, you moved through the crowd towards me, deliberately, patting people on the back to let them know that you were passing them. I felt a jolt of something. You stood next to me, pulled loose your tie. You had to stoop so that they could see your face through the bar hatch. Your arms were folded, less from impatience than to comfort yourself. You were next to be served but the man beside you shot his arm out, barked an order. You didn't look at him, just smiled. You saw me watching, widened your eyes. You didn't know who I was. I wanted to keep it that way, pretend to not have recognised you until I had to. You pressed your hand against your chest, said, 'It's important to have a strong bar presence.'

'Impressive,' I said.

I paid for my drink. You took a step back from the bar. 'So who are you here for?' you said.

The bartender was looking for someone to serve.

'You're up,' I said.

When you ordered, I saw how you leaned towards people when you talked to them, that you had a warm, chummy way of talking that seemed to duck under the formality of a situation. What was it about formality that you wanted to avoid? I imagine you felt it posed a test that you were more likely to fail, or there was a higher chance, under these rules, that someone could reject you. Your antidote for this was gentleness. I imagine you wanted it to draw out a person's kindness, to invite them to treat you kindly. I'm not sure, in that moment, if I felt I'd seen your gentleness or detected your fragility.

I looked at your lips, curling like apple peels. A back broad enough to sleep on.

When you turned back to me, away from the transaction, you seemed relieved. When I told you I was here to see your brother, you seemed disappointed. I took that as a compliment.

A couple of months later, after we'd connected online, chatted occasionally, met up a couple more times with your brother, we had a drink in a pub near King's Cross, just us, when you were down for some cooking course. I admitted that I recognised you the first time we met, pretended not to know it was you 'for some reason', I said.

You said, 'I wonder what stories he's told you.'

'Not many. He said you were glum, dark, didn't talk much.'

'I think he likes me like that.'

'He's wrong?'

'I don't know. Maybe a bit. What do you think?'

'Maybe a bit,' I said. 'I thought it was pretty funny that you'd wear a tuxedo to an amateur play.'

'I knew he'd hate it if I made a show of myself. Especially if I brought our mam and dad. Month ago, he'd told them that I'd been fired from a job. It was just a little retaliation. It's how we seem to operate.'

'And am I part of that?' I said.

You took a moment to consider this, faked a eureka face, which made me laugh. It took me a while to figure out why I found you funny. I think it's because you spoke slowly, with a dopey sort of smile, a deep Kermit the Frog quality to your voice, before rapidly speeding up at the end of a sentence with your face sort of puzzled by what you'd just said. Wanting to fuck you hadn't fully occurred to me. But I was keen to laugh.

Your train came. You reported on the strange and pissed-up passengers on your journey, your long talk with a woman who'd regretted reconnecting with a school friend. I headed to your brother's. I reported on the strange and pissed-up passengers on my journey, my quick chat with a boy who was disappointed by my ignorance of manga. You sent me a picture of a page from your course handout. 'Introduction: Definitions: Food: Anything that people eat or drink, including ice and alcohol.' I felt like we were composing our own private jokes. I felt an exciting dread I didn't yet understand.

When I got to your brother's place, more or less as soon as I set foot on his estate, I felt sort of watered down. He kept asking what was wrong. I couldn't describe it. He couldn't believe that it wasn't really something to do with us, with him. If it wasn't about him, then he didn't know what to do about it, he said. We sat on our phones sulking. He was irritated by me feeling low and I was disappointed by him not caring enough to deal with me feeling low. More often now our time together was spent like this.

Then the problem of what to eat that night came up. I said I didn't mind. He hated having to make decisions. I don't know how it deteriorated from there, but it ended with him accusing me of being complacent about the people who care about me. He said he couldn't understand how I was capable of caring for people professionally, that my complacency about others constituted a safeguarding risk. My strategy in our arguments was to not indulge his eagerness to argue, but when I ignored him, he boiled, punched himself in the head, telling me that I was fucking with him. I would cry, wondering how awful I must be to make him do that to himself.

——

During infusions, when her mouth ulcers aren't too bad, my mother likes to suck on honey lozenges. I went to the Holland & Barrett on Holloway Road to get them, but there were none on the shelf. I asked if there were more out back. The girl said they must have sold out.

'Of honey lozenges?' I said.

'Yeah?' she said.

'Do you mind checking?'

'Yeah, I've already checked.'

'The honey lozenges?'

'Yeah. Sorry.'

She held back a smile. Someone in the queue behind me sighed. I left, walked up towards the bus stop. I was watching for the bus when a white builder whistled at me from the scaffolding above. I know it was at me because I was wearing joggers and after whistling he said I shouldn't try to hide such a superb arse in joggers. This was better than last time, when another white builder said, 'I bet you've got a tight hairy cunt.' He scrolled his eyes over me like his favourite PornHub category. How could I forgive your brother for once 'innocently' calling me his 'waifu'? For once arguing, 'for argument's sake', that 'having a thing' for blonde girls or tall guys is 'unobjectionable' so it's unobjectionable to have a thing for Asians, since 'it's just a preference for what they consider superior physical traits'. Would you forgive me for feeling relief from not finding out you'd only dated women who looked like me? It's a sad relief to know that my feelings for you are protected by your death, like this builder thought he was protected by his distance above me. I wondered what was he offering. A compliment? A fuck? A relationship? A baby I'd have to raise? Some compliment. Or did he just want to make me think about him?

People were looking. Maybe I'd have felt differently if people weren't looking, or if your brother hadn't done what he did to me. Maybe I could've brushed it off, rolled my eyes, despite the fear. The uneasiness, the irritation, the prickling sweat, whatever, it could've turned into silent embarrassment. I could've walked on with my head down. I don't remember what I shouted at this builder, but I know it was an intimate overwhelming kind of anger.

If trauma is transmitted, inherited, which it is, then so is whatever causes someone to traumatise another.

A young white girl came out of the uni building, asked me if I was okay. She looked like a girl I knew at King's who once asked me if I was more Japanese or white. I'd looked at her with a bent smile waiting for her to realise. When she did realise, she was mortified, cried. I told her not to worry about it.

I told this girl on Holloway Road to go read a fucking book like a cunt.

When I got home, I opened all the windows, let in the cooling air. For a long time I stood in the bathroom, looking in the mirror.

The cold wind had pulled the eyeliner off my eyelids. Jagged black streaks pointing to the temples. I think I saw one of my own eyes move. I could smell damp. It was coming from the hand towel under the mirror. I washed the towel, all my towels, even the unused spare towels. I thought I could still smell damp. I washed them again, hand-washed in the sink, water so hot it burned my hands. No one was or is coming to stay, not for a long time. But if they did, I thought. If they did.

COMMENTS

Unknown
Women ARE sexual objects, among other things.
Reply

———

Except for his face, your brother would be cast in cement. But he wouldn't be able to move his face, couldn't speak. The cement would come up to his bottom lip, hold open his mouth. He wouldn't be able to blink. The blood vessels in his eyes would be inflamed, some ruptured. Tears would make it look like his eyes were leaking blood. He wouldn't be able to look at me. He'd moan. His oesophagus would make a clicking sound. He'd struggle to swallow. I'd reach in his mouth, pinch his tongue. It would jerk around. It would try to hide somewhere. His face would shake with trying to shut his mouth. Eventually I'd get his tongue between the nails of my thumb and index finger. It would be hot, dry, hard. I'd hold it tight as if it might slip away. I'd show him the scalpel in my other hand. He'd groan like a goat, try to shut his eyes tight, but the cement would hold the muscles in his face. I'd tap the scalpel against his teeth, scrape it across them. I'd make little cuts in his gums. The blood would be thin, the white of his teeth still showing through it. He'd gasp, breathe heavily. I'd place the scalpel on the

side of his tongue, just about the root. I'd hold it there. The first
slice would open the flesh like tofu. The second slice, on the top
of his tongue, over the puckered taste buds, would give him more
control of his tongue. I'd lift the tongue up over itself. The third
slice would sever the thin hard frenulum linguae like a daisy stalk.
Then I'd slice all the way around his tongue, but not all the way
through. The strong hard core of his tongue would stay intact,
but flaps of flesh at the sides would touch each other then separate
with strings and streams of blood. He'd wail, gargle on the blood
flowing down his throat. I'd pull his tongue with both hands using
a knee against the cement for leverage. It would rip, slowly, with a
spurt of blood. He'd scream, hack blood up out of his mouth. I'd
show him the dismembered end of his tongue. He'd stare at me.
He wouldn't believe what was happening. But it wouldn't be the
tongue surprising him. It would be the pain. He wouldn't be able
to believe you could feel that much pain. I'd drop the tongue, lift
the scalpel towards an eye. He'd try so hard to close his eyes. Then
I'd slice the eyelid around one of his eyes from the duct to the other
corner. He'd scream without his voice, just breath. I'd pick up the
tongue, stuff it back in his mouth, smother the screaming. I'd push
the scalpel to the bloodshot sclera. The lens would burst easily.
Eggy fluid would drain out the split. I'd keep cutting, gouging
deeper into his eye till it was prawn cocktail, till I was stabbing,
slicing his whole face, and I don't know what would make me stop.

COMMENTS

Unknown
I assume something terrible has happened to you to make you think
of something so abhorrent but did the guy get let off?
Reply

Unknown
This comment has been removed by the blog administrator.
Reply

———

Many times when I think of my brother, I itch. When we call each other, one of my hands holds the phone, the other hand scratches. In my bathroom, drinking wine, I put him on speaker for maximum scratching. 'Cor, am I on speaker?'

'No. I'm just in the loo. It must be echoing.'

'You pooing?'

'No.'

'Because I don't want to be talking to you when you're pooing, man.'

'I'm not pooing. Where are you?'

'I was working.'

'You're at work?'

'What?'

'You're at work now, Hiro?'

'No. I said I was. Was.'

'When?'

'The other day.'

'What day?'

'The day you're probably pissed off about.'

'I'm not pissed off.'

'All right, then.'

'Though—'

'Thought as much.'

'What?'

'This is perfect, man.'

'What's perfect?'

'This. I was just saying this.'

'What?'

'I was just saying how, like, Corina does one good deed and acts like she deserves a medal, like no one else is as good as Mother Corina.'

'What are you talking about? What deed?'

'Taking Mum to the doctor's.'

'That wasn't a deed. It's Kaasan.'

'Fuck off with that shit as well.'

'What shit?'

'The Kaasan shit. You only started it when she got ill.'

'Don't do that.'

'What are you calling me for, then?'

'I'm calling to see if you can go around and look at her laptop?'

'I've already looked at it.'

'Because it seems fucked to me.'

'It was fucked. It's older than me. I've just bought her a new one.'

'A new laptop?'

'Yeah. Why?'

'For how much?'

'Why's that matter?'

'Because I'll go halves.'

'I can afford it.'

'But how?'

'I'm good this month.'

'Don't be stupid. I'll send you some.'

'Fuck sake, Cor. Will you just leave it, yeah?'

'Well. I'm sorry, but I just can't believe you've got the money for that.'

'Want me to send a picture of my balance? Fuck.'

'How did you get it then?'

'I told you, man. Work.'

'Where you were the other day?'

'Yeah.'

'When you couldn't take out a couple of hours for her?'

'I'm going to be with her any minute now.'

'On a Saturday, yeah. Why weren't you with her when I was with her though? Hiro?'

'I'm heading up. I got to go.'

'Hiro?'

'What?'

'Why weren't you with her when I was with her?'

'Fucking all about you.'

'What?'

'Honestly. You act like you really care about people but it's only to make them feel bad about it and so you feel better about yourself.'

'Don't say that.'

'Fuck, man. Don't say this. Don't say that. It's fucked, man. Honestly, do you even see it? How fucked you are. Honestly, I was thinking about this the other day. When you're out with me or Mum, all you do is look around at other people. You're seeing if they're looking at us, if we're embarrassing you or something, and if we are, if someone is looking at us, you'd drop all this head of the family shit, poor, burdened Corina, and you'd act like you barely fucking know us, like, it's all for show, man, like you keep offering me money, yeah, pity money, like your money's more real, more earned than mine, like you're the only one working and everyone else is fucking coasting, like, poor, burdened Corina, she went down on her poncey ex again, felt ashamed of herself, and acted like the fucking bloke raped her, just so everyone'd feel sorry for her. It's fucked. You're fucked. You're not Mum. Never will be. So I don't want your fucking pity money. I don't need anything from you. All right?'

'You never believed me.'

'Well.'

'You didn't.'

'Well. Just returning the favour.'

———

My mother calls when I'm on break to say she's had an email from my father.

I don't say anything.

'Did I lose you?' she says.

'I'm here,' I say. 'What's it saying?'

'Just simply to wish me happy birthday, which is weeks late, of course, but that's no matter.'

'That's it?'

'Well, he asked me how I was and I told him and then he said that he would be in London next week. I suppose he wants to say goodbye properly.'

'Fuck.'

'Well, there's no need for that.'

'Beg to differ.'

'He said he would like to see you. Both of you.'

'Right.'

'Yes, but I wasn't sure.'

'What about? Hiro?'

'Well, yes. I wanted to ask if you wanted to see him.'

'I don't, but I'll be there when you do. Hiro, I don't know.'

'Yes. I wasn't sure. What do you think?'

I lift my head from between my knees. I say, 'I think it's best if he didn't.'

'Yes? Are you sure?'

'Yes.' I put my head back between my knees, close my eyes so hard my head roars. 'I talked to him not long ago,' I say. 'It would only hurt him. Trust me.'

SCAN OF RECORD OF INTERVIEW WITH CAMERON STRUTH

19 SEPTEMBER 2014
27 DAYS AFTER ASSAULT

RECORD OF INTERVIEW

ROTI	URN	01	NE	00673	14

Person interviewed: Cameron Struth

Place of interview: Plaistow Police Station, 444 Barking Road, London, E13 8HJ

Date of interview: 19 September 2014 (190914)

Time commenced: 0920   Time concluded: 0932

Audio tape reference nos.:

Interviewer(s): Det Insp 7871 John Finch, PC 3009 David Chaplin

Other persons present:

Police Exhibit No: CDS/03

..............*John Finch*..............

Signature of interviewer/transcriber producing exhibit

Duration of interview: 12.32

Visual image reference nos.:

Tape counter times	Person speaking	Text
00.02	DI 7871	Okay. I'm John Finch, Detective Inspector for the Metropolitan Police and after two breaks we're continuing to talk to Cameron Struth about an alleged rape. Here conducting the interview with me is.
00.18	PC 3009	David Chaplin, Police Constable for the Metropolitan Police.
00.21	DI 7871	Right. Cameron you've given us your account. Thanks for that. So let's go over Corina's statement with you now. PC Chaplin.
00.33	PC 3009	Yes. Thank you. In Ms Slate's statement she mentions that she allowed you into her bed because you had no other place to stay that night.
00.46	CS	That's correct yeah.
00.49	PC 3009	Why didn't you go home?
00.52	CS	I didn't have any money for a taxi.
00.56	PC 3009	Could you have gotten an Uber?

Signature(s): .....*John Finch*.....

2014/09

Person interviewed: Cameron Struth

Tape counter times	Person speaking	Text
00.59	CS	I don't have the app. I can't get the app. I've forgotten the password to download apps.
01.07	PC 3009	Corina states that you asked to stay because it was closer to your rehearsal space.
01.13	CS	Well yes. That was a factor also.
01.16	PC 3009	Where is the rehearsal space?
01.19	CS	The Young Vic. The Cut. Waterloo.
01.23	PC 3009	And that's easier to get to from Fulham than Canning Town?
01.27	CS	Well no not easier no. But by the time I'd have gotten home I would have had to leave again probably.
01.34	PC 3009	What time were your rehearsals?
01.37	CS	9 a.m.
01.39	PC 3009	How would you have gotten there?
01.41	CS	Tube probably.
01.43	PC 3009	Okay. So you're in bed with her. How were you both positioned?
01.49	CS	How were we both positioned?
01.51	PC 3009	Yes. How were you both positioned?
01.54	CS	How were we both positioned? I'm not sure. She was on her front and I was on my back I believe. Beside each other of course.
02.03	PC 3009	Did you talk at all?
02.05	CS	Sure.
02.06	PC 3009	Do you remember what you talked about?

Signature(s):..........*John Juul*..

Person interviewed: Cameron Struth   Page No. 3   of 12

Tape counter times	Person speaking	Text
02.09	CS	Do I remember what we talked about? Not clearly. It was nothing memorable obviously.
02.18	PC 3009	And was there physical contact at this point?
02.21	CS	No.
02.23	PC 3009	No?
02.24	CS	No.
02.27	PC 3009	In her statement Corina says you were lying on your side facing her and when she told you she worried about the volume of the party you put your arm around her back.
02.45	CS	Well aye I might have done that. It's possible. In that moment I felt she needed comforting maybe.
02.53	PC 3009	Corina goes on to state that she asked you why you didn't say hello to her during the party even though you said yourself that you had seen her dancing. And after she asked you you kissed her.
03.07	CS	No. No. That's not true.
03.09	PC 3009	She didn't ask you that?
03.11	CS	No. Aye. She did. But she only asked that to express disappointment at the fact that I didn't say hello.
03.19	PC 3009	How could you tell that?
03.21	CS	Well from the manner in which she asked.
03.25	PC 3009	But what wasn't true about what she said?

Signature(s): John Ful

Person interviewed: Cameron Struth   Page No. 4   of 12

Tape counter times	Person speaking	Text
03.28	CS	Well that I kissed her. It wasn't that clear-cut. Our faces were nose-to-nose when she asked me that. There was a pause after she asked and her intention in asking was to express disappointment at my not saying hello and simultaneously to express the affection underlying that disappointment. Then we both just started kissing.
03.50	PC 3009	Corina then states that she said, and this is a quote, "I can't" when you kissed her.
03.57	CS	She said she shouldn't, not can't. And in any case she said it while kissing me. She was kissing me and for that reason I didn't think she meant what she said. I thought she was just saying it to save face or something to that effect.
04.12	PC 3009	Corina also states that you then got on top of her, behind her, pinning her arms, pulling down her pyjama bottoms and forcing your penis inside her vagina.
04.23	CS	No. No. No. Well yes I did do that, those actions technically but not forced and it was clear to me that it was going to happen or what we wanted to happen is what I mean to say. She was kissing me and touching me and pulling me closer to her. It was clear what was happening so aye it was clear what was happening.
04.48	PC 3009	Corina then states that she asked what you were doing.
04.52	CS	Aye again but it wasn't accusatory. Like I said earlier I was having trouble with.
05.01	DI 7871	Maintaining an erection?
05.05	CS	Well aye. Sure,
05.08	DI 7871	So tell us again what happened after that.

Signature(s): John Job

Person interviewed: Cameron Struth   Page No. 5   of 12

Tape counter times	Person speaking	Text
05.12	CS	Well not much. I couldn't. I couldn't you know.
05.19	DI 7871	Maintain an erection?
05.20	CS	Yes. So I apologised of course and we stopped and we laughed about it and we went to bed.
05.29	DI 7871	And what happened after that?
05.32	CS	Nothing. We went to bed. End of story.
05.35	DI 7871	Right.
05.37	PC 3009	Corina actually states that you stopped briefly to put on a condom saying, quote, "Oops. Sorry, petal" and then you continued to force your penis into her vagina pressing your elbow between her shoulder blades and with
05.45	PC 3009	(cntd) your other arm, which was pinning her arm, shifted up to clinch her around the neck.
05.49	CS	This is mad. This is mad. I didn't choke her. No.
05.55	DI 7871	What were your hands doing?
05.57	CS	Christ. How do I. What were my hands doing?
06.00	DI 7871	Yes. What were your hands doing?
06.02	CS	What were my hands doing? They were. They were probably holding myself up.
06.07	DI 7871	How?
06.09	CS	How? With my hands on the bed probably. There's no other way to do that is there?
06.13	PC 3009	Corina states you had pinned her arms to the bed.

Signature(s): ....John John...........

98

Person interviewed: Cameron Struth

Page No. 6   of 12

Tape counter times	Person speaking	Text
06.17	CS	No. That's absurd. No. I couldn't have pinned her down if I tried.
06.22	DI 7871	You mean to say you're not physically capable of restraining her?
06.26	CS	No. No. Corina can take care of herself. My body isn't as strong as hers by any means.
06.32	DI 7871	Not even when she's drunk?
06.34	CS	She wasn't drunk. Not at that time. She wasn't slurring and she slurs when she drinks so she wasn't drunk.
06.42	DI 7871	So what you're saying is because of her physical strength and because of your.
06.48	CS	Because of my infant cryptorchidism.
06.50	DI 7871	Which is. For the tape.
06.54	CS	It's an undescended testicle. When I was young. It affects. Well.
07.00	DI 7871	Sexual performance.
07.01	CS	Sure.
07.02	DI 7871	Right. So what you're saying is because of these factors you were incapable of committing this act?
07.09	CS	Exactly. Yes. That's exactly what I'm saying.
07.10	DI 7871	Right. Now can you describe yourself for me? What sort of build you are and size.
07.16	CS	For you?
07.17	DI 7871	Well yes. For the tape.
07.20	CS	My build is I would say, I don't know. Kind of scrawny probably. I'm 5'10".

Signature(s):......... *John Jul* ....

99

Person interviewed: Cameron Struth   Page No. 7   of 12

Tape counter times	Person speaking	Text
07.25	DI 7871	5'10".
07.26	CS	More or less.
07.28	DI 7871	I'll put between 5'8" and 5'10". Any distinctive features?
07.34	CS	Sorry?
07.36	DI 7871	Do you have any distinctive features?
07.37	CS	Distinctive features? Well I have a broken nose. It was broken during birth. My mam says I was so ugly the midwife slapped my face.
07.51	DI 7871	Anything else?
07.54	CS	No.
07.56	DI 7871	Right.
07.58	CS	I'm missing two toes on my right foot.
08.01	DI 7871	I'm sorry?
08.03	CS	It's okay.
08.05	DI 7871	No. Can you repeat?
08.07	CS	I said I'm missing the piggy that went all the way home and the piggy before that. On my right foot.
08.13	DI 7871	Right.
08.14	CS	The right. Aye.
08.18	PC 3009	For the tape I'd like to say that Mr Struth is not scrawny. He is more of an athletic build.
08.25	CS	Athletic? I'm not athletic at all. I couldn't even tell you the last time I fucking ran. Sorry.

Signature(s):...... *John Ful* ....

Tape counter times	Person speaking	Text
08.31	PC 3009	But for the tape Mr Struth is not scrawny.
08.36	CS	But for the tape Mr Struth is not athletic either.
08.39	DI 7871	Right. Let's just say you're of a slim build.
08.42	CS	Great.
08.44	DI 7871	Okay. Now would you say the woman is of a similar build?
08.49	CS	Who? Corina?
08.50	DI 7871	Yes. How would you describe her build?
08.55	CS	Well I'd have to say she's more of an athletic build. She runs a lot. Or used to. We ran together.
09.02	PC 3009	You said you weren't athletic.
09.04	CS	I'm not but she liked to run at night which I consider dangerous so I accompanied her.
09.08	DI 7871	You ran with her too.
09.11	CS	To protect her. Potentially.
09.12	DI 7871	Right.
09.13	CS	Aye.
09.15	DI 7871	Right. So can you think of any reason why this woman would make such a serious allegation against you?
09.18	CS	Honestly it's beyond me. It's absurd.
09.24	DI 7871	This is totally out of the blue from your point of view.
09.28	CS	Well yes.
09.29	DI 7871	Right.

Signature(s): *John Job*

Person interviewed: Cameron Struth

Page No. 9   of 12

Tape counter times	Person speaking	Text
09.30	CS	Though I should say she's done this kind of thing before.
09.34	DI 7871	What kind of thing?
09.36	CS	She's done things to get back at past boyfriends.
09.40	DI 7871	So you're saying.
09.44	CS	She'd spread humiliating things about her exes, send them pictures of her having sex with other people. But that's only if they've cheated on her.
09.52	DI 7871	How do you know this?
09.54	CS	She's told me.
09.56	DI 7871	She told you she'd done this? In person or.
09.59	CS	In person. She told me if I ever cheated on her that's what she'd do.
10.04	DI 7871	So what you're saying is the woman has a history of seeking revenge on her past partners?
10.09	CS	Exactly.
10.11	DI 7871	Right.
10.12	CS	Whenever we argued she'd tell me this as a threat most likely.
10.17	DI 7871	But a threat only in the event of your mistreating her.
10.21	CS	Sorry?
10.22	DI 7871	You said she would seek revenge on partners who had cheated on her.
10.25	CS	Aye.

Signature(s): ....

Tape counter times	Person speaking	Text
10.26	DI 7871	So can you think of any reason why this might be one of those occasions?
10.30	CS	No. No. All I can think is that this is some terrible misunderstanding.
10.35	DI 7871	And you said the relationship ended on good terms?
10.37	CS	We've already gone over this haven't we?
10.39	DI 7871	Right but let's go over it again.
10.41	CS	Okay.
10.42	DI 7871	So you would say good terms?
10.43	CS	As well as any.
10.44	DI 7871	Who decided to end the relationship?
10.45	CS	I've already said this.
10.46	DI 7871	Remind me.
10.47	CS	It was more me. But it was largely mutual.
10.48	DI 7871	It was largely mutual?
10.49	CS	Yes.
10.50	DI 7871	And Corina would corroborate that?
10.51	CS	Well of course she probably wouldn't
10.52	DI 7871	Why not?
10.53	CS	She would like to think that I caused the break-up.
10.56	DI 7871	Caused the break-up or decided to break up?

Signature(s):....._John Jul_...

Person interviewed: Cameron Struth

Tape counter times	Person speaking	Text
10.58	CS	Caused. No. Decided. I decided. She didn't like me focussing on my work as I've said so I thought the relationship had run its course.
11.02	DI 7871	So by mutual you mean she was dissatisfied with how the relationship was going on account of you focussing on your work and neglecting the relationship so you broke things off?
11.11	CS	I wouldn't say that I neglected the relationship.
11.14	DI 7871	What would you say?
11.15	CS	I would say that the relationship had run its course.
11.16	DI 7871	As you've said.
11.17	CS	As I've said.
11.18	DI 7871	Right.
11.21	CS	She didn't like that I was moving into a different phase of my life which didn't involve her.
11.26	DI 7871	One where you focussed on your career?
11.29	CS	She was jealous. I think she was jealous, if that's the right word, of me concentrating on matters that didn't concern her.
11.34	DI 7871	Like your career?
11.35	CS	My career. My family.
11.36	DI 7871	Your family?
11.37	CS	Aye.
11.38	DI 7871	What family matters were you distracted by?
11.40	CS	My brother killed himself.

Signature(s):..

Tape counter times	Person speaking	Text
11.46	DI 7871	Your brother committed suicide?
11.49	CS	Well he tried to. He got closer this time than the other times.
11.52	DI 7871	When was this?
11.53	CS	This was the end of May.
11.56	DI 7871	Right.
11.58	CS	Aye.
12.01	DI 7871	Right. Well thank you Cameron. I think that's all we need at this stage. Is there anything else you'd like to say? Right. For the tape Mr Struth shook his head. Now Cameron we're going to keep you here for a while. We're going to take your fingerprints and a DNA sample. Then we're going to take you to a cell where you're going to await further instruction. Okay?
12.24	CS	Am I being charged with this?
12.28	DI 7871	That's what you're going to wait to find out. Now is everything I've said clear to you? Right. Mr Struth nodded. This interview is being terminated at 9.32. Thank you.
		End of tape.

Signature(s): *[signature]*

SCREENSHOT OF EMAIL SENT FROM HIRO SLATE TO CAMERON STRUTH

12 SEPTEMBER 2014

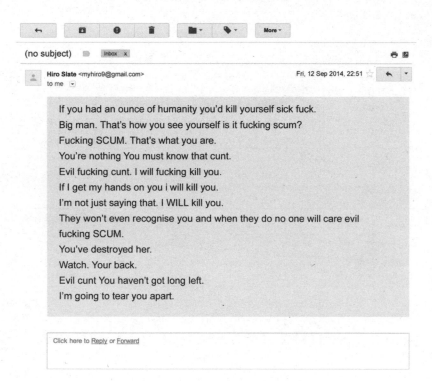

COPIED WORD DOCUMENT FROM CAMERON STRUTH'S PERSONAL COMPUTER

LAST SAVED 21 SEPTEMBER 2014

Happening Blog Sketch #1 – 19/09/14

To be honest, when I looked down at three police pressing my buzzer this morning, I did wonder if I was finally finished. In the interrogation later, I felt much better. Upstanding citizens with doubts and insecurities and families to disappoint/damage will fall apart in an interrogation because they don't conceive it as a game that can be won. The primary objective is keeping your emotions controlled. If you're self-possessed, you're practically invulnerable. The real danger isn't getting agitated and incriminating yourself, but rather allowing yourself to be pacified, susceptible, and thus compliant as a caught child. Most often detectives particularly talented in the art of psychological manipulation will get a confession by fazing you with basic respect and decency. Immediately you'll soften, feel akin to the rest of the human race, and you'll seek relief in fraternity and admitting responsibility. An inspired tactic! I could learn a lot from the police. These two performed quite well at first, apologising for the early hour and asking if I wanted a more comfortable chair, and I felt my tongue start to seize, my eyes couldn't look any higher than the table—I felt young and weak, in short—but my account still came out sound, I'm sure, abetted by the fact that a Teesside accent, to Southern ears, can herald a gentle div, and I made a habit of asking them to clarify their questions, which foxed them, I think, and soon enough they lost focus and got frustrated, pitching questions that secretly agreed with my answers, such as, 'So what you're saying is the woman'—the woman!—'has a history of seeking revenge on her past partners?' And that's when I felt I might be in the clear.

After a few hours in a cell whose window looked out on this majestic rust-coloured church on Barking Road, I even managed a nap, and when I was granted bail I bought myself a Scotch egg and a Ribena. Instead of going home I walked up to Stratford through an estate's dancehall BBQ and through the humid cemetery near there. Riding around the underground I felt accomplished and happy. The Central line had the air of an amateur theatre, with smells of grubby coins and fusty costumes, and there was a trapped heat that filled my overcoat and itched the skin inside. The cell's starchy bedsheets had given me a rash on my left cheek that felt lumpier than it probably looked. When a few people got off at Mile End, I stood with my back to the doors so I could assess the rash with my phone, and no sooner had I settled into a pool of liberty than the enormity of Corina's accusation made my gut plunge, just like waiting in the wings, because I realised then that the truth of what's happened is immaterial; it all depends on persuasion, on the alien language of law, and now it's out of my hands—*très* Aeschylus—so I imagined following someone who could lead me to something/somewhere different, or at the very least distract me.

A stop later and the only possible targets had been a couple of lasses coiled around the support pole with little crucifixes wiggling off their bellybuttons. They'd been taking pictures of themselves and bunching up their huge frizzy hair only so it could tumble down again. They laughed about the clouds outside that threatened to turn their tops translucent with rain. They were practically begging for my attention, but before I could plot which role and scenario to pursue, they'd left at Bethnal Green saying I might as well have taken a picture and giggling viciously. I imagined telling them that I was in fact a fashion photographer, and it was indeed a picture that I was after. They'd giggle differently then. Giggle for themselves. I imagined taking them to a bar because I was out of my overdraft for once in my fucking life. One of them always gets drunker than the other.

But their laughter weakened me. My eyes were glazing over this huge yellow poster on the platform wall bearing the slogan 'YOUR CAPITAL IS AT RISK' and I was about to disembark and head home, when, like angels who'd heard my thoughts, two pitiable men got on at Bank and immediately I knew that it should be one of them. Even if these men were unaware of it, the three of us were allies. The man who turned out to be mine was oversized, like a monument animated. He wore a blue suit so tight around his shoulders that the jacket rode up with taut ripples all over, and the cuffs were halfway down his forearms, the trouser legs turned up above his ankles. As I didn't know then that he had the same bottomless suffering eyes as Sam, The other man was a kind of wild dishevelled Pakistani. People were glancing at him because he had a big, full rucksack, but I felt like picking him would seem racist, and not a moment later I knew I'd chosen right. The first man, the giant, gestured to a woman sitting on one of the foldable seats by the doors. She held a baby against her chest. Wordlessly he was asking her to move the collapsed pram blocking the next seat. She snorted, shook her head, and yanked the pram between her legs. Once he'd squeezed himself beside her, this man's head reached above the window and half his arse hung off the seat. Sweat rolled down the cheeks/neck, which bulged over his sharp shirt collar. He glanced sadly at the woman like a told-off dog.

Pity washed through me, dressed up as affection: the deepest sorrows belong to the fat. What must have happened to him to make him this way? Those lasses, so seemingly invincible, with their cruel laughter, how would they have belittled him? Now watching his briefcase buoyed up on his gut, the unavoidable problem of morality emerged. This had happened the other times—as the Labour Party canvasser in Kensington/the mugged immigrant on Fleet Street/the homeless hostel volunteer/the preteen, shaved bare, undressed on a webcam for those slouching helpless men; the times when the whole world came to me—but then, like before, the more I looked at it the more I saw how easy it is to peel that word, *immoral*, straight off the surface of a performance like this, and once I'd done that, as simple as picking up lost cash from the pavement, I couldn't decipher what it was that would unite that word and the act that it described in the first place. These exploits of mine are shady, maybe, but *deceit* is an inflated word and it's not like anybody has got hurt.

At Notting Hill the woman beside my man got off. As she went, she said, 'Fat wanker.' The people around pretended not to hear it. My man shook his head. Where does he go after being insulted by a High Street Ken yummy mummy who appears to subsist on Yakult, dust and castigation?

By the end of the line there were only a few people left. The la-di-da voice ordered all of us to change. We stepped out of different doors, my man and me, and I went the wrong way down the platform so that he'd be ahead. It was marvellous to see an angular woman rush past him in the tunnel, causing him to bump against the wall, because he turned almost completely sideways but carried immediately about his business, back on course, just like an insect. From ten feet behind him, I could copy his habitual movements, pretending to text so as to keep his pace. He used his credit card to exit, and I used the Oyster I'd stolen from a house viewing in Knightsbridge.

Over Broadway the clouds had a marble veneer, reflecting sandy light in air that melted just off the surface of manhole covers and cars and those green electrical cabinets by the kerb. Just above the rooftops, the sun smeared the covering clouds a dandelion yellow.

My man walked with a seesaw motion, not actually tilting left and right, but his legs and arms made that effect by swinging in little semi-circles around his body. Are those he lives with, his friends/ partner/children, rooted in some pact of negligence—are they in a similar state?

When I was young I would ape my mother in a similar way around the house, until, one morning, before she left for work, as she darted about in search of her bag, hissing to herself, and I followed behind her, she turned and clamped her cold fingers around my face, just below my eyes, and told me to fuck off. Through tears I'd told my father what she'd done and he had merely laughed. He said I was lucky it wasn't my balls she grabbed, and doubly that she didn't keep them. The man's not given me a single word of advice that was his own, and my mother thinks advice is for the thick.

Outside an Oxfam my man stopped to look in the window. Now this is it—plot development. It's to let him see you. It's to find his eyes with yours. He was standing before a mannequin in a black suit, his reflected face hovering over the mannequin's head in the manner it's done in films when the character dreams a better version of themselves, and as my ghost walked through his ghost in the glass, our eyes did meet. Ahead of him now, I strode on, drunk with the idea of him following me. Did he notice me? Did he wonder about me? Did he notice the instability on my right foot and know by some sublime perception that Sam had knocked the TV over onto it when we were bairns, crushing the two smaller toes beyond repair?

It wasn't enough to see his eyes see mine so I turned off down the side of a site where the front wall of an old building was held up with scaffolding. In the dark down here I fisted my hands to work out the tingling. A few minutes passed while I kept my eyes on the smashed-up phone box on Broadway. When my man sailed past I felt star-struck. I gave him a minute's head start before I went back to the street.

Further along, where the shops and businesses broke off to hedged fences, brown houses and blocks of flats packed in clusters between parking areas and random strips of grass, the man pulled a lager can from his jacket pocket, cracked it, and drank. He crossed the street diagonally, not looking either side of him, and he turned down a road nodding as he passed a lone roadworker sitting through a manhole, half-inside the road. After turning a few times we came to a square court surrounded by concrete balconies. The clouds pressed lower, thickening the air. Hanging back, I watched him vanish from the court into the darkness of the opposite stairwell. With my hood pulled up, I followed.

On the balcony there was nothing but a slab of light from an open door. My plan was to glance in, carry on, and leave, but near the light I slowed, stopping to look. The hallway led straight to the living room. The main lights were off, but I could hear a theme song, a televised crowd, a talk show, and I was wondering what film or what role it was that would get me on the talk show sofa when my man appeared at the end of the corridor. He stood there half-silhouetted, only the edges of his body illuminated, looking at me. He still wore his suit, but he was barefoot. And then he walked up to me. His chest was as high as my face. He had Sam's aching eyes, so dark that what made them look infinitely agape might have been the dense blackness of their very surface. He smelt sour—raw mince gone rank.

'I saw you on train,' he said. His voice creaked. His accent was Polish, maybe. What kind of pain did he feel when he thought about those he'd left behind?

I nodded.

'All way from Bank,' he said.

I nodded again.

'You followed,' he said.

'No,' I said. 'I'm visiting my aunt. Mrs Deeds.'

'Mrs Deeds?'

'Yeah. Do you know her?'

'What flat?'

'Flat 40.'

'There not 40 here.'

'I mean 14.'

'14? Just below here?' he said.

'Yes.'

'I know her.'

'You do?'

'A tall lady.'

'Yeah, the bald lady,' I said. 'Totally bald. That's her.'

'Bald? I see no bald ladies.'

'Yeah,' I said. 'Yes. What did you say?'

'Tall.'

'Yeah. Tall. She's tall and she wears a wig.'

'Dreadlock wig?'

'Yeah. Yeah. Dreadlock wig. That's her. That's my auntie.'

'So dreadlock lady is bald lady is—'

'My auntie. Yeah. We're not blood relatives.'

'Yes,' he said. 'But now problem. I remember dreadlock not 14. Dreadlock other side of court.'

'Well, that's her husband across the court,' I said. 'You must've seen her leaving his house. They're divorced but live close because of Ben, their son. He's twelve. He must play football around here a lot so you must see him about, don't you? They divorced because she got sick. That explains the baldness. She's bald because of cancer. Because of the chemo, I mean. She got the cancer, got the chemo, got bald. That's the order. Obviously. Cancer. Chemo. Bald. Bald auntie. Totally bald.'

'I'm going to stop you,' he said.

'Okay,' I said.

'There no Mrs Deeds here.'

'There is.'

'*Stavi ludzu*,' he said, I think. 'Dreadlock woman is Olaniyi. No Deeds.'

'Maybe I am at the wrong place, then,' I said.

'Maybe you just want come in here,' he said.

'Here?'

'Here.'

'I don't know.'

'What do you want?' he said.

'I don't know,' I said.

'Are you scared?'

'I'm not scared.'

'Then maybe you want come in.'

'I don't know.'

'So why you follow me?'

'I'm visiting my auntie, like I said.'

'Why you *follow*?'

'I dunno. I couldn't help it,' I said. 'Something good might—I don't know. Something.'

'Did you want me to find out?'

I shook my head.

'But you did want as well.'

I shrugged.

'You didn't care?'

I shook my head.

'You want control?'

I shrugged.

'Or you think because you can follow you are better?'

'I don't know.'

'Or you just want different.'

'Yes.'

'Even though pretend.'

'It doesn't matter.'

'No,' he said. 'Doesn't matter. And I can pretend. I can pretend the imposter is not found out.'

'I don't know,' I said, trying to find the bottom/surface of his eyes. 'I don't know. Are you sure you don't know Mrs Deeds? I was supposed to visit my auntie.'

He looked at me. He seemed set in wax. Then his eyes opened wide, and slowly, his rigid tongue reached out of his mouth.

The tongue swayed up and down as he leaned towards me.

I stood still, the tongue sliding down my cheek and between my lips. It sank deep into my mouth.

Let me stay here forever, I thought. *Let me be this person now. Let me be his.*

He clutched my shoulder with one hand. The other hand stretched for the door, which must've been behind me, I realise now. We struggled in the open doorway; I couldn't let myself go on; I knew he couldn't save me. Pulling myself away, I skidded, sending my feet behind his feet, my back to the floor. As I fell I tore the pocket from his jacket. He stood over me, panting. There was a magnificent moment of stillness, of the nothing between us, before I scuttled through the doorway and onto the balcony and he shouted in his own language, *Fuck off! Fuck off! Fuck off!* (Or maybe he was saying *come back*?) In the stairwell my feet moved too fast and I slipped down the stairs, cracking my face against the cold court floor below. Then I ran back to the underground.

The fall has given me a black eye/weepy sutures above the brow. Subject to the swelling, my vulturine understudy Jamie will take over the Raskolnikov role. At rehearsals the following day, he made a point of shaking my hand in front of the cast. He asked me who it was who'd hit me. Then the other leads, those playing Porfiry and Sofya/Sonya, rushed up to put a hand on my shoulders. They were just about to ask that question themselves, they said, and they chattered around me like seagulls around chips.

The rest of the cast and the crew kept their distance. Was it because I kept asking them if the cut looked infected, or did they know that I was out on bail? Do any of them know Corina? Were they wondering if I look like I'm capable of rape? Were they thinking I've got the cool green eyes of a rapist, the gapped smile of a rapist, all the hallmarks of a rapist they'd only just noticed? Often I myself catch the whiff of depravity exuding from me, and I saw it collect in their nostrils, too, narrowing their averted eyes. I felt afraid, but also I didn't care.

When I got home, I smoked a spliff and watched TV, rubbing my man's jacket pocket softly between my thumb and finger.

You have to try to find solace in what's beyond your control. The only way to survive until the next hearing is to savour the feeling of this glitch, remember how tremendous and exhilarating it is to be a suspect on bail, feeling flashes of genuine dread, and above all, you must act like you're already free.

Having soothed myself I sewed my man's pocket to the inside of my overcoat. It made a new pocket in there, but the stitching doesn't stay: the threads loosen, leaving gaps between them. The pocket won't hold an object too heavy/too small. It doesn't matter. I like to keep the pocket empty.

SCREENSHOT OF EMAIL FROM ANONYMOUS ACCOUNT ACCESSED SOLELY FROM CAMERON STRUTH'S PERSONAL COMPUTER

20 SEPTEMBER 2014

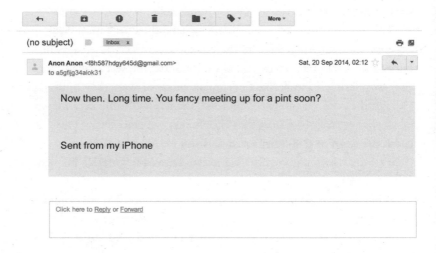

(no subject) Inbox x

Anon Anon <f8h587hdgy645d@gmail.com> Sat, 20 Sep 2014, 02:12
to a5gfijg34alok31

Now then. Long time. You fancy meeting up for a pint soon?

Sent from my iPhone

Click here to Reply or Forward

COPIED POSTS FROM CORINA SLATE'S BLOG, 'WITNESS'

SEPTEMBER 2016 (2)

The General Manager of the Kidney Service Team stood to let us know the meeting was over. The drug rep gathered her pamphlets, her samples, left the branded mugs, pens, coloured Post-its on the office table. Tasha and I said goodbye, pocketed the stationery.

'Seems convincing,' the General Manager of the Kidney Service Team said to us.

'It doesn't seem any more effective,' I said.

'But it's cheaper,' she said.

I couldn't argue with that. She looked at Tasha, whose head swayed indecisively.

'I'll ask the consultant,' the General Manager of the Kidney Service Team said. 'So what's the news on the new girl?'

'Ali,' I said. 'We're starting dialysis tomorrow.'

'She's still not eating enough,' Tasha said. 'Appetite stimulants?'

'I don't think that's necessary,' I said.

'Is she eating enough or not?' said the General Manager of the Kidney Service Team.

'Her GFR is back up to 65,' I said.

'She's not eating enough,' Tasha said.

'There's not enough evidence to say that appetite stimulants are effective.'

'Just look at her, Cor.'

'She's making progress.'

'Why are you so against it?'

'I just don't think it's necessary.'

The General Manager of the Kidney Service Team tightened her ponytail. She does this when she's bored. 'Let's see how she responds to dialysis,' she said, heading off.

'What's up?' Tasha asked me.

'I'll have a look at other antidepressants for her.'

'You,' she said. 'I mean with you.'

I looked at her, breathing instead of talking. It occurred to me that she had somehow found out about what happened, the trial, and she was urging me to let her in on it. I thought about the relief of not having to cover it over. I thought about the pain of having it exposed.

Then her eyes asked me if I'd heard what she said. I saw in her eyes that she didn't know. 'I'm fine,' I finally said. 'Busy, you know.'

'Yeah. I know,' she said.

We gathered our files. Tasha tucked her laces into her trainers.

'Your day off on Friday?' she said.

'And Saturday.'

'You busy Friday?'

'I don't know.'

'I was going to ask if want to come around ours, have some drinks, have loads of drinks, see what you think about the flat.'

'Actually,' I said, 'I can't.'

'You are busy?'

'I've got to sort something out with my brother.'

She tried to detect a lie.

'What?' I said.

'Nothing,' she said. 'He's being a dickhead again?'

'Kind of.'

'My brother was like that,' she said. 'Making bad decisions, pushing everyone away, being a dickhead. He bought a fucking narrow boat. Tough love sorts them out. Something drastic. He might even thank you for it.'

'Something drastic,' I said.

'If it's for his own good,' she said, picking up a mug, 'he'll get over it.'

I picked up the other mug.

She said, 'So maybe I'll ask someone else about the room?'

I looked at her, not knowing what to say. She smiled bitterly. Almost out of earshot, she said, 'Enjoy your mouldy windows.'

———

Her blood flows out of her body. She's surrounded by clear plastic tubes. She was here for nine days straight, had been bouncing around the wards, centres, her home, presumably, for the past four weeks. She's been assigned a counsellor, an anorexia specialist, who she sees before dialysis sessions, but she spends a lot of time here for monitoring. Other specialists come by, consult with her, with us.

Yesterday she flushed a sandwich down the toilet. I can't bring it up because she's crying. That forceful crying. Is it forced? Does she cry so that I don't feel like I can tell her off? Is that what's annoying me or is it just her crying? I'll handle it tomorrow.

She wipes her eyes, looks at me. 'You all right?' she says.

I hesitate because very few patients ask me this, because her eyes seem to see the critical thing that properly and truthfully answers that question. 'I'm fine,' I say. 'It's not me we should be worrying about.'

'What are you worried about?'

'Nothing.'

'If you say so,' she says.

I help her change into more lightweight clothes. She's mentioned feeling weighed down. She tries to hide herself with her arms. She drops down the bed. She twists a little like she's trying to compress the air out of her body. 'I just like space around me,' she says.

'That's okay,' I say, thinking, but there's a limit to the space you can have. 'Are you ready for a sandwich?'

'You don't get it.'

'You're not hungry?' I say.

'I'm always fucking hungry, mate. All the fucking time. And I'm scared, I'm scared that if I give in to it I'll never stop eating. I'll just keep eating and eating and eating and eating and fucking eating and it'll never be enough.'

Her mouth snaps a sour smile.

I nod. I say, 'Jelly?'

'I'll throw it in your fucking face.'

I nod. I say, 'Sandwich?'

———

In our mother's toilet, I hold the phone between my ear and shoulder, scratching. Would you believe me if I said I'm doing this to protect him? Could I accept it if you said I'm doing this to punish him?

'Hiro, where you at?'

'Why?' A metallic silence splits his voice. 'Where you at?'

'I'm at my place,' I lie.

'Have you been crying?'

'No,' I lie.

'Is Mum with you?'

'She's with the nutritionist.'

'What time's that finish?'

'Why?' I say.

'I was heading round hers to set up the laptop.'

'I did that already.'

'You set it up?' he says.

'Yeah. Why not?'

'Well, I was heading around there anyway.'

'Don't bother. She wants to lay low.'

'She said that?'

'Yeah.'

'But I'm heading there now. I'm basically there.'

'Where are you?'

'What's it to you?' he says.

'Where are you?' I say.

'On the 230. I'm basically there.'

'You passed High Road yet?'

'Just about to.'

'Can you get off soon as you can?'

'Why?'

'Need you to go to the pharmacy.'

'What for?'

'For Mum, obviously.'

'Yeah, but what for?'

'I'll email you it.'

'You fucking with me?'

'If you're on your way you might as well pick it up.'

'How urgent's this?'

'Pretty urgent, Hiro.'

'Why haven't you got it yet then?'

'I don't know.'

'Forget?'

'Probably. Yes.'

'Nice one. Where's it then?'

'It's down High Road. Down towards Seven Sisters.'

'What way's that?'

'Opposite way to the police station. You might have to wait a while for them to make it up.'

'But I haven't got the prescription.'

'I said I'll email it you.'

'All right. I'm getting off now then. To save the day.'

With him I hang up first. I guess it's not the sisterly thing to do. I flush the toilet paper I had held under my eyes, head back to my mother's living room, where my mother and father are sitting opposite each other, a vase of peony, hydrangea, eucalyptus between them. He turns to me, stiffly, in a suit, overcoat. He's balding now. Jowly, gloomy – no, shy, nervous. His polished shoes point to each other.

My mother stares at him coolly. She fills him in on what he's missed. I nod and smile, afraid that I might have to excuse myself again to cry. While he talks, rushed and breathless, I pick at a hangnail until it bleeds. He tells us that he'd left finance after the crunch, kicked the gambling habit and the other habits too. He's part of a recovery program, which I guess explains his candour, his reason for being here at all. Now he manages a bus tours company in Kefalonia. He has a family there, two teenage boys, Ioannis, thirteen, Jonas, seventeen. He's brought us a bottle of olive oil from his father-in-law's grove. He blushes when he presents it.

I feel like I've teamed up with my mother in his presence, but this reminds me of the distance he has wedged between my mother and I, just by being my father. I didn't learn Japanese because he claimed I didn't need to, that it would only confuse me. My mother acquiesced. When he left us, when I was eight, she tried to teach me, but I didn't want to learn.

After a long silence he says, 'If your brother's busy . . .'

I would like to have never noticed Hiro's pout on him, the same mole above his lips and mine.

He stands up, says, 'My flight is at seven-fifteen.'

'Well, it was good of you to come,' my mother says, going to open the door.

'Yes?' he asks. 'I've thought about it a few times over the years.'

'Well.' My mother smiles, holds the door. 'That's one less thing to think about.'

He coughs lightly. A film of sweat gleams over his head. He turns to me, patting the pockets of his coat. He stands there a moment looking at me. I guess he feels like he should say something heartfelt or monumental, but he just says, 'Okay.'

I hear his footsteps fading down the corridor. I feel relieved, grateful. Not for him coming, but for him not trying to make amends.

My mother closes the door. 'Didn't he look dreadful?' she says.

———

On Borough High Street, buses push bright, cold wind. The sun is hot, just far away. A rough sleeper holds himself in a ski jacket and sleeping bag by the cash machine outside the Sainsbury's. I want a Dairy Milk, 20 Superkings. It's so far from here to my bed. I want someone kind, quiet there waiting for me. A female Michael Palin. Clare Balding?

'I don't have any change on me,' I say.

I don't expect him to believe me. He nods. I think to ask him if he wants me to buy him something to eat, but nearly bump into a man in a suit in the doorway.

'Oops. Sorry, petal,' says the man.

And I find that I can't move. I feel the sun inside my clothes. The world around me deflates, flattens. Traffic. Gliding past. Everything gliding past on stretchers. Someone is stealing my breath, chasing my pulse. The buildings are toppling over like playing cards. Onto me. The roads are falling into the earth. I'm about to die. I'm about to puke. I'm about to shit myself. Black stars eat into everything. I count my breaths. That's too many breaths. Speeding up? Don't know what I can do. There's nothing I can do. Automatic doors keep trying to close. They slide a little way together, detect me stood there, eyes closed, sticky with sweat, then, embarrassed, they open again. There's nothing that I can do.

———

There was no turning back when my birthday drinks collided with your mate's stag do in Soho.

'Weird thing is that I kept thinking how great it would be to bump into you this weekend,' you said, 'and in spite of how unlikely, I did sort of expect it was inevitable.' I said I felt the same, though I'm not sure that I did.

You bought us a round. 'Where is he, then?' you said.

'He couldn't make it,' I said. 'Rehearsals, then after-rehearsal drinks.'

'Sounds about right. Well, let's forget about him.'

I was glad for the encouragement, and I don't think that I did think about him. Not when you were making us laugh with tales of kitchen mishaps. Not when we were dancing together. Not when we all ended up at your hotel bar. Not when you waited with me for my Uber. Not when you said, 'It's weird, but I feel sort of safe from the world when I'm around you.' Not even when I kissed you. Only after that, when we were on our way up to your room, but not caring.

In the morning, when you woke up, you made a sound like you were disappointed in something, which scared me, but I quickly learnt it's just a sound you made to displace silence, which you found uncomfortable. I remember lying next to you, holding your hands to my face. Your thumbs, thin at the knuckle, wide around the nail, like a spade, always tucked in behind your fingers. I would pull them out, fan your hands, slip my fingers between yours, my thumbs around yours.

'You want to hear the worst chat-up line I've ever heard?' I said.

'Go on.'

'Is your father in jail? Because, if I was your father, I'd be in jail.'

'Aye,' you said, eyes opening, 'well, that bloke's absolutely in jail.'

———

RE: Tenancy Renewal

Hi Corina,

I hope all is well.

I am writing to inform you that your landlord is happy to renew the tenancy for a further term of 12 months and he has advised us that your rent will be increasing to £900.00 upon renewal 17ᵗʰ November 2016. Please let me know if you are happy to proceed with the new rental and I will prepare and send out the new tenancy agreement to you.

I look forward to hearing from you.

Kind regards

Ana Thompson

Residential Lettings Administrator

I go around my mother's one afternoon. I'd rather be alone, but I don't like to think of her alone. On her floor I pass Leonard Down the Corridor. 'Hello, Leonard,' I say, mentally adding 'Down the Corridor'.

'Hello,' he says with a smile, a nod.

He goes into his flat. I let myself in hers.

From the kitchen end of the kitchen-living-dining room, my mother says she's making coffee. I sit at the table by the sofa, look through some of her mail. Bills. Medical forms. Covered in lists. Flowers in the vase. Hyacinths? My mother mutters, half to herself, half to me, describing what she's doing around the kitchen, getting out the cafetière, choosing mugs, wiping down the countertops, taking this opportunity to finish the washing up. Her chatter invades the room with something like a conversation, replacing the conversation that isn't happening. I look at the doormat, its cloud of dirt, the shoes beside it waiting in line. The kettle boils. She makes an enthusiastic sound, her version of voilà.

'Would you like coffee?' she says.

'I'd like a Coke,' I say.

'What?' she says, her head in a cupboard.

'I said I'd like a Coke.'

'A Coke! Do you think you need a Coke? I wonder if you need to calm down, not rev up.'

'There's more caffeine in coffee than in Coke,' I say.

'You and your brother. I wonder if both of you need to calm down a bit.'

'But compared to him,' I say.

'Yes. He has his moments. I like to remember when he was learning guitar, in his bedroom just practising his scales, and he was very still when he was sat there, very quiet and still. Still and safe.' The memory soothes her. 'I did cherish those moments. But he also had a taste for Coke.'

'I know,' I say. 'He has it every weekend.'

'Once a week is not so bad,' she says, loading a tray.

'You don't think? It's an expensive habit.'

'I wouldn't have it, personally, because I want my teeth to outlive me, but I can understand an occasional treat.'

'He's probably on it tonight,' I say.

'I don't think so,' she says. 'He should be here soon.'

'Here? I thought he was doing something with his mates.'

'He couldn't afford it, he says. Do you suppose he should be alone on his birthday?'

'When is he coming?'

'He didn't give a time, of course.'

'I might have to leave before he gets here.'

'Yes?'

'I have an early morning.'

'It is nice to congratulate someone on their birthday.'

'I'll call him later.'

'It would be nice for you to see him,' she says. 'I wonder when was the last time we were together.' She brings over the coffees. 'Are you hungry?'

'I ate before I left,' I say, 'but eat if you're hungry.'

'I'm nauseous.' She holds the cup to her face, the steam a cure. 'I think the crab I ate last night was bad.'

'The treatment can do that.'

'Thank you for informing me.' She takes a slow sip, turns slightly to the window.

'I was just saying.'

'It could have been the egg sandwich today. It didn't feel right going down. Is there a reason you won't wait for him?'

'I found a chair for you,' I say, pulling out my phone to show her the ad, the pictures. She's been napping more and falling asleep on the sofa. She wakes up crooked, she says. A sciatic pain in her bum. I found someone giving away a recliner.

'What's that on the side of it?'

'They're stickers, I think.'

'Stickers?'

'Just kids' stickers. Kids must have put stickers on the side of it.'

'How silly. What are they? Barnacles?'

'I don't know what they are. Shells. Seashells. Fruit. Unicorns. The man says he'll take them off before I get it.'

'What man?'

'The man I'm getting it off.'

'The man? What man? Where does he work? Why would they sell a chair with stickers on it?'

'I'm getting it for free.'

'They're giving it away? What business gives things away?'

'It's not a business. It's a family. They want to give it away. I saw it on a site that allows people to give their stuff away.'

'This was someone else's chair?'

'We'd have to shell out so much for a new one.'

'I understand,' she says, smiling.

'It's pretty amazing to get one for free.'

'Someone has died in that chair,' she starts to chuckle, 'and now I can die in it.'

'Don't say that.'

'Then you can give it away for someone else to die in it!'

I drink my coffee.

'Oh, lighten up.' She prods my arm. 'You're so serious.'

'No, I'm not.'

She takes my phone, hums, deliberating. 'I think it looks quite good,' she says.

'It is good. It's not even that old. The only damage is where a cat has scratched it, apparently, and maybe there'll be a mark from the stickers.'

She nods. 'And this man will deliver it here?'

'I'll have to pick it up, somehow. I'll figure something out.'

'Hiro will hire a van and drive you.'

'I'll figure something out.'

'It's worth asking him.'

'Listen. About Dad being here,' I say, 'I don't think we should tell—'

A key in the lock. Hiro lets himself in. My mother stands up, holding her arms out. I turn to see Hiro step in, not knowing where to look. He pulls up his joggers, rearranges his hair.

'So how old are you today?' our mother says, which she says to us every birthday.

'Twenty-eight,' he mumbles. He glances at me, smiles at her. Did he know that I'd be here? Does he know already that I kept him from our father? I turn back to my mug.

'Yes,' she says. 'I remember. At this time, you would have just slipped out. You came out so easily, unlike her.'

I hear him unzip his jacket, throw it on the sofa.

'Come sit with us,' she says. 'But hang that.'

He takes the jacket to the hooks on the door, sits between us. He drums his hands on his thighs. He doesn't seem angry, like he wants to destroy me. He must not know.

'Coffee?' our mother says.

'Coke?' he says.

'Oh!' She laughs, going back to the kitchen end. 'Your sister has beaten you to that one!'

'Sorry,' he says.

'Nothing to be sorry about,' I say

'I know,' he says. 'Don't know why I said that.'

'I heard you had to cancel on your mates.'

'Didn't have to. I wanted to. Wanted to see Mum.'

'I didn't mean it like that,' I say.

He pulls at his knuckles. Our mother passes him a mug.

She says, 'Or would you like something stronger? To toast?'

'Yes,' I say, not realising it was Hiro she asked.

'All right,' he says.

'What would you like? I have beer or beer.'

'I'll go for beer,' he says.

'Okay,' she says, getting up again, a bit stiffly this time.

After a silence he can't help but cross, he says, 'What's new?'

'I found a chair,' I say.

'What?'

'Yes,' our mother says, 'and she has to pick it up. Will you drive her?'

'A chair?' he says.

'It's a recliner,' I say. 'She's been falling asleep on the sofa.'

'I know that,' he says.

'I know. I was just saying.'

'Can't you get an Uber?' he says.

'I'll figure something out.'

'If you rent a van, you can drive her,' our mother says, popping the bottles.

'It's fine,' I say. 'I'll figure something out.'

'Kanpai,' she says.

'Kanpai,' we say, linking eyes for a moment.

'I don't see any other way to bring the chair,' she says.

'It's really fine,' I say.

'Do you expect this man to help you move it?'

'Maybe.'

'And I suppose you will drag it over here?'

'Could use a courier service,' Hiro says.

'And should you be going to some man's house on your own?' our mother says. 'Maybe there isn't even a chair. You shouldn't be on your own.'

'Why?' I say. Is this a general rule about women's vulnerability for her, or about my own particular vulnerability?

'It could be a scam,' she says. 'The only way is Hiro rents a van.'

I want to say that I am able to go to some man's house on my own.

'Right?' she says.

I don't say anything.

'And you wouldn't mind, would you?' she says to him.

He doesn't say anything.

'What's happening?' she says. 'Am I a ghost?'

I tilt my head to Hiro. 'That okay with you?'

He shrugs, sips his beer.

'There,' our mother says.

I down most of my beer. 'I've got to go,' I say.

'Wait!' she says, heading for the kitchen. 'I almost forgot.'

Our peeks at each other overlap. We turn to our mother. She's holding out slices of cake on a tray.

'I made honey kasutera!' she says.

COPIED WORD DOCUMENT FROM CAMERON STRUTH'S PERSONAL COMPUTER

LAST SAVED 22 SEPTEMBER 2014

Happening Blog Sketch #2 – 21/09/14

Denis Laws-Wilson (aka Claire Le Packen in the drag scene), swallowed by bedsheets, spoke with a scraping voice: 'My Ken doll is back at long last.' With arms aloft, he drew me into an antiseptic kiss. 'How do I look?'

'With your eyes,' I said.

That morning, in preparation for Denis seeing me, I had watched *Pink Narcissus* and danced to Janelle Monáe and I had a good long wank to the lads on Chaturbate to recalibrate my sensibilities, then I stood in front of my mirror practising the slanted smile of Ben (formally known as Kendall in the drag scene), the person Denis knew me to be.

'Cute,' said Denis. 'Me. I mean me. How do I look to you?'

'A—'

'—maciated?'

'No,' I said, remembering to cross my arm over my midriff and hold a cheek with the other arm's hand: Ben's default pose. 'Amazing,' I said. 'I was going to say amazing.'

'Amazing,' he said sourly. He closed his eyes and held the back of his neck. 'You lie sweetly.'

Denis and I met after I'd moved to London, in 2011, when I was working in a call centre and a Pizza Hut and living in a Poplar high-rise owned by a housing association that offered short-term lets in buildings scheduled for demolition or refurbishment. The bedroom window overlooked an already-razed site with Canary Wharf in the distance. It was supposed to be a six-month lease but they mailed eviction letters three weeks in. The night I got the letter I told my senile neighbour that I was his grandson and scored a little pocket money and I got arseholed and decided, quite on a whim, to go to The Black Cap in Camden. This is where I first saw Claire perform. She had a silver bouffant, black lipstick and a silky white dress and she lip-synced to 'Immortality' by Celine Dion while crushing rotten fruit against her body, and I scratched my cheek to hide a tear. She was one of the most beautiful people I'd ever seen. Her smile was no act. It was Denis's smile, too. Anyone with an atom of mettle can get their queen on, but it's magic to see the person, the vulnerability, beneath. The smile was so open I knew that he'd believe whatever lie I told him—about my mother's TV remote weapon, her disowning a poof, my bed- and hostel-hopping, bin-raiding, nocturnal life to avoid territorial attacks in the night. A week later he offered me a sponsorship of sorts and an invitation to live in his spare room in the flat near Hampstead Heath that he's had since the '80s. A year together and then I fled when he was diagnosed.

From his bedroom window, you could see the grassy hills of the park through the trees, where we had stumbled and groped, giggled and gasped. With one finger he touched both cheeks (measuring their concavity?), and I imagined the immense pallor of disillusionment over his face, each desperate question vying to reach his trembling lips, each memory replaying to an altered tone behind his eyes, when I told him who I was and in whose story he'd been playing a tertiary role—how I might constitute the most momentous person in his life.

A leaf, for a moment, clung to the glass of the window, then fell below, presumably onto the street.

He plucked the cup from the bedside cabinet and placed it between his legs and flicked ash into it.

'Still blow a perfect smoke ring,' I said. 'Menthols?'

'I tell myself they're diet cancer. I tell myself I'm buying time. I tell myself, when I'm really on a roll, that they're one of my five a day.'

'Want me to open a window?'

'No need,' he said. 'Pawel's not back till next week.'

'Where is he?' I said.

'You know,' he said, 'when I smoke, my lungs feel brand new.'

'They like to be stimulated.'

'You wouldn't have made me quit.'

'Is that a good or a bad thing?'

'Probably,' he said, holding a cough, squeezing the urge away, 'bad.'

'You don't need my help. You're indestructible,' I said.

'I've always felt like I'd get my comeuppance for surviving "gay cancer" and, well, here we are.'

'Stop,' I said.

'Oh, don't you start. I'm already shacked up with Ofcom. What's the matter with you anyway?'

'What do you mean?'

'You don't seem yourself.'

'I am,' I said. 'How am I different?'

'I don't know. Too—something. Pawel's not coming back till next week, you know.'

'You said.'

'What is it, then?'

'Nothing.'

'Well, I'm convinced. Is this all too much for you?'

'No.'

'You're embarrassed for me, then.'

'Of you?'

'I said *for* me. Are you embarrassed *of* me?'

'No.'

'You hesitated.'

'I'm not.' It was his fragility that embarrassed me, to begin with, though I felt breezes of sadness remembering how roughly we'd fucked.

'Shit,' he said, 'then is it—oh—what—is it boy trouble?'

'Kind of,' I said.

'Well, there's no plus-ones at our wedding.'

'I wouldn't need one.'

'You wouldn't?'

'Because there's no him.'

'What's that?'

'There is no him.'

Denis didn't understand. I saw on top of his face, like a mask, the face that he would make if I told him who I am.

'Anymore,' I added.

He stretched out his palm across the bedsheet. 'Do you want to …?'

'No,' I said. I felt the warmth of his eyes all over me. 'It wouldn't do any good anyway.'

He made a sympathetic sound.

'Don't,' I said, practically impersonating Vivien Leigh now, 'you'll make me—' and I held my breath/listened to him sigh some delicious pity.

'I'm sorry, Ben,' he said. 'I am, truly. If it does work out you can bring him. Of course you can bring whomever you want.'

I had Ben pull himself together. 'What would Pawel say?'

'Well, a lot, obviously.' Denis shifted in the bed. 'But I haven't played anywhere near as many cancer cards as I should have. He'll have to say yes.'

'He hates me,' I said.

'He's just jealous.'

'Jealous of what?' I said, sitting on the edge of the bed and searching his face.

But Denis didn't speak; instead, he turned his head to the window. Light draped shadows off his cheekbones. 'It looks like rain,' he said. 'I hope it holds off till the big day.'

'It'll be wonderful,' I said, 'even if it rains.'

'You did get your invite?'

'I did,' I said.

'Yes. I saw you liked the announcement.'

Saying nothing, I pinched my lip between thumb and ring finger, a gesture of Ben's that I'd forgotten but which resurfaced automatically like Ben had been there all along, asleep inside my skin.

'You probably think it's stupid,' Denis said.

'I don't.'

'That we're just assimilating,' he said. 'Is that why you're not coming?'

'I didn't say I wasn't coming,' I said, picking up the nail scissors from the bedside table. 'I suppose you'll need me to smuggle in cigarettes.'

'They would be appreciated.'

'When is it again? Is it—' *soon*, I was going to say, but stopped, before Denis inferred the rest.

'Third week of October,' he said. 'The 18th.'

The bail hearing. Part of me was glad that I'd miss the wedding and part of me wished he were already dead.

'You're busy,' he said. 'You're elsewhere.'

'I am,' I said.

He seemed to slumple into the bed and I looked up at him from under my eyebrows, a look that had saved me before and would save me again.

'Well,' he said, sitting up to square his shoulders with mine, decorous in the way that always made me tense up, 'at least I've seen you.'

And I managed to smile.

Before leaving Denis to rest, we drank tea and I looked through photos on his tablet. Paige had crossed the Atlantic; Cookie got battered on a stag and couldn't face it anymore; Tweet, transitioned, ostracised by some; Cruz, suicide.

'Who's that?' I said, pointing out this fishy queen in a red pressed-velvet dress and a vast smile.

'Are you joking?' Denis said. 'That's you!' And as I watched the image of me becoming me, I felt a dank crack open up inside me.

Denis said: 'I suppose for you it was just a phase.'

We sat there quiet for a while before his breathing slowed and I said I had to go, promising that I'd try to make the wedding. With a hand on the door handle, I looked back as he said: 'There's still so much to figure out.'

'Well, I can do the seating plan,' I offered, 'and book the hair appointments.'

'No,' he said. 'That's not what I mean.'

By the time I got home, it was night. A hoodied pack of blokes were smoking and jostling down the street under the only burnt-out streetlamp. On the wall outside my block, there was new graffiti. In the dark I had to use the torch on my phone to see: in red, the London Eye, but instead of capsules there were four severed heads. At first I thought nothing of it, but then I had to check that the severed heads weren't mine—but they did resemble mine. A coincidence, surely. Even so, I couldn't get inside fast enough, taking six steps in a single stride. For some time I sat on the floor against the bed and I felt the glue that holds me together become brittle and snap.

COPIED POSTS FROM CORINA SLATE'S BLOG, 'WITNESS'

SEPTEMBER 2016 (3)

Tasha and me were sitting at the nurses' station reviewing care plans. Next to us the Sister assembled a chair.

'For Tracy, in bed six,' I said, 'test for UTI and remove bladder catheter accordingly.'

'Hypervolemia in bed seven,' Tasha said.

'Appropriate urinary output after eight hours and absence of oedema.'

'Got it,' she said.

I leaned over Tasha to take Ali's charts.

'Excuse me,' Tasha said.

'No worries,' I said.

She scoffed. I shook my head, took the charts to Ali's bed.

'Lunchtime,' I said to Ali.

'What time is it, though?' she said.

'It's half-twelve.'

'What time did we say?'

'Half-twelve, Ali.'

'I thought you said half-one.'

'Half-twelve. We wrote it down together. See?'

'Fine.'

'So you have to take in 200 calories. Any preference?'

'Nothing.'

'You can't eat nothing, unfortunately.'

'Yeah, I can. See?'

'That's swallowing.'

'Which is the most important part of eating.'

'I'd say food is the most important part of eating.'

'Each to their own.'

'So what would you like to eat?'

'Does it matter?'

'Yes.'

'You're just going to give me something to eat. So just give me something.'

'Preference?'

'Something plain.'

So I got a packet of crackers, put it on the table in front of her. With her fingernail she flicked up the tag that unzips the packet. Then she opened it quickly. This was promising. But she only opened the packet, left it on the table.

'That's not swallowing,' I said.

She didn't say anything.

I took away the packet, put one cracker on a plate. She picked it up, put it down. I broke it up into bits. She ate a bit, slowly. She couldn't eat the whole thing.

Since then we've tried the smashed cracker method twice. Another time I left her to it. When I came to check on her, she'd put the pieces together and found out I'd smashed up two. There was no spectacle, just the frigid stare. I didn't want to say I'm sorry. I hoped that I looked sorry enough, but also hoped I looked resolute enough for her to know there was a good enough reason for doing it.

'I really didn't think you'd do that, mate,' she said. 'I hope that's just the job doing that and not you.'

I hoped so too, watching her eat the crackers. She ate them out of spite. I'm not imagining it. She ate them saying, 'There you go, Little Miss Ritz.'

'Thank you,' I said, then went on break.

I drank coffee, nodded off. I used to like to think that you could trust a patient regardless of their affliction, but I feel my heart only warming to Ali when she cooperates, even if it's begrudgingly.

Back on the ward, feeling sort of wilted, inaccurate, I saw Ali's bed empty. At the nurses' station, Tasha's head was in her hands, leaning over forms, reports. I asked her where Ali was. She chewed on a biro, grunted something that sounded like toilet.

'Was that *toilet*?' I said.

She looked at me as if I was fucking with her.

Inside the toilet, I heard a flush. I washed my hands. Ali came out, washed her hands.

'You need to let me know when you go to the toilet,' I said.

'Shall I raise my hand before I speak as well?'

'Do you know why you have to let me know?'

'Because you have to monitor my fluid levels?'

'Yes.'

'Really?'

'Yeah.'

'What a guess!'

'It's not a joke, Ali.'

'I'm not joking. I'm well impressed with myself.'

Her laugh smelled of vomit.

'Did you just throw up those crackers?' I said.

'No.'

'Ali.'

'I didn't.'

'I kind of need to know if you did.'

'I didn't throw up the fucking crackers.'

'Sure. Your breath just smells like puke.'

'Yeah. I guess it does just smell like puke. Fucking hell.'

'Nothing just smells like puke, Ali.'

'Parmesan smells like puke.'

'Well, yeah, parmesan does but—'

'Well.'

'—have you eaten any parmesan?'

'Was there any parmesan in the crackers I ate?'

'All right, just stop it.'

'Stop what?'

'All this little kid shit.'

'What little kid shit?'

'You're not a kid, Ali.'

'Yeah, I know that.'

'Then what is it? You want to have people monitoring your every fucking move in case you die? Nobody wants to have to do that. So don't make them. Don't be so fucking complacent about everyone around you. It's not fair on people who care.'

She was looking in the mirror at the door behind me. She nodded vaguely, whistled softly, like looking at a plump spot. 'You should thank whoever gave that speech to you,' she said.

———

My mother had agreed, when I talked to her after Hiro's birthday, that there was no point telling him about our father's visit. What has happened has happened, she said. It's our duty to shield him from the pain that it would cause him. If he goes to find him of his own accord, that'll be a first. Hiro says a lot, does little. So now I'm free to be as angry with him as I am angry with him. On the drive to Leyton, I own the silences. I also own the talk because I'm on directions. He directs his anger to other drivers, potholes, lights. I can tell the van feels cumbersome to him. When he grumbles I allow myself little sighs to chip away at him. I imagine flicking his cheek would clank.

The house we park outside is on the end of a terrace. On the lawn there's a mini football net, toy trucks. We sit here for a moment. Hiro might think I'm on my phone finding my correspondence with the man, preparing for the transaction, but really that's what

I'm pretending to do.

'You want to go ahead?' I ask.

His eyes glaze, asking himself if this crosses a line, then he grunts affirmatively and we get out of the van.

The curtains are drawn but I can see lights on through the cracks. There's no answer when I knock, but I find myself pressed against Hiro when a boy comes around the drive, saying, 'Hello, hello, hello, hello, hello, hello . . .'

'Hello,' we say.

'Hello, hello, hello, hello, hello . . .'

'Jesus,' Hiro says.

Then a bellied white man, apparently interrupted in the middle of trimming his beard, comes around the corner. 'Can I help you?' he says.

'Hi,' I say, 'I'm Corina. About the chair.'

'Sorry?' he says, frowning, brushing the shorn half of his face.

I look at Hiro to see if I didn't make sense. He looks at me as if to tell me I did make sense. What the man doesn't understand is this accent coming out of this face.

'Hello, hello, hello, hello . . .' The boy wanders around the lawn.

'Hello, mate,' Hiro says to the man. I see him inflate a little, taking a step towards the man. 'We're here to pick up a chair.'

'You're Connie,' he says to me, shaking Hiro's hand.

'Yeah,' I say.

'Hello, hello, hello, hello . . .' the boy says. He kicks a truck into the goal.

'I can give you a hand with it, mate,' Hiro says. 'That's why she's brought me.' He chuckles, points at me.

145

'You've come on the wrong day,' the man says.

'Hello, hello, hello, hello . . .'

'Wrong day?' Hiro says.

'I thought it was the 12th,' I say. 'Wasn't it? Sunday the 12th.'

'Sorry about this, mate,' Hiro says.

'Shut up, Hiro,' I say.

'No,' says the man. 'No. It was a Saturday. Definitely. I wouldn't have said a Sunday. No chance.'

I hold up my phone uselessly. 'But it was definitely the 12th. I remember.'

'You fucked up the days, Cor?' Hiro says.

'No,' I say. 'I haven't fucked up the days.' I look at him, push out my phone. 'You want to see?'

'Hello, hello . . .'

He looks at me.

'You want to see?' I say.

What does he see in me that makes him change?

'Okay,' he says. 'Well, today is the 12th, mate.'

'I told you,' the man says. 'I wouldn't have said a Sunday.'

'But you told us the 12th,' Hiro says.

'Not if it's a Sunday.'

'Well, today is the 12th, and it's Sunday, so can we get that chair?'

'You're too late.'

'Yeah, yeah,' Hiro says. 'It's Sunday.'

'Nah,' the man says, 'it's gone. You missed it.'

'Missed it?'

'Hello, hello, hello, hello . . .

'I waited around all day yesterday for you and you didn't show. Someone else wanted it and they were free.'

'So you haven't got the chair?' I say.

'Don't know what to tell you.'

'Hello, hello, hello . . .'

'You couldn't have rung us or anything?' Hiro says. 'We rented a van.'

'I waited around all yesterday for you,' the man says.

'Brilliant,' Hiro says. 'Nice one.'

'Come on,' I say to Hiro, pulling on his arm.

'Hello, hello, hello . . .'

'Yeah,' he says in the monotone that precedes a sucker punch.

'Hiro, come on,' I say and link my arm with his.

He mutters vicious words, turning stiffly.

'Sorry,' the man sings.

'Sorry, sorry, sorry, sorry . . .'

Hiro squeezes his hands, the man's neck in his mind. We get in the car. Hiro watches the man go inside his house.

'You all right?' I say.

He nods. 'You?'

'I'm okay.'

We look at the row of cars ahead.

'What a cunt,' he says. 'Sorry.'

'No,' I say. 'Enormous cunt.'

He shakes his head.

'How long have you got this for?' I say.

'You pay hourly. I just need to find somewhere to drop it off. I can pick it back up, or another one, tomorrow.'

'Tomorrow?'

'If that works for you.'

'I'm free till, I don't know, five.'

'Okay.'

'I just need to find another cunt giving away a chair.'

COPIED WORD DOCUMENT FROM CAMERON STRUTH'S PERSONAL COMPUTER

LAST SAVED 24 SEPTEMBER 2014

Happening Blog Sketch #3 – 22/09/14

Except infrequent and admittedly inconsequential theatre and a couple of Wonga adverts, the only acting job from which I've made money is the one in which I was—until earlier today—employed part-time. Twice a week I dressed up in a suit for a network marketing company called Fig Leaf to perform an ersatz admin role. There were only two main duties stated on my contract: boost morale, and report office dynamics back to the managers. My twenty-odd colleagues were under the impression that I sorted payroll/rota/updated records—simple, boring tasks that required no expertise. One of the managers, a man-weasel crossbreed called Freeman Newer, set up a desk for me at the back of the office facing the other workers and the wall of glass behind them, where the managers' offices are. My computer screen faced the wall behind me.

Before coming in this morning I was sure that I wouldn't make it to my desk before Freeman took me into his office and fired me, assuming the police inform a suspect's employers that they're on bail. If so, Freeman didn't seem to have told the rest of the office. If he had, their powers of pretence rival my own. The plan, then, was to make myself indispensable; to demonstrate my value.

The office was full of clacking keys and the Shakespearean tones of sales pitches and customer service. The air droned. The ceiling lights have not been working for a couple of months and so the only light, natural or otherwise, comes from the desktop screens, the small windows on one side of the room and, from the other side, the enormous electronic targets and awards board: a table correlating a list of our names with columns of competencies and deadlines, across which rows of yellow, orange and red smiley faces flash erratically like a fruit machine.

When the glass door closed behind me, my colleagues turned their heads and smiled the smile you smile at a bairn who's scored a penalty. Walking to my desk I looked at Freeman shuffling papers on his desk inside his glass-walled room. He looked up at me with the dead eyes of a shark.

The two assistants closest to my desk, Tom and Sally, were typing without pause. Tom raised his head and grinned. He's gawky with a £4 haircut—£1 a side—and the most complimentary person I've ever met. A few people in the office find him excruciatingly nice, with which I have to agree, especially in their company, but they don't realise how useful a namby-pamby man like Tom can be for making one feel good about oneself.

A couple of months ago, the day he'd forgone attending his own graduation because someone in the office wanted to switch shifts, I followed him into the office toilet, pretended to leave while he was still in the stall—washing my hands and letting the door close again—and I held my breath and listened to him masturbate.

But his pain is not my pain; he is not my ally. Last year, when the managers and duty managers were at the Xmas conference, Tom took it upon himself to give a staff briefing, in which he delegated the duties listed on our job descriptions, and appended this with 'And finally, to have fun!', an injunction I myself opposed by simply saying, 'Please don't say that'—i.e. it's abhorrent to suggest that our enjoyment of work is, firstly, a priority, and secondly, our duty—but, after blushing at the exposure of his own grandiosity, as we went back to our desks, he said to me, 'You're right. I never made the team, never mind captain,' and added—I shudder just thinking about it!—'Oh, Cam, you've got a black smudge on your forehead.' And after pretending not to care, when I checked myself in the toilet, I saw that there was no smudge!

Today I would condemn him to Freeman.

'I was just thinking,' Tom said as I sat down, 'that is a really, really great coat. Do you mind if I ask where you got it? I bet it was expensive.'

'Just some charity shop in Holloway, Tom,' I said. 'I don't remember what it was called.'

Sally crammed a handful of something in her mouth. 'My fiancé has one like that,' she said through the chewed food. 'I bought it for him.'

It was early to start snacking, even for her. A sack of cashews lay open on her desk spilling nuts among other scrunched wrappers, a yellow smiling Fig Leaf stress ball, and a *World of Warcraft* mug. Once, in the little office kitchen, she blubbed to me that she didn't know why she wasn't losing weight. I had noticed that she'd lost weight, I'd said, and anyway it wasn't her fault; she suffered from body dysmorphia, I'd said. She'd simpered, nodded, and sipped her midday cocoa.

'My fiancé can't even dress himself,' Sally continued, looking at Tom until he laughed. 'I bought his wedding suit for him. For our wedding. I bought the groomsmen's suits as well. My mother says I should've been a celebrity's personal assistant.'

Then she went to the toilet again. For all that disgusts me about Sally—engaged to God-knows-who and living rent-free with her mother, fingers yellowed from last night's curry, taking the lift when we're only one floor up, etc., etc.—I admire her ploys to run down the clock.

From my locked desk drawer I took out a notepad and logged it. In last month's performance review, the deputy manager Leah took me to a café in Soho and asked me if I thought I was performing my duties proactively. She'd bought me lunch, even offered me a beer, which I turned down, figuring it was a test, and maybe that's why I said without really thinking: 'I could do more, I think, and I'd like to.'

She asked me how I might 'action that aspiration', and I knew immediately: I'd compile a comprehensive list of Sally's absences, her movements (bowel or otherwise), the complaints she's received from others about her personal hygiene, and I'd learn all I could about Tom's anti-anxiety medication (which he'd been prescribed after I sprinkled MDMA into his broccoli soup one lunchtime, triggering a spate of 'panic attacks').

With Sally gone I stopped what I was doing, which is what I'm always doing—skimming articles/filling out personality tests/class tests/finding out which *Friends* character I should marry (Phoebe, as a matter of fact)/rereading past reviews of shows that predicted a spectacular career, all while keeping a fake spreadsheet open in the corner of the screen, ready to swap in and maximise if someone comes near. Instead, I zeroed in on Tom. He'd just put his phone down and entered the action into his log, making the smiley face next to his name on the targets board flash yellow.

'Did you get the text from Leah?' I said.

'Was it the one saying how lucky she is to help manage such an awesome team of people?' said Tom.

'No,' I said. 'It was the one about what the cleaners found in the toilet.'

Tom's eyes swivelled as if every object in the room surveyed him. 'What did they find?' he said.

Looking over his shoulder, making him glance back too, I said: 'You know.'

'I don't,' he said. 'I don't know. I really don't. What do you mean, Cam?'

He came closer, imploring me to whisper, but then Sally came back groaning.

'What's wrong, Sally?' Tom said and glanced over to me. (Fuck, that glance! Subservience. Supplication. It was glorious. Is blackmail the only way to achieve that?)

'It's nothing,' said Sally. 'Probably just a cold, I hope.'

Sat down, she forced a round of coughing through her throat. After the performance, she held her breath, one hand against her chest, and shook her head. 'Oh, God. What's wrong with me? What shall I do?' she said.

'You should go and get a drink of water,' I said.

'Yes,' she said. 'Worth a try.' And she waddled towards the kitchen, shaking her head in frustrated discomfort for the others to see. 'Would anyone like a cup of tea?' she said at the other end of the office.

She eagerly counted the rising hands as Freeman watched her, then he looked past her to me, and I scrawled something in my notepad. When I looked up, Freeman had turned his back to the office again. He was talking on the phone. On the targets board, a face on Tom's row flashed orange. He saw me looking at the board, and twisted around himself. He made a little sound, a whimper, and typed like a boy erasing a depraved Internet history as his parents knocked on his bedroom door.

I hate how easy he makes it for me to fuck with him; it makes me want to fuck with him all the more. Every so often, after watching a video on how to pick simple locks, I leave things in his locker. First it was a wallet with £20 in, and I was delighted when, on the first day, he took the £20 and left the wallet on the top of the lockers, and the next day, he went around the office asking if it belonged to anyone. Then it was a magazine which included an article by a sex addict who wanked at work. Then I sent him a photo of some girl's pussy from an anonymous number saying, 'Guess who?', and after a night's flirting over text, I hinted that the pussy belonged to someone in the office. This taught me a lot about who he considers romantically eligible, who he thinks would be interested in him, especially when I saw his eyes dance over the finance manager Natasha's face with a sly smile as she talked to him, even though she's married with two bairns. From another anonymous number I texted him that his father had had a stroke and that he should come home to High Wycombe and say goodbye while there was time. He missed a couple of days of work and when he came back in the office, after finding his father in excellent health, he burst into tears.

'Who would do that?' Sally had said. I'd hugged him. I'd felt every twitch of his body, every sob in my ear. My appetite for that could never be satisfied—the taste of having so much control over someone that you can tell them to do something, and they just do it.

Now Tom was blinking a lot. It had escalated too quickly. He needed to be brought back to a state of deluded reassurance. But before I could lure him further, Freeman stood on our side of his glass door.

'So,' he said, 'I've just been on the phone with Greg and we need someone to head over and help run an event tonight at Canary Wharf. I wouldn't want to put any pressure on you, and it will be a late runner, but it's extremely important. Some big potential clients that we can't afford to miss. It would pay our wages for a while, that's for sure, maybe even a bonus, and who wouldn't want that?'

Tom half-stood up. 'I can do it,' he said.

'Good man,' said Freeman.

And Tom sat down and I took my break. Outside the office on Soho Square, I rolled a cigarette in the stink/din of roadworks and beeping delivery vans. The door I'd just left opened again and one of the cleaners, Daniela, stepped out, lifting a cigarette to her lips. We've spoken a couple of times before, smiling at each other in passing. Her voice comes out slowly and softly. After saying hello and talking about mundane things—weather, etc.—I suggested we turn down a narrow alley between two buildings. It was hard to hear her in the roadworks clamour, I said, which was true, but it was not the reason why I suggested moving; in this tighter scene we stood much closer, having to let people pass now and then, and I knew that she was the perfect height for us to walk together with my arm around her shoulders. With each time we moved to let a person pass, me changing sides of the alley to stand next to her, she lowered her head and turned away. Was she unnerved by my proximity/my height/me? Did the cross that dangled in the opening of her shirt speak warnings in her ear?

Stood in the middle of the alley, not a foot between my face and hers as she kept trying to loosen a stray hair from the corner of her mouth, I looked at Daniela's thick dark eyebrows and wondered if her armpits were smooth but dark with the hair still thick beneath the skin; I wondered if she's the kind that shaves her pussy all over despite stubborn hair or whether she leaves the top patch untouched and just shaves the lips; I wondered if her arsehole was shaven, or waxed, and whether it was dark like the rings around her eyes, as Eastern Europeans do often have. Is she on the pill? Does she have chlamydia? Would I have to wear a condom? How would it go— fingers, mouths, cowgirl, missionary, doggy; the set menu? Or would she agree to peg me? She told me she was on her way to another job at the Bulgarian embassy and I said, 'Aye, I wouldn't blame you taking up another job, not with having to clean up after Tom in there.' And though I know I could've done better than that and I wasn't even sure that she understood all of what I said, she cracked her composure for a laugh that blasted from her throat, like a crow/ my mother. My mother would laugh like that when I found her coddling Sam and would ask for a hug myself; she'd laugh at my boyish needing of her. But I was a boy, and I did. 'Maybe,' Daniela said, still smiling, 'you could come to mine for food tonight. I cook very well.' She texted me her address.

She lives in Croydon; too far away.

When I went back in, Freeman met me at the glass doors. 'A word, Cameron,' he said and went into his office. When I went in, he had sat back down and was typing on his computer as if he hadn't noticed me, so I sat down and looked about the office: opened packet of luxury cookies, framed picture of him with his dog, the *Keep Calm and Carry On* poster by the window at the back of the room.

'Just had a chat with Tom,' I said. 'He's thinking about leaving. He says the job's not satisfying him anymore.' But Freeman didn't say anything. Instead, he turned and pulled a piece of paper from his printer and slid it over to me. Then he stood up and looked out the window behind his desk.

When I asked if he was firing me, Freeman said: 'Course not. We just feel that the position has become redundant. It's unnecessary for our plans going forward. There's a payment if you read on.'

His hands held each other behind his back—mock authority.

155

'But I value the work I do here,' I said.

'Yes,' he said, 'and we appreciate your contribution. We didn't imagine how successful you were going to be. It's quite alarming, to be honest. But we feel the position is unnecessary for our plans going forward.'

When I asked him why, he said, 'I've got a meeting with Greg in a minute and so I can't go into the details. I'm sorry, but that's the way it is.'

Still he didn't turn around, and I watched his neck, his shoulders sloped to one side, the side that bore a brittle collar bone, broken often, as he drunkenly confided to me on a leaving do, from mountain-biking tumbles.

'What if I don't wish to leave?' I said, picking up the dog picture.

'That's not how it works, Cameron.'

His weakling shoulder blades jutted inside the non-iron/sweat-exacerbating shirt, and I remembered when he waited for the company to scrap their policy of providing London weighting before offering a temp assistant a long-term contract, and I remembered also when he fired another administrator for stealing milk from the kitchen to give to her senile, welfare-denied mother (which, I must admit, he learned through the surveillance of yours truly), and I said, 'How would it work after I told the office and maybe a newspaper that I'm only employed here to snoop?'

His hands unclasped, arms folded across his chest, and his head shook.

'So I believe there's been a mistake on this letter,' I said.

'A mistake?' he said.

'I believe the payment number is incomplete.'

'Is that right?'

'I believe the decimal point is in the wrong seat, too. It should be a place along.'

Freeman pocketed his hands, and finally turned around. He'd forgotten to pluck a division between his eyebrows and rogue hairs revealed their natural connection. When I looked at his brow and smiled, he covered it with his hand as if scratching an itch, and he sat down. With his other hand, he pointed his pinkie at me. 'When you took the position I knew you were unhinged,' he said, 'but I didn't realise the full extent.'

'You made the job, Freeman,' I said, placing his picture face down.

'That's not the problem here.' He swivelled to look out the window again.

'What are we talking about, then?' I said.

'Cameron. For Christ's sake.'

'Say it, Freeman,' I said.

But he said nothing.

'You can't even look at me,' I said.

'You'll get what you want again, Cameron,' he said. 'You can go now. You don't have to come back. We'd prefer it if you didn't.'

Tearing the wrapping loudly, I took a cookie and left.

Only once I'd shut down my computer and filled my bag with stationery did I realise that my muscles were swimming beneath the skin.

'Is it still your break?' Tom said.

'Doctor's appointment.'

He stood up and pulled me into a hug. We linked like two bicycles locked side by side.

'Tonight,' Tom said before we parted, 'a load of my buddies are going for a drink. It'd be great if you came along.'

I couldn't look at him. 'Your buddies,' I said.

'Yeah. We've all been friends most of our lives, and then it's their friends from uni and my friends from uni. The whole gang!'

'That's a lot of friends.'

'Well, I'm an only child,' said Tom, 'and my parents are, too, so I had to make my own family.'

Staring at him, I knew that, even if I were to try and thrust my fist against his nose, he'd stand there grinning idiotically, unscathed.

'You'd be welcome anyway,' he said. 'I think you'd particularly get on with Abdul.'

'Why's that?' I managed to say.

'Well, he's just a great guy.'

'Okay,' I said. 'I'll be there.'

He made a high-pitched hum. 'We haven't decided where to go yet, but what's your number?' he said.

'Don't worry, Tom,' I said, 'I've got your number.'

As I passed the rows of desks each person looked up and smiled. Freeman glanced up at the office then immediately back down at his desk. With a hand on the glass door handle, I turned around. 'Everybody,' I called, turning their heads. 'You should know that I was employed by Freeman to spy on you. Whatever you've told me, he knows. He knows everything.'

A moment, their eyes tracing the air as if my words were hung there, and then a bubbling up of laugher, which swelled as I walked away.

SCREENSHOT OF EMAIL FROM ANONYMOUS ACCOUNT ACCESSED SOLELY FROM CAMERON STRUTH'S PERSONAL COMPUTER

22 SEPTEMBER 2014

(no subject) Inbox x

Anon Anon <f8h587hdgy645d@gmail.com> Mon, 22 Sep 2014, 00:53
to a5gfijg34alok31

Came into a bit of money dude so it's on me. Same place?

Also got a good one for you: how do you annoy your gf during sex?

Sent from my iPhone

Click here to Reply or Forward

COPIED POSTS FROM CORINA SLATE'S BLOG, 'WITNESS'

SEPTEMBER–OCTOBER 2016

On the way to deliver our mother's chair, we stop for lunch at a Morley's. I got two legs, chips. He got a strip burger. We sit at a tiny steel table that tilts each time we move. We say sorry when it happens. I watch him take the chicken strips, the lettuce, out the bun. He eats it like a salad.

'No carbs?' I say.

'What do you mean?'

'What do I mean?'

'By that?'

'I didn't mean anything by it.'

'Sorry. I don't mean to be . . .' he says, then says, 'I'm cutting.'

'As opposed to?'

'Bulking.'

'Right.'

He pushes the chicken with a wooden fork. 'Works for me,' he says.

'I wasn't getting at you,' I say.

'Okay.'

'We could've gone somewhere better.'

'It's fine.'

'Healthier, I mean.'

'You said chicken. No point spending much on chicken.'

'There's the nostalgia factor too.'

'Yeah,' he says uncertainly.

'Not for you?'

'I never really got it. Everyone going chicken shop at lunch.'

'I remember seeing you there.'

'Not eating though. And that, man.' He gestures at my box.

'The bones?'

He nods with a sour expression.

'Keeps it juicy,' I say.

'I beg you don't say that word.'

'Juicy?'

'Bleugh.'

'I never knew it was a thing for you,' I say.

'Why would you?'

'I don't know. I feel like I should've known that. I feel like I should've noticed at some point.'

He looks at me. Because you want to control me, I expect him to say.

'It's not a big deal,' he says.

'It sounds stupid,' I say, 'but I guess I worry sometimes that I don't really know you.'

He snorts, as if to say, 'Me too', then he says, 'There's nothing really to know.'

'Or just, I don't know,' I say, 'I worry that I'm not doing right by you, that we are . . . I don't know.'

He rubs a knuckle on his chin. He's wondering whether to say what he wants to say. 'I wish I could tell you stuff,' he says.

'You can.'

'I mean, without,' he says, but sighs. He keeps dipping a chicken strip in mayo, but he doesn't eat it. 'I'm sorry for saying all that shit,' he says, barely audible, 'you know, when I went off on one.'

'I know.'

'Probably too late for that.'

'Is a bit.'

'But I was vexed, you know.'

'Yeah. I know you were.'

'But more that I was feeling . . . I don't know.' He rubs his cheek. The hair rustles. 'You were making me . . .' he says, but frowns the thought away. 'I was feeling sort of like a nuisance, you know, like a useless nuisance, and you . . .' he says. 'I'm just sorry, you know.'

I don't want to force him to answer what I want to ask, which is, Were you just saying it to hurt me? Do you believe what you said, or me? I say, 'You shouldn't feel like that.'

'What? Sorry for it?'

'Like a useless nuisance.'

'I think I probably should, though. It's true, isn't it, sometimes?'

'Sometimes.'

'Thanks for that.'

'Any time.'

He stares at the bones in my box.

'So what was going on with you?' I say. 'What is going on?'

He lifts his eyebrows as far as they can go. Stretching his eyes to keep them dry? He presses his mouth against the words, says, 'I don't know.'

'You don't have to tell me.'

'Nah, it's just,' he says.

'You don't have to tell me,' I say.

'Nah, I know, I just I think it's, like, I don't know,' he says, 'I don't know what I care about, you know.' He clasps the thought between his eyes. 'I see people sort of defining themselves by what they care about, like you, but for me, I just don't know what it is.'

I say, 'It's not that great being defined by what you care about.'

'But what I'm saying is you've got something you care about, you know, something that makes you feel useful and worth a shit, and I've always wanted that, what you've got, and I've always been kind of amazed by it, and then I look at myself and I've got . . .' he says, trying to grasp it in the air, before his hands drop onto the table, his head bowed, 'I don't know.'

I watch him, not knowing what to say.

'Been struggling to find work,' he says.

I feel like I could reach through his chest, like through cobweb, to touch his heart. 'Yeah?' I say.

'I got a job for this old bloke, dad of the girl down my floor, just resyncing his accounts, easy, but when I got there, there was so much else going on, so I told him, I said he's got to replace his motherboard, right, and I could do that for him, and you know, he just thinks I'm scamming and that got me so vexed, man, because . . .' he says, but just shakes his head. 'Didn't do well for word of mouth.'

He looks up warily, knowing what I want to ask him. He tells me that he's been chatting to one of his oldest mates who's always been keen to involve Hiro in his 'enterprise'. I taste acid. He closes his eyes, waiting for my lecture.

'Is it safe?' I say.

The question makes his eyes open, shift about. 'I think so,' he says.

'Do you want to do it?'

'No, man,' he says, 'I don't. Really.'

'But you feel like you have to?'

'I don't know.'

'Okay.'

'You vexed?' he says.

'No,' I say. 'No.'

'But?'

'No but,' I say. 'I'm just a bit worried, obviously.'

'Yeah,' he says. 'Fuck.'

'All I'm going to say is you don't have to if you don't want to.'

He closes the box on his burger.

'You know you don't have to, right?'

He nods.

'Well then,' I say.

'Yeah,' he says, sighing. Then he points at my Mirinda.

'Go for it.'

He takes a sip, cringes. 'That's mad.'

'The man that thought you were scamming about the computer, though,' I say.

'It fucked me up,' he says.

'I bet.'

'Honestly, I felt it in every fibre of my bean, man.'

'What?'

'I felt it, like really felt it.'

'No. What did you say? In every?'

'In every fibre of my bean.'

'Bean? Are you saying "bean"?'

'Yeah?'

'Being.'

'Being?'

'Yeah. It's every fibre of my being, not bean.'

'In every fibre of my being?'

'Yeah. Why the fuck would it be bean?'

'You know. Fibre. Bean. What? What's funny?'

'Nothing. What did you think it means?'

'I don't know. It's just something you say. It means the full thing. All the fibre of the bean.'

'Like the essence of the bean?'

'Well, yeah.'

'Amazing.'

'I don't really see the difference, to be honest with you.'

'Yeah,' I say, 'you're right, actually.'

'Fuck, man.'

'Sorry.'

'Nah,' he says, 'I'm glad you told me. Been saying "bean" my whole fucking life.'

———

Ali weighs half a pound more than she did. The yellow tinge to her skin has faded. She's eaten a tomato this morning. A bit of toast with strawberry jam. A small glass of almond milk.

We've been tense around each other. We could only look at each other when the other was looking away. Quietly she said sorry for not having eaten more. I told her that she was progressing.

Now I rub betadine over the arteriovenous fistula on Ali's upper arm. In case you don't know, a fistula is any abnormal connection between two hollow spaces, two epithelialised surfaces, medically speaking, like blood vessels, abscesses, hollow organs. A fistula can result from an infection or inflammation, maybe developing between the anal canal and perianal skin, or within the urinary tract organ, or between parts of the intestine, or it can be surgically formed to enable treatments like haemodialysis. Here the fistula functions as an enlarged venous passage between the brachial artery and cephalic vein, allowing two wide-bore needles to take blood to and from the machine. The treatment has allowed us to talk.

'How scared should I be?' she says.

'Of what?' I say.

'This.'

'Dialysis?'

'No,' she says, meaning, I guess, her future.

'Not scared,' I say. I hold the arterial needle below the plump fistula, purple like a plum. I slide it through the flesh, picturing the enlarged blood vessel pierced, tapped, gushing blood up the tube. I tape the needle in place against her arm. Her blood flows out her body. I say, 'Just careful.'

I slide in the venous needle, tape it against the skin. I run heparin through the lines. It keeps the blood from clotting.

'Did you ever get scared doing this?' she says.

'Dialysis?'

'No,' she says. 'The job, generally,'

'Not really.'

I smooth the curve of the tube. I feel pulled into her eyes.

'So you're saying you never get scared, ever?' she says.

'Sometimes,' I say.

'But more when you were younger?'

'Well, I used to always wear a facemask when I started.'

'What docs that mean?'

'It means, when patients came in, no one could see me making this face.'

Ali's laughter dissolves the tension between us.

Ultrafiltration goal (UF goal) (fluids taken during treatment) = 1900ml.

Treatment time (TT) = 4.5 hours.

Ultrafiltration rate (UF rate) = (UF goal / TT) / patient weight.

UF rate = 9.5960 mL/hour/kg.

I turn on the machine. Acidic, hyponatraemic, hyperkalemic blood flows out of one needle towards the machine. The machine beeps, makes ambulance sounds. This scared Ali the first time we did it, but here the cleansed blood comes back into her and she is still laughing. It makes her cough up a hard dark ball of phlegm.

'I feel loose, mate,' she says. 'Loosely holding together. Like, loose.'

———

You seemed obsessed with food, cooking. You'd mentioned other fleeting fixations. Fantasy football, for a season. Gardening, for a summer. Wood engraving. Hardcore punk. African literature. French philosophy. But cooking was the only one you could make a living from. It was also how you wanted to show me that you cared about something, that you were good at something.

One time you were down, making us dinner. An expensive fish with three types of turnip. Or two turnips made three ways. You rushed about my poky kitchen. Confident. Deft. You tasted the sauce. 'Not bad, that,' you said.

I asked you how you'd got into cooking. You said Philosophy and R.E. had been 'your thing' at school. You'd unexpectedly gotten a few high grades. The teacher liked you. By sixth form, being good at this subject defined you. But then you couldn't hand in work. 'I got a pretty shite mark in a mock once,' you said when we were eating, 'and I thought, well, if I'm not good at this then what am I good at? If I'm not the Philosophy lad, then I'm just any old lad. So I figured if I didn't hand in my homework, I'd fail, but not because I wasn't any good, just because I never tried, preserving my reputation. So obviously I failed my exams, lost any will to go to uni and got a job peeling potatoes. And I was good at that.'

When you failed the exam, you quit the subject. Is that the logic that you took to the end of your life?

We're panting either side of the block's front door, either side of the chair.

Hiro, on the entrance steps, says, 'Up your end.'

My mother, in the foyer behind me, says, 'You need to lift it up.'

'What will lifting do?' I say.

'Up your end, Cor,' says Hiro.

'Why? Why up? It needs to twist, doesn't it?'

'Can it twist?' my mother shouts to Hiro.

'Twist?' he says.

'We need to twist to get the legs around,' I say.

'Take the legs off,' my mother says.

'I'm not putting it down again,' Hiro says.

'That's it,' I say. 'Bit more.'

'A bit more!' my mother shouts.

'He can hear me,' I say.

'Woah, woah, woah!' he says, a leg creaking against the jamb.

'Someone is coming,' my mother says.

'Fuck!' says Hiro.

'Okay,' I say. 'Coming back your way.'

'I think I'm going to die, man,' he says.

The chair swings back out, onto its side. A woman tinier, frailer than my mother shuffles past us without a word.

Hiro takes off his sweatshirt.

169

'Now you can take the legs off,' my mother says.

'Let's cut the fucking thing in half,' he says.

My mother makes the sound she makes when one of us swears.

'It's not the legs,' I say.

'We just need to get the angle right,' he says.

'Exactly,' I say. 'Ready?'

We try again but only grunt it into the same problem.

'It's looking better,' my mother says.

'Doesn't feel any,' he says.

'There's more people waiting to leave,' my mother says.

'You might have to take the legs off,' a woman says behind me.

'Why can't they do it?' the woman's child says.

'Pull it at the corner,' Hiro says.

'I am,' I say.

'More.'

'I am!'

'No!' he says. 'No!'

'What do you want me to do?'

'Twist it, but don't turn it.'

'What's the fucking difference?'

'She said a swear,' the child says.

'I know,' the woman says.

'Stop swearing,' my mother says. 'They don't usually.'

'Twist!'

'Stop saying twist!'

'Be nice,' my mother says.

'Being nice won't get this fucking—'

'How's it going?' a man says behind me.

'Pull it!' Hiro shouts.

'Do you need a hand?' the man says.

'Could you?' my mother says.

'We're fine!' we say.

'Let the man help,' she says. 'You're failing miserably.'

'I'm not,' says Hiro.

'Me?' I say.

The man comes up beside me, takes a corner of the chair. I shift around to the other corner.

'We just need to lift and twist,' he says.

'Told you.'

'I told you.'

'One, two, three.'

The edge shifts past the jamb, then the whole thing veers through.

'So easy!' says my mother.

'Yay!' says the child.

We set the chair down, panting. Hiro shakes the strain out from his fingers.

'Thank the man,' my mother says.

'It's no problem,' he says, walking out the door. 'Have a good one.'

The child skips past into the sunlight, the breezy trees. 'Wait!' says the woman, rushing after her.

'Why do they make doors so narrow?' Hiro says, hands on his head.

'People would get as fat as a chair,' our mother says, turning for the stairs. 'I'm going to lie down. Good luck getting it in the lift.'

NEWHAM ASSESSMENT & CRISIS HUB DETAILED RECORDING SESSION WITH CAMERON STRUTH

29 SEPTEMBER 2014

East London **NHS** Foundation Trust

NEWHAM ASSESSMENT & CRISIS HUB, CHERRY TREE LODGE, CHERRY TREE WAY, GLEN ROAD, LONDON, E13 8SP.
TELEPHONE NO 02077715900. EMAIL ADDRESS IS ELFT.HUB-REFERRALS@NHS.NET

Detailed Recording Session

ID	▆▆▆	**Family**	Struth
Type of Session	1-2-1 Initial Assessment (1 of 6)	**Session Date/Time**	29/09/2014 18:00
Assessment or Review?	Assessment	**Session End Time**	29/09/2014 18:46

Referral information	Referrer Name: Dr Abena Ameyaw		
	Referral Date: 23/09/2014		
	Referral History:	☐ Re-Referral If so please state last contact with service:	☒ New Referral
	Is client aware of referral?	☒ Yes ☐ No If No please specify reason:	
	Has client given consent for referral?	☒ Yes ☐ No If No please specify reason:	
	Reason(s) for Referral: - Panic attacks and anxiety - Complaints of insomnia - Significant weight loss		
Who was there	Cameron Struth and Farhia Hawa (Assistant Psychologist) via telephone.		
Presentation of the client	Cameron engaged well and could express how he was feeling throughout the support session, although he was often distracted and it was difficult to focus the conversation. Cameron initially seemed reluctant to share information but opened up as the session progressed. His speech sounded slurred at times.		

Purpose of the session	The purpose of the initial assessment was: To explain the Newham Assessment & Crisis Hub service To obtain consent and explain information sharing procedures Verify and update basic information Gain understanding of Cameron's current situation and create a support plan Complete Core-10
What actually happened	Cameron Struth attended the initial assessment via telephone after two attempts to contact him. The client and I discussed and completed the following documents: Basic information Confidentiality, safeguarding and information sharing procedures Consent to store and share information Access to record procedures Client worker agreement Core-10 Risk Assessment Support plan Safety plan The areas discussed during the assessment were: The client's mental health: Cameron described experiencing daily panic attacks; he struggles to breathe and gets light-headed. Cameron is unsure why they occur, they are at different times of the day, there is no consistency with regards to timing and Cameron cannot recognise anything that may be considered a trigger. The current coping mechanisms that Cameron has established includes finding space for himself and deep breathing when it is appropriate. Cameron feels confident that he has the tools to manage the panic attacks. Cameron feels anxious in the evening as he has been having trouble sleeping. We discussed his sleeping patterns; the amount of sleep he gets varies and is often impacted by his downstairs neighbours who often talk long into the night. Cameron expressed that he feels they often intentionally keep him awake. Cameron does not have an evening routine beside two small glasses of wine per night which he feels helps him sleep. We discussed the ways in which alcohol consumption can exacerbate anxiety and other mental health issues. We explored alternative routines that Cameron could implement. Cameron would like to try reducing his

caffeine intake earlier in the day, avoiding alcohol and reading instead of using his devices.

The client's physical health:

Cameron has found it difficult to maintain a healthy diet. He has experienced a loss of appetite and loss of interest in cooking; most of his meals are pre-prepared and microwaveable. We discussed the ways that he could increase his fruit and vegetable intake; he hopes to buy fresh produce when he next gets paid. We also considered how alcohol consumption may impact eating habits.

Cameron feels that his physical health has declined and he feels weak. We explored some ways to increase his physical activity that could be incorporated into his current routine. Cameron feels that he does not have time to exercise. FH to send list of five-minute 'Get your body moving' exercises via email. We also considered how alcohol consumption may impact a regular exercise routine.

The client's support network:

Cameron struggled to identify current meaningful support networks. His parents live in Darlington, NE England. They speak rarely, a few times a year; the most recent contact was May 2014 following his younger brother Sam's suicide attempt. Sam is currently in a coma. Cameron was close to Sam and relied on him for emotional support and Cameron expressed feeling quite isolated and hopeless without this support.

Cameron had difficulty naming someone that he can share his feelings with, although he says that he feels able to confide in work colleagues. We explored whether Cameron felt as though he needed to expand his social network. He explained that there are always new people to meet on the chatrooms he uses and often feels more comfortable with online relationships.

Support plan goals	Managing mental health by identifying current coping strategies and methods and evaluating their benefit. Managing his health re: alcohol consumption. Identify alternative methods. Discuss exercise opportunities. Explore counselling options, support groups and appropriate pharmaceutical treatment.
What needs to happen next	FH to create and share a support plan and email a copy of the Safety Plan and Risk Management Plan. FH to send consent details. FH to send 5-minute 'Get your body moving' activities

Purpose and date of next meeting	05/10/2014, Support Session 2 (of 6)
Review	
Risk assessment checklist	**Current Risk (please tick)** ☒ Of self-neglect ☐ Of accidental/deliberate self-harm ☐ Of attempted suicide ☐ Risk of abuse/exploitation by others ☐ Of serious violent/harm to others ☐ To children ☐ To staff ☐ Non-compliance with medication ☒ Mental illness and drug misuse ☒ Mental illness and alcohol misuse
Additional information	FH: Three attempts were made to contact Cameron via telephone. Follow up text, email, letter sent. GP updated. Case closed 20/10/14.

CORE-10 SCREENING MEASURE
COMPLETED BY CAMERON STRUTH

29 SEPTEMBER 2014

CORE-10 Screening Measure

CLINICAL
OUTCOMES in
ROUTINE
EVALUATION

Site ID ☐☐☐☐

Client ID
| C | S | / | 1 | 8 | | | |

letters only   numbers only

Sub codes
| 4 | 2 | 1 | / | | | | / | | | |

Therapist ID   numbers only (1)   numbers only (2)

Stage Completed
S Screening
R Referral
A Assessment
F First Therapy Session
P Pre-therapy (unspecified)
D During Therapy
L Last therapy session
X Follow up 1
Y Follow up 2

Episode ☐ 1   Stage ☐ A

Date form given
| D D | M M | Y Y Y Y |
| 2 9 | 0 9 | 2 0 1 4 |

Gender
☒ Male   Age ☐ 2 9
☐ Female

IMPORTANT - PLEASE READ THIS FIRST

This form has 10 statements about how you have been OVER THE LAST WEEK.
Please read each statement and think how often you felt that way last week.
Then tick the box which is closest to this.
Please use a dark pen (not pencil) and tick clearly within the boxes.

Over the last week...

Columns: Not at all (0), Only occasionally (1), Sometimes (2), Often (3), Most or all of the time (4)

#	Statement	Response
1	I have felt tense, anxious or nervous	☒ 2
2	I have felt I have someone to turn to for support when needed	☒ 3
3	I have felt able to cope when things go wrong	☒ 0
4	Talking to people has felt too much for me	☒ 0
5	I have felt panic or terror	☒ 2
6	I made plans to end my life	☒ 0
7	I have had difficulty getting to sleep or staying asleep	☒ 4
8	I have felt despairing or hopeless	☒ 1
9	I have felt unhappy	☒ 2
10	Unwanted images or memories have been distressing me	☒ 2

Total (Clinical Score*) | 16 |

***Procedure:** Add together the item scores, then divide by the number of questions completed to get the mean score,
then multiply by 10 to get the Clinical Score.
Quick method for the CORE-10 (if all items completed): Add together the item scores to get the Clinical Score.

Thank you for your time in completing this questionnaire

COPIED WORD DOCUMENT FROM CAMERON STRUTH'S PERSONAL COMPUTER

LAST SAVED 30 SEPTEMBER 2014

Happening Blog Sketch #4 – 30/09/14

Not sleeping well. Smoke and drink seeking oblivion but this only generates juddering dislocation. My mind whirrs throughout the night. The streetlamp is too bright for my crooked blinds. My head can't lay right. My shoulders stiffen while I shift positions between checking the hurrying clock on my phone and imagining roadworks clashing outside. It's at dawn when I recall scraps of hysterical dreams that I realise I must've slept a little after all, even if I don't feel rested.

Last night, I rang Darlington Memorial to ask if Sam was still asleep but I couldn't ask and I heard the man on the other end say, 'Honestly, who would prank call a hospital?'

Then I swiftly drank a bottle of wine and rolled a spliff, but I kept waking in bedsheets twisted.

In the early hours I woke—or I found myself awake—with blood smudges on the pillow; I must have been picking at the stitches above my eye. Maybe I should steal the head-cone from next door's Alsatian, I thought, wondering if the wounds on my face were infected. Google's pictures of globby gashes told me mine weren't so bad but also instilled in me the dread of what these might become, or are already: maybe it's the kind of infection that works inwards, tunnelling evil straight to the immune system.

That night I think I dreamt about collapsing onstage like Tommy Cooper, like a drowsy circus bear, and the audience thinking it's part of the act, still laughing, and it must've been the weirdly womanly shrieking from the fox den in the litter-alley by the rusted playground that woke me, because suddenly I stood at the window looking to the dark yellow street for them.

There aren't many foxes out and about in Darlington, and when I moved down here to London, I bored everyone by gushing about them. Their beauty, I said, is because of their rural descent, their incongruity, and because of their moxie, the way they'll just stop in the street and stare at you, only trotting off if you come too close. Soon enough I stopped gushing about foxes, but whenever I come across one, my breath will stop like I'm watching something I'm not supposed to see.

That's why I went out last night: I wanted to see a fox. It was an hour or so after my curfew. Spotlighted by streetlamps I went from my building through the estate towards the playground with my shadows inexhaustibly jumping and sidestepping around me over the black asphalt, trying to be in three places at once. There were no lights on in any of the squat houses, and I was feeling the chill of eyes peering at me between curtains—like I've done myself at furtive neighbours coming home from late-shifts or drug-runs—when a man in a grey hoodie appeared from a walkway between two blocks. Instinctively I ducked behind a car, and watched the man through both door windows.

Once he'd rounded another corner I darted from car to wall to shadow in pursuit. He slipped through a passageway and turned left through the car park and into the road dead-ended by the playground. Behind the bushes around the car park I could see him facing the side of the tower, imprinting, with a spray can hiss, in red, the London Eye but severed heads for capsules—but one less around the wheel than the night I came back from Denis's.

As the man finished, he turned, and in that moment the streetlight caught his face, which I glimpsed, with a cold slab of dread landing in my gut. Could he really have been Corina's brother Hiro? The notion alone seemed preposterous, but having seen myself in the severed heads made both these notions feasible. And then what of the reducing heads, one a week? A countdown? To what?

I shrieked.

He turned again, but I couldn't get a good look at him. For all I knew, he was Hiro. Once I had gone drinking with him and his friends. What I lacked in wisecracking banter I made up for with some kind of feigned Northern no-nonsense aplomb, and they seemed to accept me for that. In the smoking pen at the end of the night Hiro was called a Chink and had to respond violently. On our way back after Hiro had been knocked on his arse and told to stay there, which he did, we sat together in a booth at the back of a Turkish grill and I'd told him it was all right to cry. We swapped seats so his back was to the rest of the place, and he did cry, very gently, so gently I could've watched him for hours. He made me promise to keep it from Corina, and I did. From then on there had been tenderness between us, and in the pub he would reveal to me the vulnerability that both Corina and their mother found embarrassing.

Could this be Hiro? Surely not. He took a step towards me, and though I still couldn't quite see his face, I was all but convinced that it was him, so I gnashed and I shook the bush I hid behind, and he looked ready to shit his knickers and bolted, and I felt capable of tearing at my own flesh with my teeth, but he vaulted the playground gate, dipped under the steel slide glistening moon and vanished in the maze of lanes and houses.

SCREENSHOT OF EMAIL FROM ANONYMOUS ACCOUNT ACCESSED SOLELY FROM CAMERON STRUTH'S PERSONAL COMPUTER

25 SEPTEMBER 2014

(no subject)   Inbox x

Anon Anon <f8h587hdgy645d@gmail.com>   Thu, 25 Sep 2014, 00:15
to a5gfijg34alok31

Call her.

What about this one: what's the difference between a slut and a bitch?

Sent from my iPhone

Click here to Reply or Forward

COPIED POSTS FROM CORINA SLATE'S BLOG, 'WITNESS'

OCTOBER 2016

My mother wears her most colourful clothes to infusions. 'Everything about cancer is so white,' she says to the nurse infusing a granulocyte colony-stimulating factor. It will boost her white blood cells, defend against infections.

'There's pink,' the nurse says, knowing my mother needs to chatter through her treatments.

'Pink, white, grey,' my mother says. 'It's all pale and colourless.'

'I'd never thought of that,' the nurse says. She's sitting at a keyboard translating my mother's body into data. Next to the keyboard is the wrapped box of cookies my mother gave the nurse as a gift. She gives her something before every infusion, a token of gratitude. I know the nurse has to let her manager know about the gifts. She has to declare whether she thinks they're a bribe for preferential treatment, whether it will affect how she cares for my mother. She must tell her manager, 'It's a cultural thing,' because my mother keeps bringing gifts and the nurse each time just thanks her.

The nurse says to me, 'Your mum makes me think differently each time she comes in.'

We agree through smiles that compliments are a useful kind of treatment.

'And hopefully I brighten up your day,' my mother says, tidying her shirt. She turns to me. I can smell the yeasty poison in her. 'I'm leaving hair everywhere I go.'

'I haven't really noticed,' I say.

'Thank you for saying.'

'Maybe it's thinning a bit.'

'A bit! I look like I have mange.' She pulls out her phone.

'It's really not that bad.'

'I found a website,' she says. She passes the phone to me. A website specialising in wigs for cancer patients. 'I shouldn't have to pay VAT,' she says.

'You think it's time for a wig?'

'Wouldn't you?'

'I don't think so, but if you'd feel better.'

'I see people looking up there when we talk,' she says.

'Or you think you do.'

'Or I think I do. Yes.' She pulls her shirt at the collar, making space between the fabric and the chemo port. 'I saw Leonard the other night.'

'Leonard Down the Corridor.'

'I don't know why you insist on calling him that.'

'Because that's his name.'

'I could tell he was looking up there,' she says. 'He's probably thinking, "My god, how old is she?"'

'You haven't told him?'

'Of course not.'

'Why not?'

'Oh, he'd be hanging around all the time,' she says, 'devoting himself to me. Awful.'

'It might be good for him to know,' I say. 'For you to talk with someone about it.'

'No one needs to know,' she says.

I ask her if she's told any of her friends. She waves away the question. I ask her about the other cleaners at the hotel.

'That's an idea,' she says, shaking her head. 'Let the employer know that I might die at any moment. Why do you think I'm looking at these wigs?'

I take the phone, scroll through the styles. 'This one is pretty close,' I say.

'I have always wanted curly hair,' she says, raising her voice to include the nurse, 'like yours.'

The nurse scoffs. Her eyes scan the screen. Data she'll use to care for my mother's body. 'Let's print this out,' the nurse says, 'and take a look at your blood.'

———

'So you said you've got a brother?' Ali said.

'Yeah. Hiro.'

'Hiro,' she said, looking impressed.

The machine was cleaning her blood beside her. I'd come in early to see her. She had been discharged a day ago.

'He's your mum's favourite?' she said.

'I don't think our mum has favourites.'

'Course she does. All mums have favourites.'

'They do?'

'Course. I was my mum's.'

'You're the youngest?'

'I was a couple of years older than my sister and now I'm five years older. Mum gave her the boot even earlier than she did me. My sister couldn't hack it on her own. Too young for that.'

'I'm sorry about your sister.'

'Fuck it.'

I said, 'Most mothers I've spoken to said the whole idea of favourites with their kids goes out the window. It's all love at the end of the day, they say.'

'That's bollocks. Far as I'm concerned, love's all about favourites. You always end up loving someone a little more, a little less. It's the whole point. There's no point to anything if you don't choose one thing or the other.'

'But I think it's different with mothers.'

'But does your mum have a favourite, though, really?'

'Sure. It's him.'

Laughing made her arm pull on the needle in her fistula. She winced, hadn't gotten used to it.

'And you're older than me, right?' she said.

'I am.'

'So you must get people asking where the kids are.'

'Not really,' I said, 'to my face.'

'I think if I had to give birth,' Ali said, 'I'd fucking die. I reckon you'd be good, though. I reckon you'd be quiet. Not make a fuss, just power through.'

'I don't know about that,' I said.

'But have you ever wondered what you'd be like?'

'Not really,' I said. 'Not recently.'

But now, in the break room, Ali gone home, a few minutes before my shift starts, listening to the kettle boil, staring at the notice board without reading it, yes, I'm wondering about myself lying there with the midwife between my legs, my mother's hips taking her revenge on me for my birth. I'm imagining myself saying it's too much. It's not right. No. I won't do that. I won't. There has to be another way. My knees will come together. The midwife will do what she has to do. She'll have to encourage me to stop thinking this way. She'll think I'm unable to give birth, that I'll need an 'active intervention'. She'll think I'm not meant for it. I'll feel that I'm useless, that my body has failed me. I'll let her hold my legs apart. I imagine she'll ask for the forceps. I will be surprised again at how big they are. I imagine I'll cry now. Can't she see how much I hate this? She'll push the forceps inside me. By now I wouldn't have thought about what your brother did in years, about losing the parts of my life untouched by pain. But then I'll be back in it. Held down. Naked. Blood, semen, sweat, shit, stale breath, amniotic fluid. Ashamed, kind of. Angry, kind of. Too late. Nothing, gone, no way to get away, can't. I will not be there anymore. They can do what they want with me, this filthy slaughtered animal I look down on from the ceiling, this faulty birth machine a proper precious person comes out of. I will have lost a lot of blood. The midwife will say something polite like, 'Sorry,' or, 'We're nearly there,' because she can see that I'm in trouble. It will make me want to close up, give up, die, no, just rip it out of me, get your hands out of there, let me wash my hair, my face, brush my teeth, but I'll know it will make sense for her to say a thing like that, and hate myself for thinking she shouldn't say it. What doesn't make sense is for your brother to have said what he said. 'Oops. Sorry, petal.' Who was he talking to? It can't have been me. I couldn't get away from it so I got away from myself. I got away from myself but I couldn't get back. Who was the condom for? If it's so I didn't get pregnant, who was that for, him or me? Was it care for me? Was it some kind of compensation? That would explain the politeness, I guess, the apology. But no, that still isn't enough. I know it will never be enough. I will never know. I will never know what this stain is. I will never be able to clean it off.

—

RE: Tenancy Renewal

Hi Corina,

Thank you for your email.

I have liaised with the landlords and unfortunately they cannot accept your offer at £25.00 for the rent increase.

The proposed amount is reflective of the current market and rental price for the area.

In relation to the admin/renewal fee this is located on page 22 of your signed Tenancy Agreement (please see attached).

Please let us know if you still wish to proceed.

Looking forward to hearing from you.

If you require anything else, please do not hesitate to contact us.

Kind regards,

Ana Thompson

Residential Lettings Administrator

One of the General Manager of the Kidney Service Team's nails has broken off. The nail left behind is translucent with mild koilonychia, protein deficiency. In the break room she asks me how Ali is taking to dialysis. I can't remember the last time she took as much, or any, interest in a patient.

'She's on the right path,' I say.

'My cousin was like her growing up,' she says. 'Nice girl. Bane of our lives.'

I laugh, amazed at the callousness she must have concealed to get to where she is. Or is that precisely what got her here?

I get in the lift. Tonight I'll order a curry. I'll order three full dishes, two naans, a bottle of their sour headache wine. The wine I'll empty watching *Drag Race*. The food will last the weekend. On the next floor down, the lift stops and Tasha gets in. 'Hey,' she says.

We've had a long day. A man died. I say, 'Hey.'

'Fri-fucking-yay,' she says.

'Praise be.'

'Plans?'

'I found this liver detox I wanted to try.'

'Jesus. That makes me want to cry.'

'What should I be doing?'

'I don't know. Sucking and fucking.'

'Who?'

'Strangers.'

'Fuck that.'

'Why?'

'I'm diseased.'

'Never stopped me.'

'What are your plans?'

'I don't know, mate.' She looks up at the lift ceiling, rubs her face under her glasses.

The lift stops at the next floor. The doors open. No one's there. The doors close. We drop down again. Tasha leans against the wall, looks at her feet.

'So my rent went up this week,' I say.

She kisses her teeth.

I say, 'Fifty quid.'

'You contest it?'

'Weren't having it. Saying it reflects the market.'

'Which means there's one greedy dick in the area who upped it and everyone else just followed suit.'

'You should see the email. I said something like, while the increase in rent might represent the current market, it's disproportionate to the unchanged living standard inside the property.'

'Landlords don't have time for logic.'

'Fuck landlords.'

'My parents rent out a flat in Manchester in my name.'

'Well, that's just smart personal finance.'

Tasha chuckles, glances over at me. I feel her surveying for resentment, assessing how guilty she should feel for what she has.

We walk out the lift towards the dark doors.

'We should do something tomorrow night,' I say.

Tasha tries not to seem surprised. 'That could work,' she says.

———

My mother pours herself another Guinness. 'I don't remember the last time we played,' she says.

'I do,' Hiro says. He's never lost a game. He says he has a system that assures this.

'I'm closing in,' I say. 'I might go for it, if I roll enough.'

He sips beer through a smirk. 'You don't have the weapon,' he says.

'How do you know?'

'You're so bait, man.'

'You're bluffing,' I say.

He says, 'I know that you think Mum has the rope and I have Mustard.'

'No,' I lie.

'I don't have the rope,' our mother says, sitting down.

Hiro applauds us.

'You're not supposed to say what you don't have,' I say.

'I'll get this over with,' Hiro says. He rolls the dice, moves Miss Scarlet from the kitchen along the dining room, stopping short of the cellar.

'Not before I do,' I say.

'Wait your turn,' our mother says. She takes the dice. 'Maybe I will make a guess.'

'You have less chance than her!' he says.

'Arrogance is not becoming,' she says.

'It is a bit, though,' he says.

She shoos the idea, rolls a one. 'Can I stay in the hall?' she says.

'I don't think so,' I say. 'I think you have to move.'

'You might as well stay,' Hiro says. 'She might as well. It doesn't matter at this point.'

'Then I will suggest,' she says to me, 'Professor Plum, in the hall, with the dagger.'

'You said that last time,' I say.

'Mum's pissed,' Hiro says.

She swats his arm, laughing.

'Fine,' she says. 'Mr Mustard, in the hall, with the dagger.'

I shake my head. She looks at Hiro. He studies his cards, shows her one.

'Well, well, well,' she says. 'I know now who it is.'

'Mum,' says Hiro, 'you don't.'

'How do you know?' she says. 'Maybe it's you who doesn't have a chance.'

'Yeah,' I say. 'Maybe your system has failed you.'

'The system never fails,' he says.

'I don't think there even is a system.'

'Yes,' our mother says. 'He just says that to demoralise us.'

'The system has many functions,' he says.

'Functions!' we say.

'The point is to make you not fully believe what you think anything is.'

'And you do that by believing in yourself?' I say.

'In the system,' he says.

'You're chatting shit.'

My mother jabs me.

He says, 'You believe in the system as much as I do, you know. That's why you spend all your time trying to figure out what I'm doing and what I know and so obviously that tells me what you're doing and that tells me what I need to know.'

My mother starts to laugh.

'Don't laugh,' I say.

He points at her. 'She's laughing because I'm right.'

'This is wonderful,' our mother says. She's slid through that third Guinness into the sentimental stage. 'I don't feel whole very often but I feel nearly whole when we're together.'

'Why only nearly?' I say. I roll a five. 'I'm going for it!'

Hiro laughs. 'You obviously don't know.'

She says, 'I don't mean because we're missing your father. He's not part of us.'

I reach the cellar, the coffin of cards.

'I don't know why only nearly,' she says.

'So,' I say, preparing my guess.

'You don't know, man,' Hiro says.

I look at my notes.

She says, 'I think we find it hard to really come together, to be together, and so I don't feel fully whole. In fact, when your father was here I felt even less whole.'

I look at her. She has no idea what's she done.

'When we were little?' Hiro says.

I say, 'You're about to lose,' waving my notes at him. 'I'm going to win, Kaasan,' I say. 'Look.'

'When was it?' she says to me.

'You're drunk,' I say. 'Watch.'

'A month ago?' she says.

'A month ago?' Hiro says. He turns to me. 'What's she talking about?'

'No idea.'

'He was here a month ago?' he says.

Now she knows what she's done. She looks down at the board.

He watches us, his eyes like screws. 'Hold on,' he says.

'Are you making an accusation?' she says to me.

'Hold on,' he says. 'Are you saying he was here? *Here* here?'

We don't say anything.

He is beginning to choke on this now. He pushes himself away from the table, sits up.

'He was here? A month ago? Here?'

My mother's hands try to find the words. 'He dropped by.'

'He dropped by? What are you saying? When?'

'When?' she says.

'When,' he says.

My mother takes in enough air to keep herself afloat.

I say, 'It was a month ago. He got in touch. He wanted to come see us.'

'He got in touch with you?' he says to me.

'No,' I say. 'Mum.'

'But you knew about it?'

'Yeah,' I say. 'I knew.'

'You saw him?'

'Yeah,' I say. 'I saw him.'

'And,' he says, but doesn't need to hear the answer he knows already.

'Yeah,' I say.

He looks at the floor under the table, a strange smile curling a corner of his mouth.

My mother presses her hands against the seat of her chair. She will put herself between us.

The compost caddy is airing in the open window.

His smile has gone. He nods slowly, almost as if he's melting.

He picks up the envelope of cards, pulls them out, looks. His eyes linger over the answer. He swallows, slides the cards back inside, puts the envelope back on the board. He stands up. He leaves.

We breathe the silence he leaves.

The compost caddy airing in the open window teeters when the wind blows.

SCREENSHOT OF EMAIL FROM ANONYMOUS ACCOUNT ACCESSED SOLELY FROM CAMERON STRUTH'S PERSONAL COMPUTER

30 SEPTEMBER 2014

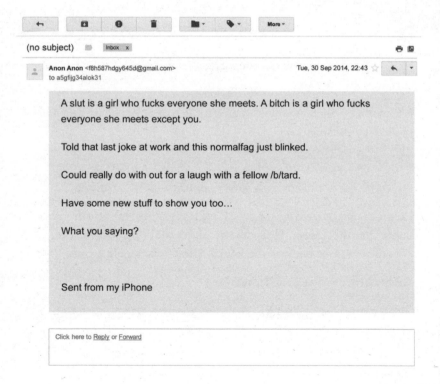

(no subject)   Inbox   x

Anon Anon <f8h587hdgy645d@gmail.com>   Tue, 30 Sep 2014, 22:43
to a5gfijg34alok31

A slut is a girl who fucks everyone she meets. A bitch is a girl who fucks everyone she meets except you.

Told that last joke at work and this normalfag just blinked.

Could really do with out for a laugh with a fellow /b/tard.

Have some new stuff to show you too…

What you saying?

Sent from my iPhone

Click here to Reply or Forward

February 2015

Her Honour Judge Gloria Mercer
Inner London Crown Court
Sessions House Newington Causeway
London
SE1 6AZ

Dear Judge Mercer,

I am writing this letter to tell you about Cameron Struth, a young man I have known for most of his life. I want to tell you about his character and about the type of person I know him to be: truly, an individual of kindness, compassion, and promise.

In Darlington, Cam's hometown, I have served as a Drama Teacher at Hummersknott School for over twenty years, served as Visiting Drama Teacher at the Federation of Abbey Schools for fifteen years, and administered classes at a leisure centre in Darlington for ten years. I taught Cam variously in school from the ages six to sixteen, and coached him in classes during this time. While studying for his A-levels at Queen Elizabeth Sixth Form, and in the summers of his time at Northumbria University, Cam assisted me in facilitating these classes. Over the years, his dedication to his craft, his sense of social responsibility, his capacity for empathy, and the generosity and gregariousness of his character has consistently, without exception, impressed me.

One memory is prominent to me as I write this letter. The young people who join our classes aren't always self-assured and outgoing, as one might imagine. Often, they struggle socially and/or emotionally, and performance can be a means by which they act out, express or come to understand the sources of their anxieties. For Cam, for instance, the class was about much more than an opportunity to get attention. There was one boy, aged twelve, who was significantly troubled. He had been expelled previously from two schools and issued an ASBO for xenophobic conduct, shoplifting, and spitting. The boy's mother was mentally challenged, his father incarcerated. A stipulation of his order was to participate in extra-curricular activities. The boy had chosen my class over other activities, he told me when I first met him, because it amounted only to "messing about". Cam, who was sixteen at the time he began assisting me, discerned an attraction to performance in the boy of which he himself was unaware. I am sure you will agree that the specific attention Cam paid to this boy was admirable in both its sensitivity and perspicacity. Cam would handpick monologues for the boy that he thought may, indirectly or directly, speak to the boy's own experiences. Cam workshopped these monologues personally with the boy, communicating with him in a way that was sympathetic without being patronising. As the boy became able to put words to his feelings for the first time in his life, his aggression overall lessened, he became more focused, less destructive, and, frankly, happier.

Cam and the boy became close friends, often using my office to rehearse and practise after school. Occasionally, Cam took the boy to the Theatre Royal, in Newcastle. Even while at university, Cam reported to me that he continued to counsel the boy when he started performing, competing, and auditioning professionally. It brings Cam and I immense pride to know that this boy has this year been cast in a major role in the Channel 4 TV show *Hollyoaks*. Accordingly, there is no doubt in my mind that I would not be exaggerating when I say that Cam saved this boy's life.

Since his move to London, Cam and I have kept in touch and even, I would say, become friends. I have workshopped a play he is working on about a devastating incident that occurred in his family when he was young. Often we have attended the theatre together. But since September of last year, I have gotten to know the new Cameron: I have witnessed him carry the stigma of being accused of rape and the social, professional and cultural effects that he has experienced. He has told me how some days it is difficult for him to get out of bed. I have personally witnessed a darkening of his demeanour. This is in stark contrast to the young man Cameron used to be, always energetic in pursuing his goals. The aftermath of this paradigm shift in his life has been incredibly difficult for me to observe, but Cameron has done the best he could to persevere through the situation.

I was not present on the night of August 23rd, and I did not witness the events that the young woman alleges to have transpired, but this allegation compels me to write to you. On that night, Cameron merely failed to recognise a series of signs that he surely would have if he or the young woman had not consumed alcohol, or she had been more explicit with her wishes. However, it is also clear that Cameron, having the good character that he does, was never out to take advantage of anyone, traumatise anyone, and especially rape anyone. He found himself in a situation and willingly participated in it, making decisions that have led to him grappling with what his life is now.

Character is a concept that transcends all other perceptions about an individual; it is the one trait that holds true for a person regardless of the situation. I believe I have been privy to Cameron's character, one that cares deeply for the wellbeing of others, and I hope this letter has contributed to revealing a truer picture of it.

Respectfully,

Beth Rowland

COPIED WORD DOCUMENT FROM CAMERON STRUTH'S PERSONAL COMPUTER

LAST SAVED JUNE 2007

<u>*Rehearsals*</u>
by Cam Struth

Inside a small garage. There are boxes, paint cans, and a motorbike covered in a sheet. Off-stage, car doors slam. The shutters open. A **Woman** *in her mid-twenties, formally dressed, enters, followed by a* **Boy***, fifteen, in school uniform, who closes the shutters behind him.*

Woman: I can't begin to tell you how fucking stupid you are. Is that closed properly? Fuck me. You agreed at the beginning never to make a scene, at the school, in public, nowhere, never. You agreed to that.

Boy: Yeah but—

Woman: What?

Boy: —why did you do it in your office then?

Woman: Fuck me. I thought you were more mature. I was led to believe you were more mature than that.

Boy: What did you expect to happen dumping me like that?

Woman: Dumping you? Oh, fuck me. Dumping you? You sound like a fucking child.

Boy: Well that's because I—

Woman: Don't even fucking say it. Don't even fucking say that fucking shit to me right now.

Boy: Language.

Woman: Don't. Don't even. Do you even understand? Do you even understand what could happen to us?

Boy: You.

Woman: What?

Boy: What could happen to you.

The **Woman** *stares at him.*

Woman: Fuck me. I can't actually—

Boy: Gladly.

Woman: —believe this. Shut up! Shut up! Shut the fuck up!

Boy: Okey dokey.

Woman: Just shut the fuck up! Okay?

Boy: Okey dokey.

Woman: Okay. Okay. Fine. Now, if you're not capable of taking it like a man, an adult, then take it like a child. I'm telling you it's over. Okay? That's that. I'm telling you. Do you understand? I tried to tell you like an adult but now—

Boy: Like a teacher more like, calling—

Woman: —it seems you need to be told—

Boy: —me into your office like—

Woman: —like a stupid little boy.

Boy: —you'd caught me cheating on homework or something.

Woman: You've just got to accept it's over. Okay? I'm not allowing it to continue.

Boy: Well that's not really up to you.

Woman: What?

Boy: It's not really up to you.

Woman: It's not up to me? Yes, it's up to me. Yes, it is.

Boy: No. Not really.

The **Woman** *stares at him.*

Woman: What do you mean? What are you saying?

The **Boy** *shrugs.*

Woman: I want to hear you fucking say it.

The **Boy** *shrugs again. The* **Woman** *stares at him.*

Woman: Okay. Listen. Do you understand at least why I think we should stop?
Boy: Do you want to stop?
Woman: Listen to me, please. Do you understand?
Boy: I think so.
Woman: Okay. Good.
Boy: I think if I showed my parents the letters and the pictures and I told them I'd been coming here instead of rehearsals, they wouldn't be very happy.

The **Woman** *stares at him, not breathing.*

Boy: They'd probably tell the school—
Woman: Look. Please. Maybe in a few years—
Boy: —and I think you would get fired—
Woman: —this could work, but now—
Boy: —and maybe go to jail—
Woman: —it's just not going to work and—
Boy: —and there'd be a newspaper article—
Woman: —your grades. Your grades. I've—
Boy: —probably a few articles and—
Woman: —I've heard your grades are slipping so—
Boy: —your husband would probably leave—
Woman: —really that should be your focus now.
Boy: —because you're a kiddy-fiddler—

Woman: No. No. You wanted it as much as me. You did.

Boy: —or nothing changes, I keep our secret, and now you don't have to keep buying me games to shut me up.

The **Woman** *stares at him.*

Woman: This was a mistake. That's all it was. We made a silly mistake.

Boy: No. You made the mistake. And you're going to have to live with it. So we'll have to be quick this time. My parents are going to wonder where I am.

The **Woman** *stares at him. She shakes her head. She tries to ask 'Why?' but the word won't come out, as if she's confused by her own question.*

The **Boy** *moves towards her.*

Blackout.

COPIED WORD DOCUMENT FROM CAMERON STRUTH'S PERSONAL COMPUTER

LAST SAVED 14 OCTOBER 2014

Happening Blog Sketch #5 – 13/10/14

The past couple of weeks I've got very little sleep, I think, not counting the gaps in my memory. The main items on my schedule have been waking dreams of Corina and Hiro knocking on my door, very much weed—Taffy Prince, a crossbreed of two Pakistani indicas, guaranteed, as Blue, the Southern cousin of my Northumbria dealer, said, to 'iron me the fuck out'—and negotiating with Sainsbury's customer service, inquiring into how many Listerine bottles I could have delivered for £150, because, if I do have to sequester myself from what seems to be Hiro's revenge plot, I figured I best stock up. These distractions did calm me, and a couple of times I got close to sleeping, I think, but one thing made my nerves clatter together: every few hours I'd get a call from a withheld number. On the other side of it, I knew there awaited a voice bearing only hatred and violence, so I didn't answer. When night came and the heating turned itself on, high, I stripped my jumper and t-shirt and decided to shut the lights and leave the curtains open. No one sleeps with the curtains open. You'd have to be in the middle of a moor to sleep with the curtains open.

So I pressed against the walls right next to the windows and surveyed outside at an angle, changing sides every thirty seconds or thereabouts. The streetlamp closest to the window flickered. Sunglasses lessened the flashing, though the street looked more shadow-soaked. For how long, I don't know, but for a while, I deliberated whether to keep the sunglasses on or not. The past week I've been struggling to accept the reality of what seem like coded messages from the police—they appear around London and on TV—and sunglasses make me see them less. One night, morning, whatever, I found a manky bag of coke in an old coat pocket and I watched *Fight Club* and when Edward Norton assaulted himself to blackmail his boss he said, 'I can do this job from home,' and I was numbly disappointed it hadn't come to that with Freeman. I emailed someone I wasn't friends with at school, a bong-eyed lad called Matty Doyle who was technically popular but who the popular kids only allowed in their clique in order to bully him. I'd stalked him on Facebook the night before. He'd become an investment banker, already on £65K and living in a Camden studio flat with a personal balcony and what must have been a 55" flat-screen TV. In my email, I asked him, 'Do you work from home?'

No reply.

The following day, Krishnan Guru-Murthy was on TV interviewing Pam Duggan after the inquest into her son's death, and because Mark Duggan and Matty Doyle share initials, I asked Pam, on a kind of half-serious whim, 'Do you work from home?' and she said, 'Well, I've been to court every day, every day, every day—and hospital,' and it seemed as though she were talking directly to me.

From there I followed a series of clues through an elaborate network and it didn't take long for me to ascertain its potential meaning. The initials M and D kept cropping up in number plates, followed by or in sequence with the numbers 134, M being the 13th letter of the alphabet, and D being the 4th. Over the next few days, now and then, I traipsed restlessly around Camden on the off-chance of finding Matty Doyle. The 134 (!) bus veered at me around street corners bearing Royal Borough of Camden signs that connected me, Cam, with the initials of both Matty Doyle and Mark Duggan.

The city is rigged around you, the code declared, and you are our unwitting agent, our linchpin, just like Mark was. We've been watching you for years, they seemed to say, because you might be the next one, the one to allow many to lash out in the only way they know how: you might be the next young lad to set the stage for the support and preservation of our power right when it looks ready to shatter.

Then I noticed that the last two letters of 'Camden' are the 5th and 14th letters of the alphabet. 5/14, May this year, the month Sam failed to kill himself. We are omniscient, they were telling me, and we are waiting for you to sacrifice yourself, not to your own death, like your brother, but to death for us.

But this can't be real, can it?

What made me keep the sunglasses on, as I cowered by my window last night, was the helicopter that suddenly chomped the sky and swung its spotlight around the buildings. Its arrival brought a call to my phone—Withheld. Was Hiro calling me out? At this point my mind was so whisked into bubbles that I felt a kind of empty invulnerability, which made me think I might as well have the police covering me, since they're apparently always with me, and in which case, I might as well induce the inevitable and beat Hiro to the punch.

Outside, the estate smelled of my neighbours' open windows, of smoked paprika and cinnamon and jerk pork, of lavender ghosts flowing under a narrow bathroom window by the closest chain of houses, where the spotlight shard caught me across the chest and I heard a lady from a balcony somewhere cry out, 'There's a topless wanker out there!' before I hunkered down in a dank skip enclosure.

Here I marvelled at the ludicrous lengths Hiro had taken. The police and their helicopter couldn't have been easy to involve. If I was going to survive the night I had to evade the spotlight, too. And this became my mission. With it cutting between rooftops I sprinted towards a nearby van. The spotlight glanced by me along the way, so I dived onto the ground and commando-crawled under a car, grazing my front, and waited. Eventually a group of lads walked past. Among them, there was that dark grey hoodie—Hiro, I assumed. I followed, dodging the spotlight, until Hiro and his cronies disappeared inside a house. We were on the far end of the estate now, and I was impressed that Hiro had rented a place near me for his HQ.

After some time the helicopter was called off and I was able to approach the house, where I heard drill booming within. Probably some kind of neo-samurai ritual, I thought. There was commotion inside and cheering now and then. Their station was the last in a row of small two-storey houses with scaffold poles for porch bannisters and bricked-in gardens at the back. The curtains were drawn in the front window, so in the alley behind, I pulled myself up to peer over the garden wall. Shadows jostled in the light through the back window. Next to this window was a door left ajar. The door opened to a utility room. A washing machine chugged and whirred. The closer I crept to that door, the noise inside whetted to human-shaped sounds. Lads bouncing, rapping along. An old lady laughing. Younger boys. So the whole family was in on it. Corina was probably in there. Past the sink and boiler and into the hall I stopped by the door separating us all, feeling such hatred for each of them.

The music stopped. A woman cried, 'Play it again!' A man said, 'I'm going to see where Stafford is,' whoever the fuck Stafford is. The door opened, but just a crack. A hand still held the handle on the other side. 'Now it's not working,' the woman said. 'Fix it.' The music started again. They cheered. As I turned to leave the music stopped again, stopping me. Then the door opened fully. And I was staring into his face. Grey hoodie. But it wasn't Hiro. It wasn't her family. In this suspended second I saw a different family holding fizz flutes crowded around a computer. On the screen—a YouTube clip bearing the red London Eye symbol that I thought counted down to his attack. A young girl said, 'The fuck?' In one moment I would feel such transcendent pain, I thought, and apparently my body craved it by the way nausea had stuffed me static, but then the man in the grey hoodie with his gentle face said, 'You alright? You lost?'

I could only nod. The man took my hand, led me into the living room. With one hand on my elbow he steered me among and through his family. He sat me on the sofa. They bristled and argued over what to do about me. Young Girl said to kick my batty arse out.

I saw the delicious fear beneath her anger. Dad said he'd get some water. Grey Hoodie kneeled before me, brushing away the grains of gravel still stuck to my skin. He draped a sunny blue towel around my shoulders. His compassion was such that he let me keep wearing the sunglasses. Mist formed in knolls behind the lenses. The tassel from his hood tickled the tiny wounds above my bellybutton. My phone hymned in my pocket, but we ignored it.

SCREENSHOT OF EMAILS FROM ANONYMOUS ACCOUNT TO ANONYMOUS ACCOUNT ACCESSED SOLELY FROM CAMERON STRUTH'S PERSONAL COMPUTER

15 OCTOBER 2014

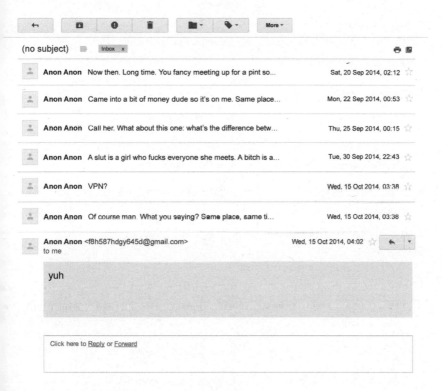

(no subject) Inbox x

Anon Anon Now then. Long time. You fancy meeting up for a pint so... Sat, 20 Sep 2014, 02:12

Anon Anon Came into a bit of money dude so it's on me. Same place... Mon, 22 Sep 2014, 00:53

Anon Anon Call her. What about this one: what's the difference betw... Thu, 25 Sep 2014, 00:15

Anon Anon A slut is a girl who fucks everyone she meets. A bitch is a... Tue, 30 Sep 2014, 22:43

Anon Anon VPN? Wed, 15 Oct 2014, 03:38

Anon Anon Of course man. What you saying? Same place, same ti... Wed, 15 Oct 2014, 03:38

Anon Anon <f8h587hdgy645d@gmail.com> Wed, 15 Oct 2014, 04:02
to me

yuh

Click here to Reply or Forward

COPIED POSTS FROM CORINA SLATE'S BLOG, 'WITNESS'

NOVEMBER 2016

In the infusion room, she snipped thorns and leaves from a bunch of roses. We weren't arguing about the best way to get home. We were arguing about the best way to find the best way to get home. 'But it's an app designed specifically to find the best way to get where you want to go,' I said.

'I know Citymapper,' she said. 'I suppose you think I'm stupid.'

'So you know it doesn't lie to you or anything?'

'I'm not saying we ask the man at the station because he won't lie. It's because he knows the best way. Best way to know the best way.'

'But what's best? What do you mean? Do you mean quickest, or what?'

'Quickest. Less walking. Best way.'

'Well, Citymapper does all that.'

'I know what Citymapper is. I suppose you think I'm senile, too.'

'Don't do that.'

'I only want to know from someone who knows.'

'But why don't you trust it? It's designed to do what we want it to do.'

'You can't depend on it.'

'You can't depend on something that's specifically designed for the thing you want?'

'I don't think there's any need to raise your voice.'

'I'm not.'

'I wonder if you could do as I ask, for once,' she said.

She closed her eyes, pulled a bra strap off from the chemo port. I remembered I used to try on my mother's bras. This was in our little yellow house in Woodford. My mother called it our fortress. We were safe in our fortress, she'd say. Our landlord was Tesco. One day Mr Tesco wanted to sell off his assets. His eviction note was friendly.

It was when I was about nine, when no one was around, that I would try them on. It was harder in the hostels because there was only one room, nowhere else to go. She was always around, or Hiro. If one of us was over 18, there would've been two rooms.

The only chance I had was when she went with Hiro to wait for a space to cook in the kitchen. I didn't like it because Hiro could come in at any time when my mother sent him to check on me.

The first time she cooked there was the last time she cooked what she wanted to cook because a man scared her by complaining about the foreign smell and someone stole our rice cooker. I remember using too much body spray before school so that I wouldn't smell foreign. I remember asking if we could have pizza, spaghetti, fish fingers, like everyone else. I made her put ham and cheese sandwiches in my lunchbox. I feel foreign to myself when I remember this. That time in the hostel kitchen made my mother feel foreign too. After that we had rice fried with egg most days. Sometimes we had fish fingers.

We moved to other hostels. She got cleaning work. I decided to hold my feelings in my toes; close enough to keep them, too far for them to come back to my head. I wasn't happy about much but I was happy when our mother went to work and we shot at helicopters in the sky with bananas, 'Pew! Pew! Pew!', when we danced the 'Macarena', when Hiro cried and I tickled him into giggles, when our mother went to cook with him, so I could try on the bras.

I remember once, when my school shirt ripped at the underarm, my mother tried sewing it together, but it kept opening up. She held the shirt in a tight grip over her mouth. 'I thought I could fix this one,' she said, 'but I can't.'

In the end we asked a station assistant for the best way to get home. It was the same way on Citymapper, but I didn't say this.

In her flat, provided by the council, in the country she might regret making her home, when she throws up into a mixing bowl, sat hunched on the sofa, and the vomit splashes over the side, down her trouser leg, I tut and shake my head. When she groans, I'm embarrassed because she's naked. But it's not her body that's naked when she groans. It's her.

———

Mottainai (もったいない) is about regretting waste, more or less. My mother would snap at me, most days, 'Mottainai!' So I'd eat every last grain of rice. We had to honour, not misuse, each grain, because each grain has value, dignity, deserves gratitude. In English, people might say, 'Waste not, want not,' but that's not quite right.

Every so often I went around a friend's house for dinner. Their parents would say, 'Waste not, want not.' They'd say, 'Corina's a good little eater.' Humiliating. I felt fat, ugly. I'd think of myself as a mottainai child, but I saw our family differently after that, couldn't decide whether we followed the mottainai spirit or whether they just didn't want to see their money rot away in a bin. So then I thought of myself as my parents' living bin. This way, the wastefulness of buying too much was invisible. In English, people might say, 'Out of sight, out of mind.'

You notice it even more when you live alone. There are no children, no dogs, no living bins. My solution is to recycle, religiously. On Tuesday mornings, bags and bags of waste food are picked up by trucks. I think of myself as following the mottainai spirit.

The longest time you spent with me, two weeks in spring, after I'd broken up with your brother, we ordered our food online, got it delivered from a supermarket. I saved about £30 that week. I felt clean.

But there was one morning, in the second week, we were stood in the kitchen in our underwear. You were making breakfast. The toast popped up burnt. 'Fuck sake,' you said, binning the toast. 'I'm sorry.'

'It's all right,' I said.

'No, it's not. How hard is it to make fucking toast?'

'It's just the wrong setting,' I said, biting down my dislike of self-pity.

You held your head in your hands. 'Some fucking chef,' you said.

Later I was sniffing a carton of milk. I passed it to you. You sniffed it. We passed it between us to decide if it was off. I tasted it. 'It's a little sweet,' I said. You tasted it. 'It's minging,' you said. 'I'd chuck it.'

I drank a cup of tea speckled with curds in the living room while you had a shower.

That night I lay next to you, staring into a dark corner of the room, afraid of how much more I might learn about you that would turn me off.

———

I watched two people pretending to be a teacher (man) and a student (woman) fucking on PornHub to see if it would turn me on. It felt like watching the Grand National. I remember my mother putting a bet on for Hiro and me when we were young. Hiro's came in last. He cried. Mine snapped its legs tripping over a hedge. Somehow I knew what that meant. I never bet again, never watched it. I know this is what your brother intended. He intended to rape me sexless, to be the one who finished me. He knew, too, that for me to manage to fuck again would be to fuck in spite of him. So what I worry about isn't just that I'll never fuck again, but that I'll never fuck again for myself.

———

Vaccination. The immune system produces antibodies when it artificially encounters an infectious disease. The antibodies are designed to fight this threat. They exist in abundance only because the body encounters the threat. I was walking through Victoria Park last October, rushing to work. The trees were just about to let their leaves go. They were incredibly full of leaves. It was bright, early morning. There was no heat in the sunshine. A man in a suit walked in front of me. In front of him a man and woman sat next to each other on a bench. There was a pram next to the bench. The second man's face was red, lumpy from rosacea. The woman had a long scar down her temple from when she must have had a plate fitted for a broken eye socket. The woman held a baby. This man was watching the first man. The woman pulled her top down a little, moved the baby to her breast. I suppose the man in the suit couldn't trust himself not to look because he turned his head to the grass on the other side. But the man on the bench knew the other man was thinking about it, watched him. 'Ow!' the woman said. The man in the suit glanced over. I guess he couldn't help himself. The man on the bench stood up. 'Get a good look, you fucking perv? Yeah, keep walking. I'll beat the fuck out of you.' I don't think the threat was the other man. The man by the bench was threatened already by what women go through and know without men.

COMMENTS

Unknown
I give up with this blog as the administrator will delete anything which is not in accord with their view. It's like being in an Islamic state where only one view of the subject is allowed, anything else will result in a fatwa on all your comments.
Replies

> **Unknown**
> I have asked and asked whether this guy she's talking about got sent down and I keep getting ignored it makes me think the whole thing never happened which is abhorrent to lie about such a thing.
> *Reply*

———

I read on break that refugees have been raping women in the Norwegian towns that welcome them. The tone of the article is regretful but also kind of unconcerned. I read one line a few times. 'We ought not to condemn the unfortunate before hearing and understanding their story.'

I put the paper down. Their story means nothing to me now. I remember a patient from back in my primary care days. He came in wearing a dinner suit, a heavy Prada overcoat, with his nose bent, eye socket shattered. He told me he'd been seeing one particular sex worker on and off for a few years. Morphine opens some people up. Sometimes they see us like counsellors or priests. He said he'd wanted to spread her own shit across her tits. She declined. The man that looked after her had brass knuckles. 'I have to pay for sex,' this man said. 'I want to have sex once a day. At least. And if I couldn't get it when I wanted it and how I wanted it, I'd have to go out and rape a real woman, I reckon, and you wouldn't want that, would you?'

COMMENTS

Unknown
I have to say there is the same amount of good and bad men and women in the world – always has been, always will be. Bad men hurt others quickly, bad women do it more slowly. There are just a few too many blogs and articles these days that are happy to point out men's bad bahavior. Women cause just as much difficulty in the world, possibly it tends to be more at home, so you see it less – but it's just as damaging.
Reply

Unknown
This comment has been removed by the blog administrator.
Reply

Unknown
Daily, young men are more likely to be the victims of random acts of violence than women of any age.

I have walked this Earth in seven decades and have been threatened with violence on public transport and in public places dozens of times over the years, the last when travelling on a train only a few years ago with my wife.

This is not a feminist issue because this is an issue where women don't actually want equality.

Directly (their genes and/or nurturing) and/or indirectly (the genes and/or nurturing of the father), women are responsible for providing the world with their violent, uncivilised offspring – discuss.

Surprise, surprise – people feel more threatened today because there are fewer employees on public transport, in public facilities and police on the streets.

N.B. Humans are never more than a few steps or a few drinks away from savagery.
Reply

Unknown

I very rarely give a second thought to the possibility of being attacked (except on the Internet) but I'm a guy. Are women really walking about in a constant state of apprehension on a daily basis?
Replies

> Unknown
> You're very fortunate, but I've been grabbed and yelled at multiple times in the streets. Just because it hasn't happened to you it doesn't mean it's not a very real concern for a lot of us.
> *Reply*

—

RE: Tenancy Renewal

Hi Corina,

Thank you for your email and confirmation.

Your mentioned points have been taken into consideration. We will liaise with the landlord and get back to you as soon as possible.

The renewal addendum is with you now waiting to be signed via DocuSign, please expect this email from Josh Mills.

If you require anything else, please do not hesitate to contact us.

Kind regards,

Ana Thompson

Residential Lettings Administrator

I come early to The Golden Cross, Stratford, but not early enough. I'd wanted to get here half an hour before Tasha and me had planned to meet. That way I could have a steadying drink without her knowing. I'm going to tell her what your brother did.

The Cross is where we often met when we were students. It's a Spoons, two floors, high adorned ceiling, a beery light, a library smell. Most of the time there's mostly men, alone, two pints each, a newspaper, lots of space between the tables. Even when it's full, it feels quiet, kind of intimate, like bar scenes in films, with the background noise faded out, away, your conversations the pronounced centre of everything.

I find a table upstairs, text Tasha. She replies, 'Do you mind if Seb comes?' I do mind, but text back, 'Sure!'

Seb is no threat, I don't think, been good to Tasha, generally, but with him about as well, I'll feel I have to be cooler, nicer, funnier than I'd have to be with only her.

I'll have to tell Tasha in the toilet, or when Seb gets a round.

My leg bounces. I wing out my elbows to dry the sweat. I check the time. It's the time we were meant to meet, which means I've got 5–10 minutes. I stand up to go for a smoke, but by the balcony I see Tasha come through the doors downstairs.

I sit back down. She texts, 'What do you fancy? Bubbles? Fuck it?' I reply, 'Sure!' but really I want a pint, more liquid, more to drink.

At the top of the stairs, Tasha holds up an ice bucket. Seb towers behind her. I stand up, hug Tasha.

'Hi, Seb,' I say.

'Alright, girl,' he says, 'how you doing? This is Jamesy.'

A short, hench guy, grinning, steps from behind Seb.

'Corina?' he says.

'Hello,' I say, shaking his hand, trying to smile.

Jamesy grins, looks at Tasha. I look at Tasha. Her eyebrows lift up.

'Were you sat here?' Tasha says.

'Yep.'

Quieter, in my ear, ahead of the lads, she says, 'You alright?'

'Yep.'

'You look hot.'

'Fuck off.'

We sit down. I can see that Tasha doesn't know how to take that. She sends me little frowns, question marks. Seb makes a meal of getting comfortable. No one wants to deal with the quiet. The lads take sips. Tasha pours us both a glass. I drink a mouthful right off.

Seb says, 'This place is so shit, man. I love it.'

Jamesy laughs a whole lot. It's actually a lovely laugh. Deep, warm, crackling out into a chuckle. His arms swell when he crosses them, the skin tightened, veins distended. I can't imagine how those arms can comfort without some kind of destruction first. I press my thumbnail hard into the pad of my finger.

Tasha says, 'Cor and me came here bare times at uni.'

Jamesy says to her, 'Yeah?' then, sweet smile, to me, 'What did you study?'

'Nursing,' I say.

He nods, trying not to show that he already knew this.

'I love that,' he says.

I finish my glass, pour myself another.

Seb says, 'I just hope it stays shit.'

'Jamesy was at King's too,' Tasha says. 'Do you remember seeing the rugby team play LSE in second year? Jamesy was playing. So you've kind of already met.'

'Are you into rugby?' he says.

'No.'

'Cor played badminton,' Tasha says.

Jamesy looks astonished. 'You don't meet many badminton fans.'

'I'm not a fan,' I say.

His face collapses. I feel bad for him. My hands feel grimy. I want to wash them.

'I just played it,' I say.

'I feel you,' he says. 'I feel you.'

'My mother made me play it.'

'Asian parents,' Seb says.

'Seb,' says Tasha.

Jamesy tries not to laugh. Seb says, 'I'm only fucking joking, man.' His elbow knocks into mine. 'I'm only joking, Cor.'

I shrug. 'I haven't played for ten years but she still goes on about it. Thankfully, she'll be dead soon.'

Jamesy laughs, then he sees Tasha and Seb not laughing, so he stops laughing and nods solemnly.

Tasha is looking at her glass. Jamesy rubs his arms, kneading knots.

Tasha says, 'How's your mum feeling?'

'Like she's got terminal cancer,' I say.

I finish my glass.

'Is it hard?' Jamesy says, looking like he already regrets what he's planned to say but thinks it's even worse to abort. 'Being a nurse and your mum's . . . ?'

'It's easier when it's not your mum,' I say.

Seb sighs. Tasha looks at him. We sit in silence for a few seconds.

'So what did you study, Jamesy?' I say.

He looks up like it's a trap. 'Well,' he says, 'nothing like nursing.'

'What was it?'

'Just sports sciences.'

'That's a little like nursing.'

'But there's no caring involved.'

Tasha says, 'Jamesy teaches football to kids in Tower Hamlets.'

'I wish I could do more for them,' he says.

Seb laughs.

'Shut up, man,' says Jamesy.

'And you think you'd be doing more as a nurse?' I say. I can see him thinking of a way out of this.

'Well, I dunno. I know, from talking to Tasha and, I dunno. I just think, when I think about it, the NHS is the only thing that makes me feel patriotic. You get me?'

Tasha takes out her phone. Seb too.

I say, 'Do you agree, Tasha?'

She looks up.

'Does the NHS make you feel patriotic?' I say.

'Yeah,' she says. 'You?'

'No.'

'I feel you,' he says. 'But I can only speak from my own experience, and I snapped my metatarsal, and I had surgery on it, and it got infected, but the nurses, man . . . I've always thought nurses are like angels.'

'I'm going for a fag,' I say.

Outside, I light up, walk towards the overground.

COPIED WORD DOCUMENT FROM CAMERON STRUTH'S PERSONAL COMPUTER

LAST SAVED 17 OCTOBER 2014

Happening Blog Sketch #6 – 16/10/14

In the brown afternoon a car alarm went off outside the flat and continued to wail well after two men came to hammer on my neighbour's door. As I left they asked me if I'd seen him lately and I told them he'd choked to death on his TV remote and his Alsatian had eaten a significant portion of his face. The one with tattoos on his forearms grabbed me by my collar but the other one held him back and I slipped out of my overcoat, leaving it with them.

All the way to the docks of Canary Wharf I pictured how I'd fell that man: duck under his grasp, boot the side of his knee, and a left hook to the corner of the jaw, just below the ear—out—just like Bas Rutten instructs.

Then, leaning over the rail along the water where the wide plaza becomes a promenade under the rolling announcement strip, I watched the metal-plate water feature in the square that makes the water look as if it streams from the trough to the top, and the gulls dipping down for chips and bits of rubbish, before following my phone, around the river loops, under tracks that shoot trains inside the buildings, to LA Fitness. Lean people wearing suits and trainers flowed out the automatic doors lighting cigarettes.

The woman at the desk looked up at me curiously.

'I'd like to have a swim,' I said.

'Okay. Well, it's twelve pound for a one-time visit. You can use the gym as well. You can use all the facilities.'

'I just need the pool,' I said.

'It's twelve pound for a one-time visit, but you can pay twenty-eight for a fourteen-day trial.'

'I just need the pool,' I said.

'Or you could buy a thirty-day trial and, if you're a student or work in the area, you can get 35% off.'

'I just need the pool today.'

'Well, it's twelve pound for a one-time visit.'

'Okay,' I said, 'and I'll need to buy some trunks.'

'They're £13.99,' she said.

'I see.'

'But you look like you need a wash,' she said.

'What's that?'

'I said you can't stay as long as you want.'

'I can't?'

'No. The one-time visit has a three-hour limit.'

'That's long enough,' I said, adding inadvertently, 'Is it clean?'

'It's a pool. It's got chlorine in it.'

'Does the chlorine clean it?' I said. 'Is that what the chlorine does?'

'Yes.'

'For some reason I thought it was for the smell,' I said.

'It's like an acid that kills bad bacteria.'

'Acid!'

'Yeah but not like *acid* acid. The pH is just above seven. It's actually the same pH as tears.'

'Human tears?'

'Of course.'

'I'll be swimming in tears,' I said, half to myself.

'No,' she said. 'No, sir.'

The trunks I bought were white with a silver streak down the side. Medium was the only size left so I had to wrap the cord strands around my waist before tying them bunched at the front. The hem reached past my knees. In the water, with one other woman soaring back and forth, my trunks ballooned and I had to dive every now and then to force the air out of them. At the deeper end I plunged once and for all into the rumble. Pulling myself down, closer to the bottom, the mounting pressure of breathlessness squeezed and filled my body and with a finger finally to the cold hard floor I looked back up at wobbly light shards in the haze, feeling weightless, unmoored, but entirely enfolded—weighted, and held. I pictured someone watching me, a mysterious smudge, a UFO, some rare and deadly shark in the water. Bubbles burbled from my laughing mouth. I was truly alone. For an instant I couldn't tell the difference between simulation and reality. Then I drank my surroundings greedily, awaiting—

—coughing, staring down at my lap, trunks still clinging to the skin. Stooped angels in soggy shorts surrounded me, sitting by the waveless pool and shivering. On the other side of the pool, the woman who'd been swimming with me was standing wrapped in a towel. An alarm was squawking.

'—he is. Here he—'

It was bright. The water gleamed like saliva. I felt so happy I hid my face and cried.

'—speak English?' I heard in a foreign accent. The lifeguard held out a bottle of water. I smiled. My comeuppance will be long delayed, if ever it comes at all.

'Is there anyone we can call?'

'What should we do with him now?'

Oh, to be a computer program, autonomous, without a traceable source, parasitically living from user to user, owner to owner, my only objective to erase people's photographs—I would feel solid then, and whole and untouchable. When ramifications go one way, and without punishment—yes, but someone will find someone to blame. We are wounds in this world. Sometimes we gape open, and if you could look inside you'd see this:

SCREENSHOTS FROM RETRIEVED 4CHAN.ORG/B THREAD INVOLVING AVATAR ACCESSED THROUGH CAMERON STRUTH'S IP ADDRESS

20 OCTOBER 2014

File: 9620FEAA-E8EA-418F-9D9B-8(…).jpg (103 KB, 600x600)

☐ **Anonymous** 20/10/14(Mon)15:13:42
No.760451306 ▶ >>760451747 >>760453811

Rekt thread

☐**Anonymous** 10/20/14(Mon)15:13:55   >>
No.760451747▶
>>760451901 >>760452541 >>760454117 >>76
0454200 >>760454591
File: 1511196282729.webm (1.36 MB,
244x360)

>>760451306 (OP)

>>

☐ **Anonymous** 10/20/14(Mon)15:14:40 No.760451901▶

>>760451747
oh no

>>   ☐ **Anonymous** 10/20/14(Mon)15:21:28 No.760452541▶

>>760451747
Not supposed to feed doggo chocolate

>>

☐ Anonymous 10/20/14(Mon)15:22:18 No.760452617▶
>>760452786 >>760452859 >>760453382 >>760453556 >>7604536
94 >>760453714 >>760454835 >>760455414 >>760455444 >>7604
55649 >>760456467
File: BabyAttackedByDog.webm (1.26 MB, 400x400)

>>

☐ Anonymous 10/20/14(Mon)15:24:09 No.760452786▶

>>760452617
Brutal

>>

☐ Anonymous 10/20/14(Mon)15:24:57 No.760453190▶
>>760453312 >>760453417 >>760455275
File: RailedInSanMartin.webm (672 KB, 854x480)

>>

☐ Anonymous 10/20/14(Mon)15:25:24 No.760452859▶

>>760452617
You sick fuck

>>

☐ Anonymous 10/20/14(Mon)15:26:55 No.760453032▶
Jesus fucking christ not the baby

>>

☐ Anonymous 10/20/14(Mon)15:26:56 No.760453033▶
Can someone please link the child that is beeing
beheaded by some, what I assume is, ISIS
soldiers?

>> ☐ **Anonymous** 10/20/14(Mon)15:30:18 No.760453312▶
>>760454052

>>760453190
If he would have kept going, I think he would of made it.

>> ☐ **Anonymous** 10/20/14(Mon)15:30:59 No.760453382▶
>>760452617
too much, you sick fuck

>> ☐ **Anonymous** 10/20/14(Mon)15:31:21 No.760453417▶
>>760453846 >>760454052 >>760454245 >>760456071
>>760453190

poor kid coulda survived if he didnt stop

>> ☐ **Anonymous** 10/20/14(Mon)15:33:18 No.760453556 ▶

>>760452617
Too far, dude. Absolutely disgusting.

>> ☐ **Anonymous** 10/20/14(Mon)15:34:44 No.760453694▶

>>760452617
reported

>> ☐ **Anonymous** 10/20/14(Mon)15:36:50 No.760453846▶
>>760453927 >>760454339 >>760454427
File: 1324837431548.jpg (8 KB, 200x183)

>>760453417
it's a suicide

>> **Anonymous** 10/20/14(Mon)15:40:43 No.760454171▶
File: SuckOnThis.webm (141 KB, 300x240)

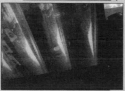

>> **Anonymous** 10/20/14(Mon)15:34:44 No.760453694▶
>>760454129

>>760453856
it's not.

Anonymous 10/20/14(Mon)15:51:59 No.760453382▶

>>

>>760452617
I know the fag who posted this >he posts this every
time one of these threads come up >We met up a
couple times irl >good laugh at first >sick fuck but
funny >knows the game >crazy amount of these
kinds of videos > plus so much jailbait Asian >so I
thought he was /our boy/ /b/ >Then this fag bitch
keeps bothering me to meet up >we hang out no
prob >chill >we come by this decomposing fox
>this guy wants to film it >wants to film me just
chatting by it like its not there >hes an actor or
something I don't know >he hasn't got his phone he
says >so we use mine >fucking faggot doesn't films
me but deletes all the shit he'd sent me pretending to
film me >I'd never grass on a /b/tard but some of the
stuff he'd send me was fucking raw >wouldn't be
surprised if he'd filmed himself >Fucking fag probs
cucked now though >I don't know much about him
except what he looks like but he shouldn't be hard to
track down >getting /baphomet/ doxxers on him >I
might be a fat beta /b/ but if I see him again I swear
he'll be on here with a belt around his throat >no lie

SCAN OF RECORD OF INTERVIEW WITH CAMERON STRUTH

18 OCTOBER 2014

RECORD OF INTERVIEW

ROTI

Person interviewed: Cameron Struth

Place of interview: Plaistow Police Station, 444 Barking Road, London, E13 8HJ

Date of interview: 18 October 2014 (181014)

Police Exhibit No: *CDS/08*

.......*John Finch*.......

Signature of interviewer/transcriber producing exhibit

Time commenced: 1412   Time concluded: 1420   Duration of interview: 06.58

Audio tape reference nos.:   Visual image reference nos.:

Interviewer(s): Det Insp 7871 John Finch, PC 3009 David Chaplin

Other persons present: Sally Moran, Special Prosecutor, CPS, Vatsal Choudhury, Solicitor

Tape counter times	Person speaking	Text
00.02	DI 7871	This interview is being recorded. The time is 14.12 on the 18th of October 2014. My name is Detective Inspector John Finch. I'm going to be interviewing Cameron Struth in relation to his failing to attend an interview with us scheduled last month for this morning in relation to his bail conditions for the alleged rape of Corina Slate. If you could introduce yourselves please, in the room is.
00.30	PC 3009	David Chaplin, Police Constable for the Metropolitan Police.
00.33	DI 7871	Thank you. And.
00.34	SM	Sally Moran, CPS.
00.36	DI 7871	Thank you. And.
00.37	VC	Vatsal Choudhury, solicitor representing Cameron Struth.
00.41	DI 7871	Good. Thank you. Now Cameron just for the tape. I know you've had to do this before. Could you give us your name and your address?

Signature(s): ....*John Finch*.......

2014/10

Tape counter times	Person speaking	Text
00.51	VC	I can speak on behalf of Cameron Struth who has indicated to me that he is not willing at this time to speak. His address is 89 Comyns Close, Canning Town, London, E16 4JJ.
01.01	DI 7871	Thank you Mr Choudhury. PC Chaplin will make a note of any non-verbal responses from Mr Struth. Can I confirm that this is still the case Cameron?
01.08	PC 3009	For the tape, Mr Struth nods.
01.12	DI 7871	So that's a yes. Now do you remember that you were supposed to come in here this morning to talk with us?
01.15	PC 3009	For the tape, Mr Struth nods.
01.17	DI 7871	And do you think you could tell us why you weren't able to come in here this morning to talk with us?
01.26	PC 3009	For the tape, Mr Struth shakes his head.
01.29	DI 7871	Now do you remember where you were when PC Chaplin and myself arrested you this afternoon?
01.35	PC 3009	For the tape, Mr Struth nods.
01.38	DI 7871	Where was that?
01.43	PC 3009	For the tape, Mr Struth shrugs.
01.46	DI 7871	You don't know. But did you know the people at the wedding where PC Chaplin and myself found you?
01.50	PC 3009	For the tape, Mr Struth nods.
01.53	DI 7871	Can you tell us how you know the people at the wedding?
01.60	PC 3009	For the tape, Mr Struth shakes his head.

Signature(s): .... *John Ful* ....

Person interviewed: Cameron Struth

Page No. 3   of 6

Tape counter times	Person speaking	Text
02.02	DI 7871	Is that because you don't know the people or because you don't want to speak?
02.05	PC 3009	For the tape, Mr Struth nods.
02.08	DI 7871	Okay. So is that the first one? Is that because you don't know the people at the wedding?
02.11	PC 3009	For the tape, Mr Struth shakes his head.
02.14	DI 7871	So you can't tell us how you know them because you don't want to speak?
02.28	PC 3009	For the tape, Mr Struth nods.
02.31	DI 7871	Yes. Right. So I'd just like to remind you Cameron that it may harm your defence if you do not mention something asked of you which you later rely on in court. Your silence here today might not look good. Do you understand that?
02.38	PC 3009	For the tape, Mr Struth nods.
02.40	DI 7871	Okay. So do you think you can tell us why you missed a scheduled appointment with us to attend a wedding?
02.44	PC 3009	For the tape, Mr Struth shakes his head.
02.46	DI 7871	Do you understand that this appointment was to talk over the conditions of your bail in relation to a crime of sexual assault in which you are the only suspect?
02.57	PC 3009	For the tape, Mr Struth nods.
03.00	DI 7871	So now do you understand that missing this appointment is an offence in itself?
03.05	PC 3009	For the tape, Mr Struth nods.

Signature(s): John Ful ....

Person interviewed: Cameron Struth   Page No. 4   of 6

Tape counter times	Person speaking	Text
03.08	DI 7871	Now you understand that this will also affect the conditions of your bail if we decide to grant you bail again?
03.15	PC 3009	For the tape, Mr Struth nods.
03.18	PC 3009	Now do you understand then that it's important for you to tell us why you decided not to meet this appointment?
03.24	PC 3009	For the tape, Mr Struth nods.
03.26	DI 7871	Now can you tell us why you decided not to meet this appointment?
03.30	PC 3009	For the tape, Mr Struth shakes his head.
03.34	DI 7871	So is there a reason why you decided not to meet this appointment and attend a wedding instead?
03.39	PC 3009	For the tape, Mr Struth shrugs.
03.42	DI 7871	You don't know. So now do you know why you attended a wedding instead of meeting our appointment?
03.48	PC 3009	For the tape, Mr Struth shakes his head. Now he nods.
03.54	DI 7871	Now were you drunk at the time PC Chaplin and myself found you this morning?
04.01	PC 3009	For the tape, Mr Struth nods.
04.04	DI 7871	Had you taken any other form of intoxicant or drug?
04.09	PC 3009	For the tape, Mr Struth nods.
04.11	DI 7871	Can you tell us what kind of drugs you had taken this morning?
04.16	PC 3009	For the tape, Mr Struth shakes his head.
04.17	DI 7871	No. Why is that?
04.20	PC 3009	For the tape, Mr Struth shrugs.

Signature(s): ....

Person interviewed: Cameron Struth   Page No. 5   of 6

Tape counter times	Person speaking	Text
04.23	DI 7871	Can you remember what drugs you had taken this morning?
04.28	PC 3009	For the tape, Mr Struth shakes his head.
04.31	DI 7871	Are you on any prescribed medication Cameron?
04.33	PC 3009	For the tape, Mr Struth nods.
04.35	DI 7871	Can you tell us what this medication is?
04.39	PC 3009	For the tape, Mr Struth shakes his head.
04.45	DI 7871	Can you tell us why you're on this medication?
04.50	PC 3009	For the tape, Mr Struth shakes his head.
04.53	DI 7871	Has it anything to do with an incident that occurred two days ago at the LA Fitness in Canary Wharf?
05.01	PC 3009	For the tape, Mr Struth nods.
05.04	DI 7871	Can you tell us what happened two days ago at the LA Fitness in Canary Wharf?
05.10	PC 3009	For the tape, Mr Struth shakes his head.
05.18	DI 7871	No. Because. From the information we've gathered from a couple of witnesses they said you had to be rescued from drowning in the pool there. Is that right?
05.30	PC 3009	For the tape, Mr Struth nods.
05.33	DI 7871	Can you tell us anything more about that?
05.38	PC 3009	For the tape, Mr Struth shakes his head.
05.42	DI 7871	Was it an accident Cameron?
05.45	PC 3009	For the tape, Mr Struth shrugs.
05.51	DI 7871	You don't know. Did you mean to get yourself in that situation?

Signature(s): *John Ful*

2014/10

Tape counter times	Person speaking	Text
05.59	PC 3009	For the tape, Mr Struth shrugs. He is visibly upset.
06.09	DI 7871	Were you trying to kill yourself Cameron? Would you like a tissue?
06.15	PC 3009	For the tape, Mr Struth nods.
06.24	DI 7871	You were. Okay. Now can you tell us why you tried to kill yourself Cameron?
06.34	PC 3009	For the tape, Mr Struth shakes his head.
06.44	DI 7871	Have you tried to kill yourself before? Have you tried to kill yourself before this time?
06.52	PC 3009	For the tape, Mr Struth shakes his head.
06.59	DI 7871	Has it got anything to do with the allegations made against you?
07.06	PC 3009	For the tape, Mr Struth shrugs.
07.12	DI 7871	So has it got anything to do with the wedding?
07.14	PC 3009	For the tape, Mr Struth shakes his head.
07.18	DI 7871	Right. Okay. Maybe we'll take a little break here. The time is 14.18. Before we do you should know Cameron that this interview is so that we can determine the conditions of your bail. So far you have not been charged with the crime that we're investigating as we're still gathering evidence to determine whether there can be a case against you and you should know that a refusal to co-operate will factor into both the conditions of the bail and how the case progresses. Do you understand this?
07.50	PC 3009	For the tape, Mr Struth nods.
07.54	DI 7871	Right. So the time is 14.20. Let's pause the recording there.
		End of tape.

Signature(s): ....

COPIED POSTS FROM CORINA SLATE'S BLOG, 'WITNESS'

DECEMBER 2016

I would break into your brother's flat, hold a knife to him. No, it would be a shard of mirror. He'd plead. I wouldn't listen to him. I'd hand him a piece of paper, a pen. I'd tell him what to say. 'There's nothing I want to say except that I did it. I'm sorry, Corina. This is the only way to make it right.' Then I'd tell him to put the paper on the kitchen counter. He'd plead, say no one would believe that he stabbed himself to death. I'd say, 'I know.' There'd be a still moment. He'd try to get past me, but I'm too quick and he's too scared of the shard, a shard as long and thick as my forearm. He'd start to cry. Crocodile tears. I'd laugh, step closer to him, the shard pointed at his throat. He'd step back. He'd reach the window. He'd plead. I'd tell him to open the window. He'd plead, open the window. I'd tell him to sit on the windowsill. He'd plead, sit on the sill. I'd tell him to put his arms outside, hold them outstretched at his sides. He'd put his arms outside, pleading. I'd come close enough to drive the shard into his throat.

I wonder if I could push him. I wonder if I could push him if I could get away with it. I wonder if I do want to push him out a window if I could get away with pushing him out a window. I wonder what I would feel after pushing him out a window. I wonder what I would feel after pushing him out a window if I could get away with pushing him out a window. In films, wronged women do this. But what if I did it? I think I would feel empty, hollow, but I imagine this emptiness, this hollowness, is folded over itself. I will be able to feel the folds.

———

'You don't have to be here.'

He doesn't say anything back. He sits next to our mother, who sits between us on the sofa. Arms folded, he prods his biceps.

'I mean,' I say, 'if you've got somewhere else to be.'

He doesn't smile but I can tell he has a smile behind his expressionless face, a smile that says, 'You can't say a fucking thing to me.'

If I could apologise, with our mother here, he would accept it, maybe. We'd be civil at first, cooperate next, a laugh might come, our standard method.

I say, 'So what do you think of her, Kaasan?'

Her head bobs from side to side.

'She's certainly qualified,' I say.

'She's too young,' Hiro says.

'What do you mean?'

'I mean her age is too low.'

'Yes. I know what *young* means.'

'Then why you asking?'

'I asked why she's too young.'

'You asked what I meant.'

'How do you think her low age, and I'm not even sure she is that young, disqualifies her?'

'She doesn't look strong enough.'

'Strong enough?'

'She doesn't look like she could handle it.'

'But she's fully qualified.'

'So she has a certificate saying she can look after people. Doesn't mean she actually can.'

'Yes it actually does.'

'It doesn't.'

'What did you think of her?' I ask my mother.

'And she's too young with the age gap,' says Hiro.

'What?' I say.

'What's her and Mum going to even talk about?'

Our mother says, 'She's too happy, I think.'

'Too happy,' I say.

'See,' Hiro says.

'Okay,' I say, making a note of it, 'though I'm not sure what that has to do with her age.'

Our mother says, 'I would like someone serious.'

'What?' Hiro says to me. 'You trying to say being young doesn't mean she's naïve or whatever?'

'Serious people are dependable,' our mother says.

'I'm just saying we should consider the fact that she has all the requisite qualifications,' I say to him.

'I would like more variety,' our mother says.

'Just because you've passed shit,' Hiro says, 'doesn't mean you're actually any good at it.'

'I would like to see someone not African,' our mother says.

'If you want to pay the extra for more experience then you can,' I say to him.

'I know there are a lot of European carers,' our mother says.

'But you told us we're getting that allowance,' Hiro says to me.

Our mother says, 'I'm interested in seeing the difference.'

'I think maybe,' Hiro says, 'just maybe, we shouldn't cut corners on the person looking after Mum.'

Our mother says, 'Or it doesn't matter what I think.'

I say, before he can say it, 'Mum's right. There's no use arguing.'

'I'm not arguing,' he says.

'Good,' I say. 'Do you want to go put the kettle on?'

'What?'

'We've got one more to see.'

'Why can't you put the fucking kettle on?'

'Hiro,' our mother says.

'Because I'm the one taking notes,' I say.

'That's bullshit.'

'Hiro!'

'I don't understand why you can't do it,' he says, standing up abruptly.

My mother and I don't flinch, but we both tense up against his movement.

'What?' he says. 'I was going to the toilet.' He tries to seem calm.

'I would like a tea,' our mother says.

I look at the notes, knowing he's glaring at me.

He goes to the kitchen.

I pull the next CV from my folder. 'Her name is Marjorie,' I say. 'She's older than the last one.'

'I don't know why he's like this now,' she says. 'He's been such a help recently.'

'Who?'

'Your brother.'

'Yeah?' I say.

'Yes,' she says. 'He's been wonderful, actually, considering.'

'Great,' I say.

The buzzer goes. It's Marjorie. I let her in the building, tell her where we are. Hiro comes back. We sit in silence, watching the door. The kettle gurgles, gets louder.

There's a knock on the door. We all stand up. I go to let Marjorie in, shake her hand. She's at least a foot taller than me, with a calm smile. The kettle clicks.

'Come in,' I say. 'Would you like a cup of tea?'

'That would be lovely,' she says.

I look at Hiro, which makes our mother look at Hiro, then Marjorie. He aims his eyes at me, smiles at them.

'Anyone else?' he says.

'Please,' our mother says.

'Thanks,' I say.

'Just milk,' Marjorie says.

'Just milk for Marjorie,' I say.

He nods like a butler. I see his head shake as he walks to the kitchen.

Marjorie and I smile at each other.

'So,' I say, but stop because we hear a clatter, a slam, in the kitchen. We wait for another sound, confirmation of a break. It's silent.

'That's my brother,' I say, 'Hiro. I'm Corina. This is my mother.'

Marjorie bows appropriately. My mother, a little surprised, reciprocates. Then Marjorie bows to me. I reciprocate. I don't remember the last time I bowed.

The three of us sit. Marjorie puts a hand inside her satchel but stops when she sees I have my copy of her CV.

'Did you have to come far today, Marjorie?' I say.

She shakes her head. 'I live on Wellesley Road.'

'I don't know it,' I say.

'It's behind Thomas Gamuel, the primary school, where my son goes. It takes five minutes to walk there, but he still complains and wants me to drive us. We walk.'

Hiro comes over with two teas, gives one to Marjorie, one to our mother. He sits down. I don't appear to be getting one. He asks Marjorie, 'Have you had a CRB check?'

'Hiro,' I say.

'What?'

Marjorie says, 'Yes. I'm fully checked.'

'That's all on the CV,' I say to him.

'Give it here,' he says.

Marjorie blinks slowly, smiling. I pass Hiro the CV.

'So you walk your son to school every morning?' I say.

'It's the most reliable time I get to spend with him,' she says. 'I pick him up whenever I can, but if I have to be at work, my sister or husband are available,' she says, letting me check off more questions I haven't asked.

Hiro says, 'Do you have a driving licence?'

'We've already established that,' I say.

He looks at Marjorie, then back at the CV. He looks at it like a page of *Where's Wally?*, quietly says, 'I didn't know, did I?'

I send Marjorie an apologetic look. Her eyes tell me she's had worse.

Hiro says, 'Why did you leave your last job?'

Marjorie nods sadly. 'Unfortunately, the mother of my last employer died.'

Hiro looks back at the CV. I see him swallow.

'Were you with that family for long?' I say.

'Six years,' she says. 'It was a wonderful experience. She had been an emergency nurse and I trained as an oncology nurse so there was a lot of common ground between us.'

'What's this gap here?' Hiro says.

Marjorie lifts her head as if to ask what he means.

He says, '2004 to 2006. There's a gap here.'

Marjorie draws in a lot of air. 'I went back to Ghana.'

'Why?' he says.

'I went back to Ghana to convince my mother to move to England so that I could care for her. She did. She had a six-month life expectancy. She lived for two years more. I would say thankfully, but in fact she lived in a lot of pain.'

248

Marjorie smiles to let us know we shouldn't feel uncomfortable.

'That is very noble of you,' my mother says.

'Oh,' Marjorie says, waving her hand. 'My husband was willing to work a little more so I could work a little, or quite a lot, less.'

'I have noticed in this country,' my mother says, 'that people are just too quick to let others take care of their family.'

'Yes,' Marjorie says, 'it is a luxury that sometimes does more harm than good. But sometimes it is necessary, when it is not possible financially, and especially when specialised care is needed.'

My mother smiles, takes Marjorie's CV from Hiro, looks over it. She makes quiet sounds of approval. She hands the CV to me, stands. Marjorie stands. My mother bows deeply. Marjorie reciprocates. Hiro and I stand tentatively. Marjorie bows to us. We bow. I don't know what's happening. My mother sees Marjorie to the door. I thank her as she leaves.

'There you go,' our mother says. 'If you're certain I will need someone, whenever that may be, then I'd like it to be Marjorie.'

'Hold on,' Hiro says. 'We barely asked her anything.'

'Mum seems happy with Marjorie,' I say.

'But we didn't even ask if she smokes or anything.'

'I agree she's the best candidate,' I say.

'But, Mum,' says Hiro, 'do you really want a smoker coming in here stinking the place out?'

My mother considers this.

'Do you really want a smoker cooking meals for you?'

'I will cook my own meals,' she says.

'But when you can't, do you want a smoker cooking your meals for you?'

'We don't even know if she smokes,' I say.

'And that's why we can't just green-light her, man.'

'If Okaasan is happy with Marjorie—'

'But she's less qualified than the last one and you were banging on about that.'

'I just think we should accept what Okaasan wants.'

'Stop that shit. You're not thinking of what she wants.'

'No?'

'Nah, man. You're just shooting everything I say down.'

Our mother says, 'I'm going to lie down.'

'I'll call Marjorie tomorrow,' I say, 'let her know she's our first choice.'

She doesn't respond, goes in her room. I sit on the sofa. I start to order the folder, pack my bag. By the window, Hiro watches me.

'Don't you think it's a bit early for all this?' he says.

'Do you want to be scrambling to find someone when the time comes?'

'But why are you rushing this?'

'Why are you nit-picking?'

'Nit-picking!'

'You need to get it together, man,' I say.

'Fuck you talking about, get it together?'

'It's going to have to happen.'

'I know that.'

'Do you?'

'Fuck you talking about?'

I zip up my bag. 'All right,' I say. 'I'll ask you. Do you think we need to get a carer for Mum?'

He looks at me. He looks towards her room.

'Exactly,' I say, standing up.

He walks from the window towards me, stops by the door. I sigh, wait for him to speak. He doesn't. I take out my phone to check the buses.

'It's just fucking classic, man,' he says.

I shouldn't say anything, should just leave. 'What do you mean?' I say.

'What would you have done if Madeline was shit?'

'Who the fuck is Madeline?'

He points his thumb at the door, says, 'Madeline. Fucking Madeline.'

'Marjorie?'

'Whatever. What if she had a fucking Fuck Japs tattoo on her neck?'

'Well, I would have taken that into account.'

'And what if Mum still liked her?'

I don't know what to say.

'Exactly,' he says.

I put my bag on my back, stand in front of him, say, 'I need to go.'

He says, 'Going to choose the coffin?'

I push him hard in the chest. He slaps me in the face. We stare at each other. Then I start smacking him. I hammer him into a ball on the ground. He grabs my legs, pulls me over. He tries to grab my arms, pin me, but I keep smacking him. I hear our mother say, 'What's going on?'

We stop. Hiro sits back. His face is red. There are scratch marks starting to bleed, blood in his nostril, smudges of bruise.

I stand up, grab my bag, step over him to leave.

Happening Blog Sketch #7 – 20/11/14

No more happenings. This coincides with other adjustments: a prescription of antipsychotics, which allow me to sleep and to achieve, if not unclouded clarity, then a dull coherence together with antidepressants; moving to a studio flat on Chatsworth Road in Clapton above an Ethiopian café owned by an *EastEnders* actor who was inspired, it says on the website, by overseas charity work; a minor surgery on my eyebrow, which had bulged to bursting with infection and threatened blindness and swelled over the sight in that eye without my realising it, a more disturbing fact for me because it means that, for weeks, I haven't once looked into a mirror; and the play starting without me. They erased my name from the posters. The reviews are positive, but I've not been to see it. The past week, I've spent my time smoking, pacing, running scenes to muted movies, and delving deep into the Internet. Nights I watch footage of myself. With the rest of my severance package, I bought a new overcoat and a few cameras and I arranged the cameras around the flat to record throughout the day. But what I record won't go online, not like before. This is just for me. Taking the pills and watching the footage lets me sleep—good full sleep.

There were ideas for happenings, but the urge to enact them went when I watched the footage; other times, the urge arrives unwelcomed and unpersuasive. That situationist avocation was put to bed last night, after Sam's funeral, in Darlington. The whole day, boxing his stuff in the morning then at the ceremony and memorial service, I was holding an immense silence and hoping not to overhear some murmured gossip about me. The *cliché du jour* was that Sam's death is not just sad, but *tragic*. I was nauseated by jealousy—all those kind, regretful words about his character and his unrealised talents; the fact that he was dead and didn't have to listen to any of this. The priest kept using his full name, Samuel, and I hated him for turning Sam into some historical figure, some saint. When the priest read a prayer, my father cried, low and loud, the first time I'd seen him cry. My mother told him to shut up so I told her to shut up. Denunciations were whispered between us while we followed the coffin out.

By the hearse on the street outside the church, the fingers pointed. 'It's all your fault,' I said to her: she's neglectful and vindictive. 'It's all your fault,' she said to me: I'm selfish and cruel. My father shook the mourners' hands as they left, saying, 'There's a bun fight at The Deacon.'

After that, we went back to Sam's. We hadn't eaten anything at The Deacon, just drank, so my mother started stewing what was left of Sam's tins.

'What time is your train back then?' she asked. She was cutting up some garlic we'd bought on the way from The Deacon. She had her back to me and she stopped chopping now and then to suck on a cigarette. I was stood by the window behind her.

'Open return,' I said.

'Well, call yourself a taxi whenever you're ready.'

'I was just going to walk.'

'Bit late for that, don't you think?' she said.

'I mean in the morning.'

'And where were you planning on sleeping?'

'Here.'

'In his bed?' she said. 'In his *bed*?'

'Why not?'

She had stopped chopping. 'I would sooner bury you in the ground than let you sleep in his bed.'

I heard the tip of the knife notching the board.

'Might as well go now, if that's what you want,' I said.

For a moment, I thought she wouldn't answer, but she said, 'You know what I want.'

I stared at the back of her head while she waited for me to leave. How many times had I wanted to grab her head and crush it or hold it close to me?

If I replied, she'd only try to hurt me further, so without another word, I went to gather my things. In the hallway, by the door, I heard my father making a thrashing sound in Sam's bedroom. Through a crack in the ajar door I saw him ripping Sam's clothes from the drawers and cupboards and lashing them into binbags. Then he just held the bags in his hands and beat them against the floor.

It was a trek to the station, through the estates and by the river, past the hospital and through the centre, and I drank beer and listened to podcasts to stop me thinking. On the train, I drank as many beers as they would sell me and got to London about nine o'clock, going straight to Denis's flat in Hampstead. For a good while there was no answer, and I wondered if their honeymoon had become something permanent, when the robotic intercom voice of Pawel said, 'Yes?'

No sooner had we had opened a bottle of wine by the bay window, with Pawel rubbing his steep forehead and twisting his face in disapproval and exasperation, than I realised Denis must not have told Pawel about my arrest and Pawel told me that Denis was dead.

The night after they were married, Pawel said, in a hotel in Whitstable, Denis woke up convulsing, his throat choked. Pawel had given him the Heimlich but only managed to snap a couple of his ribs. In the ambulance, the paramedics sliced open Denis's windpipe and inserted some kind of a snorkel. He was unconscious for most of the next day. Having rushed out the hotel topless, Pawel had had to wear Denis's t-shirt, which pinched at the armpits and hemmed off just below his bellybutton. The nurses could've given him a larger shirt, Pawel said, but he didn't want to take it off. Just before midnight, Denis woke up, and sometime later he could breathe independently. Pawel had told him it was his greatest performance and Denis chuckled through his embarrassment and his tender midriff and the scare seemed to have passed but in the early morning the nurse woke Pawel in the waiting room: Denis had gone. He'd been texting one minute, she'd said, and the next—gone.

The funeral is at the end of the week, said Pawel, and we sat there quietly. Then, for some time, we chatted practicalities. The money and the flat will go to his son Thomas—eventually, that is, because Denis's ex-wife Donna will oversee it until the boy turns eighteen. She plans to evict Pawel, rent the place out. He isn't exactly strapped—Denis gifted some albeit heavily taxed cash to him—but he can't afford to live in London on his own, let alone in Hampstead.

He said, 'I have some friends in Brighton. I will stay with them before moving somewhere cheaper. Maybe I will move north,' he said, flattening his eyebrows.

'There's nothing in the will for you?' I asked.

He didn't seem to know. There was a little section about him, Pawel said, but most was set aside for Thomas, so Donna said Pawel could take whatever he wanted from the wardrobe. When he told her that Denis had promised him the flat was his as long as he wanted it, all she said was, 'Oh? I can't see anything to that effect.'

'Like my mother says,' I said, 'that woman needs shagging with the raggy end of a pineapple.'

Then we opened another bottle of wine and reminisced about the time Donna caught Claire on stage. 'It was like Claire was looking in a warped mirror across the bar!' Pawel said, and I replied: 'I think what upset Donna most was realising her husband was a more beautiful woman than her.'

Loosened on the fourth glass, Pawel looked at me like he had before I left Denis the first time. 'I forgot how cruel you can be,' he said, and smirked. 'That meek Virgin Mary manner was just an act, wasn't it?'

'It's all an act,' I said, not knowing if he thought that I was joking.

Across the room a phone buzzed. 'Is that you or me?' I said, but it was Denis's phone. Each time it buzzed, Pawel said, he clamped his jaw to stop from tearing up, but he couldn't manage to turn it off either, so for some reason he'd plugged it in to charge.

Sometime later Pawel put his glass down carelessly, spilling some wine on the bed. With his finger levelled at me, he asked why I'd bothered coming back into Denis's life. Pawel was caring for Denis just fine, he said, adding, 'That's not supposed to be a dig,' and I felt such an unexpected and unfamiliar pain, embedded in my failure both to care for and stop myself caring about Denis, that I said, 'He cared about me.'

Pawel watched me through his sceptical squint. Then, recognising some belief in me that he'd previously shared, he smiled. 'You felt saved when he took you in?'

'Perhaps,' I said.

Pawel laughed out that word, 'Perhaps.'

Without reacting, I said, 'And I think I wanted to save him somehow.'

'Which is ridiculous.'

'Is it? Why?'

'Well, it's mighty noble of you,' he said, 'but completely fucking stupid.'

'I don't think so,' I said. 'Why?'

'Well, because there was nothing you could do that would have saved him.'

'Yes, but what I mean is I wanted to return the favour. What's so wrong with that?'

'You mean you wanted to care for him because he cared for you?'

'Exactly. What's wrong with that?'

'Nothing, if it was true, if that's what you were doing.'

'It was what I was doing.'

'Come on,' he said. 'You coming back into his life was not about when he took you in. It was about when you abandoned him.'

'No,' I said. 'No. I don't agree.'

'You were just hoping that the guilt would go away.'

257

'I wanted to care for him because he cared for me.'

'You can tell yourself that all you want.'

'And how are you so fucking sure that's not what I was doing?'

'I am sorry if this offends you,' Pawel said, looking as if he didn't recognise me, with a manner of victorious calm.

'It's just something I don't think you can be sure about,' I said. 'I don't know how you can be so sure of what you think. It's a fair question.'

'You're asking how I know that you were not trying to care for him, or *save* him, as you say?'

'Yes,' I said. 'How are you so sure of that?'

'Because you were not willing to sacrifice anything for him. You were just waiting for him to forgive you so that you could go about your life. All you were going to do was put in a little time, show your face, and hope for a pardon, to feel absolved.'

'Sacrifice anything?' I said. 'Like what?'

'Well, like yourself,' he said.

'This is stupid. We're drunk.'

Pawel drank slowly from his glass and sighed. He said, 'If you knew anything about what it takes to prioritise another person over yourself, you would know that you were only thinking about yourself when you came back.'

I could only look at his cheek, just below his eyes.

He said, 'There's this story I think about a lot that my father told me. It's about my grandmother, and my grandfather, who lived in Sobótka, in Poland, in the Second World War. Let me tell it to you.

'So, one morning, German soldiers were trooping through the town looking for Jews. They weren't Jews themselves, but the problem for them was that they happened to be sheltering a young Jewish woman. She was working as a kind of maid for them, dusting and cooking and making the beds, looking after my father who was a baby, all the usual domestic things except grocery runs, obviously, which is what my grandmother happened to be doing when the soldiers came and when they banged on their door demanding papers from my grandfather and the woman. Can you imagine what my grandfather must have been thinking? Maybe he wasn't thinking. Maybe it was a fundamental instinct to keep people around him from harm, or maybe he knew right then that to tell the truth, to say that they had been sheltering this woman, would send them all to the camps, but either way, he had no choice but to lie, and he told the soldiers that this Jewish woman was his Catholic wife.

'He knew that the likelihood was that he had passed the problem onto his wife, that the soldiers would find her in the town without her papers. Which is exactly what happened. And now what choice did she have? She could tell the soldiers that the woman they had met was not my grandfather's wife but actually a Jew that they had been sheltering, which might buy them all a ticket to the camps, or she could accept the lie that my grandfather had to tell and confess, falsely, that she had nothing to do with anyone the soldiers had inspected, and that she could not account for herself, which would send her to the camp, and therefore save them, which is what she did,' said Pawel, leaning close to me now, his breath strangely without smell. 'Make of that what you will,' he said, and he reached for two cigarettes in the bedside cabinet and lit them both.

For a moment, we sat there on the bed and said nothing and smoked. Then he said, 'Well,' and went to the toilet. Sitting there on the bed that I'd once shared with Denis, I felt pleased that he'd spent the final days of his life with Pawel. In feeling this, though, I couldn't remember a time I felt so worthless. While Pawel was gone, I took Denis's phone, which had the same password as the one when we were together, and I wrote out a text to Pawel and left it unsent. It said: 'I hope what comes next will be a relief like the relief I've felt whenever I've looked at you.'

When Pawel came back, I told him I had to go. 'Denis sent me a text that day,' I said. 'The day he died. It was just saying thanks for coming to the wedding. You should check his texts with you to see if he tried to send something while he was in the hospital.'

Pawel looked at me, perhaps coming to terms with never seeing me again, perhaps asking himself if he would ever want to, and

I drifted into the night, wind gusts whipping hail against the car windows. The hail poured off roofs and speckled the hedges below.

Before I went underground, I checked my phone. Someone on Facebook said that they'd seen a huddle of homeless people rampaging in Elephant and Castle outside the hostel where I volunteered a few years ago.

When I got there, most of the homeless lot were already asleep outside the hostel, covered in tatty sleeping bags. There was no hail here, but the night was sharpened with sleet and puddles had formed in pavement cracks by the recycle bins. One of them, a self-appointed ringleader, I assumed, talked to me as soon as I was close enough to hear. 'They've locked us out. There's beds in there. I know there is. They do this when they're low on staff.'

What a bunch—if I can even use that word, *bunch*, since they didn't merge together as one. There was a 'crazy bag lady', meaning that I couldn't tell if she was wearing clothes of her own under a bouquet of bags—Sainsbury's orange, House of Fraser pink, M&S green, Next black—which were hanging from her shoulders, stuffed under her pits, scrunched up in her hands. Her hair looked like a nest and she twitched just like a bird. There was one in a Del Boy coat, flat cap, and a tartan silk scarf, who smelt like a leather shop in the summer. A dusty one with dreads down to the floor, a sleeping bag wrapped around her waist. One whose face was so sunburnt the skin looked wooden. One with broken shoes, the left side of his bottom lip lifting up over the upper in a quizzical look. And this last man, the ringleader, hooked his arms around the woman with dreadlocks, and said: 'They lock us out because they don't like to bed us wet.'

Del Boy said: 'But we don't want to cause any trouble for ourselves.'

'Nonsense,' I said, and suggested kicking the back door in. The one with the wooden face and I gave it a good go, but the door stayed shut.

Del Boy made a meal of gathering his stuff, both annoyed and vindicated by our failure. 'I knew it wouldn't work,' he said.

After that I drank Special with the one with the wooden face, who was in fact tediously good-natured, and some man she knew who wore a black bomber jacket with pink wings on the back, in Newington Gardens by the Playhouse and the job centre and the Court. It rained heavily, gurgling in the gutters.

That night, last night, something sort of miraculous happened, a moment when I couldn't feel myself separately, as if the secret porosity of bodies was revealed to me. In an underground club on Covent Garden square, I bumped into some strong young men wearing suits and repulsed expressions. One of them pushed me and I was in the toilet, yelling, 'Don't fuck with me, fellas!' With their brassy laughter behind me, I watched my piss come out like an old rope.

A short bloke with a square, flat head and a twitchy mouth, who looked at me through the mirror while washing his hands, was talking to me. 'Cracking night. Cracking. The lads I'm with I've known for ages. They're mad. I fucking love them, like proper love. So I'm seeing this girl, yeah? It's our third date tonight, right, and she'd got to meet the lads, yeah? So I thought I'd let her meet them before they go on and we go on, you know what I mean, yeah? She's in the loo, like us, like now, yeah? Fuck knows what she thinks of them, like. Fuck knows. But this is mad, like, listen, so these lads are mad, yeah? When we was younger, like real young, we had this thing, yeah? We'd pick up girls in Danny's car. Didn't matter who, like anyone really, yeah? We had booze. We had pills. We gave them booze. But they'd never want the pills, like all wary, yeah? So I'd— oh, it's fucking mad, like proper mad, but funny, yeah? I'd take a pill with them, like with the girl, yeah? And they were mad pills, like fucking mad ones. I'd wake up later, like missed the whole night, yeah? But these guys would take care of me, no matter what, like they'd be so happy and grateful for me in the morning, like proper mates, yeah? But fuck knows, man. Fuck knows,' he said, and slapped me—'top lad'—on my back and left.

In the smoking area, I asked to borrow a lighter and cigarette, but each person said it was their last one, so I went out to find a shop.

There was no rain any more.

And a toothless man in an immaculate trilby let me roll up and smoke with him and his friends by a bench in Jubilee Gardens beneath the static, lightless Eye. They were asking if I had any booze on me, holding cans themselves. Laughing at my apologies, Toothless pulled me down to sit with them.

There were four of us—Toothless; an old punk with his yapping puppy; a wiry, giggly androgyne and me. We drank for a while, promising to find and hurt the young West Country lad who'd stolen Toothless's spot on an elevated corner by the steel gates of Waterloo car park.

When we got there the young lad was weeping. It was his first week on the streets, he said, snotty and apologetic. The punk still threatened him with a rusty penknife and the lad scurried off with his blankets. He was in such a rush he left behind a bottle of gin.

What luck! The four of us drank it down, tearing it from each other's grasps like elixir. The punk was telling us his story and the androgyne giggled till their throat was sore but the puppy yapped at them, bouncing around. The more the puppy yapped, the more the androgyne giggled; the more the androgyne giggled, the more the puppy yapped. 'Shut up!' the punk yelled at the puppy. 'Shut up!' he yelled. And Toothless asked him why he even got the fucking thing. The punk ignored him and resumed his story, but the puppy: *yap, yap, yap, yap, yap, yap*. Then the punk snarled, grabbed the puppy and strode off into a dark graffiti-covered tunnel under Waterloo.

'What's he doing?' I asked Toothless, but he just sighed, and the androgyne giggled till their throat dried out again and they coughed, shaking their head at whatever the punk was about to do. 'What's he doing?' I said again, and went towards the tunnel, where I heard the dog still yapping. 'Hey?' I said into the dark. 'Hey?' Then the dog yelped, and a little *ow*. Walking faster with the tunnel's opening light in my sight, I almost didn't notice the punk right there on my left slashing the pup's throat with his penknife. His head snapped towards me, and I said, 'Oh.'

'What?' said the punk.

'Nothing,' I said, and took off running out the other end of the tunnel.

How long I was running, I don't know, but I remember leaning on a corner on the Strand with the man in the angel-winged bomber.

'I know a girl if you want her. She's not expensive,' he said, pointing down the street at a woman with a cast over her leg, propped up by crutches.

'She's got a cast on her leg?' I asked.

'I guess she does,' he said.

'What happened?'

'We'll give you a discount,' he said.

'Will she pretend to be someone else?'

'As long as you don't rough her up, mate, you're golden.'

'Rough her up?'

'You know. Tell her what you want, then let her take over.'

'Let her take over?'

'You know. You're getting, mate. You're not giving.'

'But there has to be some kind of dynamic.'

'Dynamic?'

'I mean, if there's no dynamic,' I said, 'then we might as well draw up a contract.'

'A contract? What the fuck you on about? You homeless, really?'

'Yeah,' I said, but too late—my face had already given me away.

'All right, here's what's going to happen,' he said. 'We're going to a cash point.' He grabbed my elbow and led me up towards Covent Garden. 'Don't fucking move, mate,' he said.

'Why not? You got a knife?'

He didn't answer, then he said, 'Sure.'

Occasionally he inverted my elbow to remind me of my position, but when I saw a crowd of people by the square, I twisted my body, pushed the man in the throat, and slipped into the crowd heading for the queue outside a club. Approaching the bouncer right away, I told him over the protests of those in the queue that the guy in the bomber jacket had tried to mug me. 'He's following me,' I said, pointing at him. The bouncer looked and shook his head in recognition. When the man saw us watching him, his shoulders dropped like an arsey teenager and he walked away. The bouncer jerked his head, so I went down into the noise.

By the bar, I stood with a beer, listening to the lyrics of the music, which were about how great a night anyone listening to this music would have. Through the crowd I saw the man I met in the toilet. He was in a booth with two drinks on his own. Gingerly he brought the drink furthest away from him, a dark cocktail, towards his chest, propped his elbow next to the drink, covering it from the dancefloor, took something from his pocket with his other hand, and casually dropped it in the drink. His eyes darted about, then the villainous hand stroked and stretched his beard. He had an immense density in this room now, and it was amazing to me that nobody else could feel the gravitational pull of his malevolence. As I waited for him to notice me watching, a slender girl with a tight blue dress came over and sat in the booth. I watched them cheers. I watched her drink it. I left.

Or maybe one of those miraculous moments never came. Maybe, like all feelings, it was a dream—forgotten, but still remaining.

Later, on the middle of the Millennium Bridge with blue lights along each side of the walkway pointing straight to St Paul's, I stopped to delete every one of my online accounts, resolving—as I am still resolved to do, sometime soon—to give away my money and join the homeless, or do something else to untether myself from the world—because I can do anything! It was then that I saw on Facebook that Sam's friends were still messaging him. His friends? His audience? Witnesses? Onlookers? Let's say onlookers. Most of them said how much they miss him, while others reminisced in spiralling ensemble storytelling, an endless wake. The first message I read was from Tom Harbottle, who used to eat his own scabs, if I remember correctly, and by secondary school, scars covered him like his skin had grown nails. He used to steal Sam's pencil case and throw it on the school roof. He's the one who started Sam's nickname—Gorilla. The lads would chase Sam up the trees around Cocker Beck near our estate despite the fact that he could fit four headlocks in his arms at once. One such time (was it in the tree overlooking our tiny back yard? Wasn't that where my father built a wobbly treehouse to shut us up, where we snuck out late one night and found my mother asleep up there already?) they threw stones and shook the branches. Sam tried to transfer from one tree to the next, but he fell, directly onto his shoulder, pushing it down and forward forever, like he was looking around a corner, or like a gorilla. If he'd wanted more time in life, if he'd stayed a while longer, I hope I would've said sorry for calling him that name myself, for knowing how to hurt him, and hurting him.

It was Heather Davis after Harbottle, the girl with two shrunken arms who lived in a mansion opposite Broken Scar weir and who I was too ashamed to admit even to myself that I fancied. She said: 'It's been months and I'm still in disbelief. I wish I could've done more to help. My thoughts and prayers go out to your family.' That's me; that's Dad; that's Mam. Did I feel her thoughts and prayers? No. I didn't because she didn't send us anything. She only held up a picture of her own face, and inserted it into our open wound.

Sam, the wind was booming on the Millennium Bridge as I scrolled through your onlookers' questions. You'd find that funny, wouldn't you, Sam—them asking questions? The expression you'd make is a kind of feigned curiosity, slightly camp, and secretly scathing. Often I used your expressions. You'd snort at that like Mam snorts whenever I mention acting, but you made faces and I talked, and that's how we worked—at least before the pills Mam thought you needed turned your face into a mask. Your face. Your face—I was remembering your face, with the eyes so black and narrowed by high and round red cheeks with the forehead so wide with its perpetual knoll of furrows in the middle above the nose, and with the expression so aghast like that time we found Dad's precautionary MY FUNERAL spreadsheet—I was remembering your face when you messaged Heather Davis back.

'Thank you,' you wrote back somehow.

Now, listen, there are sights I've seen in London that would make you think you're dreaming, Sam. One night from my old bedroom window in Newham I saw through the rain a barefoot woman wrapped in tarpaulin and newspaper shreds beside a skip wolfing down a squirrel. On the DLR another night, arching along dark yolky yellow office building windows either side, I watched a welding flash ahead of the bend over Heron Quay, and as I swung in line with the welder crouched in sparks on the next track, I looked up and saw a man in the window behind, hanged by his belt from the dim light fixture, which, whenever I remember it again, will make me picture you. But a dead lad talking takes the award, Sam.

I felt then, seeing your words, just like I had boxing up your stuff, and I found the Han Solo figurine you mail-ordered from a magazine after first seeing the film. Han Solo was your hero, though to me, you more resembled Chewbacca. When it arrived all the way from America, the figurine was unfinished. It had an unpainted face, a belt without its holster. Dad wanted to send it back, but you kept it, either in spite of him, which was not really your style, more mine, or because you found it unique—perfectly incomplete. Did you try to make yourself that way? Tell me, Sam, is that what you were doing when you dropped from the treehouse while Dad and Mam were hiding me? Or did you just drop so they would stop? Did you love me that much?

I was close to crying on the Millennium Bridge late last night. I was close to crying because I knew I could've saved you—from falling, from all of it—but no tears would come. No tears, I think, because bastards' eyes see clearest. When St Paul's bells rang out I ran home grinning and now I laugh with my morning alarm, thinking of you saying, 'Thank you.'

As the first pink glimmers of daylight grow in the mist outside, laying a tint of rust across my bottom two wonky blinds, and there, on the edge of the gleaming grey street, a fox slinks bendily under a fence by a bank and into an alley, its white-tipped tail disappearing behind the bins, I laugh because I know you wouldn't have said, 'Thank you.' You would've said, 'Coming to get you' or 'Hitler's still alive!' or 'Boo!' But me asserting who you were won't beat the injustice of your death. Your speaking in spite of where you are—or where you're not—does that instead. That is not you, and of course it is you. Your onlookers liked what you said. They liked what you said enormously. This is your afterlife. This is eternity.

Guilt is hell on earth, the dress rehearsal.

COPIED POSTS FROM CORINA SLATE'S BLOG, 'WITNESS'

JANUARY 2017

Ali came in barely speaking, eyelids sagging. I asked her if she'd done any exercise. 'Ate an apple,' she said.

'Have you done anything to burn off the apple?'

She nodded.

'Star-jumps?'

She nodded.

I asked her how many she'd done. She held up two fingers.

'Two?'

She shook her head.

'Twenty?'

She shook her head.

'Two hundred?'

She shook her head.

'Ali, have you done two thousand star-jumps this morning?'

She smiled. Pulse was 38 BPM. She slipped away, unconscious, myocardial infarction.

I called the crash team, got out the way, had to go back to my own work. I was sick with thinking of her. At the end of my shift I found her in the acute ward. Her kidneys were failing. I asked a nurse there about her, but the nurse just shook her head.

'What does that mean?' I said.

'I don't really have time for this,' she said.

'Time for what?'

'For her, for girls who should know better.'

I went to find the Sister to complain. The Sister nodded, tired, said something about following it up.

I found a bed near the kidney unit, slept, went back to acute. It was 3 a.m. Ali was asleep, stable. I found another nurse. 'What's going to happen?'

'So her BMI is 18, which is not quite within the anorexic range. We've admitted her here. She'll be here a couple of nights, we expect.'

'Then what?'

'It depends on her organs, if they fail. If an organ fails, she'll go to the ward that treats that organ.'

'If not?'

'The mental health team know, so, depending, she'll be with us or them.'

She was in acute two nights before being taken to Cardiology. It's a ward that's been cut significantly. I heard about a girl like Ali who'd ended up in Cardiology. She'd got sick of being in bed, tried to get up. A nurse had restrained her, broke her arm. The nurse avoided legal repercussions because the girl had osteoporosis.

I visited Ali in the evening. She was crying, trying to pull herself out of the bed.

'What's the matter? Are you in pain?'

She pointed at the bed, hanging off the side of it.

I expected to find piss or shit. 'I can't see anything,' I said.

She slapped the bed. I heard the sound of the metal frame. The mattress had deflated.

'How long has it been like this?' I said, but she didn't say. Hours, I guess, by how she cried, the marks on her body.

I found the Cardiology Sister peering up with puckered lips from the nurses' station.

'How has she been?' I said.

'Non-compliant.'

'What do you mean?'

'We try to talk to her, but she just cries.'

'Crying isn't non-compliance.'

'It is.'

'How long does she have to be here?'

'Look, it's not like we want to have her here.'

'Has anyone contacted St George's?'

'Of course. That's who we want to have her.'

'What do they say?'

'They want us to have her.'

'When will they decide?'

'I don't know. Depends if they have a bed for her. Depends if someone there gains weight.'

'Are they equipped to care for her there?'

'Not in the current state she's in.'

'When will she be ready?'

'Tomorrow morning. If she gets through the night okay.'

I sat with her. The mattress had been inflated.

'Do you know what's going to happen next?' I said.

She shook her head.

'Someone from the Eating Disorders unit will come to assess you.'

'Assess me how?'

'They'll take your weight, ask you some pretty invasive questions.'

She nodded.

'Do you want me to prepare you on the kind of questions they'll ask?'

An open smile. Had her mouth always been so big, so many big teeth?

'I know what they'll ask me, mate. When did this start? What's your relationship with your mother? Has your BMI ever been over 20? They want to know if I'm mad or sick enough to treat me.'

I felt hot in the face remembering the questions I've asked her. The nurse came to tell me to leave. They were going to wash her.

———

You were reluctant to have a bath with me. This was after we'd fucked a bunch of times, so your body wasn't unusual to me, but maybe it was always in some way unusual to you.

'It'll be better if you slide in once I'm in,' you said, 'or we'll have a Deep Impact sort of situation.'

'Shut up,' I said.

'There'll be no space for the water.'

I stepped in between your legs, lowered my back against your front. 'Don't look at my arsehole,' I said.

'Too late,' you said.

That made me drop down too quickly, knocking the wind out of you. Water splashed over the sides. We squirmed into a position that was kind of comfortable.

'Have you got enough room?' you asked.

'Yeah,' I said, feet flat against the taps. 'Have you?'

'Too much.'

I can't remember the word you used to describe your body. Was it tubby, chubby or chunky? Would it hurt your feelings to hear me even imagine it was either tubby, chubby or chunky? It was something like that, something that would hurt you to hear someone else say, which is what had been said to you when you were younger, you said, which is why you learnt to say it yourself. For me the only word to use is big. Your dimensions were tall, wide, thick. I couldn't get enough of you, of trying to gather you in my arms until I was stretched out like a squirrel on a tree, of feeling your duvet weight on top of me, of other proportional advantages. But this wasn't enough for you to leave behind the things that had hurt you. I remember how lacing up my trainers before a run would make you remember. You felt the need to address it yourself. You made some joke about signing up for an iron man. 'My trainers are getting serviced,' you said.

Maybe I shouldn't have addressed how you felt about your body, but I was excited by the idea of having seen an aspect of you. You were generous with me, just laughed, engaged the subject openly, so unlike your brother, who fought any attempt to characterise him. You said, 'My body and me are pranking each other.'

'Pranking?' I said.

'Or punishing,' you said.

'Why?'

'I should probably exercise.'

'You're on your feet all day.'

'Never trust a fat chef, my mam always says. Must've took that to heart.'

'You're not fat,' I said.

'I have fat, I mean.'

'You shouldn't be so hard on yourself.'

'I think the problem is I'm too lenient.'

'The problem isn't you or your body,' I said.

You laughed. You laughed when you agreed. Your brother laughed when he disagreed. 'I suppose I feel as though I'm not allowed to have this kind of body,' you said. 'But knowing this doesn't help how I feel about it.'

I twisted around, propped my chin on your chest. Sheepishly, with one of your eyes pinched together, realising that I might have experience in this department, you said, 'I suppose this experience isn't limited to my own circumstance.'

I shook my head, smiling. You had a look on your face that told me you were wondering if you should ask me about my experience in my body, but I pulled myself up your body to kiss you.

I'm grateful for the joy of having been with you. It just hurts to remember how good that felt.

There's no difference between picking a scab and scrolling through Instagram. An irresistible discomfort. I tell myself I'm gathering tips about how to live my life when I'm ready or rich enough.

There's one particular woman whose life I can't help wanting for myself. Here she is in Nicaragua, on a hammock by the beach at sunset. Here she's at a music festival. Here she's swimming in London Fields Lido. Here she's in an exercise class in New York. She's leaping into the air off a platform. #ActionHero. It leads me to a video of people in leotards slapping their bodies onto crash mats in the foetal position, dodging bricks that swing on wires. Two people spring up, sprint off around the back of the scaffolding, which stands like two giant staples crossed over each other so that a bird's eye view would give you a +.

A woman says, 'In the background, you hear impact sounds. We're talking about, you know, a 160-pound body landing, and for me, there's something profound about it.'

The woman's name is Elizabeth Streb. She came up with this form of purposely dangerous acrobatics, calls it PopAction. She says, 'I believe humans can fly, and I believe PopAction is a methodology, a pretty complex technique, even though, from a distance, we look like wilding crazy people.'

A ladder, connected at its middle point to one of the top beams of the scaffolding, revolves like a propeller, just missing the mats. Along the ladder, as it spins, more people in red unitards jump on, off, climb up, down. At the height of one end of the ladder's ascent, one person, holding on by his hands, lets go like leaping off a swing. He leans forward in the air, towards the floor, straightening himself like a pencil before slapping down.

'We haven't yet been able to access quantum mechanics, but I wish we could go fast enough to disappear. I wish we could figure out how to go through each other's bodies or skip a spot in space.'

Most of the people in red unitards hold on to the ladder as one person on the floor pushes it around faster.

'Each of these action heroes have to agree to come into this room and take a hit. You feel the gravity. You are out of control. So it's really an acclamation, it's an assessment, deciding to love being out of control.'

They scream, laugh, cheer.

'Streb PopAction has been accused of being brutal and masochistic and sadistic and all that, and all I'm trying to demonstrate is there's an enormous distance between death and something ethereal, and the difference between those two points is, perhaps, where the drama of action resides.'

One by one, as the ladder revolves, getting slower with each revolution, each person in a red unitard leaps from the top beam, smacks the mat, jumps up, dashes off, stands up straight, one next to the other.

'That feeling of falling, or fear of falling, or however you want to quantify it, if you're paying attention, you're feeling those forces as you're falling, and they can't disappear because it's a present-tense technique, Streb PopAction is a present-tense technique, and you're in that millisecond at all times.'

———

My mother asks what we should make. She looks into the fridge. I look in the cupboards. I ask her what she fancies. I do not look at her fluffy tufts of hair.

'Nothing,' she says.

'Aren't you hungry?'

'Yes. I'm not very hungry.'

'Okay.'

'But I can make you something.'

'When did you last eat?' I say.

'I ate this morning.'

'You should eat something.'

'I could have made anything for you, with longer notice,' she says. 'When did you last eat?'

'Lunchtime. Three o'clock.'

'And you're hungry already?'

'How old is this okonomiyaki sauce?'

'What does the label say?'

'2012.'

'That's okay,' she says.

'Do you have cabbage?'

'Of course.'

'Mayonnaise?'

'I can make some.'

'How do you feel about okonomiyaki, then?'

'My mother taught me to make mayonnaise,' she says.

'How do you feel about okonomiyaki?' I say.

'I suppose we can, if you want to.'

'I haven't had okonomiyaki in ages.'

'You haven't?'

'You seem surprised.'

'I just remembered how much you like fried food.'

'I'll grate the cabbage,' I say.

'Can you pass me the flour, and the stock,' she says. 'Not the cubes. The packets there, please?'

We stand opposite sides of the kitchen. I grate cabbage in a bowl. I hear her tap an egg over the counter.

'Be careful with that,' she says.

'I'm in my thirties.'

'You still need to be careful. Your brother cut himself.'

'Cut himself?'

'He had a cut on his cheek.'

'What from?'

'Shaving.' He does not do it often enough. He needs to be careful.'

'When did you see him?'

'Just before you came over.'

'He wasn't staying for dinner?'

'He just left.'

'He didn't say why?'

'He said something about selling his car.'

'He has a car?'

'Or buying a car. I think he's impossible sometimes. Is that ready?' she says. 'Combine those and I'll heat the oil.'

I tip the cabbage into the pancake mix. Stirring it together, I see a hair swirl through. I move in front of the bowl, stir slowly to find it, but it seems to have vanished.

'Sometimes,' my mother says, lowering her voice as though he's in the next room, 'I think it's impossible to be a mother to that young man.'

'Yeah.'

'Sometimes he can look after himself. If we were in Japan, he might benefit from a traditional apprenticeship. Though the master and pupil arrangement always made me want to vomit.'

'Yeah.'

'I know he lies to me. I could never get him to tell the truth. He doesn't respect me enough. Now he will never be able to. Are you finished with that? Is there shell in there?'

'No.'

'Let me see.'

'No. It is shell. Don't worry. I've got it.'

'Do you know you have to use the shell to get the shell?'

'It's fine,' I say, but she comes over, sees me pluck out the hair, flick it in the bin.

She stares at the bin.

'It's fine,' I say.

She stands stiffly, hangs her head.

'Kaasan,' I say, 'it's fine.'

If she registers what I say it's only in her blinking. I put my hand on her shoulder. She scratches her head. She pulls out another bowl from the cupboard, tips flour into it. She scratches her head. She taps another egg over the counter, cracks it into the flour. She scratches her head. She scratches her head with both hands. She scratches her head, scratching fast.

'Hey,' I say. I grab her hands, but they still move as if they're scratching. Her eyes are closed. 'Hey,' I say.

'It's so itchy. It's very, very itchy.'

'Okay,' I say, keeping her hands together in the crux of my elbow so I can wet my hand under the tap, stroking the water over her hair. 'Okay,' I say as the tension in her arms starts to melt. She doesn't open her eyes.

'Do you think I need my hair?' she says.

'Need it?' I say. 'No, you don't need it.'

She nods.

'Would you like to shave it?' I say.

She frowns.

'Would you like me to shave it?'

Her eyelids twitch. A tiny nod.

'Okay,' I say. 'Let's shave it.'

I lead her to the toilet. Her eyes are still closed. I sit her down on the toilet, run the tap warm. It fills the sink. I lather my hands, her head, with soap. I take the razor I keep here from the shower.

'Are you sure?' I say.

She nods.

I shave at the temple first. The soft hairs gather in the razor. I wash them off, draw the razor over the same place, picking off hairs the razor missed. She doesn't open her eyes, breathes slowly.

'Okay,' I say, 'take a look.'

Slowly, she stands. She faces the mirror a moment before opening her eyes. She covers her mouth. I've left her with a downy mohawk. I love to make my mother laugh. When I go to shave it off, she stops me.

'No,' she says.

'What?' I say.

'You don't want me to look silly, do you?'

———

Ali is an inpatient on Avalon Ward, South West London and St George's Mental Health Trust. She's been there a week. I've come every other day for her dialysis, most days at visiting hours, when she is more awake, but I've missed the past two times, too tired after work, had someone else assist her treatment. We're in her room. The walls are bare. A window looks out onto a lawn.

Since being here, Ali's weight has gone just above the limit that allows her to go outside once a day, for 15 minutes, when a nurse has time to take her. Ali refuses to go. She weighs enough to have physiotherapy, but she won't. She won't speak. She resists every meal. She spends most of her time alone.

The skin around her eyes is flaking, sore. She stares at her hands, a nest between her knees. A little horizontal crease forms at the top of her nose. I feel like she's gearing up to tell me some secret of her misery, but instead, she starts to cry. I force myself to look at her, feeling some resistance to me looking at her, probably coming from her wish to be formless. Then at once I know this has nothing to do with her mother, like her specialists seem to think. She knows she is starving herself, but not for anything. Her starvation isn't for anything, but of things. Of time, of friends, of a life with a body that others have without worry. She tells me that she just wants not to worry about eating, about meals. She just wishes she could sustain herself on light, by looking, by keeping her eyes open. She is indignant about how complex the body is, with all its complex needs. Her body feels more like it belongs to ideas about bodies than to her. She wants to live outside her body. I don't know what to say. I say I'm sorry I missed the past two treatments. I tell her that I'll come back tomorrow.

'Don't say that if you're not going to,' she says.

I say it again.

———

'Before you can learn how to fly, you need to learn how to fall. But before you learn how to fall, you need to learn how to land.'

In a studio in a warehouse under the overground tracks by London Fields, I glanced around at the six others on the mat. We stood in rows of three. Our teacher Cali had a purple mohawk, tattoos on her arms, legs. She smiled. Gold tooth.

First she showed us how to make a ball with our bodies. Our shins, our hands, flat on the mats. She showed us how to push up off the mat, extend our body, 'feel that foot of air under you', land flat on our stomach, our thighs.

'Good!' she screamed, clapped her hands. One of the men and one of the women had clearly taken the class many times before. I felt clumsy.

We stood up in our rows again. Cali called out, 'Head!' We jumped, spinning 90°, bowed heads.

'High bend!' Another 90° spin, bowing shoulder height.

'Fold! Crouch! Ball! Stomach!'

We stood up, panting.

'Isn't this fun?' Cali screamed, arms outstretched. She looked insane. I half-shouted 'Yeah!' with everyone else.

She told us to get in single file. I stood at the back of the line. The woman in front turned around, whispered, 'This is ridiculous. I love it.'

I managed a smile.

Cali said now we'd each learn to fall on our backs from standing, fall like a tree. One by one they turned to face the next person in the queue, stretched their arrowed arms up in the air, leapt backwards, blindly, landed. Cali guided them at first so they could feel what it feels like to land flat on your back without bending. Each time they did it solo, Cali cheered, handed out high-fives.

On my turn I faced the empty room, everyone behind me, my arms stretched up.

'Go!' she screamed.

I tried, but I guess my back didn't want to be horizontal. It jolted up when I sensed the mat coming, my hands shot out to brace.

Cali said, 'That's okay. That's okay.'

I felt the others watching, wanting me to do it so they didn't have to watch me fail.

'Let's try again,' Cali said.

I turned around again, falling again, but my body disagreed. I apologised to Cali. She pulled me up.

'Okay!' she said. 'That's okay!' She shouted, 'Mag, Level 3!'

One woman peeled off, ran up the scaffolding at the back of the studio. The rest of the class stepped back off the mats, looked up. I felt wooden.

Mag stepped up to the platform edge. She stood there for a moment looking straight ahead of her like there was no space below. She lifted her arms above her head, lowered them, sprang off the platform.

The bottoms of my feet tingled. I stopped breathing. The air seemed to grab her, hold her, as her arms swung in unison from her hips to over her head. For a moment she was completely still in the emptiness, so gracefully helpless now, plunging so fast, gravity remembering to act.

I remember thinking she couldn't stop, she would just vanish through the mat, through the world, but *whack*! She hit the mat, spinning immediately onto her back, sitting up. We cheered, clapped, whooped, whistled, high-fives all around.

Then we roly-polied. We leapt into balls. We leapt onto our stomachs. We threw ourselves onto the floor. We treated our bodies with a calculated kind of fearlessness, putting our bodies through the slightly painful intersecting space in the Venn Diagram of risk and safety.

Cali stopped us and asked if I wanted to try that fall again. I said I did and I felt no fear as I leapt back, my back smacking on the mat. Their applause, a wave of triumph, seemed to dissolve the borders of my body.

Afterwards we all went to the pub. I ached. I laughed. I loved that ache.

*Living room of small house in Darlington, North East England. The
furniture is pushed to the sides. Sheets cover the floor.* **Paul** *(56; miner's
build but shrivelled with age) and his youngest son* **Sam** *(23; harelipped;
tall and burly but gentle) are crouched under the front window, at the
back of the stage, both in workwear. They're chiselling away mouldy
wallpaper and cleaning the stained wall behind. Between them is a
scattering of cleaning products, chisels, tins, knives, a bucket, a paint
roller, Paul's toolbox. The oldest son* **Cam** *(25; wiry; an elegant but
practical manner) sits on a chair to the right of them, wearing dark
chinos and an overcoat, smoking a cigarette.*

Paul: Whole fucking point of the cavity is protecting this wall
here from all the rain and shite that hits the other wall out
there. The gap between the walls is a barrier basically so if
you stuff the gap with insulation, all this absorbent material,
right, you've just made a sort of connection between two
things that were always meant to be kept apart. So when
you've got all the rain and shite seeping through the wall out
there it starts seeping through the insulation and seeping
through this wall here. It's basically one wall with a spongey
centre, a fucking custard cream.

Cam: Right. *(knowingly)* And who put the insulation in?

Paul *tries not to rise to it, but can't help himself.*

Paul: It was fucking freezing in here, man. Like a having a tent for a house. And no soundproofing. No privacy at all. You could hear her next door pluck a fucking pube out her arse.

Cam: Out her arse?

Paul: Oh you know what I mean.

Cam: Imagine what she could hear.

Paul *glances up at him, puzzled and slightly affronted by the possible implications. He chooses not to entertain it. Cam stands and looks out the window and down the street. Seeing nothing, he sits back down.*

Paul: *(smirking)* Any minute now.

Cam: What?

Paul: She'll be back any minute.

Cam: I was just looking outside. Does—what's his name?—that lad who ate pebbles?—do they still live at 44?

Paul: Aye. They've just bought theirs. Fuck knows where the money's coming from.

Cam: Nice lad actually. But nice in a didn't-get-enough-oxygen-at-birth kind of way. One time, when I was around his, we were playing on the Xbox in his bedroom, and his mam must've woken up from a nap or something because she came into his room completely naked. Happened a couple of times actually. And the lad's dad, Mam saw him necking a lass from Sam's year in a car park. He paid her not to tell anyone. Is that right? Two-hundred quid or something? She know what time I was coming up?

Paul: Aye. She knew.

Cam *watches them work. He watches his brother. He picks up the toolbox and reads the label.*

Cam: 'Dad'.

Paul: What?

Cam: Not you. It says 'Dad' on here.

Paul: Well spotted.

Cam: You put 'Dad' on here? Not 'Paul'?

Paul: It was my dad's.

Cam: So he put 'Dad' instead of his own name? Or was it his dad's?

Paul: I put 'Dad' on it. I gave it him for his birthday.

Cam: But he died before I was born.

Paul: I'm aware.

Cam: So you had 'Dad' on your toolbox before you were a dad.

Paul: Guess so.

Cam: *(trying to get Sam's attention)* So that's why you started reproducing? To have the right name on your toolbox?

Paul: Didn't have much choice in the matter.

Cam *looks at* Sam, *confused and disappointed by his detachment.* Cam *stubs his cigarette in an ashtray on the windowsill and takes off his overcoat.*

Cam: Howay then. Is there owt I can do?

Paul: Do?

Cam: Aye.

Paul: Like what?

Cam: I dunno. Anything.

Paul: You just keep sitting still and looking pretty.

Cam: I could get rid of the wallpaper.

Paul: *(snorting)* You'll only cock it up.

Cam: Getting rid of paper?

Paul: *(amusing himself)* You'll probably get a papercut and faint.

Cam: But it's all damp and soft.

Paul *just laughs.* Cam *doesn't know how anyone could cock up something so simple. He doesn't know why he deserves this. He looks to his brother for backup. But* Sam *just glances up at him, embarrassed*

either of him or for him.
Sound of car pulling up outside.

Paul: That'll be her.

Cam *peeks out the window then steps away from it. He takes out another cigarette and lights it. He checks himself, half-tucking his shirt. He glares down at* **Sam.**
Sound of key in door.

Cam *braces himself.*

SCREENSHOTS OF EMAIL CHAIN BETWEEN KAY DEEDS AND CAMERON STRUTH

18–24 APRIL 2014

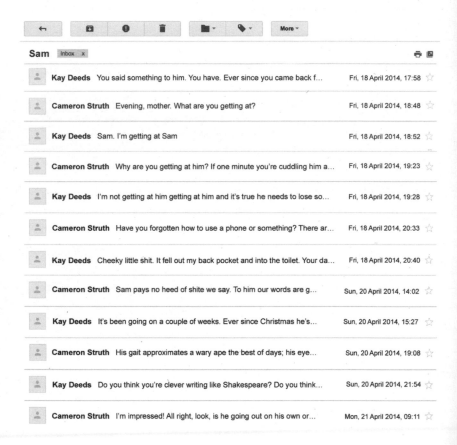

Sam   Inbox   x

Kay Deeds You said something to him. You have. Ever since you came back f…	Fri, 18 April 2014, 17:58	
Cameron Struth Evening, mother. What are you getting at?	Fri, 18 April 2014, 18:48	
Kay Deeds Sam. I'm getting at Sam	Fri, 18 April 2014, 18:52	
Cameron Struth Why are you getting at him? If one minute you're cuddling him a…	Fri, 18 April 2014, 19:23	
Kay Deeds I'm not getting at him getting at him and it's true he needs to lose so…	Fri, 18 April 2014, 19:28	
Cameron Struth Have you forgotten how to use a phone or something? There ar…	Fri, 18 April 2014, 20:33	
Kay Deeds Cheeky little shit. It fell out my back pocket and into the toilet. Your da…	Fri, 18 April 2014, 20:40	
Cameron Struth Sam pays no heed of shite we say. To him our words are g…	Sun, 20 April 2014, 14:02	
Kay Deeds It's been going on a couple of weeks. Ever since Christmas he's…	Sun, 20 April 2014, 15:27	
Cameron Struth His gait approximates a wary ape the best of days; his eye…	Sun, 20 April 2014, 19:08	
Kay Deeds Do you think you're clever writing like Shakespeare? Do you think…	Sun, 20 April 2014, 21:54	
Cameron Struth I'm impressed! All right, look, is he going out on his own or…	Mon, 21 April 2014, 09:11	

Kay Deeds No. Your dad says he's seen in him the Tanners most nights with...	Mon, 21 April 2014, 12:39	
Cameron Struth Well, that sounds better than normal, to be honest, Mam. H...	Mon, 21 April 2014, 18:29	
Kay Deeds He was home on the Find Friends thing but when I went over the...	Mon, 21 April 2014, 18:35	
Cameron Struth Fuck me, Mam. Has he shared his location with you willingl...	Mon, 21 April 2014, 20:01	
Kay Deeds He's the one who showed me it in the first place! It's not my fault ...	Mon, 21 April 2014, 20:10	
Cameron Struth So he's avoiding you. He's ignoring you. He's a grown ma...	Tue, 22 April 2014, 18:46	
Kay Deeds Of course that's what your leadheaded dad said but I can see for...	Tue, 22 April 2014, 19:53	
Cameron Struth Consider how it might be healthy for you both if you were t...	Wed, 23 April 2014, 18:20	
Kay Deeds Thank you Dr Struth. I didn't you know you knew so much about mot...	Wed, 23 April 2014, 19:27	
Cameron Struth Well, I know him, and I can think of him without involving m...	Wed, 23 April 2014, 21:52	
Kay Deeds What have I done to hurt him? I'm only thinking about what's bes...	Wed, 23 April 2014, 23.43	
Cameron Struth Bravo, Mother Teresa. In any case, what could I have said to h...	Wed, 23 April 2014, 23:58	
Kay Deeds I noticed after Christmas. Then things really turned after he cam...	Wed, 23 April 2014, 00:21	
Cameron Struth When was he in London?	Thu, 24 April 2014, 07:37	
Kay Deeds When he was doing seeing you! Don't take the mick now Camer...	Thu, 24 April 2014, 20:30	
Cameron Struth Well, I didn't say anything. Again, what exactly have you di...	Thu, 24 April 2014, 20:35	
Kay Deeds All Christmas you two were always off having little sidebars and s...	Thu, 24 April 2014, 20:41	
Cameron Struth You barely gave us time to ourselves, Mam. What devastati...	Thu, 24 April 2014, 20:56	
Kay Deeds Oh Lord I didn't bother you one bit. Don't lie about that to me plea...	Thu, 24 April 2014, 21:02	
Cameron Struth So what if we talked about it?	Thu, 24 April 2014, 21:08	

| | Kay Deeds | Don't play thick now. That lad's on a knife edge ever since seein... | Thu, 24 April 2014, 21:21 | ☆ |

| | Cameron Struth | Well, it's encouraging that you're catastrophising this, M... | Thu, 24 April 2014, 21:29 | ☆ |

| | Kay Deeds | Jesus wept you're as leadheaded as him. Queen Ethelburga's is... | Thu, 24 April 2014, 21:47 | ☆ |

| | Cameron Struth | Believe it or not, I don't. What—did he actually get in to Que... | Thu, 24 April 2014, 21:58 | ☆ |

| | Kay Deeds | I do know it was a long time ago and enough time for most folk t... | Thu, 24 April 2014, 23:21 | ☆ |

| | Cameron Struth <cameronstruth@gmail.com> | Thu, 24 April 2014, 23:53 | ☆ | ↩ | ▾ |
| | to Sam | | | | |

Now then, Sam. How you getting on? Mam's concerned about you. She seems to think your possession of something approximating a social life constitutes some kind of abysmal misery. What does that say about her, eh? She also tells me you're seeing someone. Has that been for long or what? Do I know her? Sorry to ask but do you mind calling Mam (off)? She'll act as if you haven't crossed her mind, obviously, but I thought perhaps you ought to see (below) how worked up she is. Take care if you are having trouble. Call if you need. There's an empty side of my bed if you felt like visiting ever.

...

---------- Forwarded message ----------
From: **Kay Deeds** <kaydeeds@gmail.com>
Date: Thu, 24 April 2014, 23:21
Subject: Re: Sam
To: **Cameron Struth** <cameronstruth@gmail.com>

I do know it was a long time ago and enough time for most folk to see it as nowt more than a fart in a hurricane but Sam's a different beast. He is. Every day's a fucking midlife crisis for the poor lad. I can see it. He doesn't have to say anything for me to see what he's seeing. His eyes glaze over but not like a thicko. His eyes glaze over like someone at the end of some Holocaust film. Lord knows he's not obsessed with himself like you or your dad but these pits he falls in are in himself and I can see he's dreaming about the kind of life he'd have for himself with better a time of it at school but we all know it wouldn't have made an hapeth of difference if I let him go to Queen Ethelburga's because Sam is Sam. He is what he is God bless him. It's no one's fault. Not even mine before you jump on that one. Do you really think judges' sons would've given him an easier time of it? Of course not. Of course not. Sam is Sam and posh lads can hurt you as much as rough lads. There's nowt worse for a lad like Sam to be stuck boarding with those pricks and perverts. There's nowt worse than a boss' son. The best thing was hoying the invitation in the bin. But he might not think that so it's better he hasn't the temptation to dwell on that sort of thing. It's done now and there's no point dwelling on it. But that's the sort of thing that's happening now. I see him dwelling. And Christ knows we can give him things to dwell on if we want to and don't go putting on like you've not in the past so I want to hear it from you so I can him. Lord knows no one else is going to or can.

COPIED POSTS FROM CORINA SLATE'S BLOG, 'WITNESS'

JANUARY–FEBRUARY 2017

She comes out the toilet with her wig on but her work shirt open. 'Can you help me with this?' she says. The treatment has numbed her fingers.

'I have asked if they could provide shirts with pop-on buttons,' she says, standing in front of me, 'but they just said they didn't know.'

I start to button her shirt. 'You could replace them with pop-ons.'

'If I could replace them myself, I wouldn't need them to begin with.'

'You might need to talk to them about reducing your hours.'

'Yes?' she says.

'It's not getting harder?'

'Harder? I wouldn't say so.' She holds her chin high when I reach the collar. 'The cleaning products do seem a bit stronger. They make my eyes water. And I struggle with the trolleys sometimes.' She makes a dismissive sound. 'They're clumsy things anyway,' she says. 'The wheels have not been changed in years.'

'Do other people have problems with them?' I say.

'How should I know?'

'You don't talk?'

She makes that sound again. 'What are we going to talk about?'

'I don't know. Anything.'

'Anything,' she says. 'Anything is everything that isn't cancer.
Everyone there is someone who hasn't got cancer. They're people
who eat normally. They're people with eyelashes. What do you
suppose we have to talk about?'

'There are other things to talk about,' I say.

'Yes, possibly,' she says. 'There must be. Possibly I'm not quite
myself. Well, that's exactly what it is. That's exactly the problem.'

———

'I've made up my mind,' said Ali. She'd been on Avalon Ward two
weeks now. Her voice sounded like she was about to laugh. Not as
reassuring as you might think.

'Yeah?' I said.

'I'm going to gain a kilogram by the end of the week,' she said.

I knew my face wasn't matching up to her enthusiasm.

'What?' she said.

'What does your therapist say about it?'

Ali bit her fingernails.

I said, 'It just feels a bit sudden, Ali.'

'It hasn't felt sudden for me.'

She spat a curl of nail on the floor.

'I can imagine,' I said.

'No, you can't.'

'Why do you keeping saying that?' I said. 'I can't imagine. I don't get it. Of course I can. Of course I can imagine.'

'Because you don't know me, mate. We don't know each other. Why are you here?'

I picked up my bag, put it on my lap. We didn't say anything. I looked at her to see if she meant what she said. She stared out the window.

'Do you want me to go?' I said.

'Do what you want,' she said.

'I don't want to go.'

She watched a girl in a wheelchair outside. I watched her.

'I'm not off it for thinking I'll gain a kilogram by the end of the week,' she said.

'I never said that.'

'All I'm saying is I'm going to gain as much as I can. I'm in control of it now.'

'And I think that's good. It's great.'

'It is,' she said. 'I think it is.'

Ali assessed the damage she'd done to her nails.

'So the therapy is good for you?' I said. 'It's working?'

'It's a fucking mare.'

'How come?'

'Some of the people here,' she said. 'It's like they've been forced to work here.'

'I know what you mean.'

'I know it's because there's not enough of them, but I feel like they know I'm relying on them not to die and so they make it so much fucking worse than it has to be that I've got no choice but to make myself better so I don't have to rely on them anymore. You know what I mean?'

'I do.'

'They butter my fucking bread for me. I've never slashed myself. They know that, but they don't trust me with a plastic fucking knife because I look like someone else who has.'

I only nodded.

'What's the matter now?' she said.

'Nothing. Well, I'm not being funny, I'm not starting anything, but I'm just a little confused by it all.'

'What's confusing?'

'Well, you're saying that you're in control now.'

'I am.'

'And no one trusts you, because they just see the outside.'

'They do.'

'But you're saying you're going to gain weight.'

'Yeah.'

'So you know you should gain some weight, to be healthy.'

'Yeah.'

'But you're not. You're barely eating.'

'I will. That's what I'm saying. I will.'

'But you haven't. You're not.'

She bit down on her nail again, frowning, eyes blinking.

'I'm not having a go,' I said.

'You're being supportive, then, are you?'

I didn't know what to say. I didn't know what I wanted to say. I guess I didn't believe her.

She looked at me, her nail, at me. She said, 'Sometimes it's in control. Sometimes I'm in control. Sometimes I'm in control of it.'

'And what about now?' I said.

She took a moment before saying, quietly, 'I am.' She stared at her arm, or a spot on the bed. 'I just need them to give me a bit of space.'

But there is no space. After rounds, I thought about her drinking warm water with lemon or apple cider vinegar before breakfast to boost her metabolism. Making porridge, I thought about CBT to rewire her instinct to overvalue shape and weight.

Three weeks later, I get a call from Ali. 'They say I can leave now,' she says. 'I gained enough for them. You want to help me with my bags?'

———

My mother walked, little steps, to her kitchen, to make us coffee. She was irritable. I don't press her much to speak these days. There has been a turn. She just does things, slowly. I watch. I listen, try not to yawn. It was early afternoon, still chilly, quite dark. There was a crack, a scatter, from the kitchen. She'd dropped a bowl. It was cracked in two.

'It fell out my hand,' she said.

'It's a clean break,' I said. 'It's fixable. Have you got any glue here?'

'Yes. I need to go and get some gold.'

'Did you say gold?'

'To make gold glue. Yes.'

'Just use normal glue,' I said.

'Mind your step.' She headed for the door.

'Where are you going?'

'To get the gold,' she said.

'Just use the glue here.'

'I think I'm capable of going to the shop.'

'What shop?'

'I'll find one.'

'Please just use the glue. Or throw it out. You never cared before.'

'You might think I'm silly and old-fashioned,' she said, 'but I think it's the thing to do,' meaning kintsugi (金継ぎ), with gold glue, it will be more beautiful than just a crack, meaning, a crack filled with gold is more beautiful than just a crack, meaning, it's gold that makes the crack beautiful, meaning, a crack is just a crack.

When I got back from the Wilko on the high street, the DIY centre on Lea Bridge Road, God's Own Junkyard on Shernhall, in the industrial estate, caught in a constant draught, with brass powder to mix in the glue, the cut she got on her palm from picking up the pieces would not stop bleeding, meaning, possibly, the cancer has spread to her liver.

———

I duck into the toilet when I see the General Manager of the Kidney Service Team with her back to me in the corridor. I sit on the toilet. When the door opens, I lift my feet.

'Corina?' says Tasha.

I breathe through my mouth because my nose is a little blocked.

I hear her grumble, the door close. I count to 30, then leave the cubicle.

Tasha stands there by the sinks, an eyebrow raised.

'Hi,' I say.

'Hi,' she says.

I wash my hands. 'Did you call my name?'

'I did.'

'Thought I heard something.'

'What's up, man?' she says.

'Sorry?'

'What's the matter with you?'

'I just went for a piss.'

'That's not what I'm on about.'

'Then I don't know what you're on about.'

'I'm on about the fact that you're actually hiding from me in the toilet now. You've barely said a word to me since The Cross and I know it was maybe a bit shitty of me to blindside you like that, and I'm sorry, but it's too much now. Something's happened. What's happened?'

I shrug, hold my hands under the dryer. She shouts my name over the noise.

'Nothing's happened, Tasha.'

'What?'

'I said nothing's happened.'

'You wouldn't have acted like that if something wasn't wrong though.'

'How do you know how I would've acted?'

'Because I know how you would've acted.'

'Apparently you don't, though.'

'You can tell me, man. Obviously.'

'Okay.'

'Well?'

'Well, what?'

'Are you taking the piss?'

'No.'

'You're telling me nothing's wrong, that nothing's happened?'

'Yeah.'

She stares at me. I can't meet her eyes. She nods. She shakes her head. It feels like the end of something, an irreversible change.

'Cool,' she says, sounding like she's about to leave, but she stays here looking at me to let me know it is the end of something, an irreversible change.

When she finally leaves, I look in the mirror. I can't meet my eyes.

———

The job centre security guard fills the doorway.

'Are you two related?' he says.

Ali and I look at each other, then back to him.

'You can only accompany her in if you're related.'

'I'll be out here,' I say.

'Thanks a lot,' Ali says to him.

'It's the policy. Otherwise you've got a community centre up there.'

'God forbid,' she says.

I light a cigarette at the corner of Mare Street. Across the junction a woman strides out the William Hill, looks about, antsy. She speaks to a passer-by who shakes his head. She doesn't seem bothered by it, steps into the road. A car halts, beeps. The driver knifes his hand at her. She shrugs, crosses the road. She sees me watching. I shift my eyes so I'm looking down the road, feel bad for doing this, then look at her.

She nods to me. 'Excuse me, darling,' she says.

'You all right?' I say.

'I don't suppose you've got any spare change on you?'

'I've got nothing on me. '

'Do you reckon I could borrow your phone, then?'

This has happened before. I chased a schoolboy for five minutes then lost him by Lee Valley Park.

'Please,' she says.

I look around to see who else is nearby, what choice she might have made in asking me. I'm always looking around to figure out how I've been perceived in relation to others. I say, 'Yeah, okay.'

'Thank you, darling. Thank you.'

I watch her type the numbers, watching for a burst of energy. I could have said I haven't got any data.

'Hello,' she says. 'It's me. Yeah. I'm going to be a little late. Yeah.

Like five minutes. Fifteen minutes. Yeah. Yeah. There. All right. No. No. I'm not. Had to go back. Yeah. All right. Yeah. Bye. Love you too. Bye.'

She hands back my phone, thanks me, walks back to the William Hill.

Ali comes out.

'That was quick,' I say.

'Bunch of cunts,' she says, walking up the road.

'What happened?'

'Bunch of cunts, mate.'

'What happened, Ali?'

'Sanctioned.'

'What for?'

'Bunch of cunts.'

'Ali, stop a minute, will you?'

'How am I supposed to apply for jobs when I'm allowed outside once a fucking day?'

'Did you tell them about all that?'

'Fucking obviously.'

'It didn't make a difference?'

'The Decision Maker made his fucking decision.'

She looks down the long, loud road.

'How long for?' I say.

'Eight weeks.'

'Shit. What are you going to do?'

'Lay fucking low. What else?'

'You'll get sanctioned again.'

'Then I'll get fucking sanctioned again.'

She takes out a cigarette, scrapes a lighter.

'I can help you out,' I say.

She spits out smoke.

'No?' I say.

Her shoulders are jacked up around her eyes.

'Suit yourself,' I say.

'I've owed people before, mate,' she says.

'You don't have to "owe me" owe me.'

'Sure,' she says. 'Heard that before.'

'Honest,' I say.

'Well maybe I won't owe you the money.'

'You won't owe me anything.'

She eyes me. 'And what if I end up fucking off to Monaco?'

'Then you'll fuck off to Monaco,' I say. I want to say, 'But I'd like a postcard,' but I don't.

'I'll get a job,' she says. 'I've worked before. Warehouse stuff. St Mungo's. I volunteered a lot once.'

'Sure,' I say.

She sighs. 'Thanks.'

We walk across the road towards the cash machine.

'Bunch of cunts,' she says.

The mother is going to die. She knows this, generally. She knows she is losing, will lose. This is why she's irritable. She's irritable because the loss is inevitable.

One night the daughter dreamt that her mother had died but then came back to life. The mother's eyes and tongue had been devoured by worms. Her limbs had withered, rotted. Her whole body was crawling with ants. She only moaned, gasped for food and water. What worried the daughter, in the dream, was knowing that the mother could never die, that she would have to feed the mother, squeeze the shit out of her, change her bedsheets, every day until the daughter herself died. The daughter woke up the moment she realised that, before she died, she'd have to find someone else to take care of her mother.

Early one morning, a few days later, the mother called an ambulance for herself. All she told the daughter when the daughter got to the hospital was that she felt 'great, great pain'.

Her oncologist Dr Datta asked the mother what she planned to do once she left the hospital. The mother told him that she wanted to go to Kew in the spring with her daughter. The oncologist asked her if she'd thought about hospice care, or community nurses. She said no, of course not. He told the daughter what he was seeing that he thought the mother didn't know.

Now there are four things the daughter needs to know. Does the mother know her prognosis? What is she afraid of? How does she want to die? How much suffering is she willing to endure for the sake of added time?

In the oncology ward, the daughter says, 'I just spoke to Dr Datta.'

'Strange man,' the mother says.

'He told me you said we're going to Kew.'

There are pauses between hearing and speaking.

'Yes.'

'I talked to him about how you're doing,' the daughter says.

The mother faces the ceiling. Her eyes slide from the ceiling to the daughter, dreamily. She says, 'Yes.'

'I looked into it as well,' says the daughter. 'Do you want me to tell you what I found out?'

Silence. The daughter knows it's important to let there be quiet. In quiet, the mother will understand what she wants to know, or not to know.

The mother's eyes turn back to the ceiling.

'Not right now,' the mother says, 'if you don't mind.'

SCAN OF INDICTMENT NOTICE

INNER LONDON CROWN COURT

The Queen v Cameron Struth
charged as follows:

STATEMENT OF OFFENCE
Assault with intent to rape, contrary to Sexual Offences Act 2003

PARTICULARS OF OFFENCE
On or about the 23rd day of August 2014, in London, United Kingdom, the crime of RAPE, contrary to section 1 (1) of Sexual Offences Act 2003, was committed by Cameron Struth who did rape Corina Slate.

SCANS OF DEFENDANT'S APPLICATION
FOR PROSECUTION DISCLOSURE

DEFENDANT'S APPLICATION FOR PROSECUTION DISCLOSURE

(Criminal Procedure and Investigations Act 1996, section 8;
Criminal Procedure Rules, rule 22.5)

Case details

Name of defendant: CAMERON STRUTH

Court: INNER LONDON CROWN COURT

Case reference number: LF5087437

Charge(s): RAPE, CONTRARY TO SECTION 1 (1) OF THE SEXUAL OFFENCES ACT 2003

Note: You <u>must</u> give a defence statement, and allow the prosecutor time to respond, <u>before</u> you can make an application for prosecution disclosure.

How to use this form

1. Complete the Case details box above and answer the questions set out in the boxes below. If you use an electronic version of this form, the boxes will expand. If you use a paper version and need more space, you may attach extra sheets.

2. Attach to this form:

   (a) a copy of your defence statement, and

   (b) copies of any correspondence with the prosecutor about disclosure.

3. Sign and date the completed form.

4. Send a copy of the completed form and everything attached to:

   (a) the court, and

   (b) the prosecutor.

1) What material do you want the prosecutor to disclose ?

The content of all text messages sent and received by complainant on the 24th of August 2014.

The content of all text and Facebook messages sent from complainant to complainant's previous sexual partners.

2) Why do you think the prosecutor has that material ?

The defendant has reason to believe that the police will have accessed this material during their investigations and, having consulted with the police, the prosecuting team will have had access to and reviewed such material for evidence to support the case against the defendant.

3) Why might that material:

    (a) undermine the prosecutor's case against you, or

    (b) assist your case ?

If the content of the first collection of telephone evidence demonstrates a degree of nonchalance or satisfaction on the part of the complainant with reference to the party in which the offence is alleged to have taken place, this will undermine the reliability of the complainant's witness and impact statements.

If the content of the second collection of telephone evidence demonstrates a history of the complainant retaliating against previous sexual partners by way of defamation of humiliation, this may support the defendant's contention that the complainant's allegations are predicated on a desire for revenge instead of suffering a non-consensual sex act.

4) Do you want the court to arrange a hearing of this application ? YES / ~~NO~~

If YES, explain why you think a hearing is needed. (If you do not ask for a hearing, the court may arrange one anyway.)

The defendant has reason to believe that the prosecution has not given full disclosure of the evidence which may support the defendant's case. A hearing is necessary to give the defendant a proper opportunity to assert his case.

The defendant faces a potentially significant period of imprisonment if he is found guilty of this offence. It is thus essential that disclosure is properly completed. A hearing would ensure the defendant's right to fair trial on the evidence is secured.

The Crown Prosecution Service has failed in several previous cases regarding sexual assault to disclose all relevant evidence. The disclosure in such cases thus requires scrutiny by a judge.

Signed: ..._VChudury_........................... defendant / defendant's solicitor

Date: ....._28/11/14_..............

RECORDS OF TEXT MESSAGES FROM CORINA SLATE'S MOBILE PHONE

A) 24 AUGUST 2014 (THE DAY AFTER THE ASSAULT)

Date Time	Record Type	Outgoing	Incoming	Text
2014/08/24 14:29:22	MOBILE TERMINATING	███████	███████	
2014/08/24 14:31:45	MOBILE TERMINATING SMS	███████	███████	How are you feeling then? I've just back on it… We're at the Mitre if you feel up to it
2014/08/24 14:36:23	MOBILE TERMINATING	███████	███████	
2014/08/24 17:50:19	MOBILE TERMINATING SMS	███████	███████	███ What you saying? Mitre? I WILL keep ringing you.
2014/08/24 17:58:33	MOBILE ORIGINATING SMS	███████	███████	Sorry, no, I'm fine, just can't face getting out of bed.
2014/08/24 18:12:26	MOBILE TERMINATING SMS	███████	███████	Oh no! Fair. You had a good time last night?
2014/08/24 18:56:51	MOBILE ORIGINATING SMS	███████	███████	Yeah it was fun. You?

B) 16 JULY 2010

Date Time	Record Type	Outgoing	Incoming	Text
2010/07/16 14:31:45	MOBILE TERMINATING SMS	███████	███████	Can't we just keep this between us?
2010/07/16 17:58:33	MOBILE ORIGINATING SMS	███████	███████	Why? Are you ashamed of it or something?
2010/07/16 18:12:26	MOBILE ORIGINATING SMS	███████	███████	I've told everyone who's asked exactly what happened. You're a cheat, ███. You cheated. People need to know exactly who you are before they let you fuck them over.
2010/07/16 19:56:51	MOBILE TERMINATING SMS	███████	███████	Can you delete your fb post? My parents will see that. Please. Be reasonable.
2010/07/16 19:59:03	MOBILE ORIGINATING SMS	███████	███████	This is what you get. Dickhead. Fuck you. Bye!

C) 24 JULY 2010

Date Time	Record Type	Outgoing	Incoming	Text
2010/07/24 14:31:45	MOBILE ORIGINATING MMS	███████	███████	████████████

SCANS OF APPLICATION FOR SPECIAL MEASURES FOR WITNESS

Not Disclosable

WITNESS ASSESSMENT FOR SPECIAL MEASURES
Information required for an application to the court by the CPS
(Anticipated not guilty plea only)

Name of witness: Corina Slate	URN	01	YR	00673	14

Age: 31   Date of Birth: 18/02/1983

---

1. Identification of Witness *(one form per witness)*
Tick which box(es) below apply to the witness   [* automatically eligible]

Vulnerable		Intimidated	
a) Youth under 18 *	☐	e) Witness in fear/distress about giving evidence	☐
b) Witness with mental disorder	☐	f) complainant in sexual case *	☑
c) Witness with learning disabilities	☐	g) Weapons offence	☐
d) Witness with physical disability/disorder	☐		

---

2. Eligibility for 'Special Measures' [Intentionally left blank because the witness is automatically eligible for special measures]

Explain briefly the nature of the witness vulnerability and show how Special Measures are likely to improve the quality of their evidence. Factors to consider: circumstances of the offence, age of the witness, their social and cultural background/ethnic origins, their domestic employment circumstances, any religious beliefs or political opinions, any behaviour towards the witness of the accused, his/her associations, family.

Evidence of disorder/impairment or witness fear/distress:

The effect of the evidence (seek expert advice if necessary):

---

3. Special Measures
Explain to the witness what is meant by 'Special Measures', the measures that may be available and what this would involve for them. Tick below the measure(s) which would be likely to maximise, so far as practicable, the quality of their evidence.

Consider: the needs of the witness, age, development or disability, communication difficulties, the state of mind (distress, shock); the type and severity and/or the circumstances of the offence (offender known to the witness); the purpose and likely value of a visually recorded interview on this occasion, perceived fears about intimidation and recrimination.

310

Not Disclosable

Special Measures			
Screening witness from defendant	☑	Visually recorded interview as evidence-in-chief	☐
Evidence by live link	☑	Intermediary	☐
Evidence in private	☑	Aids to communication	☐
Removal of wigs & gowns	☐		

4. Witness views

What views has the witness/person acting on his/her behalf expressed about:

♦ his/her eligibility?
The complainant is automatically eligible.

♦ whether Special Measures would be likely to improve the quality of his/her evidence?
She believes it would greatly improve the quality of her evidence. She believes the presence of the accused would hinder her ability to give evidence. She is significantly distressed by the prospect of giving evidence and seeing the accused in court.

♦ the measure(s) proposed?
She would like to give her evidence in private as some of the evidence involves details of injuries she sustained to her vagina and vulva.

5. Views of any other interested parties/agencies involved e.g. Parent/guardian, Doctor, Social Services, Schools, etc. (include details and address(es)).

Is there any other supporting material attached? Yes/No. If 'Yes' please list:

6. Special Measures Meeting

Is a Special Measures Meeting required? Yes/No

Assessing Officer:
Name: Eleanor Davidson   Rank/job title & No.: PC 6732   Date: 03/01/15
Tel.: ▮▮▮▮   Mob.: ▮▮▮▮   E-mail: ▮▮▮▮

COPIED POSTS FROM CORINA SLATE'S BLOG, 'WITNESS'

FEBRUARY 2017

'In recent years, across a number of jurisdictions, the position of the crime victim in the criminal justice process has achieved unprecedented prominence in the minds of scholars and policy-makers. In England and Wales, this has led to the Labour government pledging to put victims "at the heart" of the criminal justice system' (Hall, 2007). 'As a consequence of such moves, victims in England and Wales are now promised high levels of support, facilities, and information from many criminal justice agencies and voluntary organizations. These include a Witness Service at every court, explanations from prosecutors on various aspects of the process, the possibility of making a statement as to the impact of the crime, and the potential to give evidence during criminal trials via "special measures"' (Ibid).

'The reforms under the Youth Justice and Criminal Evidence Act 1999 are limited because they reflect an "accommodation approach" preserving the traditional adversarial model and the orality principle' (Ibid). 'Criminal trials are structured as a contest between victim and defendant. The adversarial nature of this arrangement can be particularly traumatic for victims of violent crime. Rape victims often have to provide graphic details of an assault and endure detailed and highly personal questions about their sexual history' (Parsons and Bergin, 2010). 'Live oral testimony by witnesses is the preferred means of presenting evidence at trial' (Ainsworth, 2015).

'A greater percentage of the witnesses giving evidence through special measures demonstrated fewer negative reactions (such as anger, fear, tearfulness, etc.) compared with those that did not' (Ibid). 'Measures which deviate least from this traditional model are also least effective in alleviating witness stress and securing the best evidence' (Ibid). 'There have been tragic examples of the need to find ways to reduce the distress that victims can suffer from cross-examination. Ms Frances Andrade (an adult complainant of "historic" abuse) took her own life after giving evidence at the trial of her alleged abuser; three days before her death she texted her friend to say that after appearing in the witness box, she felt "raped all over again"' (Ministry of Justice (MoJ), March 2014).

'Figures published by the MoJ show that, in recent years, there were around 1,000 Crown Court trial hearings annually that were delayed due to the absence of a prosecution witness. It should be noted that this annual figure covers all offences tried in the Crown Court and the reasons for witness non-attendance are not recorded. However, it is possible that a proportion of these trial witnesses would have been victims in a sexual offences case and they failed to attend the trial hearing out of fear of the cross-examination or the criminal justice process as a whole' (Ibid). 'A factor said to contribute to the trauma for victims is the manner in which cross-examination is conducted. In trials of sexual violence offences victims are required to recount their ordeal and be challenged about personal and sensitive experiences and information' (Ibid). 'On the stand, complainants report feeling as though they are the ones put on trial' (McManamon, 2014). 'There have been examples of cases, reported by the press and media, where it is said that cross-examination was aggressive, with victims, for example, repeatedly being called a liar' (MoJ). 'In essence, the defence's overall questioning approach was to use a sequence of questions, in parts, to build a foundation of facts which was then used to expose inconsistencies in, and make accusations against, the complainant' (McManamon). 'The defence scrutinised the complainant by noticing inconsistencies which were built using contrastive devices. For example, the defence contrasted statements such as "being happy" with "a terrible man". Together the statements created a puzzle inference [the juxtaposing of two facts in order to create an inconsistency that poses a puzzle conveying negative inferences] as to why the complainant expressed happiness towards her alleged rapist . . . The discrepancies were created over the complainant's general credibility – not to the facts related to the offending itself' (Ibid).

'Witnesses using special measures were less likely than those not using them to experience anxiety (63% compared with 73%). Use of special measures was also associated with the impact of cross-examination, with 41 per cent of those using measures saying they had been upset a lot compared with 56 per cent not using measures (not significant)' (Hamlyn et al, 2004). 'It is relevant to note that those who used special measures were slightly less likely to have been upset "a lot" compared to all prosecution witnesses (38% and 48% respectively), although this was not statistically significant' (Ibid).

'Video-link is one of the most widely used special measures' (Hall). 'Here, the witness is presented with a video screen showing only the face of the person talking, and can only hear that person's speech. Hence, the witness is spared the intimidating experience of the court environment and the presence of the defendant and his family in the public gallery' (Ibid). 'This meant that although the defendant and counsel could see and hear the witness, witnesses did not have to see the defendant, only the lawyer questioning him/her. This was thought to be less intimidating for the witness than giving live evidence in the courtroom' (Hamlyn et al).

'Concerns have been expressed regarding the potential impact of the complainant's credibility' (Ellison and Munro, 2013). 'Video transmission or the use of other forms of special measures may imbue witness testimony with undeserved credibility, whilst others have argued, to the contrary, that the removal of a witness from the courtroom may somehow undermine her perceived reliability or trustworthiness in the eyes of jurors' (Ibid).

'"She's giving evidence from a separate room, which, when she first came in, that's swayed me straightaway because I thought, 'Bless her.' She can't even face him"' (quoted in Ibid).

'When a male juror confided that he had been affected by seeing the complainant "distraught on the screen", another juror immediately retorted that women can easily get themselves into a distressed state, implying that the complainant could simply be a good actress, and resisting any temptation to afford her additional credibility on account of her performance via the live-link' (quoted in Ibid).

'"You didn't get any sense of her physicality"' (quoted in Ibid).

'"You can't get a presence of somebody"' (quoted in Ibid).

'The "vividness" of video-mediated testimony may be diminished relative to in-court testimony' (Ibid). '"To me, the video link took away that reality. And I'm not saying it's right to bring a rape victim into a court . . . where they wouldn't be able to give evidence properly, but it just lacks a little bit of reality for me"' (quoted in Ibid).

'"I think it would have helped if she'd gone to court rather than do the video link, to see what the interaction was between them"' (quoted in Ibid).

'One female juror was vociferous in expressing her dislike of the live link. She asserted that the complainant would have "come across a lot better" and her testimony would have had more of an emotional impact had she appeared in court. As she put it, "If you saw her face-to-face crying you'd think, 'Oh my god,' and you'd get more upset." Expressing a slightly different, although related, concern, moreover, another female in the same group complained that it has been impossible to assess the complainant's "true emotions" during her testimony due to her physical absence from the courtroom' (quoted in Ibid).

'The difficulty revealed through observations is that this distancing of the witness from the courtroom can also be confusing and frustrating [for them]. In particular, because witnesses only see and hear one person at a time through video-link, they were often puzzled when someone else in the courtroom asked the presently viewed lawyer/magistrate a question or vice versa. Thus, the witness sees the person on screen looking "off camera" and speaking to an unseen, unheard other' (Hall).

TRANSCRIPT OF NEWS ARTICLE FROM
THE NORTHERN ECHO

MONDAY 12 JANUARY 2015

MOTHER TESTIFIES AGAINST SON CHARGED WITH RAPE

The mother of a man on trial for allegedly raping his ex-girlfriend at a party in Fulham, London, gave witness today at Inner London Crown Court.

One of five witnesses for the prosecution on the second day of trial, Kay Deeds, 58, of Darlington, alleged that Cameron Struth, 30, an actor, has a history of abusive behaviour.

When asked by Prosecutor Megan Greene whether there was anything she knew about the defendant relevant to the charges against him, Mrs Deeds, a clerical assistant for JobCentre Plus, alleged that the defendant had abused his younger brother, Samuel Struth, who attempted suicide on May 28th last year, three months prior to the alleged offence, and died on November 3rd 2014.

The witness added: 'I am certain that [Struth] pushed Sam out of our treehouse. It nearly killed him.'

When asked by Greene if Struth's allegedly abusive behaviour was sexual in nature, the witness said: 'They played dress-up. They played husband and wife. It was always Cameron's idea. He was always making Sam do it.

'Cameron would put my knickers on and my bra. Sam never liked any of that. He really didn't. But he looked up to

Cameron and he was scared of Cameron so much he didn't have much choice.'

The witness recalled one specific incident in which she had come home from work and that, 'from the bathroom window at the back, I saw at the end of the garden Sam naked but for my bra and knickers hanging all baggy from his little body.'

She added: 'So I run downstairs and ask him where his brother is and he tells me Cameron ran away after playing dress-up.'

At this point, Struth stood up in the court and protested his mother's story. For the entire trial, Struth had remained silent and unmoving. The only other instance in which he exhibited emotion was when excerpts from his journals were read out to the court, and he cried.

Mrs Deeds covered her face with her hands before she was asked to step down.

Cross-examination will begin tomorrow.

Dear Corina

I know it must be a shock to see my name. I got your email from an old email Cameron sent to all of us about one of his plays. I know it must be painful to see his name here too. I'm sorry. I am.

You are probably wondering why I am writing to you. Well I want to say sorry on behalf of Cameron who won't give you the apology you deserve. I wrote to him just before the verdict telling him why I went against him in the trial. I said everything I needed to say to him about why I reckon he has turned out the way he has and why I am disgusted by him. Hand to God I was only surprised he did not do something like that sooner.

I do not want to make this all about me. I am only saying this so you know I am not trying to hurt you or dredge it all up again. I am on your side Corina.

I have been thinking about you lately. My life has changed a lot since the trial. My husband Paul has left. I don't know where he has gone. To be sure I often wanted him gone but I admit I was not actually prepared for him to go. I did not expect him to go. I wouldn't say he was all bark and no bite because of course he did bite but he made a lot of empty threats over the years. So I've had to sell up and move on. I came back to Hartlepool my hometown and I rent a little flat here and I don't really feel alone because there's loads of folk around me in their own little flats. Lord it is good just keeping to myself in my little flat with only what I need and no one to worry about but myself feeling safe and secure and stable finally. I go swimming in the sea before eating my porridge. It has cleared up my psoriasis. I just got back from a swim when I started writing this. Something about coming back to my little flat and sitting down with my porridge made me think about you. Of course I am sure your life has changed a lot too. I do not want to make this all about me.

I am just sorry for what Cameron did to you. I will never truly understand him and I have never much liked him if I am being honest. But you must be wondering how he could do something like that. I am not normally one to be pointing fingers but I am sure that having Paul as a father was something to do with why Cameron is Cameron. To be sure he is his own person and a lot of him has nothing to do with Paul or me or anyone else. I know we are all made of the people who make us and make us suffer and this is mostly why I felt the need to write to you but Lord what is life except choosing how you act in spite of all of that?

But the fact is that Paul failed him as a father. It was a blessing when he left. It was. I just wish that I had left myself and much sooner. He has hardly worked the past few years. Funny how watching someone lose respect for themselves makes you lose respect for them too.

I reckon you would've been better off with someone like Sam. He was a gentle lad God bless him. He was also a very smart lad. Did you know about this Corina? He was gifted as they say. Honestly I wished it was not true. I did. I wanted him to be a big dopey lad with a steady job who would not dwell too much on it all. The problem with smart folk is that they keep trying to figure out what everything is all about. When the world does not lay itself at the feet of smart folk they will feel let down by the world and the world will swallow them up.

Of course Paul said the heavier the weight he bears the stronger he gets and of course I knew he was right. But with a lad like Sam you have got to protect him. I tried protecting him from all of it but it wasn't enough with Cameron and Paul in the mix and the school he went to. What more could I have done? How was I to know how bad it would get? No mother could have dealt with that better than I did. I just wish he could have stood up for himself once in a while. He ended up a very lonely man Corina. That's the truth of it. I wish he could've found himself someone like you. I reckon someone like you could have saved him. Lord knows about Cameron. It doesn't bear thinking about.

Anyway I am also sorry the trial went the way it did. I hope you have found a way to live with it and I hope this letter helps somehow.

I have prayed for you.

Kay Deeds

COPIED POSTS FROM CORINA SLATE'S BLOG, 'WITNESS'

MARCH–APRIL 2017

What was the weight of having her as a mother? Was this weight easier or harder to bear as her favourite? Was it love that you felt as her favourite, or just a shadow of gratitude for not shaming her as much as everybody else, including herself? What about the weight of your brother's envy, his aching for what you had? Did you see a share of this weight on me, in my own family? Is it what drew your brother to me? Is this what drew me to him? What would you both have been without her? Would he have done what he did? Would it have let you stay alive? If you'd stayed alive, still bearing the weight she'd put on you, what marks would I have come to see? What loads would you pass on? What resentments? What limits of care? Was it inevitable that you would shatter me somehow too?

———

At four a.m. A&E sends a woman who's vomiting severely. Fever of 39.3°. Hypertension. She admits to ingesting approx. 3,000mg of ibuprofen, 0.5l of vodka. A renal biopsy shows acute interstitial nephritis, glomerulonephritis, 30% fall in eGFR since admittance.

Her husband and new-born son visit. The husband nods bluntly. He holds the baby so its face looks over his shoulder. I see the back of its fluffy head. I go to the mother, say, 'Your family is here. Are you ready to see them?'

She tries not to cry.

I tell the husband that she's resting. 'We need to keep her overnight.'

He makes no effort to pretend to be concerned. Like hearing an announcement over the tannoy that's not for him. He turns, walks away. I see the baby's face, sleeping serene.

My shift ends. In the break room I turn on the kettle, go to the fridge for milk. In there I see the stack of the General Manager of the Kidney Service Team's yoghurt pots. They fill half a shelf. I count them. The kettle clicks. I pick up one of the pots. Strawberry. I scratch a little indentation in the foil lid. I open the lid, drink the yoghurt in a few gulps. I take another pot, pineapple, drink it down. I take a coconut. I drink it. I take another, peach, start to swallow, but it struggles in my throat. I rush to the toilet with the empty pots in my hands. They fall rattling to the floor as I hold open my mouth, waiting for the gush. But the feeling settles. I swallow, breathe. I put the pots in the bin by the toilet. I cover them with paper towels.

———

Studies in cell culture indicate that short-term fasting reduces chemotherapy side effects by selectively protecting normal cells (Safdie et al, 2009). Challenging conditions like fasting stimulate organisms to suppress growth, reproduction, diverting energy towards cellular maintenance, cellular repair.

With the body in protective mode during fasting, it may be that normal cells arrest, go into a kind of hibernation mode, while transformed cells, their genetic pathways stuck in an 'on' mode, continue to proliferate, remaining vulnerable to anticancer drugs. In theory, the cancer cell, by continuing to try to multiply, commits cellular suicide. It tries to compensate for the effect of fasting, but it can't.

Take a 66-year-old Japanese woman diagnosed with stage IV breast cancer and widespread metastatic disease to liver, spleen, pancreas. After two mastectomy procedures, she received adjuvant chemotherapy, consisting of docetaxel, cyclophosphamide.

During all four treatment cycles, the patient fasted prior to a chemotherapy administration. The fasting regimen consisted of a complete caloric deprivation for 48–140 hours prior to chemotherapy, 5–56 hours after, during which she only consumed water, vitamins. The patient completed this prolonged fasting without major inconvenience, lost 8lbs.

After the first fasting-chemotherapy cycle, the patient experienced mild fatigue, dry mouth, hiccups. She was able to carry out daily activities, working up to 22 hours a week. In the subsequent treatments, she received chemotherapy accompanied by a regular diet, complained of moderate to severe fatigue, weakness, nausea, abdominal cramps, diarrhoea. The effects of this significantly interfered with daily activities. She had to withdraw from her regular work schedule.

By the fourth chemotherapy cycle, self-reported side effects were lower in spite of the expected cumulative toxicity from previous cycles. Platelet level decreased by 7–19% during cycles 2 and 3, but did not drop during cycles 1 and 4. After the fourth cycle, a 180-hour fast, her neutrophil counts and white blood cells and platelet counts reached their highest level since the start of chemotherapy. By this time, however, a PET scan documented further metastatic disease to the bones.

While fasting stimulates the cellular system into a protective mode, and has thus been shown to alleviate adverse chemotherapy side effects, the procedure cannot completely prevent tumour growth or metastasis. Complete prevention is impossible. Life can be devastating and devastated at any point, but this is exactly why it can be beautiful. When you're vulnerable you're close to death, but you're even closer to another, more painful kind of death if you're immune to life. If you're not vulnerable, you won't need care, and if you don't need care, or someone else, can you ever really be in love? Can you? This is not a rhetorical question.

———

After work I walked along the river. The sky looked like it had been washed too many times on a high heat. The light was chilly, sieved through the clouds. I'd spent the last hours redrafting care plans, reviewing dosages, recalculating dosages, maintaining the machines. I'd supervised a white student making her calculations. She said, 'Fuck my life.'

I said, 'I'll trade you.'

She had smiled shyly.

'It is hard,' I told her. 'You'll have your lowest moments here. If you have any lower anywhere else that's just tragic. And the thing is, if you take on any more responsibility here, it doesn't get any more satisfying. It just gets worse. And you'll end up taking the brunt of other people's fuck-ups. You can be the best, but it won't matter. There'll be someone responsible for caring for someone who isn't up to it and you'll have to clear up the mess. Basically, some people can care for people and some people can't and the people who can't shouldn't even fucking bother.'

The student was chewing on the corner of her lip. 'Yeah,' she said, looked at the floor.

I avoided her for the rest of the shift. Then I walked to the skate park along the South Bank. I leant on the railings. There was a wiry topless guy screaming into his board. He threw the board clattering in front of him. A little girl near me asked her mother what's the matter with him. 'He's upset he can't do what he wants to do,' she said.

Other lax, skinny guys sat along the back wall looking at their phones. The skater ran onto his board, pushed hard off the ground, swerved towards the ledge that ran beside a set of stairs. He popped up on the very edge of the ledge, slid along balancing only on his front two wheels, but the board stopped sliding, he kept going, flailed in the air. I closed my eyes, heard gasps, 'Ooooooooo', then I saw him in a bundle on the concrete at the bottom of the stairs. He lay there for a moment, slammed his fist on the floor, got up. He hobbled a bit. His anger had turned into a kind of blinkered determination. He rode back to where he started, stretched his back. He leant on his board, stared at the path he'd just taken.

He ran at it again, scraped the board under his feet. This time he managed to pop off the ledge, flip the board mid-air, land on it, but it shot out from under him, sending him back on his arse. He shouted, turning passers-by's heads. He tried it over and over, each time falling in different and similar ways. He was exhausted. The seat of his trousers was dark with dust, sweat. After one attempt an older man wearing a bum-bag, polo shirt and shorts muttered something about stupidity. I glared at his miserable white face. He saw me glaring, walked on.

The skater broke skin, grazed his shoulder, his elbows. He kept trying. He popped up, slid, fell, popped up, slid, popped off, flipped, fell, popped up, slid, fell, popped up, slid, fell, popped up, slid, fell, popped up, slid, popped off, fell, popped up, slid, fell, popped up, slid, fell, popped up, slid, popped off, flipped, fell, popped up, slid, popped off, flipped, landed, rode on. The group of other skaters erupted. They applauded, smacking their own boards on the floor. Three or four of them chased after the skater, cheering. When they reached him, he had his arms stretched up. They grabbed him off his board, hugged him, jumped with him. I clapped from where I stood. He nodded to me, rode back to the group, fist-bumped each one. Then he put on his t-shirt, his backpack, rode off along the river. When he wasn't pushing off the ground, he rested with his hands on his knees. He shook his head in relief, disbelief, pride, gratitude.

That night I went to PopAction, managed to fall off Level 1, a 10-foot drop. Now my body knows when it is horizontal, can land horizontal instinctively.

Tonight we're working in groups of three. Cali wants two of us to stand in a kind of lunge position, facing each other at the end of a mat. The third person will stand on one thigh of each person, back to the mat, holding onto the supporting persons' shoulders. This third person will bend their knees slowly. The other two will make a chair of themselves, putting one hand on the third person's back, one hand on their bum. Then the third person will push down on the thighs, not that forcefully, just enough to get a foot up in the air, leap backwards towards the mat. When the third person does this, the other two will give a gentle guiding push on the third person's bum, sending them topsy-turvy. The aim is for the third person to land flat on her back.

'Who wants to flip?' Cali says.

I remember once my mother and father had been arguing and sometime later that night he said to me, 'Never volunteer for anything.'

I volunteer.

'What if I land on my head?' I say.

'It will really hurt,' she says.

———

'What about my birthday? Will I be here for that?'

'I don't think so.'

'Will I be able to go to Kew?'

'I don't think we can get you to Kew.'

'I suppose so. Is there something else you want to ask me?'

327

'Do you want to talk more about this now?'

'Of course.'

'Okay. Where would you like to go when we leave the hospital?'

'Home.'

'Okay. And how would you want that to go, once we're home?'

'Can I look after myself?'

'I don't think so. The community nurses will come around to treat you now and then. Then it will have to be me, Hiro, or a carer. Do you remember Marjorie? I can see if she's still available.'

'No, no.'

'I thought you liked her the best.'

'I did.'

The daughter waits for the mother to correct herself, but the mother reaches over to the daughter, grabs her thumb, squeezes it impatiently. The only way that she can ask me for care.

'It will mean me seeing you in some compromising positions,' I say.

'Consider it payback,' she says.

———

I meet Ali in The Victoria, Dalston. The pub is dim even though there are enormous windows. It's got wooden walls, a wooden horseshoe bar. Two old blokes stand at the bar where I imagine there used to be seats before a refurbishment. One of them is rolling a cigarette, spilling tobacco down his jacket. The other frowns across the bar at a group of students.

The band from Ali's church is playing downstairs. I've had one pint, feel pissed. Ali sips a ginger beer, has made a few comments already about ginger beer being an insufficient substitute. She eyes up my pint.

'Fancy going for a fag?' she says.

'Too soon after for me,' I say, 'but I'll come out with you.'

'No, it's all right. I just thought you might before we go down.'

'I'm good.'

She flashes a surprised face. I see myself through her eyes, know that she expected me to need a cigarette before going into the gig.

'Let's go down,' I say.

'Give me a sip of your beer, then.'

I hold my hands up to let her take it. She sips slowly, shallowly. 'I'll be shitfaced now,' she says.

We go down. The crowd sound expands around us. We join it. I wouldn't be happy to say I'm shy but I'd admit I'm not one to push through a crowd, speak up if someone barges. Ali is. I've not seen her in a crowd before. I smile at how I thought she'd flinch at people pressing into her.

The band come out: three singers, keyboard, drums, bass, guitar. They smash out two caffeinated gospel songs. Then one singer stands by the keyboard. The keyboard plays alone. It sounds like an upbeat song he's trying to tame. Then the singer's voice is low, steady, like it's getting pulled out by a rope. 'What is this that I feel deep inside?' Her face scrunches up. 'That keeps setting my soul on fire?' She squeezes her fist so tightly it shakes. 'Whatever it is,' she sings, 'whatever it is,' her voice trying to go higher but collapsing, 'it won't let me,' inhaling deeply now, resolving to go higher, then singing, slightly higher, 'hold my peace.' A stone in my throat. 'What is this that makes folks say I'm mad and strange?' I feel the stone aching to cry out. 'Whatever it is,' she sings, 'whatever it is,' snapping her voice off, shaking her head, then singing, quickly, trailing off, like an apology that shame won't let you own, 'it won't let me hold my peace.' I can't not cry, as much as I try. I turn away from Ali. I look up at the ceiling, hoping the tears won't spill.

Ali taps me on the shoulder. Close to my ear she says, 'All right, mate?'

I glance back, hoping she didn't see enough of me to see my eyes but enough of me to see a smile.

She asks again if I'm okay. I turn to her, facing the ground, mumble something about the toilet. I squirm through the people. At a tight knot in the crowd, I realise that Ali is following me. I try to steady broken breathing.

Ali says, 'Corina?'

There are two girls in the toilet. I say to Ali, 'I just need the toilet.'

One of the girls says, 'Number one or two?' I get in a cubicle. Ali tells the girls to shut up. They leave laughing. Something about the close walls, the closed door, gives my body permission to stop trying not to cry, but I hold my hand over my mouth to stifle the sounds.

'Corina?' says Ali. 'Can I come in?'

'I'm pissing,' I say.

'I'll wait.'

'Okay. I'm not pissing.'

'Can I come in, then?'

I let her in. Our feet nearly touch. She watches me cry, watches it peter out to snivelling. She doesn't say anything. I sniff, blow my nose.

'You okay?' she says.

I think of what to say. I think of saying yes, but then what? I think of shrugging, but then I'll still need to think of what to say. I think of saying no. But I don't want to. I don't want her to know. I don't want to confirm it. I don't want there to be anything to know. If I give her a share of this weight, will it make it any lighter for me, or will the giving only bring about another kind of weight we'll have to bear together, something so awkward to hold it makes us contort, stumble, wince? Will it flatten or twist or skew whatever holds us together? When she looks at me, will I see that my pain has become an eyesore? I feel worn out. I sit on the toilet. I say, 'No. I'm not.'

I look at her. She knows. Her eyes are shiny.

'You don't have to say it, mate,' she says.

'I do,' I say. 'I should.'

'You really don't,' she says. 'Not now.'

I dry my face with my palms. 'I can feel myself blushing,' I say.

'It suits you.'

'Every cloud.'

'I'm sorry, mate,' she says, 'about what happened to you.'

'Yeah,' I say. 'You know?'

'Yeah. I know.'

'Is it obvious or something?'

She shakes her head, but shrugs too. 'Found your little blog,' she says.

COMMENTS

Unknown

I've pretended that it didn't happen. But I realized I have PTSD too and just started dealing with it. 15 years of torture. I'm glad you're coming out . . . God bless.

Reply

Unknown

Me 2

Reply

Unknown

I have felt so alone, like I'm part of a great big dark silence I can't
see out of but reading this blog helps me to look back and try to
deal with what happened. You don't know me but reading this blog
I feel you're listening to me even though I'm the one listening to
you!

Reply

———

Love, I think, is where two open wounds press against each other
so one wound becomes a kind of gauze for the other wound. Each
wound protects the other wound from the world. But the wounds
are still wounds. A wound can't heal a wound by covering it. Only
time away, apart, some air, can allow the wound to heal, even if this
exposes the wound to the world. I could be wrong.

———

I do think about dating again. I know I must have given the
impression that I'm a committed widow, but despite the fact that I
love you, want only you, I refuse to accept that I'm faulty, obsolete.
I know there must be someone kind that I can have a drink with.
I'll still watch him with my drink. I'll still want him to be you.
But maybe I can trust him enough that I'll forget to monitor him.
Maybe I'll stop questioning, for a moment, whether he's just
interested in me because of my mother's genes. Maybe I'll stop
questioning, for a moment, what he's expecting or wanting from
me. Maybe then I can enjoy him. Maybe he'll turn me on. Maybe
I'll want to fuck him. I tried very hard just then not to say 'Maybe

I'll let myself want to fuck him.' I'm not sure if that is something you can let yourself do, but I know I can smother desires I can't stop myself from having, even if they're desires I want to be able to act on. I know there must be someone kind that I can have a drink with. I just hope he will be kind enough, after a handful of great dates, to stop himself from asking why I start to cry when we get in bed. I hope he'll just lie there silently, still, then be gone when I wake up.

———

I did think about coming to see you when you were between your life and your death. I was going to come when I knew your brother was working, but then I couldn't bear to see you like that. I was going to come one time when I had stopped caring whether your brother found out about us, but then I was too angry with you for doing that to yourself, and to me, you stupid, selfish prick. Then it was too late. I guess I hadn't let myself accept that you were gone. I protected myself from it, opting for a different, not lesser, kind of pain.

———

The last time we saw each other was on a video call. It was just your head I saw. On a video call, eye contact is impossible. We both just see the other person seeing the other person. I felt close, felt faraway. I kept glancing at myself, rearranging my hair, tilting the screen for a more flattering angle. You told me you couldn't come down the week after, as we'd planned. 'Low on funds,' you said.

I said it was okay, that there were other things I could do instead. That wasn't true, and even if there were other things, I knew I wouldn't do them anyway. It wasn't a special talk. There's not much to say about what we were saying. It was just the simple, beautiful, humdrum act of touching base.

There was a look on your face, though, the way your expressions came and went, the slowness of it, the struggle of it. I don't know if I've added that in because that's what I imagine you did because that's what I remember happening in a film I can't remember now. There was a little silence right before I said I had to go off to see my mother.

'Fair enough,' you said.

I said goodbye, but I didn't go. Neither of us went. We looked at each other in our screens, each of us looking slightly down, as if at each other's chins, smiling, kind of embarrassed, kind of glad, then I saw your eyes look into mine. I saw you look at me, even though I know you didn't. You gave up the sight of me so I could see your eyes look into mine, even though they didn't. You knew the last of me you'd see was the webcam's dark eye, and what you were going off to do. I saw you look at me, even if you didn't, then you left. It surprised me, made me laugh. It let me feel closer to you. It let me hold you, albeit like I hold you now, like a window holds its view.

—

'**Mate, is this** going to hurt?'

'Maybe.'

'Maybe?'

'I don't want to lie to you.'

'Did it hurt when you did it?'

I shake my head.

'It did!' she says, peering over the platform. 'Fuck this, man.'

'No,' I say, 'it doesn't hurt. Not really.'

'Not really?'

'You'll be fine.'

'Can't I just fall from standing like the other times?'

'You are standing.'

'You know what I mean,' she says.

'You'll be fine.'

'And even if you're not!' Cali shouts.

I widen my eyes at Ali. She nods as if to say, 'You were right about her.'

'Just don't look down,' I say.

'Oh, that's great fucking advice. Did you come up with that yourself?'

'I mean when you're falling,' I say.

'What am I supposed to look at?'

'Look right at that back wall!' Cali shouts. 'Let your eyes keep you straight!'

I smile as if to say, 'She's not wrong.'

'Fuck. Do I actually fucking jump or am I falling?'

'It's a bit of both,' I say.

'Fuck it,' she says. Then she just does it. She springs slightly off her toes. I hear her gasp. I see her jaws clench as she falls. I see the moment her body feels it's too much fall.

A quiet, compact sound!

We all cheer. Cali shouts, 'Yeah!'

But Ali groans. Cali and I run over. I go to lift her up, but she shakes her head violently. I lower her down against the mat. She's winded. Cali shouts, 'Relax!'

Slowly Ali's breath comes back. I ask if she's okay. She tries to push herself upright, laughing, but winces, lies flat on her back. I press her side, ask her if that hurts. She gasps, then laughs again, still wincing.

'She might have broken a rib,' I say.

'That was amazing,' Ali says.

———

I'm sitting up at the head of the bed, legs crossed. She's sleeping foetal, her head lying in the crook at my pelvis. The table fan hums in the dark. You are stroking my thigh. I pretend not to notice so you won't stop. You're wearing a bobble hat with leafless trees on it. You smile with one eye open. I understand that we've been to a dog shelter. The dog stands there at the bookcase in my bedroom pulling out plays with both paws, snickering at the blurbs. The dog is Muttley. I understand that you've been fucking the girl at the dog shelter. She has wet yellow hair. I stand with the dogs barking in their cages while she pokes and flicks her tongue in your ear. 'You only care about yourself, Corina.' But no, it's night still in my mother's bed. I feel her stirring before she wakes. I ask her if she needs the commode. We whisper, I guess, because we don't want to wake the light up.

'Maybe a little,' she says, shuffling forwards.

I hoist her upright. The light by us, by the window, is dark green. There's a shadow on the ceiling streaked dark and light. I think of a Guylian seashell. I feel sick, feel hungry.

My mother sits at the end of the bed. She's breathing heavily. Often the things most difficult to do are the things we can't help doing.

I pull her pyjama bottoms down. There's a point, even if you've spent your whole life led by shame, when the rules and values of the outside world just don't seem so important. Morphine helps.

I kneel down. Even in the dark I can see the crest of pubic hair, its silver whiskers, pressed down to one side from the sleep, smelling tangy and sweet in the way a plant can smell sweet. I think of leaves, of soil, of mushrooms. I think of chutney.

I take the bottoms off over the end of her feet. Her toes are curled in, the tiny toenails hiding. I see all the bits of her body, from a million memories throughout my life, the parts I love that are beautiful, her fingers that never seem at rest, always bent or tensed in some sharp position, the green needle-point freckle below her collarbone, the patch of skin on her overactive sternocleidomastoid region that's permanently goosebumped, her earlobes that join straight to the jaw that I used to nip and stroke when she let me sleep with her when I was scared or sad or lonely, the parts I've heard her call too big, too small, misshapen, old, and I don't know what I'll do when they're still here and she's not, when there's no more of her voice, no more of her thinking, or loving.

I hold her hands. She wobbles at each joint onto her feet. There's so little of her body, her, left. With my arms hooked under her underarms, I crutch her around the commode by the door. I know that lowering her down, my hands holding her tightly at the top of her ribs, will pinch through the morphine numbness, but she'll remember the only other way is a hoist. There is no dignity, she'd say, in a hoist, or less dignity, anyway.

She slumps, relieved. The piss comes down in heavy drips. When it seems to stop I ask her if she's finished.

'I don't know.'

'Does it feel like there's more?'

'Do I feel like there's more?'

'Yes.'

'Yes.'

'But it won't come?'

'Yes.'

'There's probably no more,' I say. 'It'll go when you lie back down.'

'It will?'

'Yeah.'

'You're not just saying that?'

'No.'

'Okay.'

She lifts her hands. I duck my head under them. She hangs them on my shoulders. I pull up her bottoms as far as they'll go with her still sitting, then I lift her with one arm around her waist. With my other hand, I pull up the bottoms all the way.

Slowly, I get her back in bed. Sometimes it's hard to lift a body, but if it's a body you love it's as easy as lifting yourself. Though even that is not always easy.

I draw the duvet up to her chin. She settles. Every little calorie comes out in long exhalations. She holds her chin up, as if to tauten the skin around her throat. Where there's no shame there's also so much elegance.

I find myself staring at her face. These days I spend so much time staring at her face. Recently she said she doesn't feel like a person anymore. A 'human' is what she said. 'I don't feel like a human. Just a thing that feels pain.'

Suddenly she sucks in air. I lean closer, adrenaline spikes, hoping she gathered the breath to speak.

'For a second,' she says, 'I forgot that you were here.'

'Charming.'

'I'm sorry. I didn't mean it that way.'

'Don't worry,' I say. 'Are you comfortable?'

'Am I comfortable?'

'Yes.'

'Yes. Very.'

'Good.'

'What time is it?' she says.

'It's just past four.'

'It's late. You don't have to be here.'

'It's fine.'

'Not on my account.'

'It's fine,' I say. 'Do you want me to leave you here a while?'

'If it wasn't so late,' she says, 'you could take a taxi.'

'They still run this late.'

'I know that.'

Her eyes glint in the dark. The pupils look silver.

'I don't know what to do, then,' I say. 'What should I do?'

'What should you do? I can't tell you that.'

'But I don't want to do anything you don't want me to do,' I say. 'Do you want me to be here or do you want to be alone?'

'I wouldn't worry about what I want.'

'Of course I'm going to worry. Why not?'

'It can't be helped.'

'What can't?'

'You don't understand.'

'You're right,' I say.

She scratches her cheek. 'Don't worry so much about what you want. Sometimes you want so much. It's wonderful,' she says, 'to want so much. But all that wanting is very painful. But it is also wonderful to want so much and want that pain. But sometimes you don't want anything or cannot want at all. Useless to say it can't be helped. You just make do.' She steadies her breath. 'I'm quite tired,' she says. 'I might try and sleep now. Will you be here when I wake up?'

'Yes,' I say. 'I'll be here.'

'And you won't mind if I sleep until morning?'

'Not at all.'

'You'll be okay on your own?'

'I'll be okay.'

She swallows. 'I think I'll feel better in the morning. I think I'll be hungry in the morning.'

'Is there anything you would like?' I say.

'Scrambled eggs.'

'Scrambled eggs?'

'Yes. Why not?'

'No reason. Okay. Scrambled eggs.'

'And you'll be here in the morning?'

'Yes. I'll be here.'

'You're very kind.'

'It's nothing.'

'No, it's not,' she says.

Her eyes close. I watch her breathe. Her mouth opens like she's yawning. She isn't. It just hangs open.

'Kaasan?'

She makes a little noise.

'When you said I couldn't get a taxi because it was late, what did you mean?' I say.

Her teeth tap together. 'I said that? When?'

'Just now.'

'I said that? I can't remember.'

'Well, you mentioned,' I say, but feel as though it's something I have to let go.

'I would remember if I said that, wouldn't I?' She tilts her head to me. I guess I could ask her again. She might say, 'With all you've been through.' She might say that she meant nothing.

'Yeah,' I say. 'Yes. You would. Don't worry.'

'No?'

'No. It's okay. Don't worry.'

She sighs, out of breath. I watch her. There's a smell I recognise. It's the water at the bottom of a vase, water that's cloudy and needs to be changed. Yes, I know that smell. I don't know when it will be, but it will be very soon. I don't imagine she'll talk much now. Not much at all. Blunt, shallow inhalations. Her body will slow down even more, impossibly down. Then there will be no more her, Kaasan, Itō Mitsu, 伊藤 蜜. I'll hold her head, press my mouth to her head. I might ask her to come back. I've seen many dead bodies. Over the years I've come to feel that they're beautiful. I think my mother's will come to be the most awful and the most

341

beautiful thing. I'll feel alone, less, proud, in love with her, and it. I'll feel drenched in seawater, stiffened once dry.

お別れ.

I look out the window. Roofs give the dark out there some edges. Soon I'll slice some fruit. Oranges. Plums. Pears. Neither of us will eat them. She just likes the smell.

COPIED POSTS FROM CORINA SLATE'S BLOG, 'WITNESS'

APRIL 2017

I was clearing out her bedroom. Hiro was clearing out the kitchen. He had let me register her death, apply for cremation, talk with the solicitor, arrange the funeral, etc. He didn't feel the need to defend himself for not helping out, or accuse me of doing it all to make myself look good. At the funeral, he had a swollen, split lip. He hadn't cleaned his shoes.

We started on the flat a few days after the service. That morning I'd texted him saying I'd be there, and to let me know if he wanted me to keep anything. He didn't reply, just came, got going on the kitchen. I wanted to tell him what and what not to throw away, but I knew I'd go over what he'd done anyway so I left him to it.

In the bedroom I had four designated spaces. I'd pushed the bed right up against the back wall to make room for one corner by the door for stuff to bin, the other corner for stuff to keep, the doorway for donations, the bed for stuff I'll decide on another day.

For an hour I just touched things. At first, once I'd designated the spaces, I worked quickly, jostling around the room, making piles: yes, no, maybe. Then I had one of her shoes in my hand. I sat on the floor, tracing my fingers along the laces, the creases in the leather where her feet bent as she walked. I must have been there for ten minutes before I decided to go through each thing I'd moved, get to know it like I got to know this shoe. These things told me facts about her that I knew but hadn't really realised. Knowing something before realising you know is a weird kind of remembering. You know it, but only vaguely, in the way you know the sun is somewhere behind the clouds, then it's there in your mind, clear, distinct. I remembered how narrow her waist was, how small she was. I remembered silly jokes. In a shoebox of receipts, photos, deeds, forms, handmade birthday cards from Hiro and me, an old diary in Japanese, I found about twenty brass 5-yen coins. When we lost teeth, this is what the tooth fairy brought us. We'd complain because we couldn't spend it. She'd laugh, say, 'Show some gratitude. She flew all the way from Japan!' Squeezing the coins in my hand, I laughed. Tears came too. I really got a sob going, folded over myself on the bare mattress at the end of the bed, among her things, startled eventually to feel Hiro pull me into a hug. I felt him also shaking, snivelling. Once the sobs had given way to sniffles, whimpers, he sat on the edge of the bed, waiting to make sure I wouldn't cave in again.

'You don't have to,' I told him.

'I know,' he said.

'You're not obligated, I mean.'

'Am I not required to either?'

'Then why are you?'

'It's not because I've forgiven you, if that's what you're thinking.'

'That's not what I was asking.'

'Yeah, it was.'

'Well I haven't forgiven you either.'

'Good to be on the same page.'

'In the same boat.'

'Of hating one another.'

'Good times.'

He stood up, but he didn't leave. He looked at the things in the room. His mouth twitched.

I said, 'Hiro,' but he shook his head.

He said, 'I do get it, you know. I never didn't get why you kept him from me.' He stretched his swollen throat. 'And I think that's what really hurt, man. That there was a reason for it.'

I can see in his face, a steely stillness, that he will never truly forgive me for this, even if he forgets it often enough for it to seem like our relationship has healed. I guess I'm talking about a scar.

'It wasn't a good enough reason,' I said.

'Well,' he said, preparing himself to leave.

'I don't even know.'

'You do. You knew why. You know why, and I do as well. If I went out there to him, it wouldn't be long before I was crossing borders with stolen cash stuffed up my arse.'

'Maybe,' I said.

'But that doesn't mean—'

'I know,' I said. 'I think I just needed to punish someone for, I don't know.' I pressed my toe against the shoebox on the floor.

His gaze stroked over the things around us.

'I never got to ask her about it,' I said. 'About what she thought. About how she'd been to me. About what happened to me. She said something just before she, you know, but we never got to really talk about it.'

'She couldn't talk about it,' he said, looking tired. 'She couldn't let it be something to even talk about.'

'Why, though?' I said. 'What happened?'

He didn't know. Only she did. I wiped my face. I groaned. I said, 'I guess I should make do with that.'

We were there in silence for a while before Hiro said, 'Got to make do,' and went back to the kitchen.

I carried on grouping her things. I was looking at her toiletries, creams, when I heard Hiro from the kitchen say, 'What the fuck?'

When I went to see what the fuck, I found him kneeling into the cupboard under the sink. He noticed me, stood, jerked his head towards the cupboard.

'What is it?' I said.

He told me to look for myself. I knelt down, saw about a dozen jars filled with murky liquid. I pulled one out.

'Is it piss?' he said.

'Piss?' I said. 'I don't think so.'

'I thought she was collecting her piss, man.'

I shook the jar to see what was inside. Hiro cringed.

'Because I've heard about people collecting their piss,' he said.

'They're eggs,' I said.

'Eggs!'

'She's pickling eggs.'

'Do you think all those jars are eggs?'

'I don't know.'

'Maybe one of them's piss.'

'Do you want there to be a piss one?'

'First I thought they were thumbs and dicks and shit.'

'Piss is better.'

'I did feel better thinking it was piss. Then I thought about her collecting jars of her piss. Then I felt bad again.'

I took out another jar.

'She's brewing Guinness, man!' he said.

'Can you imagine?'

'That would be sick,' he said. 'How old do you think this stuff is?'

'No idea. Shall I open it?'

'I don't know, man.'

I twisted the lid. There was a loud pop, a hiss, a fizz. We gasped like watching fireworks, laughed at ourselves. I felt tears come again. I clenched them down. I took off the lid, lifted the jar to Hiro's face.

'Allow it, man!'

'Doesn't smell bad,' I say.

'Will it make you puke?'

'Don't think so.'

'Man, I'm hungry. When did you last eat?'

'Yesterday. I think. You want to order something?'

'I've been waiting to ask that for ages.'

'I can't be fucked with cooking.'

'Fuck cooking, man.'

'What do you fancy?'

'I don't know. Something easy. Pizza?'

'What about something that'll go with what's in the jars? What goes with pickled eggs?'

'I'll eat anything.'

'All right. Pass me my phone.'

'I haven't got any cash on me.'

'Don't worry,' I said, adding, out of habit, 'My treat.'

He nodded, head staying low, as if he felt me holding this over him. I looked at my phone pretending not to notice, feeling the slightly mended ties between us fray again.

'I'm going to wash my hands,' he said.

'Okay.'

'Can we get a curry?' he said.

I looked at him. 'Sure.'

'Cool,' he said.

He went to wash his hands, but I could hear him watching something on his phone. I knew what he'd want to get so I ordered for us. I forked out an egg, cut it in half on a plate. A yellow chrysanthemum yolk. For a while I waited for Hiro to come back to show him, then I started again with the bedroom.

When the food came we laid it out on the floor like we did to watch TV when we were young. We must have drunk three beers each before an irritating tension passed, or the force of its cause had faded.

'Can you believe Leonard Down the Corridor, though?' Hiro said.

'I've never known anyone cry so much.'

'You didn't pay him to cry that much, did you?'

'He couldn't help himself.'

'He was putting us to shame, man.'

'Did he actually love her or something?' I said.

'Shit,' he said, 'maybe.' He shook his head, smiling. 'Tragic.'

'Sweet guy,' I said. 'He probably did love her.'

'And she never gave him the chance to tell her.'

We reminded ourselves of her.

Hiro said, 'When do we have to be out of here?'

'I don't know,' I said. 'She put our names on the tenancy so I didn't know if I wanted to try to live here.'

'Here?'

'Yeah. You know. Unless you wanted to or something.'

'Nah,' he said. 'That'd be all right.'

'I just mean in case you needed a better place right now.'

'Nah,' he said. 'I'm going away for a while actually. Going travelling.'

'Travelling?'

'Setting off in a couple of weeks.'

'A couple of weeks.'

He looked at his hands. 'So I've still got time,' he said, 'to help out.'

I told him I'd like that. I didn't feel the need to ask him where he's going. He seemed grateful for that. We didn't seem to need to talk about it. I asked if I could try the food I ordered for him. He passed me the container. We ate together.

I woke up just after dawn. Hiro was still asleep on the sofa. I felt fuzzy, made of lint. A honey light filtered through the window. I felt myself pulled into it, pressed my cheek against the glass. Slowly the sun infused the room, warmed the window, my cheek, brightening the condensation from my breath. Hiro coughed himself awake. I sat beside him on the sofa. We looked at each other. Please take care of yourself, I wanted to say. Come back. Let's be together again sometime. I wanted him to say, We'll talk every day, I'll be back before you miss me. He lifted his eyebrows instead of smiling. He looked tempted to ask if I'm okay. I looked at him, tempted to say, Yes, often I am okay, meaning, unhealed, undestroyed.

———

You might think 'repair' means two things reuniting, becoming a pair again. But actually it comes from the Latin for 'repatriate', as in, 'to return to one's country'. I'd read this as my mother drifted around the border of sleep. Do you know how we can repair when we're separated from the closest thing we have to 'our own countries', our bodies? I mean, did we ever have a country to call our own? Were what we thought were borders only features of always being already separated from ourselves, crossed by others?

———

On break I weigh up whether to smoke. Back on the wards there's the aftermath of a homeless shelter fire. They wailed in just before my shift was supposed to end. We needed to make up numbers in the A&E night team. I came through with two other nurses, two psychiatrists, a chaplain.

'Expect smoke inhalation, chest pains, burns, fractures, confusion, trauma.'

Every patient had carbon monoxide poisoning to some extent. We gave them oxygen through facemasks.

'What about Mark? Is Mark here?'

Every patient wheezed. We gave them steroids, salbutamol. Every

patient had pneumonitis to some extent. Panic made them breathe
more rapidly.

'Breathe in, and breathe out on three. One, two . . .'

'Aaaahhhh!'

It was my job at first to provide each bed with cyano kits in case of
cyanide poisoning.

'Can someone get someone to turn off that siren, please?'

I took the tests.

A second wave of five casualties came through.

'Are you still in pain?'

We checked a patient for soot in his mouth, singed nasal hairs,
listened for hoarseness in his voice. Another patient had burns on
his upper airways. We gave him general anaesthetic. I heard one
man moaning with what looked like very bad burns. It was a shame
that he was still conscious. He knew that he would die soon. In ten
minutes he did die.

At the end of my break I can still smell barbeque. I stub out my
cigarette, half-smoked, let the clear sky strain through my eyes, go
back on the ward. It's quiet now. The nurses move carefully, calmly.
A consultant asks me to change a patient's dressings. I pull on new
gloves, go to the patient's bed. Sooty hair surrounds the oxygen
mask.

'Hello. I'm Corina,' I say, picking up the chart. 'How are we doing?'

He doesn't answer. I say, 'I think it's time for a new dressing, isn't
it?'

I scan the chart, eyes snag on the name, a plunge under my ribs,
look up. His green eyes. I look through the hair, the mask, his
features gathering in front of me. It can't be him, as much as it is
him. An immense weight. Of his looking at me. I'm fleeing without

moving, falling off the cliff he left inside me. He looks away. I try to remember the advice. My pores prickle with sweat. Depth drains from my vision. I try to think only of my breathing. Slowly he sharpens in my eyes. He pulls down the mask, glances up at me, like a rough sleeper asking for help. I guess that's what he is.

'You were in that fire?' I manage to say.

He nods. He's gaunt, a splinter.

'What?' I say.

'Aye,' he says.

'You're staying in that hostel?'

'Aye,' he says. 'I am.'

I wince at his voice. Is that what my body has been sweating out?

But I can also hear your voice. I hate him for sounding like you, for hearing you now, through him.

He looks behind me as if to ask for someone to replace me. I try to imagine how I'll feel if I did leave.

I put down his chart, stare at his arm for a few seconds, trying to forget it's his arm.

He says, 'You don't have to—'

'Shut up,' I say, moving to the side of his bed.

I manage to touch his arm. The muscles in my arm are primed to twist his arm till it snaps. I take my hands off him. His arm lies there trembling. I begin to think of the causes of the trembling, but stop myself. His eyes are closed. He must be trying to separate himself from this arm like I'm trying to separate this arm from him. I stare at the dressing that needs changing. My mind won't let me forget the dressing is on him. Almost automatically, before I can think further, I douse it in saline, peel it off. He breathes in sharply.

'Shut up,' I say.

The burn beneath looks like a dog bite. The skin that stretched to form a blister lies in a collapsed bundle over the wound.

I hear him breathing. 'I don't even want to hear you breathe,' I say.

'Sorry,' he says.

'Or talk.'

He nods.

'Or move.'

He doesn't say anything.

With more saline, a soft wipe, I debride the wound. With the exudate, the slough gone, the wound shines pink. I pat it dry with gauze, prepare another dressing.

'Cor?' he says.

His voice feels acidic. This must show on my face. He doesn't say anything else. I look up at him. He's frowning. This isn't an angry frown. This is a permanent frown. It's new. I smell, within the smoked smell, the dank genital reek of unwashed clothes.

'How long were you staying in that hostel?' I say.

He glances at me out the corner of his eye.

'How long were you staying there?' I say.

'Couple nights,' he says.

'How long have you been like this?'

'Couple years.'

I try to see on his face the familiar manoeuvres of his lies, but there's just a sad see-through mask.

'Since?'

'Not long after.'

'The trial?'

'I couldn't keep hold of anything,' he says. He bares his teeth, pushes his tongue through the holes.

'Lost a couple of teeth, did you?' I say harshly. 'That must have been difficult.'

He looks from under his eyebrows. A mangy fox.

I lay gauze over the burn, press it gently in place. I feel his eyes flit over me, assessing the damage he's caused. I look at him. He looks away.

'Were you at Sam's funeral?' I say.

He seems insulted by the question, but stops himself from showing it. 'Of course,' he says.

I want to ask what it was like, but I don't want to hear what he has to say.

He tries to fill his lungs, breathes out jagged rocks of air. 'To be honest,' he says, 'it was bound to happen eventually.'

'I don't need to know,' I say, going around to the end of the bed. I amend his chart, thinking of you. I thought that I'd been trying to find answers for why you did that to yourself, why your brother did that to me, why my mother couldn't believe me, answers too terrible to hear, but really I've been trying to find a way of living, of loving to live, with vulnerability, the likelihood of pain, of cruelty. I haven't found it, I probably won't, but I hope that the likelihood of cruelty is the price we have to pay to love.

I look at your brother, hoping it's for the last time. A smirk comes into his mouth. He says, 'As a matter of fact, I thought you were having a thing with him.'

'I was,' I say. 'I loved him. He loved me.'

The smirk slips. He stares at me.

'Did that ruin your apology?' I say. 'Is that not how you wanted this to end?'

He shakes his head, but not to say no.

'Is that why?' I say.

He rubs the dirt in the creases of his palm. He says, 'Maybe I just—'

'Shut up,' I say.

He looks at his hands. He stops breathing, holds his breath.

Will I unfold my fists?

I say, 'I don't feel sorry for you.'

He looks at me. Eyes full of uncried tears.

'I don't,' I say.

He nods.

'I don't,' I say. 'I don't.'

ACKNOWLEDGEMENTS

In the Seeing Hands of Others began as a component of a PhD thesis, so a vast thanks is owed to the supervisory team who midwifed it: Maria Hyland, Douglas Field, Frances Leviston and John McAuliffe. Without their generosity, encouragement and perspicacity, the novel would be largely unintelligible and probably abandoned. I'm indebted more broadly to the Centre for New Writing and School of Arts, Languages and Cultures at the University of Manchester for financial support.

I can't account for the publication of the book without thanking Mark Blacklock, Anna Webber, Hayley Shepherd, Lucie Worboys of Crow Books, Patrick Taylor, Graeme Hall, Hannah Westland and Luke Brown, for their guidance, diligence and wisdom.

The novel revolves around forms of suffering that I haven't and can't experience. If a novel deals with another's experience, specifically another's trauma, then it should in some way serve – take care with – that experience. The imaginative leaps I made to this end were prompted and informed by countless conversations with friends and family alongside the invaluable work of these writers in particular: Sohaila Abdulali, Linda Martín Alcoff, June Alexander, Elizabeth Miki Brina, Joanna Bourke, Susan Brison, Cathy Caruth, Akiko Hashimoto, Judith Lewis Herman, Itō Hiromi, Cathy Park Hong, Liz Kelly, Bessel van der Kolk, Chris Kraus, Rachel Loney-Howes, Audre Lorde, Marie Matsuki Mockett, Sameena Mulla, Eileen Myles, Maggie Nelson, Nancy Venable Raine, Nawal El Saadawi, Cassie Premo Steele, Alice Sebold, Janet Treasure, Megan Warin. I view *In the Seeing Hands of Others* as a dramatic vehicle for the confluence of their words. It works, I hope, to bear witness to the systemic misogyny that undergirds sexual violence and how this intersects with other forms of oppression and exploitation. It was written in the hope that the urgency of its subject will seem to future readers inconceivable. It is to all victims/survivors of rape and of all forms of sexual and domestic violence that this novel is dedicated.

The demands of writing were alleviated by the support, advice and sometimes actual contribution of friends and comrades: Alex, Ali, Anna N., Anna O., Danny, Duncan, Jonny, Ollie, Patrick, Richard, Ted, Willy. Rob provided the first reading and he, along with the Small and Androutsos families, have given support of countless other kinds. The most generous people I know are my parents and step-parents, especially in light of my bone-idle and taciturn propensities, and I'm beholden to them – Mam, Dad, Tony and Marion – for their love, forbearance and belief.

I owe, by far, my greatest debt of gratitude to Anna. The encouragement, comfort, patience and fortification that she has given in relation to this novel is just a fraction of the supreme grace with which she has filled my life, saving it, making it possible. This novel is about 'life held precariously in the seeing / hands of others.' Mine is held in hers.